John Morison

Australia as It Is

Facts and features, sketches and incidents of Australia and Australian life - with

notices of New Zealand

John Morison

Australia as It Is
Facts and features, sketches and incidents of Australia and Australian life - with notices of New Zealand

ISBN/EAN: 9783337313197

Printed in Europe, USA, Canada, Australia, Japan

Cover: Foto ©Andreas Hilbeck / pixelio.de

More available books at **www.hansebooks.com**

AUSTRALIA AS IT IS

OR

FACTS AND FEATURES, SKETCHES AND INCIDENTS
OF AUSTRALIA AND AUSTRALIAN LIFE

WITH NOTICES OF NEW ZEALAND

John Morison

BY A CLERGYMAN

THIRTEEN YEARS RESIDENT IN THE INTERIOR OF NEW SOUTH WALES

THIRD EDITION

Let thine eyes look right on,
And let thine eyelids look straight before thee.
Ponder the path of thy feet,
And let all thy ways be established *—Proverbs*

LONDON
LONGMANS, GREEN, AND CO.
AND NEW YORK : 15 EAST 10ᵗʰ STREET
1894

PREFACE

THE observations in the concluding chapter are to
be understood as applying to the interior; population being the basis of representation, there is little
or no parliamentary representation of the thinly
populated interior. In those trying their prentice
hands at legislation, there is the ever recurring
subject, the Crown lands, called also waste lands of
the Crown. Why waste? The land is already applied
for all the purposes to which it can ever be profitably
applied, *grazing*. One of the many evils attending
the administration of the land in withholding from
the people the rights to the land is deferred payment.
Those in possession of all the rights to the land they
occupy will always be found valiant defenders and
upholders of the integrity of law and government.
'Truth seen springing out of the earth and righteousness looking down from heaven '—in deferred payment on the purchase of the land, there will be
nothing seen springing up but dragon's teeth

troubles and difficulties increasing and multiplying without number and without end. Something of this may be already seen in every new administration. Coming in with a new land law, there would have been none of these distracting measures of Government, if the words of wisdom had been listened to of the late President of the Council, Sir John Hay, appropriating all the high table land for the benefit of those who desired to settle on the land and make homes to themselves. Those occupying stations far inland have no thoughts of permanently remaining there ; they are there as are those on board ship, making money and nothing else, and the *cuisine* in no way differs from that on board ship, in preserved vegetables, for the simple reason they cannot be grown there. With their tens of thousands of acres, they often find it difficult to hold their own during a severe drought ; those with their hundreds of acres would be certain here to be involved in total ruin, and the great safety and protection to life and property far inland is the paucity of the population, everyone being a marked man, no one having business there but in connection with stations.

CONTENTS

———◆◇◆———

CHAPTER I

PRELIMINARY OBSERVATIONS

CHAPTER II

THE BUSH

CHAPTER III

PIONEERING

CHAPTER IV

SQUATTING

CHAPTER V

GOLD-DIGGING

CHAPTER VI

SHEPHERDING

CHAPTER VII

LOST IN THE BUSH

CHAPTER VIII

DROUGHTS AND FLOODS

Coast and Dividing Ranges—A Drought and its Terrible
Effects—Singular Origin of a Fire—Hot Winds—Agriculture in the Interior—Travelling on the Road—Sandy
and Swelling Blight—Bullock Drivers—Carriers—Stock-

CHAPTER XII

DEMOCRACY AND ITS RESULTS

AUSTRALIA AS IT IS

CHAPTER I

PRELIMINARY OBSERVATIONS

Chinese Expedients for Communicating Information to Chinese
Settlers—Reasons for Emigrants Refraining from Letter-writing
Precarious Condition of New Settlers - Cautious Gold-diggers
- Australia, Tasmania, and New Zealand—Mistakes of Emi-
grants in not ascertaining the Districts Suitable for them
A Local Governor's Advice Cotton-growing Manners and
Customs Peculiarities and Uncertainties of Colonial Legis-
lation.

ON one occasion I entered a shepherd's hut, which
formed one of the numerous out-stations of a large
grazing establishment, and found a Chinaman, who
acted as hut-keeper, busily engaged in reading a
Chinese volume. Having signified a desire to be
informed as to the nature of the contents of it, and
of a number of other Chinese books which lay
beside him, he replied in English, ' All this country
this Chinaman write—other Chinamen write—all
write China,' pointing at the same time in every
direction around him, and finally in the direction
of China. In traversing bush tracks, and the main

lines of roads, one not unfrequently sees trees
which have been neatly stripped of their bark a
few feet above the ground, with Chinese characters
carefully written in ink on the white surface—one
of the many expedients resorted to by Chinamen
with the object of communicating information to
their countrymen, and saving them from loss and
disappointment. A volume of letters of recent
dates from some of those observant foreigners who,
engaged in different pursuits, have settled in
different parts, would probably be one of the best
handbooks of Australia which could be published.
Not the least of the writer's objects in the following
chapters is to give a trustworthy view of life and
manners, for the guidance of those who may be
interested in the subject. What is true of one
place may not be true of another place, and what
is true at one time may not be true at another
time ; and the fitful changes—periods of prosperity alternating with periods of depression, which
have unfortunately been of frequent occurrence
in the Australian colonies—are very unfavourable
to letter-writing ; hence much of the uncertainty
which exists in the public mind as to the real condition of society in those regions. A carpenter
told me that on his arrival at a large seaport town,
which happened at the time to be in a most
flourishing condition, he obtained employment at
the rate of twenty-five shillings a day, or half a
crown an hour. The climate was agreeable, beef
was sold at one penny per lb., and Australia seemed
to him to be a very land of Goshen. He wrote to

inform his comrades at home of his good fortune, with the object of inducing them to follow his footsteps ; but he deeply regretted afterwards that he had done so, for his letter had not reached the equator when he was thrown out of employment, and instead of receiving half a crown an hour, he could not get employment at any rate of wages. He made a shift—as many are obliged to do when hands of their own craft are too numerous—and became a gardener. A treacherous dependence may be sometimes placed on first impressions ; and the shame of having to contradict themselves, to say that they were altogether wrong in what they had previously written, leads many emigrants to forego correspondence. The affections are very apt to go along with the interests ; new ties of friendship are formed, old ties are broken ; and there are those who *forget*, those, too, always very numerous, who wait ' to-morrow and to-morrow,' to write more favourable intelligence. To-morrow, with its favourable intelligence, does not come, and they do not write. One young man, who had emigrated very much against the will of his parents, said to me that he had not written to them for seven years. In his case it would have been rather disagreeable to have written to state how he was situated, as he had resigned a good situation in Glasgow, and was not receiving one-sixth part of the salary which he had been in receipt of at home. He wrote at last, but, like many others, not until he felt himself justified in doing so—that is, when his pecuniary circumstances were more favourable.

The spirit of commercial enterprise is so much abroad ; the arts of money-making are so numerous and the power of self-interest is so strong, that failing the aids supplied in trustworthy correspondence, no alternative would seem to be left to newly-arrived emigrants but to grope their way. When a new gold-field—regarding which flattering accounts may have been circulated in the newspapers—has been discovered, the more experienced and better-informed diggers employ and pay a party of reliable persons to visit it and furnish a report, a fact of some significance, proving the necessity for caution on the part of intending settlers.

Every one who has been resident in any of the Australian colonies very soon becomes familiar, however, with the leading local characteristic features ; some things standing out very prominently, and distinguishing one quarter from another. The first colony in the line of the overland mail from England, and calling at King George's Sound, is—

WESTERN AUSTRALIA—Capital, *Perth.*— It has a large unexplored interior, and newly discovered gold-fields.

SOUTH AUSTRALIA — Capital, *Adelaide.*— Mouth of the river Murray, draining the interior of Victoria, New South Wales, and Queensland, navigable for 2,000 miles, dividing with Queensland the present right to and interest in the projected new colony of Northern Australia. Products : wheat, copper, and wool.

VICTORIA—Capital, *Melbourne.* ' Go-a-head ' population. Products: wool and gold.

NEW SOUTH WALES Capital, *Sydney.*—Fine harbour. Parent of all the other colonies. Products: wool, gold, coal, silver, lead.

QUEENSLAND—Capital, *Brisbane.*—The latest formed colony. Warm climate. Products: wool, gold. Squatting in the ascendant, with a vast unoccupied territory, forming the newly projected colony, Northern Australia.

TASMANIA (Van Diemen's Land).— Principal towns: Launceston, Hobart Town. English climate and English hedgerows. Products: potatoes, oats, and apples.

NEW ZEALAND, though about the same size as Great Britain, extends over thirteen degrees of latitude. There are very considerable differences in the climate of one place from another; the southern extremity being cold, the northern warm. There are about sixty thousand natives, ' Maories, in New Zealand, and of this number there are not more than five thousand in the middle island, where Southland, Otago, Canterbury, and Nelson are situated. The northern island, the principal settlements in which are Auckland, Wellington, and New Plymouth, being warmer than the middle island, is preferred by the Maories, as it would also seem to be by the European residents.

More enlarged observation and better acquaintance with the Australian colonies would have convinced some Europeans whom I met in the southern settlements of New Zealand, where I had gone in 1850 on a health-seeking excursion, that they had committed serious mistakes in settling there. Such places as Southland and Otago are not at all adapted for persons who suffer from pulmonary complaints, in consequence of the frequent rains and cold south-westerly winds, and those emigrants ought to have gone to the high upland parts of Australia, in the gold-digging regions, where the climate is more favourable, where they could have obtained employment easily at remunerative rates, and would not have been required to do manual labour at sheep stations. A great deal has been said of the healthiness of the Australian climate ; this must be understood, however, to apply chiefly to the high, mountainous parts of the interior, where the atmosphere is very rare, dry, pure, and warm. Along the coast, and in low-lying parts of country, the atmosphere is much denser ; stifling heats prevail, and some affections, such as dyspepsia, might be aggravated instead of being relieved in such places. The seats of commerce and large towns would seem to be far more favourably adapted to those—such as clerks—who have been accustomed to the occupations of town life than the embryo agricultural settlements. Those settle-ments, always bidding high for public favour, are in need of a different class of emigrants. The consumption of excisable commodities by those persons amply reimburses the Government for the expenses incurred in granting them free passages. The advantages to the labouring class are certainly

great when they find employment at high wages.
Those who are in possession of small, carefully-
accumulated capital generally require, however, to
be cautious as to the mode of investment. ' Don't
trust anyone ; judge for yourself. Look at two
sides of a shilling,' were the words which I heard
spoken by the superintendent, or local governor,
of one of the New Zealand settlements to two
young men who had entered into conversation
with him regarding their intentions of settling.
Ignorance may be ruinous. There are many
important things to be learned on the spot, a
knowledge of which cannot be very well dispensed
with ; for in Australia, as elsewhere, instead of the
man overcoming the difficulties, the difficulties
may overcome the man. ' Two are better than
one ;' and the term ' mates ' is a very favourite
expression, well understood by all experienced
colonists. The human heart was formed for friendship, and, generally speaking, it will not be found
good on the part of either individuals or families
to be alone in Australia. There is very little to
be said about the old and established settlements,
the population of towns, and those in the neighbourhood who are engaged in agriculture, in vine
and in tobacco growing. In those places channels
for labour and industry have been opened up and
very clearly defined, indicating to emigrants the
safest course to follow. In newly-formed settlements, however, there are often difficulties in the
way of ascertaining the proper season for the
sowing of grain, and the kind of cultivation suit-

able to the locality. A 'land-order' emigrant in
Queensland told me that a friend of his had sustained great loss from these difficulties. After much
labour and expense in clearing and trenching ground,
the fruit trees which they planted died in spite
of every available precaution. In a more elevated
part of Queensland, and in a sheltered situation,
there would have been less risk of a loss of this
nature. What may be grown with advantage
in one place may not be grown with equal advantage in another. Wheat and maize are the
two cereals most extensively cultivated. In all
the hot districts they are liable, however, to be
attacked by the weevil in stack or in bin; the
cold in winter is not sufficient to check the
ravages of that much dreaded insect. Australia
being of very great extent, there is a variety of
climate, and climate will always determine the
kind, as well as the mode, of agricultural industry
to be adopted. There was a great deal of good
sense in a Sydney merchant whom I met, who
had brought five hundred coolies from India in
one ship, with the object of cultivating cotton
on his land in Queensland. Coolies would be
much more likely to succeed as labourers in a
cotton plantation than English, Scottish, or Irish
immigrants. Besides, they can live very cheaply
on rice and sugar. The following extract from
the editorial article of a Queensland newspaper, if
not conclusive, contains some truth on the subject
of cotton-growing :

' Instead of cotton cultivation increasing in proportion

to the increase in our population, it has decreased, and now [1868], after six years' trial, there seems less probability than ever of its soon taking its place with our wool, hides, and tallow as one of the large staple products of the colony. The public companies which were started for the purpose of cultivating cotton in Queensland under the stimulus of choice land on easy terms, and a Government bonus on the cotton produced, have all either become insolvent or have given up the cultivating of cotton ; and of all the small farmers who commenced with the cultivation of cotton four or five years ago, scarcely one can now be found who has a single plant, except it be in his garden as a curiosity.'

The squatting, or grazing, cattle-breeding, wool-growing parts of the country—Australia proper—have many characteristics in common, and the observations of the writer have a wide general application in relation to those districts. There are many things in Australia, as elsewhere, for which no reason whatever can be given, and it is sometimes rather idle and unprofitable to inquire for a reason. Manners and customs operating in a country, and regulating the conduct of its people, ultimately attain the force of law, and it is for the advantage of everyone interested to be made acquainted with them. It was not in the bond, it was not according to the letter, that those who went and took possession of the unoccupied lands should hold those lands in perpetuity, and claim rights to them almost tantamount to purchase in fee simple. The words in the bond were, that the land was to be taken from them when required for

agriculture. Very, very little, indeed, will ever be
required for agriculture ; and the majority of the
occupants of the land are not likely to be much
interfered with in their possession, so long as
they continue to pay the small rental to Government with which they are charged. They have
acquired a right to the land by discovery or
by occupation. ' Possession,' it is said, ' is nine
points of the law,' and use and wont, King-
custom, rule rampant. The present occupant may
not have discovered the land, but, he paid very
highly for his right of occupation to the previous
occupant, who, if *he* did not discover the land,
also paid for *his* right of occupation. There was
a district in New South Wales which was sold
in this way, without a sheep, horse, or hoof of
cattle upon it, for 40,000*l.* ; sold not by the Government, but by one private person to another.
Grievances arise, and will always arise, from such
questions where population increases. Smith cannot see the fairness of *his* buying land at twenty
shillings per acre, whilst his neighbour, Thomson,
retains possession of twenty, sixty, or one hundred
thousand acres, and does not pay one penny per
acre of rental. More than one penny might be
paid, however, in Victoria, and less in Queensland.
Thomson has undoubtedly the best of it ; his land
requires no fencing, ploughing, or sowing, for there
is an excellent crop of natural grass upon it. But
Smith, after all, has not much good ground for
complaint. There is plenty of unoccupied territory, and if he desires the advantages of Thomson,

he has only to do as Thomson or his predecessor
did : go and 'take up country,' or, what one Smith
cannot do, ten Smiths can accomplish, and purchase
a station, of which there are many for sale.

The larger number of mankind are born to live
on trust, and to think little of the laws by which
they are to be governed, save how to obey
them. They leave legislation to the study and
occupation of those who have leisure for the task,
to those whose presumably superior wisdom and
intelligence they would much rather confide in
than their own ; and it is very annoying to many
poor struggling emigrants, looking out for the
means of subsistence for themselves and their
families, to find that no sooner have they set their
feet on the shores of Australia, in Victoria, and in
New South Wales, than they are instantly installed
politicians, called on to give their votes for a
member of Parliament, and often to express
opinions on matters of which they actually know
nothing. Indeed, it would seem to be necessary
for one's safety and security to study colonial
politics. A member of the New South Wales
Parliament, whose hospitality I frequently enjoyed,
said to me on one occasion, in self-congratulation :
' I knew what was coming—I have sold out.' All
the people cannot be members of Parliament, and
all have not the opportunities which this gentleman had of hearing that the newly-elected Liberal
representatives, and those who were at the helm of
State, intended at that time to reduce the value of
all the best land in the colony, and that land for

which he had paid 1*l.*, 2*l.*, and 4*l.* per acre would soon not be worth more than five shillings per acre. Other highly disturbing changes frequently take place. A diminution in the revenue occasions an alteration in the tariff; there is an imposition of new duties, and merchants, if they will not suffer loss, must watch political movements. Bankers also, and indeed every class in the community, are involved in those changes ; for politics reach to, and often shake, the foundation of the whole fabric of colonial society.

CHAPTER II

THE BUSH

'BUSH' is the name given to the natural forest or uncleared land, of which there is much, especially along the coast, extending considerable distances inland, and characterised by dense vegetation. In the interior, however, there is very little to be met with ; the country generally presents a park-like appearance, with ridges, hills, valleys, and mountains covered with grass, dotted here and there with trees. On the first sight of Australia seaward, a *vastness* discovers itself in hill ranges and high mountain peaks which appear in the far distance, in many directions, and the view thus obtained, though very extensive, is dull, heavy, and monotonous. All the land seems to be covered with trees, and there are no green hills or parts of country entirely clear of timber to relieve the eye from the oppressive, dusky, and sombre shade of the Australian forest.

The similitude of Australia, in its great physical outlines and configuration, to the *dropping from a cow*, though very homely, is not a bad illustration. There is greater or less unevenness on the surface beginning at the coast, and the irregular and ill-defined ridges, hills, valleys, and mountains form a gradual steepness of ascent in travelling towards the interior ; and this steepness continues till the Australian Alps are reached—ranges of high hills and mountains running parallel to the coast, at elevations of two, three, and four thousand feet above the level of the sea. Passing beyond the Australian Alps there is a descent, though scarcely perceptible, into the interior. The climate here is warmer, the country more level and more thinly wooded than the quarter which has its fall of water to the coast. The *eastern* and *western falls of the water* are well understood —the eastern being the fall of the water into the ocean, the western the fall of the water into the large basin of the interior, of which the river Murray at Adelaide, navigable for some hundreds of miles, is the great outlet. All the other rivers are navigable only for very short distances.

There are great differences in the climate according to latitude, elevation, and situation. In regard to latitude, a mountain in Queensland, for example, may be as high as a mountain in Victoria or in New South Wales, and whilst there will be snow in winter on the mountain in Victoria, and

on the one in New South Wales, there will be none
on the one in Queensland, the last place being
farther north and nearer the tropics. There are
some parts of Queensland which are extremely
hot in summer ; too much so, one would think, for
the English constitution. There are other parts,
again, in high, mountainous districts which are very
agreeable, where the heat is not felt to be so
oppressive. There are always cooling sea-breezes
blowing a long way inland, and in the high upland
districts the pure balmy atmosphere is most
delicious all the year round. Even in the interior
during the hottest days in summer a gentle
westerly wind generally commences about ten
o'clock every morning, tempering the great heat of
the rays of the sun ; serving as a fan, and drying,
as it were, all the perspiration on the body, so that
one would never seem to perspire, unless he is
engaged in manual labour, or is exerting himself,
as in riding. This is not the case in lowland parts,
however, such as those near the coast, the atmosphere there being much denser. The nights in
hot districts in Queensland are frequently extremely
cold, and the days extremely warm. The two
great extremes of cold and heat would not seem,
however, to be prejudicial to health. The climate
is very dry, and catarrh and many other diseases
are almost unheard of.

Botany Bay was a very appropriate name for
the part of Australia which was first discovered,
for that region is thickly covered with large
flowering shrubs of a varied and beautiful character ;

but the whole continent might well admit of the
designation ' Botany Land.' There seems to be
an endless variety of vegetation, differing in different parts of country according to climate, soil,
and situation ; and the economy of nature is very
striking, every quarter being occupied by, and
appropriated to, the growth of some description
of vegetation suitable to the locality, and found
nowhere else.   In a temperature and soil, for
instance, similar to those of New Zealand, the
ground is thickly covered with fern, including the
tree fern and the cabbage tree.   In the great
variety of climate there is a corresponding variety
in the forms of the vegetable world, and what may
be found in one place will not be found in another.
One of the greatest hopes of the graziers in New
Zealand is the naturalisation and the rapid diffusion
of English grasses.   There is nothing of this kind
wanted in Australia, however, as it is already
stocked with natural grasses, of sorts exactly suited
to the particular districts in which they are found
growing. English and other grasses have been introduced, and some of these, as the white clover, may
be found growing most luxuriantly in alluvial spots.
It only grows, however, for a very short period, the
great heat and dryness of the climate being unfavourable to spreading.   The natural grasses
strike their roots deeply into the soil and are very
hardy ; though exception might perhaps be taken
to them in many places where they appear to be
tufty, thickly spread, and not covering all the
surface, whilst they are liable to be seriously

injured by over-stocking. This is not so much the result of the nature of the grasses as the faults of the soil and of the climate, as in more favourable situations the land is thickly matted with grass, and over-stocking would seem to benefit instead of injuring it. It is not merely grass, however, but a great variety of nutritious herbs, upon which sheep, cattle, and horses are dependent for pasturage. During a day's journey over the open pasturage land of New Zealand one might see little else than stinted flax and fern tussock, grass and anise plant. During a day's journey over some of the pasturage land in Australia, one would see wild flax, the same as that which is cultivated in Great Britain ; wild tares, wild oats, wild hops, trefoil, chickory, camomile, sarsaparilla, horehound, daisies, buttercups, hyacinths, violets, wild carrots, parsnips, and an innumerable variety of other vegetables. It would be futile to attempt to give any general description, however, as one part of the country differs so greatly from another, whilst what is found in one place may not be found in another. The astonishing variety of vegetable life is certainly one of the great leading physical characteristics of Australia, but one must travel far and wide to appreciate this fact. It does certainly appear most remarkable that, amid the apparently endless variety of vegetation, poisonous plants are rarely heard of. In some parts of South Australia the *tute*, so annoying to sheep-farmers in New Zealand, is found : but, with this solitary exception, no one ever hears

C

of sheep or cattle dying from poisonous plants in Australia.

It is a beautiful arrangement of Divine Providence, and a good illustration of the special care of Him who doeth all things well, that in a part of the world of His creation liable to severe droughts and want of seasonable showers of rain a special remedy should have been provided to meet the want, and a kind of coverlet should be made, altogether of a singular texture, to be thrown over the land to protect it, and thus to render it adapted for the purpose in the great design of its creation. Had all the human beings since the creation of the world been employed in digging, trenching, casting up large mounds of earth mixed with stone, gravel, and boulders of rock, to prevent the soil from being washed away by floods, the whole sown with nutritious grasses, and finally planted all over with trees to prevent the grasses from being scorched and burnt up to the roots by the fierce heat of the sun's rays, it never could have been done so well as it has been done by the great Creator. The trees which are spread all over the land are just of a kind specially adapted to give covering and shelter to the grasses without destroying them. They are ever-green, and the most prevailing kind of them shed their bark and not their leaves ; not their whole bark, but the outer layer, like the scarf-skin of the human body. The leaves are of a narrow elongated shape, of hard gummy texture, and they all droop down towards the earth ; the heat of the rays of the sun in passing through them and the trees' spangled branches is thus broken, and genially tempered to the tender grasses underneath. The value of these Australian trees for shelter has been appreciated by the sheep-farmers in New Zealand, who are importing seed of the gum-trees—which grow very rapidly and to a large size—and planting part of their farms with them ; the pasturage land in New Zealand often resembling the bleak, bare hills of Scotland. The timber is valueless for cabinet-making purposes, however. In some places a considerable distance from the coast there are clumps of forest to be met with, similar to the forest in New Zealand, which contain a large variety of hardwood trees, pine, rosewood, satinwood, cedar, and many others which for cabinet-making purposes are quite as good timber as any which can be found in New Zealand. In the interior there is nothing of this kind, and the only serviceable woods for building and fencing are the stringy bark and iron-bark : failing these, the box. The iron-bark, as its name denotes, is an exceedingly hard and durable description of wood. There are similar hardwood trees along the coast, and small pieces of them form an appreciable article of export to Great Britain for the use of shipbuilders. The so-called cherry-tree, with the stone outside, resembles a large shrub of the pine species, having small red berries upon it, like the pine-trees in New Zealand. The myall is in great repute for making handles for stock-whips ; it is very close grained, highly scented, and never grows to a large size : cattle are very fond of eating the leaves, and, as a

consequence, ' Myall country ' is usually considered
first class. The apple-tree, so named from the
leaves bearing some resemblance to the leaves of
the ordinary apple-tree, is the only other tree for
the leaves of which cattle and horses would seem
to have any liking. There are many of the trees
with peculiar names which are sometimes calculated to mislead. The oak resembles a pine-tree,
and is never found save where there is water, by
the side of a creek or a river. The honeysuckle
is a tree which appears to have received the name
from its deep green and shining leaves.

' Limestone ranges,' ' box,' ' myall,' ' apple-tree,'
' salt-bush,' ' gum and stringy bark,' ' plains,' and
many other names are seen in the advertisements
of ' runs ' for sale. There is one general description applicable to these runs—they are thinly
covered with trees, and the plains are not an
exception to this. There may be plains, and of
very considerable extent, without trees, where the
mirage beguiles the wearied traveller, but they bear
no proportion to the country described as *plains*
which have trees growing upon them. There are
scrubs existing in some places ; those on the eastern
side of the dividing range, visited by the coast
rains, from which the cedar and other highly-prized
wood is obtained, are dark, dense, and impenetrable
forests, surpassing anything of the kind to be met
with in New Zealand, containing countless varieties
of plants, bushes, and trees, like some epitome of
the whole vegetable kingdom, differing in the
luxuriance of growth from aught found elsewhere,

and seeming as if a part of Borneo or some other
tropical region had been transferred to Australia.
Many of the trees, such as cedar, pine, and rosewood,
are of gigantic proportions. Parasitical and creeping
plants are very numerous ; the wild vine hangs
down in festoons so much woven and interwoven
in the branches of the trees that entrance into
one of the scrubs is impossible without the aid of
a hatchet, and even with this auxiliary it is not
very safe for the uninitiated to attempt an entrance.
In addition to the risk from snakes there is a
nettle-tree which has been fatal to horses and
cattle which may have come in contact with it,
and it would not likely be less sparing of a man's
face or hands. There are bricklow scrubs in some
parts of the northern interior, which served in
the early days as a harbour for blacks, and which
now occasion great difficulty in getting the cattle
out of them when they are wanted. Scrubs appear
here and there, but it is very seldom that they
are heard of as impeding the operations of the
grazier.

One is very apt to imagine that families
dwelling far apart from each other in the pastoral
districts, three, four, six, or eight miles, must be
liable to suffer and be distressed by a painful feeling
of solitariness. This is rarely the case, I think ;
at least I never knew of anyone making the complaint. Persons who are out with their flocks of
sheep from morning to night, from one year's end
to another, may indeed frequently complain, but
they always look forward to a more settled mode

of life when they have earned sufficient pecuniary means to establish themselves in a township, and follow the occupation to which they had been originally accustomed. There is a great deal in the topographical features of the country and its teeming abundance of life to amuse, interest, and relieve the mind of the feeling of loneliness which might otherwise prey deeply upon it. The adaptation of external nature to the human mind is here wonderfully manifested. There is a *largeness*, *openness*, and *sincerity* in its natural aspect, every part being distinctly marked and visible in the pure gleaming sunshine. There are no dark dells, places of concealment for the mind to conjure up objects to alarm ; and there is no want of the most cheerful and innocent companions in innumerable feathered songsters, from the early dawn of the morning to the setting of the sun. It is said that the birds of Australia do not sing, that they merely chirp and chatter. Some of them chat most hilarious notes, like the tinkling of bells. The 'laughing jackass' is a prodigy, unexpectedly giving out a loud, uproarious noise sufficient to awaken the 'seven sleepers.' Many of the birds are of the same type as those of Great Britain ; but they vary a little in their plumage. There is our domestic pet, the robin, with the wren, wagtail, crow, curlew, plover, and snipe. There are also the harbingers of spring and summer in the several varieties of swallows, and the cuckoo. The cuckoo is only heard at night. There are bats, owls, and hawks in great abundance, and the mountain pheasant, or

lyre bird, which, however, is rare. The eagle-hawk
is very large, and destructive to young lambs : there
is one species of pure white colour. There are
many varieties of pigeons ; one is very small, being
about the size of a house-sparrow : it is seldom
that more than two or three are seen together ; and
there are no large flocks of them such as are seen
in the forests of New Zealand. The fleshy berries
with which the pine-trees are covered in that colony
furnish them with the greatest abundance of food,
and they do not appear to have the enemies which
they have in Australia. The macaw, a large black
parrot, and the quail seem to be the only two
birds exactly alike in the two countries, with this
remarkable difference—the macaw in New Zealand
is very tame, permitting one to come near and kill
it (at least I know that one permitted me to
approach it), but in Australia it is exceedingly
wild and, indeed, almost untamable. There are
some large birds in New Zealand which do not fly,
and some of singular habits, like the mutton bird,
which burrow holes in sandy places in the ground.
The natives have their seasons for catching them,
and adopt ingenious methods of preserving them
for future use, in a preparation of fat and
aromatic herbs. There is the robin, too, in New
Zealand, where it is very tame. Once in
my travels, one perched on my shoulder.
There are many other birds of hallowed associations which make the forest resound with mirth
and melody. The most remarkable perhaps is the
' tui,' or ' parson bird ' ; the latter name having been

given it in consequence of its being jet black, and having two small white feathers like a clergyman's bands hanging out from its breast. It is of the same size as the blackbird, and is the most noisy of all the New Zealand birds. There are parrots in New Zealand, but not in any proportion to the very great variety which exist in Australia. The climate in Australia being so widely different, there is a corresponding difference in animal life. Among the birds, the most prevalent are parrots. The large white parrot-cockatoos are always seen in flocks, and are great pests to the farmers. The greatest favourite is the magpie, which may always be observed hopping about the door of a dwelling, piping out a long carol of friendly salutations. Of the wild turkey, more properly the bustard, one seldom sees more than two together. The brush turkey, very like the Norfolk, but much smaller, and found in the scrubs in hot districts, is very remarkable for laying a large quantity of eggs, for covering them with leaves and sand, and leaving the sun to hatch them. The emu is nearly as large as an ostrich, to which it bears some resemblance, but it is dark in colour ; it lays about a dozen eggs, and hatches them in the same way as domestic fowls. Large numbers of them may be seen together ; they do not fly, and owe their safety to their fleetness in running. A stroke from one of their feet will stun, if not kill, a dog. The ' native companion ' is a gigantic crane, which is very easily tamed ; but it is dangerous for children who may come near, as it has been

known to make a sudden dart with its long
narrow bill at their eyes. It evidently takes great
delight in companionship, and flocks of them
may be seen together, where there is plenty
of water, employed—as one would very readily say
—in amusing themselves, fluttering about, chatter-
ing, and performing antics. The pelican and black
swan are often seen sailing with great gravity
amongst numbers of other water-fowl in the sheets
of water in the courses of the rivers in the interior.
Wild geese are of migratory habits, and are only
seen occasionally. Wild ducks are very plentiful,
and abound everywhere in the rivers, creeks, and
lagoons. The aborigines adopt a curious method
of catching them, which borders strongly on the
ridiculous. Covering his head with a green sod, a
native quietly swims towards and drops in amongst
a flock, seizes a bird by the feet, and pulls it
under the surface of the water, despatches it there,
and carries on the work of death in this way till
nought remains save the dead bodies floating on
the surface. There are also wood ducks, which are
so-called in consequence of their roosting on trees
at night. They are very abundant in some places,
and are not easily distinguished from common wild
ducks. The musk duck, which smells very strongly
of musk, has the bill of a duck, cannot fly, like its
co-partner, the widely-celebrated water mole, which
forms the connecting link between birds and
beasts ; the latter always diving under water when
anyone approaches it, but it soon rises again.

There is the greatest abundance of cod-fish in

the deep parts of the rivers in the interior, and they
form one of the principal means of subsistence of
the aborigines, who are very expert in spearing
them—whilst catching them with hook and bait
serves as a very agreeable and profitable pastime
to their white brethren. Where there are no cod-
fish, as in the eastern falls of the water, plenty of
eels are usually found.

The kangaroo and opossum have a right of
precedence over all the class *mammalia*, as they
supply the aborigines with food. They appear
to be found everywhere. Kangaroos may be
observed sometimes in unfrequented parts of the
country in considerable numbers together, quietly
browsing like a small herd of deer. They are
very easily frightened, and if any of the females
have young beside them when danger is appre-
hended they instantly put them, by means of their
small fore-feet, into their pouch, or the young leap
in themselves, when the parents hasten away, not
running, but leaping—sometimes incredibly long
distances, as if they were actually flying, over fallen
trees, rocks, and gullies. When chased by dogs,
and hard pressed, the females carrying young take
them from their pouches and drop them on the
ground. They are very harmless ; but it is scarcely
safe to come to close quarters with some of the
males, which are called 'old men.' In one instance
which came under the writer's notice, a gentleman,
possessed of sixty thousand sheep, narrowly escaped
being drowned by an 'old man.' It was rather

amusing to this gentleman to cry 'hilloo' to his kangaroo dogs when hunting. All the amusement ceased, however, when an 'old man' came leap, leaping towards him, clutched him round the waist with its fore-feet, and commenced hop, hopping away with him to a large water-hole to drown him—a well-known and dangerous practice which kangaroos have of fighting their enemies. He cried out lustily, as he might under the circumstances be very well excused for doing, and the faithful dogs came to his rescue. Their hind-feet are the kangaroos' weapons of defence, and, being possessed of immense muscular strength, they will rip up a dog at one stroke, and they very frequently do so. The wallaby is a smaller kind of kangaroo, and harbours amongst rocks. It is a harmless little beast, though there is always pleaded in apology for the cruel sport of killing it, that it is for 'the tail to make soup,' the only part of the carcase which is used by the white Nimrods.

The opossum is the great article of dietary of the aborigines; it is also much valued by them— as it is sometimes by Europeans—for the sake of its skin, which is used for making opossum cloaks and blankets. It is not much larger than a good-sized rabbit. It is found in hollow trees, which the aborigines may be always observed narrowly scanning for marks of the claws of the animal's feet. It subsists on foliage of trees, but it is very partial to maize and fruit, and multiplies with astonishing rapidity where they are growing

The flying foxes and squirrels, in hot districts, are charged with a great amount of depredation. All these animals are nocturnal, and, like other night prowlers, escape the just reward of their misdeeds by coming out of their hiding-places at dark and never being seen during the day. There are a large number of creatures of which very little is known, and there are many peculiar to certain places. They are all of small size, with the exception of the wombat, or native bear, an animal which burrows holes in the ground and lives on leaves of trees—a kind of sloth, but resembling a bear ; it is very harmless, however, as are all the others.

The native cat is a beautiful speckled little creature, but, unfortunately, it has nothing save its beauty to recommend it ; it is the great devastator of poultry-yards, and the source of much vexation, loss, and grief to housewives. There is a large tiger-cat, but it is rarely seen. The native dog deserves all the bad names which are given to it. If in killing a sheep it would content itself by satisfying its hunger in feeding upon it, like the lion, there would not be much to be said against it. The native dog never does this, and the whole pleasure it would seem to have is in destruction—in the biting, maiming, and worrying of as many as possible. It is a pity it should ever have been called a dog, as it bears a much closer resemblance to a wolf or a jackal ; it howls, and does not bark. It has nothing of the cunning of the fox ; it takes bait very readily in small enclosures ;

and the liberal use of strychnine in bits of meat in places which they are seen to frequent has resulted in almost a total riddance of the grievous pest in some places. In consequence of sheep being always kept closely in hand during the day, and the shepherd following them attentively during the night, the opportunities for the native dog to attack sheep are strictly guarded against. It is very different with young calves, however. A cow conceals its calf when newly dropped, and before it is able to follow. It is when thus concealed that the native dog takes the opportunity of falling upon it as prey. There would never seem to be any danger of a native dog killing a calf alongside its mother, and a native dog attempting to do it is one of the grandest sights in nature. The loud, distressing lowing of the cow, when danger is thus threatened to her calf, is a signal to the whole of the herd to come to her assistance. The signal of distress is answered in a loud bellowing by all the cattle within hearing, and is despatched, as it were, in telegraphic calls far and wide. On, on they all rush to the cow and calf at a most terrific pace roaring and bellowing the while, heedless, apparently, of their own safety in leaping over fallen trees and gullies, and as much infuriated as if a stream of liquid fire were passing through their veins. The best appointed army in the world would not withstand the onset of one of these herds of cattle, as thousands may be collected in hastening to the rescue of a calf.

Lizards and guanas are very numerous ; and, speaking of them as one species, they may be seen from two to three inches to two to three feet in length. The smaller ones live upon flies and other insects ; the larger upon mice, other vermin, and young birds. There is one very large kind, like a miniature alligator, having rather a formidable appearance; it seems to live chiefly on vermin, but may be observed very frequently climbing trees, like some of the others, in search of birds' nests. They are all very harmless and, like the snakes, are never seen save in the summer months.

Everyone very soon learns to take care during summer where he places his foot on the ground, especially when treading on grass, which one does with all the horror that is entertained of snakes; and a kind of patriotic sentiment is evinced in always endeavouring to kill every one of those reptiles that may be seen. The unvarying tale, if the valorous exploit of having killed one is performed, is that it was a 'big one '—always a *big* one—just as we talk of a big rat. There is one thing for which snakes deserve some commendation—they always strive to get out of the way; but if trampled upon they will bite, in which case it is not so much their fault as the fault of the trampler. Instances of persons being bitten by them are of rare occurrence, in consequence of everyone being on his guard against them, and the almost universal practice of travelling on horseback. They are very prolific, but the system of always burning the grass when it will

burn, in addition to bush-fires, serves to keep them
down. They have holes in the ground, in dead
trees, and in the rocks ; they prey upon frogs,
lizards, mice, and birds. They sometimes go in
search of mice and rats, and thus find their way
into houses, and, when they have ensconced themselves beneath the flooring, they are regarded with
no very agreeable sensations. In these cases cats
are always found to be very useful in constantly
keeping their eyes upon the intruder, but they
never dare to approach it. Snakes are also accused
of robbing hen's nests. There are several varieties
of them—black, brown, diamond, carpet, whip ;
there are others, one of which, very rare, is about
fourteen feet long. The average length of the
other kinds is about three feet. They will not
move if you happen to meet their eyes first—in
this way they will permit one to come near and
kill them ; but at the moment the eyes are taken
off, they glide away. They are easily disabled by
the stroke of a stick over the back, and, when thus
struck, they are frequently seen to turn round and
round, biting their own body. The aborigines eat
them, but it is only when they kill them themselves,
as their flesh, when self-bitten, would be poisonous.
The antidote of the aborigines for a snake's bite is
perhaps the most effectual—scarifying or cutting
with some sharp instrument the bitten part, and
sucking the blood, at the same time using a tight
ligature above the wound. There is something
deeply significant in the gleam of a snake's eyes,
which cannot be better described than as a ' ray of

intelligence.' This, in reference to a repulsive body and inconceivably disgusting tail, is a figure of degradation ; intelligence and impurity meeting together, not always assented to, and not much reflected upon. A gentleman informed me that in crossing a small plain he observed a bird whirling round and round in the air, and always coming nearer towards the earth ; at last it dropped, and did not rise again. On going to the place where the bird fell, there was a snake. The bird had fallen into the snake's mouth through the well-known power of fascination. Bad as snakes are, they are not nearly so bad as deaf adders, for a bite from one is always supposed to be followed by death. They are about eighteen inches in length. They do not move out of the way, like snakes, but will permit themselves to be trodden upon ; and this readily happens, from their resemblance to a charred piece of wood ; but, fortunately, they are not very numerous, and are never seen in cold districts.

The entomologist would reap a rich harvest of delight in Australia. The whole ground and much of the vegetation in summer are literally alive with insects of very great variety, differing in different places—affording another remarkable contrast to New Zealand, where there are very few insects, and where one may lie on the ground with as little fear of them as he would have on his bed. There are great numbers and varieties of centipedes. The tarantula, a poisonous spider, and the scorpion have no doubt some great purpose in the economy

of creation here, and · are useful in their place.
The greatest amount of harm the insects would
seem to do is to create an uneasy feeling whilst
resting one's-self on the ground, which it is almost
impossible to do without the knowledge of the
certainty of smothering hundreds of them. The
centipede, however, is quite able to resent an injury
of this kind. In lifting firewood fear is always
entertained · of some poisonous insect.

Ants are spread all over the surface, and they
live as if they claimed to be the sole and rightful
owners of the soil. The branches of the highest
trees are not exempt from their excursions and
marauding expeditions. There are many varieties
of them, one of which, the soldier-ant, about an
inch in length, will stand up on its hind legs, and
in this threatening attitude face a man on horseback, as if disputing the right of way. They have
settlements all over the bush, with paths leading
to them, beaten hard and plain like a great public
highway. Some of these settlements are very
conspicuous objects ; and the stranger is sadly
puzzled in endeavouring to guess what they are,
assuming, as they do, the form of conical-shaped
mounds of red earth, occurring at intervals, some
of which are as large as small hay-cocks. These
are ant-hills. There are also ant-beds of greater
or less size, all teeming with life, and not much
elevated above the level of the ground. There
is a species which is provided with wings at a
certain period. The wings drop off after they
have flown about for a short time, and the

D

ground seems strewn with them. The ants are proverbial for their untiring labour and industry, and their thoroughfares through the bush are crowded with them going to and fro, from the early dawn of the morning till late in the evening, those returning to the settlements carrying spoil of some kind or other. In the manna country and season they appear as if conveying bags of flour on their backs. They are the great bush scavengers, and make prey of all the dead animal matter and all the insects which they can get hold of. Great numbers of them may be often observed engaged in a severe contest with a live butterfly or beetle, which they are careful at first to denude of the wings. Unable to draw it along the road whole, it is cut or sliced into small pieces, to admit of easy and speedy carriage. The law of co-operation seems to be well understood by them—help being always rendered where help is required—and if one of them has been unfortunate in laying hold of too large a piece for carrying, there are always plenty ready to give a helping hand. They have evidently some means of communicating information to one another—a language of signs—and they may be frequently observed on their journeys to put their heads close together as if receiving and imparting intelligence. The very diminutive black ants are the most troublesome. They have settlements underground, and come out in myriads, when the scouts have discovered some delectable stuff, such as honey or sugar, in any part of a house. They are always seen in a line like a train of gunpowder, following one after the other, passing and repassing. Every conceivable expedient is resorted to for keeping sugar, preserves, and other sweets out of their reach. The white ant would seem to be one of the principal agents in earth-making in Australia, causing the trees to supply a vegetable mould from the trunks and branches, which is not done with the leaves. In fact, they may be very serviceable in this way, as they will make a heap of earth in a very short time. It is not so agreeable, however, when they effect a lodgment in the pine flooring, and the other timber of a finely painted and furnished dwelling-house, for they will soon make a heap of dust of it.

There is a great abundance and variety of spiders, butterflies, beetles, and moths, and some of the last are very large and beautiful. Every-one complains of the common house-fly being far too plentiful in summer, and a very great annoy-ance. The March-fly, the same as the gad-fly, is very tormenting to horses and cattle. The blow-fly occasions immense anxiety, and, though a great foe to strivers after domestic economy, is a great friend of hungry dogs. It is remarkable that sheep never seem to suffer from it, not even when newly shorn, and when the Australian sheep-shearers appear almost indifferent as to shearing the skin off with the wool. No doubt the great dryness of the climate will account for this.

Mosquitoes, from the bites of which new-comers complain, are not much known in the interior ;

the sandy, bushy, low-lying parts of country, where there is water, being their favourite places of resort. It is only when first bitten that their bites are attended by very disagreeable eruptions upon the hands and face. The sand-fly in New Zealand is almost as annoying, but neither insect is much worse than our midges.

Grasshoppers, caterpillars, and locusts are great plagues in certain seasons in some districts, eating up the green grass and the crops of the farmer. They keep always moving in one direction, like a desolating army. It is only during seasons favourable to the hatching of their ova deposited in the earth that they suddenly appear in such multitudes. The aphis is also a great destroyer, and a very frequent one, no district being, and very rarely a season, exempt from its ravages. There is also many a sorrowful tale told of the ravages of the aphis in gardens.

There is a large fly called a locust, which comes out of the ground in summer, leaving its grave cerements generally at the grave's mouth. In some districts the trees are completely covered with them, and they make a most deafening noise.

There are none of the flying insects so much deserving of notice as the bees. The native bee has no sting, is dark in colour, slender in body, and not much larger than the common house-fly. The aborigines adopt a very ingenious method of discovering their hives ; catching one, which they can always readily do where there is water, they fix with gum, which is easily obtained from any of

the trees beside them, a small particle of white
down upon its back, let it fly away, and keep
running after, keeping their eyes intently upon it, till
they see it alight at its hive, which is always found
in a hole in an upstanding tree. One native, with
a tomahawk or a stone adze in hand, cuts notches
in the tree for his big toes to rest upon, and in this
way, making notches as he ascends, using them as
steps in a ladder, and holding by the tree with one
of his hands, he mounts and very speedily cuts
out the honeycomb at the place where the bee
was seen to enter. The bark from the knot of
a tree serves for a dish to hold the comb, and it
is soon devoured at one meal. Hives of English
bees were regarded, until a comparatively recent
period, as great curiosities. It is most surprising
how fast those bees have multiplied, and how
rapidly they have spread. Farther and farther
every year they are found making their way into
the interior, to the great delight of many who had
not anticipated the arrival of such welcome visi-
tors. With the countless numbers of milch kine,
and the honey lodged in the trees, it is no longer
a figurative expression to say of Australia that
it is 'a land flowing with milk and honey.'
There are none who have benefited so much from
the introduction of English bees as the shepherds
and their families. Out all day with their flocks
of sheep, and straggling after them amongst the
trees, it is a pleasant recreation to look for the
treasures of honey, and a profitable way of spending their superabundance of spare time. There

was one hut which I knew of where the man
employed as hut-keeper had been very industrious
in laying up a large store of it in casks for sale.
The atmosphere in some quarters is strongly
impregnated, at a certain season, with the smell
of honey ; and this is the case especially where
a heath much resembling the Scottish heather
abounds. The mammosa-tree is one mass of
sweet-scented golden blossoms and sprigs, and
there are other flower-bearing trees of a larger
kind, furnishing no end of pasturage for bees ; the
climate would also appear to be highly favourable
to their increase. Many of the trees are hollow,
in consequence of the destruction effected by the
white ant, and these hollow upstanding trees are
excellent places of shelter for bees as well as for
opossums.

The peppermint is a tree which grows to a large
size, and is found only in cold regions ; it is noted
for dropping the manna, an exudation from the
leaves which falls early in the season, and with
which the ground underneath is strewed as
with flakes of snow, or peppermint drops. It
is considered to be very wholesome, and is the
delight of children. There is a great abundance
of it at the proper season in high, upland districts.
There are strawberries, currants, an uneatable
orange, and pears, with varieties of small berries in
the scrubs, but all are of little account. The
native currants, perhaps, claim some importance
from being seen in great quantities in Sydney
markets for sale. They are sent there in a green

state, and are used in making tarts. The only
really valuable wild fruit is the raspberry—more
properly, the bramble—found in cold districts, and
largely used by the settlers in making preserves.
One seldom hears complaints of the want of fruit.

The seed stones of the peach and nectarine are
very easily carried, and as easily put into the
ground ; and the young trees grown from them
will, in three or four years, produce an abundant
supply of fruit. The more expeditious method,
however, and the one usually practised, is to
obtain young trees, which are seen in profusion
in neglected gardens. Grafted young trees, when
they can be obtained, are always preferred. Peach,
apricot, and nectarine are the most common of
imported fruit trees, and may be found near
every dwelling. Grape cuttings and slips from
fig-trees are also easily carried, and there is not
much in the climate of any part of Australia to
prevent one from indulging in the anticipation of
sitting under his own 'vine and fig tree.' One
always requires, however, to know the nature of
the climate and situation before thinking of
planting fruit trees ; and the latitude of a place
will not always serve as a rule for guidance.
Along the coast the climate may be very favourable for the growing of bananas, oranges, lemons,
citrons, pomegranates, guavas, and loquats. In
the same latitude, but at a higher elevation, the
climate may be well suited for mulberries, almonds,
walnuts, quinces, pears, and plums. At a higher
elevation still, about two and three thousand feet

above the level of the sea, and in the same latitude,
the climate differs greatly, being much colder and
adapted only for the growing of English fruits and
vegetables, and the gardens there are found
stocked with the same varieties as those of Great
Britain : apples, pears, plums, cherries, strawberries,
raspberries, gooseberries, currants, peas, carrots,
parsnips, radishes, leeks, onions, potatoes, cabbages,
and greens.   The flower plots, containing the much-
cherished roses, dahlias, daisies, &c., resemble, if
they do not surpass, equally well-attended plots
in Great Britain.   Pumpkins and all the melon
species are easily grown, and many of them, as
the rock and water melon, are good substitutes for
fruit.

'What a fine country Australia would be if
provided with navigable rivers!' is a frequent
remark.   Yet, if there were many navigable rivers,
it would not be the remarkable healthy country
it is ; whilst there would be none of that pure,
balmy atmosphere which we feel to be one of
the greatest luxuries of human existence.   There
are no stagnant marshes, or at least very few, to
hold and drink in the rain as it falls and to serve
as feeders of streams.   There are therefore no
poisonous exhalations to create a miasma in the
atmosphere; to breed the many ills to which flesh
is heir.   Slight showers of rain are not of frequent
occurrence : as a rule, when rain falls, it falls in
'bucketsful.'   Creeks, upon which nearly all the
country is dependent for supplies of water, are the
great reservoirs ; they abound everywhere, between

the ridges and mountains, and are set like pails
beneath the eaves of a house, to catch and hold the
rain as it falls into them, to store it up for future
use. They are simply waterholes at greater and
less distance, of greater and less size, and appear
in the form of the links of a chain. During a
heavy thunder-storm or fall of rain these water-
holes are filled, one after the other, and then
the superfluous water rolling over the surface
conceals them entirely from view, when the creek
or chain of waterholes assumes the appearance of
a large swollen river. During seasons of long
drought many of these waterholes are apt to
become dry, and thus cause the loss of great
numbers of horses and cattle, which, being weak
from scarcity of pasturage, often sink in the slimy
bottom, and, unable to extricate themselves, perish.
Springs are very rare, and it is from the creeks
that the rivers are chiefly supplied. During dry
seasons, therefore, many of the rivers are very
shallow and easily fordable. On the occasion of a
heavy fall of rain they rise rapidly, but the flow of
water subsides almost as quickly as it rises. The
greater portion of the country has the appearance
of having been visited by tremendous falls of rain,
which have washed away all the vegetable mould
and fine soil from the mountains, hills, and ridges,
and lodged it, as in many places of the interior, in
large heaps, ten and twenty feet deep where, unfortunately, it is of no use for cultivation, in consequence of the prevalence of hot winds which scorch
and dry up, in summer, all succulent vegetation.

A heavy and sudden fall of rain after a long drought carries away the fine friable soil, as may always be observed in these Australian downfalls of rain, as easily as meal would be carried from the roof of a house during a shower; and there are large tracts of country where there is little soil remaining—nothing being seen but the substrata of clay, shingle, and sand, with tufts of grass and herbs struggling through the surface. The most lamentable feature in connection with good soil, most usually found in heaps, streaks, and patches, is that the great proportion of it is liable to be covered by water, and the crops destroyed by floods. There are matters here of grave importance for the political economist and the legislator. There are districts where population should be encouraged; there are other places where it should be discouraged. Ten thousand acres is a great extent of land; one hundred thousand acres is still greater; but there are parts of the far interior where even a goat might not be able to subsist on such a large district at one period of the year; whereas at another period the same land might be capable of feeding half a million. Having inquired of a gentleman acquainted with the district referred to, why the New South Wales Government could not get an offer of ten pounds a-year for a hundred thousand acres, the answer was intelligible : 'You understand,' he said, 'there is great want of hills, and a very level country ; when a flood comes there is no place for the cattle to go, to escape being drowned ; they are surrounded on all sides by

water, and yet, when a drought comes, they perish
for want of it.'

Thunder-storms prevail during the months of
December, January, and February—the time of
harvesting and sheep-shearing. Hail-storms occur
at the same period, and are frequently most destructive to crops. The thunder is most appallingly
loud, accompanied by cracks like the bursting of
large pieces of artillery. The lightning, called
sheet-lightning, is vivid and incessant sometimes,
without being accompanied by thunder and rain.
The forked lightning, which always accompanies
thunder and rain, is often seen darting across the
heavens in a zigzag direction, frequently coming
to the earth in a continuous stream, like liquid fire
poured out of a vessel. The number of splintered
trees in high, mountainous regions bears evidence
of its destructive force. The course of the desolating wind, 'the cyclone,' may be found sometimes
distinctly marked in a pathway through the bush,
trees being torn up by their roots, leaving a track
like the clearance for a road or a railway. The
fall of rain is far from being general. A few
families located on the high coast ranges complained to me that it was always raining where
they were. I certainly had never been there
myself save when it was raining. A gentleman
residing far inland, about the same latitude, mentioned to me shortly afterwards that he had not
seen rain for three years. The country without
rain was decidedly the most preferable for the
grazing of sheep. The dew falls there plentifully,

as it does in similar districts ; the grasses and
herbage are of a more nourishing character ; and
the sheep are exempt from the diseases to which
they are subject in cold, wet quarters. There
are always frost and snow on the high mountains
south of Queensland during winter, but none on
the coast.

There is as great diversity of country as there
is of climate. The undulating ridges, like billows
of the ocean, which prevail to a great extent in the
interior, are dreary and desolate, monotony seeming
to hold supreme sway ; but there are many pic-
turesque districts, towering peaks of mountains,
hills and valleys, with vistas extending and spreading out in all directions. No landscape is thought
perfect without water, and a river may be observed
frequently gliding softly along, upon which there
are sporting numerous varieties of water-fowl.
The trees, too, always plentiful, resound everywhere
with the notes of birds, and lend a liveliness to
the scenery which is otherwise so agreeable and
complete.

Where nature does most, man does least. Toil,
sweat, and manual labour are very unsuitable in a
warm climate for the English constitution. Ease
may be more remunerative than labour, and it is
grazing, nothing save grazing flocks of sheep and
herds of cattle, to which the great bulk of the land
is adapted, and to which it can ever be appropriated. The ground, as I have said, is occupied
by the first discoverers, or by those who have
purchased from them or their successors the right

of occupation. These occupiers pay a yearly sum
to the Government for the use of the land which
they hold. In the large domain—it may be forty,
sixty, one hundred, or two hundred thousand acres
—which may be in the possession of one person, a
strong attachment may have grown up, and great
interest may be felt, in the place ; and, in those
instances where the owner and his family reside,
the squatter homes will always be found to bear
the aspect of thriving little villages. They are the
great centres of attraction for working people ;
and if the mansion-house of the proprietor be distinguished far and wide by a generous hospitality
to travellers, there will not unfrequently be found,
also, all the elegance and refinement which obtain
in the lord of the manor's house in England.

Gardening is always an agreeable and profitable pastime where the climate is favourable. A
gentleman occupying a station on the borders of
Queensland and New South Wales seemed rather
ambitious of excelling his neighbours in this delightful art, and nature lent him a strong helping
hand in his garden husbandry. One might guess
a long time without thinking what this was—a
quarry of bone-dust ! This was actually the case,
and I was present at the time when the gentleman
was digging and carting it away from the mouth
of a limestone cave. There were myriads of bats
in the cave, and magnificent stalactites.

Geologists and mineralogists will find everything to their heart's content in Australia ; if they
might not, indeed, have to coin new words to add

to their very large vocabularies. Shepherds have usually tales to tell of something or other which they have found. One showed me a piece of sulphur which he had taken from a layer, another a piece of lead, another a piece of copper; and one told me that he had sunk a well where the ground was covered with lava, and the water was too hot for drinking—tantalising enough in warm weather.

Much remains to be known of Australia. Every day brings with it a fresh discovery of something or other. The remarkably favourable terms on which persons are permitted to go and occupy unknown parts of the interior and follow the pursuit of grazing, combined with the great facility of transit, has served hitherto to bring to light, and advance quickly, a knowledge of much that would have otherwise remained long in obscurity. Some years ago a tribe of blacks was discovered with no hair on their heads. It was long known that buffaloes and alligators abounded within the line of the tropics in Northern Australia, but it is only very lately that pioneers, in searching for 'runs,' found themselves suddenly face to face with them. Three young lads, sons of adjoining settlers, who had gone on an exploring expedition in the northern part of Queensland in search of country where they might establish themselves as graziers, told me on their return, after an absence of nearly twelve months, of a terrible fright which they experienced on seeing an alligator lurking by the side of a river. They had no knowledge of anything of the kind before, and this was a neighbour—even worse, they thought, than the blacks— for whom they were not at all disposed to cherish any friendly feeling. They stuck, however, to the country which they had found, and called a large river which they had discovered by the name of the leader of the party.

CHAPTER III

PIONEERING

LITTLE was known of the early settlement of the interior, all the information having been confined to a small number of persons who occupied large tracts of land. Those settlers had friends and acquaintances whom they were always ready to serve, and it was not in conformity with their interest to make the public acquainted with the discoveries which were being made every day of new territory. There were some who, thoroughly inured to the life and acquainted with the mode of dealing with the aborigines, became very expert in pioneering, and profited largely by selling their right to the country which they had discovered. Some districts were good, some bad, and some indifferent ; and considerable judgment and knowledge of the natural grasses, soil, and climate were necessary in the selection of eligible spots. There was sound and healthy country, and there was country altogether unsound and unhealthy. It might be absolutely ruinous to take possession in some districts for the grazing of sheep, though those districts might do for the breeding of cattle.

Views of permanent settlement were entertained by very few, and the right acquired by discovery to tracts of land as large as an English or a Scottish county were parted with as readily and freely as a horse may be parted with in a market. These tracts are called ' runs ' ; and the sale and purchase of them continue to form one of the largest business transactions in the Australian colonies. The work of pioneering and ' taking up country ' still continues to be prosecuted with as great vigour as ever—more especially in the colony of Queensland, and also in Northern Australia. And the stimulants to money-making, by taking advantage of the great opportunities afforded for the increase of sheep and cattle in grassy districts, without purchasing the land, continue as potently in operation as in the early days of emigration.

Representatives of almost every calling and profession may be found sheep-farming in Australia ; sons of landed proprietors in Great Britain, retired naval and military officers, bankers, barristers, clergymen, clerks, and numbers of others who knew nothing of sheep before they became settlers, save when they had to think or speak of it in the shape of mutton. To learn the management of sheep was to some almost as difficult as to learn Greek and Hebrew : but, where money is to

E

be made, the way of making it will also be quickly
learned, and the sheep being a profitable animal, it
is accordingly made the subject of patient study
and investigation.   It is the same with cattle.
Those who knew as little of a cow and a bull as
they did of a male and a female rhinoceros made
themselves acquainted with the breeding and
raising of cattle, and to what tends most to profit
in fattening them for the butcher and boiling
down.   A 'run,' however, is the first thing to be
looked for under certain well-known 'Crown land
regulations.'   The land in the country to be
discovered must be taken up in 'blocks,' each
block being estimated to sustain four thousand
sheep, and six hundred and fifty head of cattle ;
and for each block there is to be paid ten pounds
annually at the Government treasury, besides a
small assessment on the stock.   The discoverer's
statement that the land will sustain so much stock
is the only guarantee which is required, but a
block originally estimated for four thousand sheep
may be afterwards found capable of feeding two or
three times that number.   There never would seem
to be any difficulty in obtaining a 'run,' which has
been occupied and partly stocked, if we may judge
from the advertisements of stations for sale with
which the columns of newspapers abound.   Adventurous spirits, however, save the expense of
purchasing the rights which others may have
acquired, by discovering tracts for themselves.

Those who have had long experience in the
bush and are accustomed to the work of pioneering

and ' taking up country,' are always careful to avail
themselves of the services of one or two trusty
black attendants before setting out on an exploring
expedition. The aborigines have something very
nearly approximating to an intuitive knowledge of
eligible territory ; and their services are in many
ways valuable, as they know the most likely
places to look for water, and are expert in catching
opossums, which are necessary in the event of
provisions falling short. Their senses of sight and
hearing are remarkably acute ; they very soon
detect the presence of other blacks in the locality,
and give timely warning against any danger which
may be likely to arise from a sudden attack,
should the natives prove hostile. Fears are
seldom entertained of their desertion, or of their
fraternising with other tribes of blacks which may
be met with. Their loyalty to the tribe to which
they belong is proverbial, and desertion to another
tribe would be met with most severe punishment.
Besides, they would be certain to meet with no
very welcome reception from another tribe. As
their services are given more from goodwill than
from hope of reward, it is only from attachment to
persons with whom they are well acquainted that
they are ever prevailed upon to lend themselves as
parties in an exploring expedition.

The kindness extended by some settlers to
aboriginal children in domesticating them, and in
giving them employment as they grow up, has been
sometimes the means of enriching the families of
the former. The black boys who have formed an

E 2

attachment to their masters' sons are always ready
to do whatever their young masters ask them. In
breaking-in refractory young horses, which are
usually the most valuable animals, a black's services
are always in request ; whilst in rough, scrubby,
and mountainous country none can compete with
them as horsemen in the mustering of cattle and in
' heading ' mobs of wild horses. Young men who
from early childhood have associated freely with
them, and are acquainted with their habits and
disposition, acquire a degree of confidence which
leads them to think little of the difficulties of
pioneering and taking up country when the blacks
are the great obstacle in the way. The temptation
to hazard an enterprise is sometimes very great, as
first-rate tracts may remain unoccupied in consequence of the blacks being numerous and hostile.
Mr. Peterson, the son of a most respected old
settler, was not more than twenty-two years of age
when he resolved to make an excursion into the
interior, to take up a station in a part of the
country of which he had heard favourable accounts
from an old stockman of his father who had been
there, and who was now the owner of a station not
very far distant from the district to which young
Mr. Peterson proposed to go. ' Yes, Micky go,
said a strapping young black fellow, apparently
quite delighted at the prospect of a long journey,
when Peterson put the question if he would accompany him. Tom and Bill, two old convicts, assigned
servants of his father, also said that they would go.
They set no value on their lives ; there was nothing

to prevent them from going, whilst they were very
likely glad of the change. Peterson said, rather
thoughtfully, as if warning them of the danger to
which he was leading them, 'We'll chance it.'
Tom said, ' As long as I have my rifle in my hands,
I am not afraid of blacks.' A mob of young heifers
and some bulls were drafted out from old Mr.
Peterson's herd of cattle to stock the district which
was to be taken up. The two assigned servants
were placed in charge of the bullock-dray, which
contained two years' supply of flour, sugar, tea, salt,
clothing, horse-shoes, etc., with implements for
erecting a hut and a stock-yard ; Micky, the black
boy, and his young master taking charge of the
cattle and a few head of horses. There was very
little expense incurred in the expedition, and, as
they had all been inured to bush life, everything
went on as they expected. If the pole of the dray
broke, Tom was quite competent to put another
one in ; and if any of the team of working bullocks
died, it could be very soon replaced by one of the
heifers which travelled alongside. After about six
months' wearied travelling in bush tracks, leading
from station to station in occupied districts, sometimes on the banks of a river, at other times over
stony ridges, through valleys thickly matted with
grass, and over mountains and hills thickly covered
with trees, they found themselves on the confines
of the territory which they proposed taking possession of from the black proprietors. Their pro-
spects did not look very encouraging, however. At
the last station on their journey they saw two men

on horseback, with carbines in their hands, tending a small herd of cattle. They might have remained there also, and supported one another ; but it was country that they wished to take possession of to which a personal claim could be established, and the right to which could be placed beyond all dispute by the mere fact of priority of occupation. One thing was clear enough, and this they learned from the men at the station—the blacks were anything but friendly ; and they had the evidence of this with their own eyes, each of them with whom they had met having darted out of sight. Peterson knew well how to deal with them : not to trust them ; to keep them at a distance, but at the same time to show no hostility towards them. It was satisfactory to learn that no one had been there before him ; that the country beyond was wholly unoccupied, and that he might take up his blocks anywhere. He continued to travel down the banks of a river, with his dray and cattle—the blacks taking to flight, like wild ducks, as the cavalcade advanced : a very bad omen, and arguing anything but a peaceful settlement amongst them. Peterson was, however, in no way disheartened ; down, down the river he still descended until he came to an alluvial flat, with some ridges closely adjoining ; and here he halted, thinking it would be a good spot for the head station. There was no time to be lost in marking out his boundaries, and in sending a description of the district which he had taken up to the Crown Land Office. Their steeds were in good condition, and, tomahawk in hand, and accompanied

by Micky, Peterson rode about ten miles farther
down the river, marked a tree as the extremity of
his run in that direction, with frontage to both sides
of the river. Peterson was not very greedy, at
least not so greedy as some persons have been ; he
was content with fifteen miles on both sides of the
river, extending ten miles backwards, which he
estimated as four blocks. Tom and Bill were set
to work, and in a very short time succeeded in
erecting a hut. They were proceeding with the
erection of the stock-yard, and had gone some
distance with a cross-cut saw to fell timber for
splitting rails. The blacks had been watching
them, however, and, unobserved, had stealthily
crept up near to them, until they were within reach,
and were enabled to make a fatal dart with their
spears. Bill was killed on the spot, a spear having
passed through his body ; Tom was mortally
wounded his cries were heard, however, by Peterson, who was instantly at his side on horseback,
with his loaded rifle ; but he could only hear from
the dying man's lips what had occurred, of which
there was fatal evidence in the spear still quivering
in his body. Peterson was quite equal to the
occasion, though he had now no one but Micky
to support him ; and it was really a most trying
situation. Micky was little better than a boy,
and was seldom entrusted with a rifle. Peterson
was there all alone, far in the wilderness, surrounded by hordes of savages, ready to fall upon
him, all thirsting for his life ; and there was the
dray, with the two years' supplies, and a herd of cattle

to be looked after. So long as he was on horseback, with the rifle in his hand, and pistols in his
holsters, he felt no danger whatever, he said, as he
could keep any number of the blacks at bay—
could dance round them and pick them off one by
one. They had evidently had experience of fire-
arms, as they carefully avoided showing themselves,
and were afraid to come near or to stand in sight
of that of which they have such aversion. Convinced that they would make another attack upon
their now very helpless party, Peterson was never
thrown off his guard, but it was impossible to keep
the hut and dray in sight all the day, when he and
his companion were both out with the cattle. On
returning one night they found that the hut had
been broken into, and that the blacks had been
helping themselves to the two years' supplies.
Matters were now becoming serious. There was
the prospect of starvation before them, or the alternative of quitting the district, with the destruction
of all Peterson's fondly-cherished hopes, added to
the loss of the two men, and it was very apparent
that the blacks kept their eyes closely upon them.
Surmising that they would soon return again, he
entrusted Micky with the charge of the cattle, and
lay in ambush within rifle range of the hut. He
had not been long concealed when he observed a
black fellow crawling stealthily towards it on the
ground ; he levelled his rifle and, taking sure aim,
fired—the black fellow lay dead. Peterson had his
plans formed. He knew that the aborigines were
very easily frightened ; he, therefore, cut off the

black fellow's head and buried the remainder of
his body ; the head he carried into the hut, and
carefully deposited it in a cask from which they
had been abstracting sugar. A large number of
blacks came next day to the hut ; they obtained
an easy entrance, and, watching their movements
at a distance, to his great satisfaction, he observed
them making out of the hut in the maddest
possible haste, stumbling over each other in their
eagerness to escape. Their sudden flight and trepi-
dation were easily accounted for : their eyes had
caught sight of the black fellow's head. I have the
authority of Peterson for saying that the blacks
deserted the district immediately, and that he was
never troubled with them again. He made some
important observations to me as to the manner in
which wild tribes of blacks ought to be treated,
which agreed exactly with the statements of others
who have had a great deal of experience amongst
them. The most of the 'brushes' (butchering,
you know) with the blacks arise from the sheer
brute ignorance of the whites. They first make
friends of them, and pamper their animal tastes
and propensities, which must be gratified, and it is
very natural for them to take a man's life, or to do
anything else which might stand in the way of obtaining a bit of tobacco, some sugar, or some flour.
The point to be observed is to keep them in sub-
jection by awe and reverence—prohibit them
from coming near the homestead—don't meddle or
disturb them in any way ; and if they want tobacco
or anything, give it merely in payment for work,

and nothing more. Kindness they don't understand. Those remarks, however, apply only to
districts where the natives are wild and unruly. In
quarters which have been long occupied tribes of
blacks may be seen roaming about from station to
station on the most friendly terms with the settlers,
not the slightest fear being entertained of them—
many of them, in fact, being strongly attached to
their masters, and making themselves highly useful
to the settlers. The females very frequently act as
domestic servants and nurses, whilst the men are
employed as bullock-drivers and stockmen, and
the boys in going messages or in tending cattle.
They will never, however, remain long at one place,
and are always ready to fly, like birds out of a cage,
back to the bush, where they live encamped by the
side of a creek, or river, subsisting on grubs found
in dead trees, opossum, or fish—or on an occasional
young calf. They seldom remain longer than one
night, however, at one place. Messages are very
frequently sent to all the members of a tribe—
some of whom may at the time be very profitably
employed at stations—to attend a ' corrobora,' or
meeting of the whole tribe, to enforce the observance
of some heathenish rites ; or, perhaps, to prepare
for battle with another tribe for some offence, such
as that of taking away one of their 'gins,' or
females.

It is always understood that to take families
into districts where there is danger from the blacks
would be highly improper, and such a course
is generally carefully avoided. Mr. Peterson

mentioned the case of a family, with whom the
writer was well acquainted, who ran serious risks
from the proximity of some of the more unruly
aborigines. The father of the family had engaged
himself as superintendent of a station on the very
outskirts of occupied country, and took his family
with him. A white woman in that quarter was a
novelty, and Peterson did not grudge a journey of
seventy miles to visit the family occasionally. He
warned them, however, of the great danger to
which they were exposing themselves by permitting
the blacks to go in and out of their house, and by
showing great kindness to them. In long-settled
districts such a course would be thought nothing
of, and indeed it prevails universally; but this
was a different case. During one of his visits, Mr.
Peterson thought it proper to expostulate again
with his host and hostess on the impropriety of
their conduct. The advice was immediately acted
on, and a black fellow, on being refused admittance
into the house, went away very moodily—seemingly
as a much wronged and injured person—and having
laid hold of his spear, which was outside, he
returned and threw it with all his strength from
the door of the house. It was intended for his
benefactress, who was at the fire-place at the time
with a tea-pot in her hand. She narrowly escaped
being killed, the spear having passed beneath her
arm and pierced the side of the tea-pot. Fire-arms
were immediately in request, and all the encampment of blacks about the place instantly fled,
brooding over revenge. A breach had, however,

been created, which it would take a long time to heal. In such cases, and in cases of stealing cattle and breaking into huts, severe retaliatory measures are resorted to, and blacks are generally fired upon when they are met in districts where their depredations have been committed, or they are driven off like wild animals. This is never considered, however, a very safe and economical method of procedure. Marauding bands of blacks, here to-day, away to-morrow, and bent upon destruction of life and property, are anything but satisfactory, and every precaution should be taken to keep them quiet. Some most lamentable instances have occurred of individuals, and even of whole families, having fallen victims to their perfidy and revenge— victims, too, it must be said with regret, of want of knowledge of the aboriginal character. It is almost impossible for any one with the smallest shred of humanity in his soul not to feel compassion for the naked, homeless, miserable, destitute-looking creatures, all wearing the image of humanity, with smiles very often too on their countenances, redolent with good nature, and apparently susceptible of great sense of kindness. The blacks do not, however, take this view of their case, as they have no consciousness of being so abject as they are supposed to be. Very likely they entertain contempt for those who, acting towards them as if they thought them so, would rob them, if they could, of their freedom and independence. They would appear, nevertheless, to have a strong sense of justice. A woman who refuses to give them all

she promised for bringing a supply of firewood
has her child taken away, and its mutilated remains
exposed on a tree before her house on the following
day. The death of an equal number of whites is
made to atone for the same number of blacks.
Details of their deeds, or misdeeds, would not be
very edifying, however. The first occupants of the
land were left to defend themselves and their
property in the best way they could, until the
establishment of the native police—a body of very
recent origin. An old shepherd pointed out to me
an old stock-yard which he had seen at one time
stuck round with blacks' heads, to deter other
blacks from approaching the homestead. He
always went armed, he said, when following the
sheep, and could not even go for a bucket of water
at his hut without another man keeping guard over
him with a musket. This old shepherd, in whose
hut I stayed one night, whilst narrating some of
his hair-breadth escapes, gave a rather curious
narrative of the adroit manner in which a black
fellow succeeded in escaping the contents of a
blunderbuss. The shepherd had an aboriginal
woman living with him, as was very customary
with old convicts. The blacks made a rush upon
his hut one day when he had been out ; ' they
escaped helter skelter, however, when I entered,'
he said, ' but there was one black fellow who had
not time to get away, he having been rummaging
about trying to get something to take with him.
I thought I was sure of *him*, and kept pointing my
blunderbuss at him ; but what does he do ? he

lays hold of my "gin" and keeps her always
between me and the blunderbuss, whichever way I
pointed it ; I could make nothing of him, so he
escaped into the bush, dragging the "gin" before
him, and going backwards.'

It is never thought sportsmanlike, or honourable,
to kill or fire at a hare in its lair, and some
consideration of this kind might be fairly pleaded
in favour of the blacks ; and if three white men, of
whom I heard, could—as they really did—surround
an encampment, and continue firing amongst them
until they were all killed, it only goes to prove that
the whites are capable of committing as great acts
of cruelty as the blacks. The eldest boy of one of
those white men had been taken away and killed,
and this fact might go far in extenuation of the
frightful barbarity—murdering the whole encampment. But there was certainly nothing of this
kind to warrant still more merciless dealing with
blacks in another case of which I heard, where
they were disposed of like vermin, by mixing
strychnine in the bread in the huts which they were
wont to rob. The devil has been called an 'ass,'
and there was certainly abundant evidence of the
fact in the case of the man who committed this
fearful crime, and whose *grippiness*—determination
not to lose anything, and predilection for driving a
hard bargain—was a point of weakness which easily
exposed him to the risk of being taken advantage of,
and ultimately rendered him the victim of a swindle
by which he sustained the loss of everything which
he had taken such unscrupulous means for holding

possession of. Merchants at the time were realising
15 and 20 per cent. by advancing money upon
stations ; he entered the lists with them, and the
opportunity was not to be lost of concluding an
excellent bargain, as he supposed, with a gentleman
who was to give him a high rate of interest for an
advance of six thousand pounds. It was a con-
certed plan to rob him ; he was waited on at his
own house, and, at the gentleman's request, gave a
draft upon the bank for the amount, deriving great
satisfaction at the thought that the payment of the
money was beyond all dispute a conclusion of the
bargain. The legal formalities by which the right
and interest in the station were to be made over to
him were to be attended to on the following day,
at a stated place and time. Nothing was seen,
however, of the 'gentleman' at the stated place
and time ; all that could be ascertained being the
fact that he had been seen very early in the
morning at the bank, and had received the six
thousand pounds. The loser afterwards left for
another part of the globe, where, perhaps, he might
find more honest people to do business with.

Whilst sympathising with the blacks, the fact
is not to be lost sight of that they are capable
of committing frightful atrocities, their conduct
sometimes being more that of ferocious wild beasts
than of human beings. The refinement of cruelty
which they have been known to practise has, perhaps, no parallel in the history of any other race of
savages in the world. One of the oldest settlers
mentioned to me that he had found one of his

convict servants tied to a tree, still breathing, his eyes having been gouged out, and portions of his flesh having been rudely pricked out as with the points of spears. The leniency of the blacks, however, is as little extended to those of their own tribe who may provoke their ire by disobedience to some native customs. A gentleman told the writer that a black boy in his service, having failed to comply with some heathenish rites, such as a tooth knocked out, or something of that sort, was seized by the tribe he belonged to, cut and hacked all over with boomerangs, was at last subjected to the very extremity of torture, and pinioned down to an ant-bed with forked sticks. In this position his employer found him, but life had fled.

During the long, weariful evenings which a clergyman in the far bush is so frequently doomed to spend in the huts of stockmen and others, it is impossible to avoid listening to stories of adventurous life. On those occasions the blacks form a very common topic of conversation; and the recital of encounters with them are sometimes not very agreeable to hear. One stockman, Neil M'Closky, who was one of the earliest pioneers, assured me that he, with two men and a black boy, was bold enough to face, and fight, and conquer, two or three hundred natives in the open field, in a fair pitched battle. It was at the time of the large emigration to Adelaide from the United Kingdom, when cattle were bringing very high prices. To avail himself of this market, M'Closky, with two men and a black boy, set out with a herd of heifers, through what at that time was unfrequented country, following the course of the Darling river. The blacks mustered in large force as they proceeded on their journey.—sometimes in their front, sometimes in their rear, all hooting and yelling at the highest pitch of their voices. No doubt could be entertained of their murderous intentions. The colours red and white—emblems of war—shone out conspicuously from their naked bodies, whilst they were all armed with spears, boomerangs, waddies, and shields. The cattle were greatly frightened, and it was very difficult to keep them together. The herdsmen left the river during a moonlight night with the cattle, with the object of escaping their foes ; their remorseless pursuers were, however, upon them at the dawn of morning next day. It was necessary to bring the cattle back to the river to drink, and there were more of the enemy there waiting them. All thoughts of the blacks were sometimes lost in endeavouring to keep sight of the cattle. This state of matters continued for some days in succession, the herdsmen being hunted and pursued at every step of their journey. Congratulating themselves that they had at last outrun the blacks, not having seen them for two days, they quietly encamped by the side of the river, and their horses being much fatigued by the reins of the bridles being always held in their hands, they were hobbled and allowed to graze freely Whilst repairing their saddles, and sitting comfortably by the fire, old Joe—one of the men

—shouted, 'The blacks, the blacks!' in a voice of
grim horror and desperation. There was no
mistake about it—there they were, coming down
upon them like a swarm of bees, completely surrounding them. The cattle, when the blacks are
in any way troublesome, always run off, and bound
away, like deer in a forest, at their utmost speed,
having a wholesome dread of the natives' spears;
and on seeing and hearing them, M'Closky's herd
dashed into the river and swam to the other side.
The blacks were rushing in upon them, 'A horse, a
horse, a kingdom for a horse;' but their horses
were hobbled at some distance from the place of
their encampment, and it was hopeless to attempt
reaching them without being speared. To have
got on their horses' backs, even at some risk, was the
only likely means of escaping, there being otherwise no hope of averting an attack from the over-
whelming horde of savages. All the provisions,
however, for the journey lay beside them—flour,
salt, meat, tea, sugar, saddles, blankets, etc.—
and to have left them would have been to lose
everything, and to expose themselves to certain
destruction. There was little time for thinking of
escape, or for calculating risks; it was a sudden
surprise—the boomerangs came whizzing through
the air all round them, and they were for some time
kept shifting about and leaping on the ground to
escape the dangerous missiles, in much the same
way as if they were treading on live coal, or were
dancing a quadrille; and they would certainly have
been struck had it not been for the branches of the

trees with which they were surrounded. How
M'Closky managed at this very critical juncture
will be best narrated in his own words : 'Steady,
men, steady ; you have got your guns and ammunition—let's fire one after the other ; stand you
there, Joe ; Jack, stand you there, and I will
stand here,' pointing towards the places where they
were to stand in a circle as it were, with their backs
to each other ; 'we'll do for them, one after the
other ; Jacky I told off for picket duty, to see that
none of them crawled on the ground near and
through a scrub not far off. I had not finished
speaking when Joe roared and bellowed like an ox
when drawn up to the pen with the green hide
rope, and the red-hot branding-iron is applied to
its ribs—a boomerang or waddy had struck him
on the thigh ; he fell forward, but quickly rose again,
determined, he said, to sell his life as dearly as
possible.' Children, but certainly not men, might
have been frightened at the 'guys' which the
blacks had made of themselves, with streaks of
pipeclay and red ochre on their faces, and fantastic
figures bedaubed all over their naked bodies, no
two blacks being alike. They had certainly striven
to make themselves as hideous-looking as possible,'
and some degree of care had been taken to draw
an image of a horrible-looking human countenance
on the face of the small bark, or wooden shields,
which some of them carried on the left arm, with
the object of striking terror into the hearts of their
enemies. By frantic leaping, shouting, and by
brandishing their spears, boomerangs, and waddies

F 2

in the air, they had heated their blood and worked
themselves into a state which was intended for the
boiling or the fighting point. They had evidently
never been under fire before, and knew nothing of
the deadly character of the weapons which they
had set themselves to contend with. They had
now nothing left but spears and waddies, having
expended all their boomerangs, which, being in-
tercepted in their flight by the branches of the trees,
failed to return to them, as they generally succeed
in making those singular weapons of warfare do
Their spears are much to be dreaded, as they can
throw them to an incredibly long distance, and
unerringly hit the object aimed at. If a small bird
perched on a tree serves as a target for the
exhibition of their marvellous skill in the use of
this weapon, they will succeed in striking it.
They marched boldly up to the front with all they
had in the world, and about as naked as they
came into it, their conduct being like that of moths
flickering round the flame of a lighted candle.
M'Closky and his men kept up a rolling fire as
black after black approached within dangerous
proximity; but the painted bark and wooden
shields were a very sorry protection against the
leaden bullets. The hubbub and screaming
amongst the 'gins' as they saw warrior after
warrior stricken to the ground, and the cries from
the wounded, appeared to discomfit them quickly,
and to unman their resolution altogether. All at
once the whole body fled, as if some invisible
power had come in amongst them, which it would

be death to one and all to stand near to, or attempt
to resist. A parting shot from M'Closky's rifle
accelerated their speed. The wounded struggled
to get away, dragging themselves along the ground,
and one of them, seeing a piccaniny, a young child,
who had been left behind in the *melée*, made
towards it, grasped it in his feeble arms, stumbled
and fell. M'Closky could not look any longer at
the horrid spectacle, and was glad to rush away
from a place that was ever attended in after-life
with harrowing recollections. The blacks were
entirely nude—at least they had nothing on their
bodies but the usual small strip of opossum skin,
like a rope, round their loins, knotted in front ; and
there was always the horrid spectacle of seeing the
effects of the firing in the gashes upon the naked
bodies of the poor savages. It was a severe lesson
which had been taught them. one which the
survivors could not fail to remember ; and it has
been by many such lessons that the aborigines
have been subdued, and the life and property of
the settlers protected and preserved. The sight of
a man with a fowling-piece, in a quarter where
there is hostility or want of confidence between the
blacks and the settlers, will cause almost any
number of the former to run away, they being as
easily scared in this way as crows from a newly-
sown field. It is never desirable, however, that
they should be so easily frightened, or that they
should be on any but the most friendly terms with
their white brethren. They are dangerous as
enemies, but as friends they make themselves

useful in many ways. A gentleman who occupied
a station on part of the river where M'Closky had
the brush with them, as a fight with them is
modestly termed, assured me that he found them
of the greatest service, and that he had no fewer
than twenty-five thousand sheep herded chiefly by
them. He had studied their character sedulously,
had made himself acquainted with the proper way
of managing them ; and, having a whole tribe under
him, he had succeeded in checking their roaming
propensities.

In the very exciting and interesting work of
'taking up country' no persons were so likely to
succeed, or were so fully competent for the task, as
three strong, active young gentlemen newly arrived
from Scotland, whom we shall call Brown, Smith,
and Robinson, and who were possessed of a fair
amount of capital, which they purposed investing
in sheep-farming. Brown had been amongst sheep
since he was a boy ; Smith and Robinson were
very willing to learn ; they were all imbued with
a strong determination to succeed, and breast the
waves of adversity, whatever these might be. They
had not heard much about the blacks, however,
and did not take them into account in their
reckoning : but one thing they were certain of—
whatever others had done, they were capable of
doing ; whatever difficulties others had contended
with, they were as capable of contending with. In
some respects their plan might be said to have
been well formed, as numbers of young men who
arrived at the same period, and who had been

induced to purchase land, had lost all their money.
The first settlers could not manage to get along
with their patches of cultivation ; floods, droughts,
fluctuating prices, weevil, with the scarcity and
the bad quality of labour, sadly dismayed them.
Those who had sheep and cattle seemed to be
placed beyond the reach of adversity : there was
but little labour required in tending them ; they
were not so liable to be swept away as a field of
wheat, nor would they be laid flat on the ground
and thrashed during a heavy thunder-storm ;
whilst even in a season of severe and long-continued
drought, cattle, sheep and horses, if not too
numerous, could find something to subsist on.
Besides, those animals had the power of locomotion ; but the case was very different with
expensively-cultivated fields of cereals. Prosperity
seemed always to attend those whose wealth consisted in live stock ; and the fine natural pasturage
of the country afforded scope for carrying on the
pursuit of grazing. When a new discovery seemed
all at once to have been made, the valuable
purposes to which the waste lands might be turned,
there was quite a *furore*. It was at that period
that the searching for runs and 'taking up country '
commenced, and from that time is to be dated the
origin of squatting—the monopoly of the waste
lands by the class called squatters ; which is such a
source of heartburnings and disaffection amongst
the people. At the time of, Brown, Smith, and
Robinson's arrival sheep were selling at two pounds
a head, cows at twenty to thirty pounds, and

horses at sixty to one hundred pounds. With such
prices, and an unlimited supply of rich pasturage
land at a merely nominal rental, no doubt could
possibly exist in the mind of any one that grazing
in Australia, with any ordinary degree of care and
management, was a most remunerative occupation,
and a most eligible mode of investing capital. So
thought Brown, Smith, and Robinson, and so
thought every one. This was a few years before
the commercial crisis of 1843 in Great Britain,
which brought sheep down in price in Australia
from two pounds to two shillings per head, cows
from twenty pounds to twenty shillings, whilst
horses suffered much the same rate of diminution
in value, bringing ruin to the door of almost every
settler. It was during the time of high prices, and
when the feverish excitement of taking up country
was at its height, that Brown, Smith, and Robinson
arrived. Their course was clear ; to do as others
were doing : to find out a run—to penetrate the
interior, and take up country for the grazing of the
stock which they intended to purchase. No one
could tell them anything about the subject, as
no one had ever been there. At least, such was
the case generally at that time, though more
information may now be gleaned from the memo-
randa of explorers. They might obtain a description of the country which had been taken up
in any one direction by applying at the Crown
Land Office ; they knew also that by far the
greater part, nearly all, in fact, of the country right
up to the Gulf of Carpentaria was unoccupied, and

that they would come upon a run somewhere or
other ; whilst they could not be wrong in following
the track of others who had gone before them.
There was no time to be lost, and instead of going
by a very circuitous road, but which was plain all
the way to where they proposed travelling, they
resolved on shortening their journey, took passage
on board a small schooner which was to lead them
to a small shipping port, intending to make their
entrance from that point into the bush, and cut
right across the country, as they had heard that
others had done, thus saving themselves a journey
of nearly two hundred miles by the circuitous route.
Agreeably to the information which they had
received, they found everything at the shipping
port which they required for their journey—horses
for riding, and carrying their blankets, clothing,
provisions, tin pots, and other necessaries. The
fire-arms which they had carefully brought with
them from home were strapped along with the
other freight to the large carrying-saddles on the
backs of the pack-horses. They set out on their
exploring expedition in the highest possible spirits,
amazed and interested by the novelty of the
scenery, by the many singular objects which
attracted their attention, and with which they were
everywhere surrounded ; birds, trees, shrubs, everything was quite new to them, and afforded an endless subject for conversation. They experienced
nothing but joyous sensations, which increased
immeasurably in the golden dreams which 'hope,
high hope,' nurtured within their breasts, of future

wealth and independence. The kindness of every
one with whom they met was everything that could
be desired—all being ready to give information,
although they were long ignorant of the full force
of the meaning of the taunting expression ' new
chums ' with which they were sometimes greeted.
They had been taught how to hobble their horses,
to prevent them from straying when encamped out
at night. Not one of them, however, could make
damper, and, instead of flour in their commissariat
stores, they supplied its place with biscuit ; whilst
they learned from a bullock-driver, beside whose
dray they encamped on the first night, the use of
the quart-pot for making tea.

The first few nights were spent very pleasantly
indeed beside the fire which they had kindled at
the usual encamping places where there was water.
There was no scarcity of firewood—plenty, indeed,
of it everywhere ; the only grievance in the world
of which they felt at the time any reason to complain was the mosquito, which is always very
annoying to new-comers ; but they sought protection from it by rolling themselves up in their
blankets ; and, having been fatigued, they were all
very soon asleep. For about fifty or seventy miles
from the place where they started the road was
distinct enough, as it had been trampled by drays ;
but beyond this there was, properly speaking, no
road, the track being merely a ' marked tree-line.'
An experienced bushman could have no difficulty
in tracing his way from one tree to another ; but it
was altogether different with those unaccustomed

to bush travelling. The marks on some of the trees would be obliterated in consequence of bush-fires, some of the marked trees would be blown down by high winds ; and once thrown off the track, it would be difficult to find it again. They had come to the marked tree-line, and commenced the ascent of the Australian Alps, described in some old maps as ' impassable ranges,' and there was nothing now to guide them in their course save the trees, which they very soon lost sight of, not understanding the great importance of the tree-line, and the necessity of looking patiently for it as if their very lives depended upon it. They were still in great glee ; always cheering themselves with the hope that they would soon be out of the forest and have a good view all about them, not knowing that Australia is one immense forest. They continued for several days climbing hills and steep mountains, crossing deep ravines, experiencing great difficulties from bluffs of rock, boulders, loose stones, and the thick underwood overtopped by branches of trees, in which they were frequently employed cutting a passage with their pocket-knives. They were not as yet in any way disheartened. They persevered, assured that ' perseverance,' as they had often heard their parish teacher say, and as they had also read in books, would ' surmount all difficulties,' and be ultimately crowned with success. As the summit of one high mountain was reached, there was always another beyond it, and that, too, must be ascended before they could hope to obtain a view of what they expected the table-land, and

descend upon the prairies, where the settlers were
all busy with their flocks of sheep and herds of cattle,
accumulating riches rapidly. About two weeks had
been expended in the vain attempt to cross the
range of mountains, which they could have done in
three or four days by following the marked tree-
line. They were unceasingly the victims of a
delusion in imagining that they must be near a
homestead, from the beautiful green swards of grass,
newly sprung up, the ground swept clean as with a
broom, from recent bush-fires which had covered
it, resembling the lawn before a gentleman's
dwelling, whilst they mistook the rocks glistening
in the sun in certain places for houses and castles.
Smith and Robinson were sure—'quite certain,'
they said—that they saw a man, sometimes a
woman, carrying a child. It was a mere illusion ;
but they could not help going to these rocks,
and much time and labour were expended in
this way, to the great fatigue of both themselves
and their horses. At last painful misgivings began
to come over their minds, though they did not say
anything to each other, that they had been too
venturesome. They had heard of persons being
lost in Australia and never heard of, and this, too,
might be their lot. They helped to cheer one
another, however, but their lips did not speak what
the heart felt. Their horses were greatly fatigued,
as they had lost some of their shoes, and were
crippling ; and they themselves were compelled to
walk on foot nearly all day under the sweltering
heat of the mid-day sun. Their clothes were very

much torn in going through brushwood and under
branches of trees their feet latterly became
blistered and swollen, and as their calf-leather
boots could not be put on again when taken off, by
bandaging their feet with strips of cloth they
travelled with greater freedom and less pain.
Indeed, few persons could have shown so much
power of endurance, and they really proved themselves to be stout-hearted fellows, to whom every
praise was due, despite their foolhardiness. There
was one thing a very great danger which they
did not understand or anticipate - their minds were
apt to become as weak as their bodies, and to be
incapable of comprehending the seriousness of their
situation, and of devising a means of escape. Once
a cloud, like a shadow of death, came over them ;
it might be called, indeed, a cloud of ignorance,
with all its attendant miseries, ruin, desolation,
death, like some palpable object which their heads
might touch. In the labyrinth of stupendously-
high mountains, separated by yawning gulfs, they
approached the brink of a precipice, which was
concealed from their view by saplings and bushes.
The pack-horse lost its footing, rolled down, down
to the abyss beneath, and with it all hopes of sus-
taining themselves—' lost, all lost, quite lost ! ' It
was a moment of dreadful agony ; their hearts
departed from them ; their feet were slipping
another instant and they anticipated rolling down
after the pack-horse. Quick as lightning Brown
called to Smith and Robinson, ' Hold the horses fast
by the heads ;' the reins of the bridle they had been

holding, loose, and dangling in their hands. Fear
was communicated to the horses by the sudden
hold laid on them, and they dragged their blind
guides from the dangerous ground. Brothers in
adversity, they wisely avoided any altercation ; they
slowly retraced their steps, intending to follow the
water up, quite contrary to the great bush-directory,
to follow the water down. When lost, it was a
most hazardous task to ascertain the direction in
which the water was running. Smith, at one place,
took off his Glengarry bonnet and threw it into
the stream ; it was soon out of sight, and he lost
it. Robinson quietly remarked to him that he
might have thrown a bit of a branch instead, and
kept his Glengarry. It was impossible to tread in
the face of almost perpendicular mountains, which
wound round and round both sides of the stream
like the letter g. Their perseverance and determination had their reward in one sense, by satisfying
their minds that they were, as they thought, always
ascending higher ; but their mistake was taught
them in a very startling fashion. The gnawings of
hunger had compelled them to kill one of their
horses ; they set out next morning with a portion
of the horse-flesh, with as much as they thought
would suffice before reaching the station on the
high table-land, which they were told they would
come to after crossing the mountains. They toiled
on, travelling where travelling was possible, and
coming always nearer, as they supposed to their
destination ; when all at once, and to their utter

confusion and consternation, they came to the very
place where they had been several days before !
There could be no doubt about it whatever : there
was the dead horse, with the large gashes in its
haunches, where they had been cutting out steaks.
They all looked on in mute amazement, staring at
the dead horse as if it had been a grave newly dug
for their interment. For some time they could
not avoid thinking that they were in some enchanted country, and were the sport of the weird
sisters of the forest. Brown at last said he knew
how it was—they had been travelling in a circle ;
Smith and Robinson nodded assent. Their knees
bent beneath the weight of their bodies, and borne
down by their accumulated load of anguish, sorrow,
and disappointment, they all sank like dead men
to the ground. They said that they had a compass,
but that they did not know how to use it. How
they ultimately succeeded in getting out of the
mountains, where they had been shut up for nearly
six weeks, they could not very well explain.
Desperation, a last effort for life, had supplied them
with almost superhuman courage and strength ;
leaving their horses' saddles, and everything that
was burdensome to carry, they had set out on foot,
keeping close to the stream, and following it to
its source, subsisted on kangaroo-rats, having
already acquired so much knowledge of life in the
bush as enabled them to cater for food without
going to the very extreme—killing a horse. Most
providentially, they came to a shepherd's hut at the

side of the stream which they had so persistently followed. An old convict who was in charge of the hut made some tea for them, and afterwards conducted them to the head-station, where they were most kindly treated by the owner. They gradually recruited their strength, and in a few weeks, after being refitted, were enabled to make another start ; this time largely benefited, one would very naturally suppose, by their experience. The necessity of using greater caution in their future endeavours, snakes even, upon which they were always in danger of trampling, might have taught them. In crossing a high range of mountains, out of reach of the coast-line, and debouching into the interior, there was a magnificent view presented to them of the vast, boundless expanse of territory lying stretched out before them like a scene on the canvas of a panorama. 'Links, links,' said Smith, being put in mind of the irregular mounds of sand or downs which he had seen on the sea-coast of his native country ; not a plain to be seen—the whole country covered with trees, except a few white specks that looked like lakes, but which they afterwards discovered were places where there were no trees. Their path seemed now very plain and easy. The country was now being occupied, and there was nothing for them to do but to proceed down the course of some of the rivers or creeks, until they came to where the last station was taken up.

They had now come to one of life's great turning-points, when all the issues of the future

seemed as if dependent on the first step. They
were ignorant of a great number of things, and
these they could never hope to learn from mere
hearsay ; none of them could make damper, salt a
bullock, shoe a horse, or handle an adze ; and they
could not tell men as ignorant as themselves how
to do those things. They did not know good
grazing country from bad—knew nothing of the
modes of management. 'Divide and conquer,' and
divide and be conquered. They separated, and
went through a course of colonial experience
which they ought never to have learned. Had
they remained together—in other words, remained
true and faithful to themselves--enjoying each
other's society, deriving mutual support, countenance, and encouragement, they would have supplied
in a large measure the deficiencies under which
they were all labouring, and made themselves
masters of the situation. They are now all dead.
Brown and Smith's tale is very soon told. They
were unfortunate, to begin with, in a selection
of bad country, taking up land that had been
passed by others. There were expenses connected
with the starting of a station for which they were
altogether unprepared, and never anticipated.
Money is easily borrowed from merchants upon
security of stock and station at exorbitant rates of
interest—15 and 20 per cent. ; indeed, as high as
25 per cent. has been mentioned, and prevails
to an enormous extent. They never could get
themselves out of the hands of the merchants, from
whom they were obliged to receive their supplies

G

for the station—another large item of merchants'
profits. 'There is no friendship in business,' so
passes the mercantile axiom, though there will be
always found a great deal of apparent friendship
in the forming of business connections. Brown
had a lot of maiden ewes which, if he had been
permitted to keep (as he said to the writer, in a
long winter night when he was staying at his
homestead, and listening to the tale of his adven-
tures), he would have got out of the merchant's
hands. They must be sold, however, as the
merchant wanted the money in payment of long
outstanding arrears.

Notwithstanding the scrambling nature of the
occupation of searching for and finding out 'runs,'
and the great jealousy which arises in observing
others who are more fortunate, in occasionally, it
may be, finding a superior class of country and
holding possession of a large tract of it, the
greatest favour and kindness are always manifested
to 'new arrivals.' Neighbourhood is valuable,
affording as it does the advantages of society, of
co-operation, and of greater security against the
aborigines ; and no complaint has been heard of
the first occupants having failed to assist by
counsel and a generous hospitality those who have
followed in their wake. Their lands are quite
secure, the boundaries well defined, and registered
in the archives of the Crown Land Office ; and a
right is granted or conceded to the land in occupation almost equal to purchase in fee simple. They
cannot suffer, therefore, in any way from others

following in search of land. Difficulties have
sometimes arisen, however, from the uneven extent
of country which may have been in possession of
one individual, and from the difficulty of not
knowing what was altogether included in it. An
amusing incident was told to the writer by one
who has gained for himself a name of great and,
indeed, of universal renown as an explorer. In
searching for a run he at last came upon a fine
district, and set to work, with a black fellow who
always bore him company, marking out his
boundaries by making marks on the trees with a
tomahawk as he went along, describing in this
way the large domain he proposed appropriating
to himself as the right of his discovery. It was
like travelling round a large English or Scottish
county, and some days were occupied in this preliminary but necessary work. Suddenly, however,
he came upon a comfortable homestead ; and he
found that the district had been formerly occupied :
so that all his labour, zeal, and fervent hopes were
instantly dashed to the ground. He had commenced his Australian career with a flock of sheep,
placed in bad grazing country ; they all died, and
at the time of which we write he had fallen into a
singular 'line of business'—that of finding new
country, and selling his right of discovery to
others. The Government of Queensland has very
wisely imposed a check on this practice, by not
recognising any individual right unless the discoverer is in occupation, and the country or ' run '
is stocked to the extent of one-fourth of the sheep

or cattle which it is estimated to carry. Matters
in regard to the ' searching for runs,' as now going
on in Queensland, Northern Australia, and the
unoccupied territory of South Australia, were
much in the same state in New South Wales at
the period of Brown, Smith, and Robinson's arrival
in the last-mentioned colony ; and some of the
incidents contained in their narrative are not
without instruction and guidance for intending
emigrants and settlers. Robinson was very fortunate, indeed, in the land which he had taken up,
and for this he was mainly indebted to the advice
of an overseer of a station, with whom he had been
acquainted at home ; indeed, he had learned all
the usual routine and many important lessons
from that overseer. A melancholy interest sur-
rounds the closing scenes of his life, the truth
of which was vouched for to the writer by a
gentleman well acquainted with him ; and it may
not be without interest to the reader. There
was an object to him of far greater concern than
his wide domain, and the multiplied wealth which
his annually increasing flocks were ever hastening
upon him—one that he loved above all, even more
than himself. It was for her to whom he had been
betrothed in his fatherland that he was treading,
with unwearying care, and unbending resolution,
the steps in the ladder that were to conduct him to
future wealth and independence. His betrothed
was to him an object above all earthly value : he
could not honour her too much ; he could not
suffer too much for her. Like some presiding

earthly divinity, it might be truly said that it was her eyes and mind that were attending all the unnumbered cares and duties in his striving and industrious life. There was a foe which his unsuspecting nature never dreaded; he had received as a guest, and most hospitably entertained in all the frankness of unreserved friendship, one who was very soon to visit his native hills. A word! what may a word *not* do? what has a word *not* done? How many have writhed in agony from a word—their hopes, once like summer blossoms, drooping, languishing, dying, under the blighting curse of a word, leaving them to be cast like ' loathsome weeds away'! ' By thy *words* thou shalt be justified, and by thy *words* thou shalt be condemned.' Think of this, ye slanderers—think of it with all its deep, all its everlasting significance. 'The power of life and death is in the tongue.' Robinson's treacherous friend, as if on some fiendish errand, whispered into the ears of his betrothed that he was a drunkard. The poisoned arrow festered in her heart, and she wrote that she would not be married to him. The world was no longer to him what it had been; in an evil hour he hastened his departure from it, and was numbered with the dead. Under the shade of an iron-bark tree, not far from the wool-shed, there still remain the letters of his name carved out in a block of wood, marking the place of his interment. Many years after his death the station which he had formed, and fully stocked, was valued at sixty thousand pounds.

The aborigines of Australia are fast melting away, and continue to disappear rapidly before British settlers. The blankets supplied to them by the Colonial Governments, with the sugar, flour, meat, and clothing which they occasionally receive from settlers, in payment of such services as stripping bark from trees, carrying water and firewood, would seem to act as so many destructive agencies, by enervating and debilitating their constitutions and hastening their decline. In districts where they might have been seen at one time roaming about in numbers of ten, twenty, or forty, there is now rarely one to be seen ; and the expression is not unfrequently heard : 'Where have they all gone to ?' Not one of the aborigines of Tasmania (Van Diemen's Land), where they were at one time very numerous, now remains, and the same tale will soon be told of the aborigines of Australia. Every part of country has its distinct tribe of aborigines, or blacks, as they are almost invariably called, belonging to it ; and when far distant it is found that they do not understand the language of each other. In districts long settled these tribes have almost entirely died out, and nought may be found remaining of them save at some settler's homestead, in the form of some decrepid old man, or gin, or both ; bearing so very little trace of the human figure and the lineaments of the human countenance that they might be very readily trampled upon by the horses' feet, and be mistaken for cast-off black wearing apparel, or black oil-skin cloth. Numbers of them,

old and young, may be very frequently seen
huddled together beside a small fire, which they have
kindled near a settler's homestead, all in a most
torpid state, from having gorged themselves with
food after a long fast. There is no lack of attention and the offices of humanity shown them by
the settlers. If the night is cold, they will receive
any quantity of clothing ; but as soon as the
sun rises and they feel warm, the clothing is
thrown aside and forgotten. They generally keep
their blankets in winter ; and the gins, or females,
are rarely without an opossum cloak. When
employed at a station, both men and women
are always clad in English clothing. They
will not remain long at one place—they must
be always roaming about ; indeed, their wild
nature would seem to be altogether invincible,
unless when they are taken young, and inured to
the habits of civilised life, and even then they are
always ready to burst their bonds. The writer saw
a black boy whose portrait appeared in a number of
the 'Illustrated London News,' he having been
taken to England by Mr. Geddes, of Warialda, an
old and respected colonist and pioneer ; but no
sooner had the black boy returned to his native
encampment than he threw off every article of
clothing he had upon him, and fled into the bush,
seemingly as delighted as a bird escaping out of a
cage.

The native police, or 'black trackers,' as they
are sometimes called, are a body of aborigines
trained to act as policemen, serving under a white

commandant—a very clever expedient for coping
with the difficulty, which appeared almost insurmountable, of hunting down and discovering
murderous blacks and others guilty of spearing
cattle and breaking into huts. There is never any
friendly feeling subsisting between one tribe of
blacks and another; they are very often at war,
and blacks taken from other tribes, usually far
distant, will heartily enter into a scheme of pur-
suing other blacks and bringing them to justice.
Consequently the native police were the very men
wanted—in accordance with the old adage of ' Set
a thief to catch a thief.' When a black is once
put upon the track of others, he will follow it up
like a bloodhound, until he comes upon the object
of his search—not by the sense of smell, but by
the astonishing power of sight, by minute observation of the impressions left on the ground of the
footsteps of those on whose tracks he has been
directed to follow. Native police, or black trackers,
are never heard of except in districts where the
blacks are troublesome—that is, in newly-settled
districts. They are all in the pay of Government,
are taught the use of fire-arms, and are clad in
uniform like other police officials. They are first-
rate horsemen, and take great pride in their gay,
soldierly appearance and high position.

The nude, houseless aborigines of Australia
present a striking contrast to the aborigines, or
Maoris, of New Zealand. Climate will explain the
cause of the different types of character of many
things on the earth's surface, but the great differ-

ence in the climate of New Zealand and Australia
will not explain the difference in the character of
the native races of the two countries. The New
Zealanders have sprung from an entirely different
stock of the human family. The aborigines of
Australia are jet black, have strong, coarse black
hair, a slim build, and not much muscular strength.
The New Zealanders are of a brown, tawny complexion, and have also black hair, but not so coarse
and strong. Their bodily frame is well developed
—each one seeming tall and muscular, and they
have finely-formed features. They have pahs, or
villages, in which they reside, though these seem
at a distance little better than a large motley
collection of thatched pigsties ; and the first
impression of them is not much improved on
approaching nearer and examining them — a
stockade formed of trunks of trees, sunk in the
ground, and close to each other, usually surrounding them. They are most industrious, cultivate
the soil, and are acutely alive to the advantages
of European civilisation. Many of them acquire
wealth, and have saw-mills, flour-mills, and small
vessels ; but in trading, however, they always bear
the character of being frightfully avaricious ; they
cannot endure to see others gaining anything that
they think they might possess themselves ; hence
their jealousy of the English colonists and the
wretched New Zealand wars. Marriages are not
of unfrequent occurrence between Europeans and
Maori women, and the children by these marriages
are generally good-looking. A German with

whom I met in the northern island was married
to one, and he said that he had found no cause
to regret it. Their children were receiving the
best education which the town of Wellington
could afford. He had fifty Maoris employed as
servants. The New Zealanders are said to be partial
to these marriage connections with the Pakehas or
Europeans ; and half-castes are numerous—chiefly
the progeny of old whalers, runaway sailors, and
convicts. In a rambling tour, the writer having
entered one of these settlers' houses, agreeably to
the invitation of the owner, found the Maori wife
the very paragon of excellence as an active,
bustling, thorough-going housewife, whilst the
house was well provided with all the usual domestic
comforts. Their children were attended to in
their education, along with Maori children, by a
missionary. The man, an old whaler, deeply
lamented the misfortunes which he had suffered
from English settlement, as he had been formerly
doing a brisk trade with the natives, and with
vessels off the coast. All this, however, was now at
an end. The following incident is worth relating,
as an illustration of the presence of mind and
shrewdness of the Maoris ; and in this case of a
Maori woman. A ship, in which the writer was a
passenger, having arrived in the harbour of one of
the settlements, a number of New Zealanders came
in their canoes alongside, for the purpose of selling
fish, potatoes, and fowls, which they had brought
with them. In the midst of a great deal of haggling
between them and the mate of the vessel, as to the

price of their commodities (they are hard, ' gripping '
persons to do business with), a Maori woman, with
the usual mat on her shoulders, hair floating in the
breeze, and otherwise very sparingly clad, took it
into her head to clamber up the ship's side. There
was no objection to this. On reaching the deck of
the vessel she stood erect as a statue, in no way
abashed ; and commenced walking about with an
amount of ease and dignity which would have
graced a princess. After satisfying her eyes with
all that was to be seen, she came boldly up to a
lady who stood behind me, and entered into conversation with her ; some of her words were
English ; and her meaning could be understood.
At last she put the question, ' What kind of
country yours ? ' The lady had come from Edinburgh, and commenced describing, by pointing to
the windows of the ship's cabin, the fine houses,
riches, and splendour of the city of Edinburgh.
The Maori woman listened very thoughtfully and
attentively to all that was said, and, with great
amazement in her face, replied, ' And what brought
you here ? ' It was a poser. The Scottish lady
gave an answer, but a very unsatisfactory one,
which must have confused the New Zealand
woman's mind more and more, as to a people who
had such a good country of their own coming to
theirs, probably to take their country from them.

Their susceptibility to religious impressions
and their attachment to the outward observance of
religion are very remarkable. More strict observers
of the Sabbath could not have been found anywhere

than at a pah at which I was present on a Sabbath.
One native declined to speak to me, pointing with
his finger towards the sky, and saying it was
Sabbath. In acting thus he was following the
injunctions understood to have been given by the
missionaries to avoid intercourse with Europeans
on the Sabbath. There is a wild, magnificent
beauty to be met with in many parts of New
Zealand. This Maori settlement was one of these
places. It was beside a large bay, having a narrow
entrance into the ocean, a strip of flax and fern
land skirted it on one side, sloping from the base
of a very large and high mountain, which was clad
to the very summit with dense, dark, impenetrable
forest, and communicated to the mind an impression
of great strength and protection ; whilst a feeling
of awe and solemnity seemed to hang over the
Maoris, nestled at its foot, and engaged in the
pursuits of peaceful industry. There were patches
of cultivation scattered everywhere about, interspersed by small streams of water, pure as crystal,
proceeding from the bendings of the mountain. It
was Sabbath, and some of the Maoris had come
considerable distances on horseback to attend
divine service. There was as much commotion as
at a fair during the early part of the day. The
quarrelling of dogs and pigs, which had accompanied some of them, was very great, and there
was no small ado in establishing order amongst
those unruly animals. There was a neat church
and belfry, which the Maoris had erected at their
own expense. The church was not used, however,

as it was a day of beautiful sunshine, and they
preferred squatting themselves on a grassy knoll
beside it. There were 'young men and maidens,
old men and children,' all wending their way
to the house of God. All the old men were
tattooed, and some of them had frightful visages:
none of the young men were tattooed, however, as
the practice had been discontinued through the
influence of their Christian teachers. There were
many clothed with their native mats- others partly
clad in English clothing ; and some of the half-
caste females were attired in the latest style of
fashion. Quietly, one by one, and without a
sound or whisper, they arranged themselves in
circles on the grassy knoll the men and the
women dividing. They had not all sat on the
ground when there commenced, in all the 'stillness
of Sabbath morn,' the tolling of the Sabbath bell.
How strange the sound of that bell seemed to me
in that place, calling to church such an assemblage of Christian worshippers ! The greatest
extremes in the world the highest civilisation and
barbarism—seemed suddenly to meet and close
in harmony ; the Christian brotherhood of men
asserting itself independently of all earthly dis-
tinctions. The hidden springs of action and
motives to conduct are far beyond the reach of
mortal eye. It is God that searcheth the heart -
man looketh on the outward appearance ; but one
might have travelled over all Christendom, and
have not seen a more devout demeanour in a
large body of Christian worshippers on a Sabbath-

day. They all appeared as if spellbound, and under the shadow of a great overawing power—in the actual presence of the Supreme—as indeed they were. They had been under the ministry of a Wesleyan Methodist missionary, but, as he had many places to attend to, he was absent on this occasion, and his place was filled by a native teacher, who conducted the services in the Maori language.

Pioneering and the searching for 'runs' have prevailed in New Zealand as in Australia, more especially in the southern or middle island—that part of New Zealand in which the provinces of Southland, Otago, Canterbury, and Nelson are situated. The natives there are not numerous, and there is no hostility to be dreaded from them. Graziers are not given to complaining ; they have the use and benefit of the land, are not required to purchase it ; indeed, they are not permitted to purchase, though this has occurred sometimes, so that a family, all things considered, with a few cows and plenty of pasturage, might not find much ground for complaint in New Zealand. If there are no native dogs in New Zealand, there are not wanting wild, ravenous animals. I heard one grazier state that his brother killed, with his rifle, fifteen hundred wild pigs in one year. They had destroyed nearly all his lambs. There was no use made of the dead pigs, and they were left to rot on the ground where they were killed. In their wild state they do not appear to fatten. There are dogs bred for the purpose of catching them, called 'pig dogs.' Some have adopted a clever method of clearing their cultivated land of fern roots, which are very difficult to get rid of, by folding pigs on the land and leaving them nothing to eat but the fern roots.

If a rebellion had broken out among the natives of Australia, two or three ounces of gunpowder would have been amply sufficient, and far more effectual than the two or three millions of good sterling English money which has been expended in the endeavour to suppress the rebellion of the natives in the northern island of New Zealand—that part of New Zealand in which Auckland, Wellington, Taranaki, or New Plymouth, are situated. The different tribes of natives in New Zealand, it appears, do not agree any more than the different tribes of natives in Australia. A chief of a tribe sells his land to the Government, at Auckland; there are other chiefs opposed to the selling of land, and they fall upon the chief who has sold his land and kill him and his men. The British authorities do not interfere, and bring the murderers to justice. 'This won't do,' say some of the more intelligent native chiefs; 'let Queen Victoria rule *her* people, and let us have a Maori king to rule *our* people.' 'Mistaken clemency is at the bottom of all our troubles in New Zealand,' says the Reverend S. Ironside, at the head of the Wesleyan Mission, twenty years a missionary amongst the natives, and personally acquainted with the rebellious chiefs, in a lecture on New Zealand, delivered and published in Sydney by Mr. Ironside—a copy of which he presented to the writer. The following remarks made are not without interest, being written from personal observation. 'The north island is mainly a system of mountains and valleys. A rugged mountain range runs down the centre, mostly covered with dense bush, scrub, and creeping vine, up to its very summit, with two or three snowy peaks lifting up their hoary heads to the sky. This range sends out its spurs either way towards the coast, sometimes abruptly abutting on the shore, with valleys of the finest agricultural land, a rich black loam, several feet in depth, between them, through which a never-failing stream of the purest water merrily sings on its way to the ocean. These streamlets abound everywhere. In the inland forests and hills nature has provided for the traveller a good substitute for ladders in climbing, in the roots of the large trees spread along the surface of the ground, while the clinging vine not unfrequently furnishes a capital hand-rail. But, at best, the getting over the ground is slow, heavy, wearisome work. Through the whole extent of the country you may travel everywhere without fear of sting or bite, for there is no ravenous beast, no venomous reptile, to be found. There are materials for a very comfortable bivouac. Wood and water for the fire and for cooking, leaves and fern for your couch, and you may speedily replenish your stock of provisions from the neighbouring stream or bush. The rivers and seaboard are well stocked with fish, from the magnificent hapuka, or rock cod, through all the

varieties down to the piharan, or delicate lamprey.
I remember once, when voyaging in the mission
boat, in Cook's Straits, my natives, with rude
appliances, in about two hours, loaded the boat far
more deeply than was desirable with baracoota.
Then the forests, lakes, and rivers equally abound
with feathered game, such as the kupuka, the kaka,
the weka, the patangitangi. There are, moreover,
the fern root, the mamuka, and other edible and
succulent roots, and stems of native plants, from
which in former times the natives derived a large
portion of their subsistence. I think, therefore,
that the rebellious natives are not to be readily
starved into submission. They can live in comparative abundance in their native country, where
a white man would starve. The best harbours on
the coast have the least quantity of available land
in their neighbourhood, as they are mostly hemmed
in by high and rugged forest-clad mountains,
rendering great outlay necessary in order to open
up the country, while the finest plains and valleys,
with hundreds of thousands of acres of rich and
fertile soil, are without harbours at all—either an
indifferent roadstead, like Taranaki, or a river with
a frightful sandbar stretching across its mouth.
The rivers and harbours on the west coast have
all their sandbars at the heads. The prevailing
westerly wind, meeting the current coming out of
the river, raises a bar across the mouth, on which
even in comparatively fine weather the sea sometimes breaks with awful fury.

'The middle island differs materially in its

II

general features from the northern. There is a
rugged mountain range, a great part of which is
above the snow line, running down the island, from
north-east to north-west, but through the whole
distance it runs nearly along the western coast ; its
spurs run right down to the coast line, and deep
blue water runs between them right up to the bases
of the lofty hills, very much like the fiords of
Norway, I should imagine. There are no sound-
ings in some of the inlets—you might take the
"Campania" and moor her to the stately forest
trees on the precipitous shore. The east side of
the island presents the fine spectacle of splendid
rolling prairies of rich natural grasses, varying in
width from fifty to seventy and, in some places,
one hundred miles, to the foot of the western range.
This grassy land, I am told, will carry in its wild
state one sheep to the acre ; in some places more
than this. These plains are as fine an agricultural and pastoral country as is to be found in
the world. There are few natives on the island
—not more than five thousand altogether. The
climate is too cold for them, and the former
cannibal raids of the northern tribes have greatly
diminished the few residents. The settlers of the
five provinces, into which the island is divided, have
a glorious future before them. They have no fear
of war with the natives ; they are only just near
enough to hear the bursting of the storm. Everything there is fair and flourishing. Many useful
and valuable minerals only wait the necessary
capital for their development. To say nothing of

the gold-fields, there are copper, chrome, iron, plumbago, coal in abundance ; and I quite expect that marvellous though the past of that island has been, its future will be more so.

. . . . .

' They have derived great benefits from civilisation. Their implements for husbandry, and for building their houses and canoes, were of the rudest description. It must have cost them weeks of patient labour to bring down a forest tree with their rude stone axe, of some six inches long and two or three inches broad, with a very blunt edge. Their dress was composed of flax mats of various degrees of fineness. I have seen Kaitaka mats of such a fine and beautiful texture, worked by native women, that they would grace the form of the loveliest of her sex. But all these things are passing away. Being well supplied with European tools and wearing apparel, their own rude substitutes are thrown aside. The Maori is very imitative ; he soon knows how to use the tools of civilisation. There is nothing in husbandry, or in the mechanical arts, that a native will not acquire, and in some instances he will surpass his teacher. His ingenuity in discovering means of increasing his ammunition during the wars was a marvel to the civilised soldier. Marble, copper tokens broken up into slugs, and other hard substances, serve him in the place of lead ; while the exploded percussion-cap is made to serve over and over again, by putting in the phosphorised head of a vesta.

' Ever since I have known the Maoris, their

numbers have been rapidly diminishing. Year by
year, the decrease is greater. In one valley I remember, twenty-four years ago, with at least one
thousand souls living there, not more than three
hundred could now be found. A large proportion
of the population is adult ; in a careful census of
the people of the district under my charge some
years ago, I found five hundred men, three hundred
and seventy-five women, and about two hundred
and fifty children ; and from late inquiries it would
appear that a like proportion obtains all over the
country. If an epidemic visits the country, it
makes fearful ravages among the poor natives—
the measles having destroyed hundreds of the
people.

   ' I wish, with all my heart, they could have been
preserved as a race. I hope the remnant may.
But "the Lord reigneth." His purpose in placing
man on the earth was that he should " be fruitful
and multiply, and replenish the earth, and subdue
it." The poor Maori could not do this, and would
not allow others to do it for him, so he is passing
away. Noble efforts have been made by the British
Government, by Christian missionaries, and by
high-minded philanthropists to serve him, and they
have been so far a comparative failure. I cannot
but grieve deeply over this untoward result. But
those beautiful and fertile islands will be the home
of a healthy, happy, prosperous community—I
hope a truly Christian one—and the remnant of
the native race will blend among the descendants
of our own people. If the dream of Macaulay

about the future is to be realised, and a New Zealander in the coming age seats himself on the broken arch of London Bridge to sketch the ruins of St. Paul's Cathedral, it is likely he will be an Anglo New Zealander.'

CHAPTER IV

SQUATTING

Rapid Appropriation of Territory—Squattage Right—Runs and Blocks—Laws affecting Grazing—Value of Stations—Gold Discovery—Unstocked Runs—Weeds—Sheep Scab—Farm Servants—House Accommodation—Cattle and Sheep Stations—Schoolmasters and Physicians—Founding of Townships—Camp Followers—Squattage Homes—Land and Land Legislation—Absenteeism and Resident Squatters.

A RIVER overflowing and bursting its embankments, rushing onwards, and spreading itself out in all directions, may serve as an illustration of the advancing waves of population, and the mode of occupation of all the known territory of Australia. It has been owing to the enterprise of private individuals, and not to any action on the part of Government, that the land has been taken possession of and occupied. Government, with its tape and measuring-line, has been completely distanced, and left helpless. Be it right or be it wrong, there it is—the stupendous system, the great Australian fact — *occupation of the land*, and all the use and benefit of the *land*, without purchase. This great fact is one that never requires to be mentioned, as people will always be found ready enough, and in sufficient numbers, to embark in schemes which promise extraordinary returns of wealth, and it requires no bounty or inducement of any kind to assist and encourage them. On the occasion of the gold discovery no step whatever was necessary on the part of the Government to induce the people to go gold-digging, and there have always been found plenty of persons ready to occupy the land on the very favourable terms which have been offered. The great natural wealth of the country spread over the surface, its adaptability to the grazing of sheep and cattle, and the great facility of transit were inducements of no ordinary character in the race for riches to stimulate to acquisition and possession. The problem of the sudden rise and prosperity, and the remarkably rapid extension of occupation and settlement of the Australian colonies, is thus very easily solved. It is easy to point out some of the great public material advantages of squatting. All the natural wealth of the country is instantly reaped, and made as available as a field of ripe wheat and barley, whilst employment is provided for a great number of people. The occupiers of the land—that class of the community called *squatters* or *Crown tenants*—not being required to purchase the land of which they hold possession, they enjoy the full use and benefit of every farthing of their capital ; and it has been this extraordinary encouragement to capital which has made Australia become what it is ; it caused it to be opened up, brought commerce and population to its shores, and provided employment for hundreds and thousands of famishing emigrants from the British Isles. It is not to be forgotten that the first settlers were not required to purchase land, as they secured grants of territory from the Governor in consideration of their employing convicts, whose labour they secured free. The foundation was thus laid at the very commencement of Australian settlement of a plan of colonisation which attracted emigrants by the encouragement which was given to capital, and that encouragement has prevailed ever since, and has thus led to the settlement of every known part of the continent. Money! money! An ass laden with gold has been known to enter a fortified city, where ten thousand armed men could not enter; and but for that great en-couragement—the use of the land without paying for it—Australia would have long remained and been no better than a walled city. If the occupants of the Crown lands reap, as it is usually said, all the benefits of the country, they must, at the same time, be considered as having rendered a large return, if not an equivalent, for the privileges which they possess, in the employment of their capital, by making the natural wealth of the country serviceable for the public benefit. Without very great encouragement to capital, persons would never have been found to embark their money in an undertaking where the issues were problematical; with hazards and uncertainties surrounding them on every side, and with no conveniences of any kind, such as roads and bridges, nor public expenditure to meet public necessities. What centuries would have to accomplish, in purchasing the land before obtaining the use of it, squatting has accomplished within a comparatively short period of time. The squatter's life has not been altogether a smooth one, without difficulties : experience had to be gained, knowledge of country acquired, modes of management to be learned ; besides, there were injurious influences at work, such as droughts, disease amongst stock, fluctuating prices in the London market, commercial crises in England—one of which nearly ruined every squatter in Australia. This is one side of the picture which is never looked at, and, indeed, completely ignored by many who cry out against the squatters—the croakers forgetting all the while that it was the painstaking, industrious hands of that class which were feeding them.

The land being taken possession of and appropriated by individuals, in accordance with Act of Parliament, a right of an important character has been acquired and grown up—namely, the squatter's right. Time has only added to the difficulty of meddling with that right, and increased the complications in which the whole subject is involved. Mr. First has sold his right of occupation to Mr. Second ; Mr. Second has sold his right to Mr. Third, and the land has passed into the hands of Mr. Sixth, or Mr. Tenth ; each one having paid large sums for his right, with the exception of Mr. First, who must also be regarded as having paid very largely for his right of occupation, in the expenses which he incurred in taking up the country, and the risk of life which he probably exposed himself to in 'brushes' with the aborigines. The Government always insists upon its right to the land, and has never, on any occasion, acknowledged the right of compensation to the squatter —except for his improvements—when it takes away any of his land from him, for the purpose of selling it to others. The upset price of 1*l.* per acre, which has puzzled so many, is easily understood ; it was intended originally as a breakwater, to prevent the squattages from being seriously encroached on. There were also some public purposes which were intended to be served in fixing on the high price. Good land is very small in quantity in comparison with bad, and is usually found in streaks and patches on the sides of creeks and rivers. The holders of Crown lands, if permitted to purchase their streaks and patches of good land, would be in continued possession of the large area of bad land adjoining. The getting hold of these streaks and patches has been called 'picking the eyes out of the country,' and the high price of 1*l.* per acre was intended for such land, and as a kind of protest against the spoiling of the country for purposes of future colonisation and settlement. William Charles Wentworth, orator, 'Shepherd King,' and inaugurator of responsible government in Australia, estimated the value of the grass lands before the gold discovery, and when the prices of wool and tallow were very low, at three-halfpence an acre ; and there is a great deal of land in the interior which might be said to be not fit for selling, especially in small quantities. A severe drought, such as that which occurred during the end of 1865 and the beginning of 1866, would be disastrous in the extreme to those whose property consisted chiefly of land. If the country were not liable to protracted droughts, and if there were seasonable showers of rain, the land, for grazing, might be said to be altogether invaluable, as cultivation could scarcely produce a better quality of grasses and herbage than those which are found growing naturally. The climate is hardly adapted to the growing of fine wool. Stations, or runs, vary in size from ten thousand acres to half a million of acres, according to the extent of country originally taken up by pioneers. A gentleman in the Survey Department of New South Wales, employed by the Government in defining the boundaries between New South Wales and Queensland, mentioned to the writer the case of one gentleman who had taken up and occupied one hundred miles of frontage to a river! The boundaries between stations are usually all well defined—as much so, indeed, as the boundaries between gentlemen's or noblemen's estates in Great Britain—and are almost entirely determined and delineated by the falls of water into creeks or rivers, and by marks on the trees. There seems to have been no restrictions as to the quantity of land which one individual might occupy ; and the settler, as the pioneer or squatter may be fairly called, is not confined to one block : he may take

up four, ten, or even twenty blocks, either all adjoining or in different parts. In Queensland, where
the taking up of country has been going on of late
years at a very rapid pace, much disappointment,
and no small amount of loss of time and money,
was sustained by many who had been trafficking
in blocks, taking up country, and selling their
right to it to others. A sudden stop was put to
this by an Act of the Queensland Parliament,
recognising no one's right to the country which he
claimed unless he was in occupation, and had
stocked it to the extent of one-fourth of its grazing
capabilities. There were many who could, with
no small degree of self-adulation, use the phrase,
'I am monarch of all I survey, my right there is
none to dispute' who were rejoicing over their
acquired possessions, and had been at great trouble
in marking their boundaries, and having their
names registered in the Crown Land Commissioners'
books as the rightful, because the first, claimants
to the part of country. They found themselves,
however, suddenly deprived of the fruits of all their
vexatious toil and adventure ; found that it was
a mere shadow which they had been clinging to
and trusting, unless in those cases where they
had cattle or sheep to stock their country. Mr.
Robertson, the Prime Minister of New South
Wales, publicly complained at the time how he
and his partner had been baulked of their Queensland territory. They had neither sheep nor cattle
upon it—some person, with sheep or cattle, had
taken possession of it, and the Queensland Govern-

ment recognised the man with the sheep and cattle
as the proper claimant. Laws affecting grazing or
squatting will be found to vary in all the Australian
colonies, as well as in New Zealand. In the case of
the first occupiers that is, those who have been
the first to take up the country the practice of
the Government hitherto has been to grant a lease
of fourteen years, and at the expiration of that
period a renewal of the lease for ten or for five years.
The stocks are at the same time liable to assessment, to meet the necessities of Government
dealt with as a whole—and are the great source of
maintenance, the pillar of support of the colony.
The assessment levied upon the stock will always
be considered with regard to the interests of the
graziers. If, instead of a penny per head of sheep,
the squatters in Victoria had been called on to pay
a shilling a head after the gold discovery, the increase in the assessment could not have been considered unjust, as sheep were largely increased in
value. The mode, also, of making the squatters
pay for the privileges which they might be supposed
to possess cannot be regarded as in any way un-
fair. The grazing capabilities of their runs are
valued after the expiration of the fourteen years'
lease by persons appointed by the Government ;
and the occupier of a run of a hundred thousand
acres may not have to pay so much as the occupier
of a run of forty thousand acres—the run of forty
thousand acres being estimated to carry more stock
than the run of a hundred thousand acres. Besides,
the squatter has always the remedy, when he

thinks the Government valuation too high, of
having the dispute settled by arbitration. The
squatters in the older colonies of New South Wales
and Victoria cannot complain of much injustice in
having to pay more for their grazing than they do
in Queensland, as they possess greater public advantages, such as roads and bridges, with a larger
population, thus causing them to obtain better
prices for their spare stock. Fifteen pounds a
year for the use of as much land as will graze one
thousand sheep, and twenty pounds a year for the
use of as much land as will graze five hundred
cattle, will not generally be considered exorbitant
taxation or *rental*; besides, the land may, in
favourable seasons, carry two or three times the
quantity of stock above what is estimated.
Previous to the gold discovery runs were not of
very great account, as the value of sheep and cattle
consisted chiefly in the tallow which they would
produce after having been boiled down, and the
rights to parts of country as large as English or
Scottish counties, with all the improvements upon
them —sometimes very valuable—were sold at exceedingly low prices. The same practice was adopted
then as that which continues to be still in vogue.
The station, with all the improvements, is given
in with the purchase-sum of the stock upon it, the
price of the herd of cattle (which might range from
eight to ten shillings; that of sheep from four to
six shillings) ; and the person buying the sheep or
cattle receives along with them the right to the
country where they are grazing, with all the im-

provements upon it, such as dwelling-house, wool-
shed, huts, &c., including the right to brand
the unmustered cattle and horses.   Before boiling
down was thought of, and during a time of great
depression, occasioned by a commercial crisis in
England, stations, sheep, cattle, and horses sunk to
an infinitesimal price, and might be said, indeed, to
have had no marketable value.   A story was told
the writer by an old colonist of a gentleman
arriving in New South Wales at the period referred
to, from England, and purchasing several thousand
sheep at sixpence a head : it was a very cheap
bargain, he thought, and he calculated on realising
a profit by driving them over and selling them in
the Port Philip district.   He failed in his reckoning, however ; after the expenses of the journey,
he had not left himself sufficient to pay the men
whom he had engaged as drovers, and he could
not find anyone to purchase his sheep.   It came at
last to a parley ; and he proposed to the drovers
that they should take the sheep for their wages.
This they consented to, and without any more ado
he turned his back on his way to Sydney, leaving
the men with the sheep to make the best of their
bargain.

The gold-diggings brought about a revolution
in the value of stock and stations, as they did in
almost every other mercantile commodity ; and
no other description of property, perhaps, has been
so much enhanced in value, and shown so little
symptoms of decline.   Population was all that
was needed to bring money into the hands of

the graziers, and the gold-diggings did this most effectually.

The consumption of animal food is very great in the Australian colonies. Beef or mutton is the principal article of dietary in the three meals a day, and every individual is estimated to consume a bullock in the year. From the increased price of sheep and cattle stations are more than quadrupled in value, whilst a fresh impetus is given to the taking-up of new country, aided and stimulated by the largely-increased prices of wool and tallow in the London market. Practically, and speaking generally, the land for grazing is out of the hands of Government altogether, and if any one chooses to commence grazing or squatting in Australia or New Zealand, if he does not go and take up country, he need not go to the Government, but to those in occupation, and bargain with them.

Occasionally there are stations which, from various causes, fall into the hands of Government; the principal cause being the desertion of those places. The Government adopts the usual course of disposing of the right to these unoccupied locations by public auction. The following is a copy of a Government advertisement in one of the Sydney newspapers in reference to these stations:

UNSTOCKED RUNS.

BY ORDER OF THE GOVERNMENT OF NEW SOUTH WALES.

Day of Sale, MONDAY, *29th January next.*

RICHARDSON and WRENCH have received instructions from the Honourable the Minister for Lands to Sell by Public Auction, at the Rooms, Pitt Street, Sydney, on MONDAY, 29th January next, at 11 o'clock,

New Leases for Five Years of the several runs of Crown Lands hereinafter mentioned, upon the terms and conditions prescribed by the Crown Lands Occupation Act of 1861, and the regulations framed in pursuance thereof.

** Full particulars of the boundaries of the several runs may be obtained upon application at Messrs. Richardson and Wrench's Rooms, or from the GOVERNMENT GAZETTE, No. 272, of Friday, the 29th December last.

The special attention of intending purchasers is directed to the following clauses in the conditions under which the leases will be sold, viz. :

The lease of each run for five years will be sold to the person who may offer the highest premium for the purchase thereof, and subject only to the annual rental specified.

The purchaser will be required to pay down at the time of sale a deposit equivalent to 25 per cent. of the premium (if any) offered for the lease, together with the rent computed from the 1st January to the 31st December 1866.

These runs will not be liable to assessment under the Increased Assessment and Rent Act of 1858.

CLARENCE DISTRICT.

No.		Estimated area. Acres.	Rent.
1	Tomara	14,000	£11
2	Marydale	16,000	13

I

LACHLAN DISTRICT.

No.		Estimated area. Acres.	Rent.
3	North Hyandra	64,000	£50
4	North-East Wallandra	64,000	50
5	Salmagundia	23,040	18

MONARO DISTRICT.

6	Murrah	10,000	10

MURRUMBIDGEE DISTRICT.

7	Argalond	16,000	13

NEW ENGLAND DISTRICT.

8	Mooraback	20,480	16

WELLINGTON DISTRICT.

9	Jumble Plains, block B	32,000	13
10	Ditto do. C	51,200	40
11	Ditto do. G	38,400	15
12	Corses Coule	16,000	13
13	Palisthan	64,000	100

The previous occupants of these stations had undoubtedly very good reasons for parting with their interest in them ; and they most likely had been at very considerable expense in the erection of their homesteads. The objection to some stations might be a want of water, and in some seasons, especially in winter, too much water ; another objection might be, that the country was scrubby and mountainous. The subject is noticeable as illustrative of the variety of country, and of some districts which might be said to be scarcely worth having, or even to be ruinous to those in occupation. The country may be all generally described as beautifully grassed, and

thinly timbered ; but the grasses in some parts
are more nourishing than they are in others.
There is the distinction sometimes made between
'breeding' and 'fattening' country ; and there is
the same distinction to be made between all the
pastured farms, some of which are more valuable
than others. The greatest drawback to some of
the best grazing land in Australia is the *grass
seed* ; the tufts of grass throw out long shoots of
seed-bearing stems like oats or barley, and when
the seeds ripen, they come in contact with the
wool of the sheep, and frequently prove injurious
to the health of the animal by penetrating the
skin. The 'thistle' and 'burr' are imported weeds,
and are extremely destructive in districts where
there is rich alluvial deposit of soil, laying it completely waste and absolutely useless—sometimes,
indeed, worse than useless—for the grazing of
sheep. Like the imported bees, they continue to
spread farther and farther every year into the
interior, the one, however, a curse, and the other a
blessing—marching, as it were, arm-in-arm. On
one station, thirty miles in length, and twenty-five
in breadth (very favourably adapted for those
pestilent weeds taking root and flourishing, con-
sisting chiefly of flats of black soil) the owner had
fifteen men employed at thirteen shillings a-week
in the endeavour, if not to extirpate, at least to
keep them down. It was rather a hopeless undertaking, however, as the next flood would sow the
land afresh with seed carried from the banks of
the river. The owner was subsequently desirous

of selling his station, which contained twenty thousand sheep, and about six thousand head of cattle, and for the whole he was willing to take 25,000*l.* This gentleman, who was a very old bush residenter, gave a singular account of himself. He had brought all his money with him from England in sovereigns: the ship in which he was a passenger was wrecked, and his sovereigns, with the ship, went to the bottom of the sea ; he got his foot safely on shore, however, and was reduced to the position of a working man. Nothing daunted, he made his way into the interior and looked out for employment ; he had been engaged as a shepherd in the station of which he was now the owner, and a rich relation had died and left him money sufficient to purchase it from his employer. Besides grass seeds and burr, there is another great foe to the squatting kingdom. The greatest terror is always entertained of it, and every foe would seem to dwindle into insignificance in comparison. This is 'scab.' The most stringent laws are in force to prevent its spreading, and the only effectual method that would ever seem to have been discovered for its removal, is the same as that which has been applied for the removal of the ' cattle plague ' in Great Britain—stamping out —slaughtering the whole flock of sheep, in which even one or two sheep may be found affected ; the Government awarding compensation to the amount of four shillings for every sheep thus killed, from a fund contributed by the graziers to the Government for the purpose. Those who fail to comply with these scab regulations, and do not

kill all their flocks of sheep in which any of them
may be found diseased, are heavily fined. Whilst
travelling over a station, in which the stamping
out process was going on, I saw thirty men engaged
in the destruction of three thousand maiden ewes
which had caught the disease from imported rams.
The men appeared to do their work very systema-
tically, but it was a fearfully revolting spectacle.
There were carts driving dried timber, and men
employed in making a funereal pile of it; with
every layer of wood there was a layer of the newly
killed sheep; higher and higher the pile of wood
and wool, flesh and bones, was raised; and as the
last carcase was heaved upon the top of the huge
mass of the recently animated matter, a lighted
match very speedily consummated the work that
had been commenced, a finishing stroke to the
work of absolute ruin and destruction in which
they had been engaged. The men stripped themselves of all their outer clothing, in accordance
with the terms of the Scab Act, and threw them
into the flames.

There is a large, wide-spread ramification of
streams and branches of labour and industry—all
having their source and dependence upon squatting.
Blocks of country necessarily require overseers,
shepherds, and stockmen; bullock-drivers are also
indispensable. The next important personage, a
representative of labour following in the wake of
capital, is the bush carpenter, to aid in making
huts, stackyards, fencing and hurdles. A bush
carpenter is worth at least a dozen of his more

pretentious town namesakes; with no other appliances than his axe, adze, morticing tool,
and cross-cut saw, he is competent with the
assistance of another man to do almost any
kind of work in the carpentering line of business required in the bush. Temporary house
accommodation is always easily provided by means
of a few sheets of bark stripped from the neighbouring trees, one extremity resting on the ground,
the other resting in a slanting direction on a pole
a few feet above the ground, fixed on two forked
sticks, in the shape of the roof of a house. This
erection is called a *gungah*—the native style of
house architecture, and the first approach that is
made to house-building. A hut is an erection of
a much more substantial character, and bears
throughout all the usual marks in the delineation
of a house, having a door, window, and chimney.
The walls are made of split timber six or eight
feet in length; one end sunk in the ground, the
other standing upright, are either nailed to, or put
into grooves in the wall plate. There are always
two apartments, with holes of greater or less
dimensions cut in the wooden walls for the purpose of admitting light, and serving as windows.
There is seldom, however, in any hut a want of
light, as the shrinking of the slabs causes innumerable openings in the walls all round and round,
and light as well as fresh air are poured in as freely
and bountifully as into a bird's cage in the open
air. A hut is the kind of accommodation provided
for shepherds and all the working-men employed

at stations, and with which the owners themselves
are contented on first starting their bush life.
House-building is never regarded as a matter of
much serious thought or concern ; trees being
plentiful, and some of them being remarkably
well adapted for being split into slabs. When
required to bestow any extra amount of care and
attention, the carpenter can make the split timber
to appear as if it had come from a saw-pit. Shingles,
that is, strips of split wood like slates, may be
sometimes used for covering the roof, but bark,
carefully taken off the trees, is generally employed. Neatness and comfort may be sometimes
happily combined with very little expense. The
owner of a squattage property and fifteen
thousand sheep, assured me that his dwelling-
house, a remarkably neat and commodious building, of eight apartments, did not cost him more
than sixteen pounds. He superintended the
erection of it himself, and the unnecessary expense
which he might have lavished on his house, he
had expended in the cultivation of a garden
and vineyard. There are not many hands required
at cattle-stations, as aboriginal boys and men
can always be readily obtained, when needed,
from the blacks belonging to the locality, who
are always roaming about from place to place,
and who very soon become domesticated ; their
services are quite as valuable in the mustering of
stock, if not more so, than the services of white
men. There is also great economy in employing
them, as clothing, tobacco, flour, and sugar is all

the remuneration they ever think of. Sheep-stations are the great rendezvous of the labouring class of the population ; and this is more particularly the case when the proprietor with his family reside there. In respect of the number of persons employed, and of the order and system of management, a large sheep-station might be said to differ little from a manufactory in a town. One large sheep-owner remarked to the writer, who was staying at his house, that he had one hundred mouths to fill all the year round ; and at the busy season of sheep-shearing and harvesting he had as many more to provide for. Lambing and sheep-shearing provide employment for a large number of persons engaged at other occupations, such as splitting, fencing, gold-digging, &c., during the remainder of the year. Two months' constant employment may be sometimes obtained at sheep-shearing by going from one part of country to another, according as sheep-shearing has progressed. The work is always done at so much per score of sheep—usually about four shillings, with rations ; and good shearers are reported to clip as many as five and six score a day. None of them, however, seem at all fastidious about clipping the skin off with the wool ; the sheep do not seem to suffer in any way from the rough handling to which they are frequently subjected. The excessive dryness of the climate soon heals the wounds, and the blow-fly does not injure them. Sheep-shearers are also expected to wash the sheep previous to shearing, at the current rate of labouring men's

wages. Shepherds are never called on to shear sheep;
and, indeed, not one, perhaps, in fifty of the class of
individuals usually engaged in shepherding could
do it. There is a store at every station belonging
to the owner, which contains supplies of clothing,
shoes, tobacco, crockery, and all the other necessaries which individuals and families on a station
might stand in need of, or be likely to ask for, thus
saving them the very great inconvenience they
would be exposed to in travelling long distances to
have their wants supplied. The grazier in Australia is not only a grower of wool, but a dealer in
slops, blankets, household utensils, saddles, shoes,
&c. When there are two or three young families
residing at the head-station, a schoolmaster will
generally be found, who adds to the duties of
teacher very frequently those of storekeeper. One
seldom hears complaints of the want of teachers,
as there are numbers of persons who have received
a good education, dislike shepherding, and are
unable to do manual labour, who take to teaching
in families as a means of earning a livelihood, and
securing for themselves a comfortable home. It is
very usual for shepherds, who have boys in their
families shepherding, to be provided with family
tutors. They can, of course, only be taught in the
evenings, and the spare time at the teacher's dis-
posal is very likely expended in such work as
cultivating the garden. The want of medical
attendance, one is very apt to suppose, must be
severely felt in the thinly-populated pastoral districts, where there are squatters residing with their

families ; however, an arrangement is often entered
into by contributing a sum of money in the shape of
a bounty for the residence of a medical practitioner.
There is also a fair sprinkling of individuals who
have some knowledge of medicine and surgery, who
can prescribe and ' put to their hands ' in cases of
emergency ; whilst there are few of the squatters
who are not provided with a ' medicine chest.'
One regularly-qualified medical practitioner, acting
as superintendent of a cattle-station, incidentally
mentioned to the writer, when halting for the night
at his house, that he had taken the situation
because he could not conscientiously charge the
fees which other medical men were doing—fees
which appeared to him to be little better' than
robbery of unfortunate people. The climate is
remarkably healthy, and in the case of working-
men requiring constant medical attendance, there
are Government hospitals in all the populated
districts to which those persons are sent. Clergymen are few and far between, and are placed at an
immense disadvantage, having literally no resting-
place for their feet. It may take one a whole day
to travel over some man's run to see a family ; and
it is a very charitable interpretation, indeed, to say
of the large bulk of the people, that they are living
in a patriarchal state, and that every head of a
family is the priest of his own house. There is
one thing to be said in favour of many, if not of
most of them, that they are always looking forward
to a more settled mode of life.

The starting of a township is regarded as

a great event, and anyone ambitious of per-
petuating his name and handing it down to pos-
terity as the founder of a city—perhaps the future
capital of a great nation—may do so any day in
Australia without exposing himself to the risk of
much loss or inconvenience.   The first to earn this
honourable distinction is usually a bullock-driver,
and all he has had to do has been merely to ask
permission of the squatter, or the gentleman in
whose employment he may have been, to erect a
hut for himself and family at the crossing-place of
the river, or some other eligible place on the station.
Sheep increase, cattle increase, wealth increases ;
more labour is required, and population increases ;
the bullock-driver, in his long, toilsome journey to
the coast, with his load of wool, brings back, on
his return load, many things which he shrewdly
guesses he can sell at an immense profit in the
neighbourhood where he resides.   He opens a store
and does a thriving business ; there is a petition to
the Government for the running of a mail ; and
the store having become a public-place, and being
conveniently situated, it is found suitable for the
post-office.   The Government is at last supposed
to be alive to the occasion, and surveyors are
despatched to lay out a township at the locality.

There is far more instinct than reason in many
of the people, with their carefully-accumulated
earnings.   The allotments of land being put up
for sale by public auction, they throw away their
money in bidding against each other for such
allotments as they may have set their hearts upon,

when they purpose establishing themselves in the
line of business to which they may have been bred, as
shoemakers, tailors, saddlers, &c. Storekeeping and
innkeeping invariably take the lead ; and in some
of the outlying townships, one individual may be
sometimes found to hold in his hands all the business
done in the place, and to be storekeeper, innkeeper,
pound-keeper, and postmaster. Many of these
worthies undoubtedly act very discreetly, and do not
take too great advantage of their situation, in disposing of articles with which the settler's stores are
not provided ; and it is to be hoped that the instance
of one, mentioned in the hearing of the writer, as
selling needles at a shilling a piece, was a purely
exceptional case. Modern civilisation may have a
great deal to recommend it, but there is a great deal
of modern civilisation which bush people could
easily afford to lose : the gratifying of the sense of
novelty not at all compensating for the expense of
purchase.   Travelling Jews with trinkets, organ-
grinders, German bands, Ethiopian serenaders,
circuses, electro-biologists, and people of that class,
are great nuisances in the embryo townships. Photographers might claim for themselves exemption
from being classed with the useless train of camp-
followers. One of these persons with whom I met
in the far bush, and who had been the first in the
field, stated that in a short time he had accumulated ten thousand pounds ; and as he thought
that he might as well enjoy the fruits of his
earnings, he went on a trip to England. After
spending all his money, he returned to the bush to

recruit his finances; but to his great disgust he found the whole country wherever he went, over-run with photographers, spreading themselves out like a string of wild geese, and could not get an opening; at every place he went to, indeed, there had been a photographer before him; and he was obliged to change his occupation, and as the people had all their *cartes de visite* of their heads *outside* taken, he commenced to take and give *cartes de visite* of their heads *inside*—phrenological charts.

The sheep-farmers would seem to be of opinion that, from the description and quality of labour thrown into their hands from emigrant ships like raw material sent ashore to be converted into useful purposes—a knowledge of the management of men is an important branch in the knowledge of their business, and as much to be attended to as the management of stock. In fact, the same talents are required for a successful sheep-farmer as those that go to make a good drill-sergeant. To teach others, they require to be well taught themselves; to know everything; to see everything done by everybody; to be first and foremost in everything. It is not easy to persuade some 'new arrivals' of this, and there are some very slow, and some unwilling to learn. Mr. Gruther, owner of several large squattages, who had a world of hard, rough Australian experiences hid within his breast, had consigned to him from England two young relatives to indoctrinate into the mysteries of sheep-farming, and to lead them in the same path as that by which he had been

conducted to opulence. He was as kind to them
as any one could have desired. After an early
breakfast one morning, he asked them to go with
him to the wash-pool, where the men were washing
the sheep, previous to shearing. It was a very
busy time and everyone was employed. Mr.
Gruther was a man of few words, and on arriving
at the wash-pool, he said to his young friends:
' Strip, strip.' They could not believe that he
meant them to divest themselves of their superfinery and go into the dirty pool amongst the men;
but Mr. Gruther was in earnest, and, without saying
another word, watching his opportunity, when they
were both standing near the brink of the wash-pool,
he placed a hand on the back of each and shoved
them both in, superfinery and all.

Not the least of the many important considerations connected with squatting, is the claim which
has come to be established, and recognised, of *bona
fide* settlement; and the statement made in the
preceding chapter of ' no attachment being formed
to place ' would require to be corrected here, for
through the lapse of time a very strong attachment
will sometimes be formed to place. The best
evidence of this is in the stylish mansions, houses,
gardens, and vineyards, which are occasionally
met with at stations where the proprietor resides,
and it is scarcely possible for fancy to conjure up
more pleasant homes, and luxurious retreats from
the rude bustle of the world, than some of these
squattage residences. Through the effect of the
operation of the great law of custom, it will

generally be found that the man who pays his
yearly rental, say forty pounds, for the land, from
which he is grazing three or four thousand sheep,
or a thousand head of cattle, feels his position in
every way as good as the man who purchases his
forty acres for forty pounds. This observation
applies to the large bulk of squattage properties.
No doubt the squatter may be deprived of his
property when the Government requires the land
with a view to selling it, as it may be stated, for
public uses or for agriculture. To what other public
uses, however, can the great bulk of the land be
applied than that to which it is already applied—
grazing? And as to agricultural land at twenty
shillings an acre, very little indeed can ever be
cultivated and sold at that price. There was one
squatter in Queensland, known to the writer, who
had twelve thousand acres taken off his run by the
Government for the purpose of selling it to land-
order emigrants. In a large squattage of a hundred
thousand, or two hundred thousand acres, twelve
thousand does not count for much, and in this
instance, as in others, the gentleman who had lost
this portion of his run very likely found the
remainder enhanced in value—a market being
brought to his door for his stock. The subject is
well understood, the squatter purchases as little
land as possible ; the purchase of land he always
regards as throwing away money, and when he
does purchase, it is merely to keep others off his
run. Buying land is an English idea, and were a
real Australian settler asked to buy the land of

which he holds possession, at a pound an acre, he would look with as much blank astonishment as a captain of a vessel would do in mid-ocean, if Neptune, with his trident, suddenly rose from the deep and asked him to buy the salt water of which he was obtaining the use and benefit. But squatters do buy land, they are, in fact, very partial to it. By buying certain spots on their runs they can secure themselves in possession of large adjoining areas of their grazing land ; and they have derived enormous advantages from ' pre-emption right '— the right in the first place of purchasing a square mile of the land where the head station is situated, and from the scarcity of available land which may occur at intervals in streaks and patches, this may include, in no small number of instances, all the available land on the run.

Every one has heard of the Victoria great land swindle, and the great tossing up of cabbage-tree hats by the squatters there during the administration of the land in that colony by Mr. Gavan Duffy, of *The Irish Nation* fame. Nothing could have exceeded the ovation given Mr. Duffy, on his arrival, by the radical brotherhood of Sydney and Melbourne. ' The right man in the right place.' A testimonial in money was given to him, to enable him to support the dignity which they intended to bestow upon him, in the shape of high legislative honours in Victoria. Daniel O'Connell used to say that a carriage-and-four could be driven through any Act of Parliament ; had he lived, he might

have seen an Act of Parliament, made by his
henchman, in which the rights to three millions of
acres of the best land in Victoria were driven through
an Act by card shuffling, dodging and making
use of what, in colonial phrase, is called ' dummies.'
In New South Wales, where radical rule also
prevails, in the case of a squatter who wished to
retain hold of his run, when in danger of losing it
by others coming in and settling upon it, the wife
of his overseer said to me, that the infant at her
breast, and the rest of her children, were ' free
selectors'—that is, the owner of the station had
made use of their names in picking up the best
parts of the run, not for the land itself, but to
remain in undisturbed possession of the grazing
land adjoining. This is, in general, very easily
done, from the peculiar geographical character of
the country, and by purchasing the narrow strip of
alluvial land at the sides of creeks, rivers, and
water-holes. The immense areas of country without
water are absolutely valueless, save to those who
are in possession of these water frontages. The
Government of New South Wales cannot be supposed to be ignorant of the fact that dodges, such
as that related above, are practised, and of the
spoliation, or ' manipulation ' of the Crown lands,
as the *Sydney Morning Herald* calls it. Several
merchants and others in Sydney having interest in
runs, frankly confessed to the Minister of Lands—
Mr. Robertson—in remonstrating with him on the
enormities of his Land Act, that they had practised
these dodges themselves.

K

'The good old rule, the simple plan,
That they shall take who have the power,
And they shall keep who can.'

All this has taken place, and is taking place, under
radical rule. The Government of Queensland is
more conservative, however, than the Governments
of Victoria and New South Wales, in not being so
liberal, or, to speak more correctly, so prodigal of
public property, whilst they would seem to be
influenced by the consideration that the colony will
last longer than their life-time, and that the world
is not yet coming to an end. Hence, the squatters
in Queensland are not permitted to 'dodge,' botch,
make use of 'dummies,' purchase select parts of
their runs, simply to keep others off, or to destroy
the country for all purposes of future colonisation
and settlement.

One is entirely driven out to sea in not knowing
what to think of squatting, in regard to its most
important political bearings. The grass land is
necessarily limited, and it is not every one who
can share in the boon of having sixty thousand,
one hundred or two hundred thousand acres of
land at a small rental. The squatters are a
privileged class of the community, and are therefore regarded with great disfavour and jealousy by
those classes of the community who are called the
people, *par excellence*, and none but those who
have lived at the antipodes can understand the
antagonism which exists between them. Over the
larger extent of the interior, throughout nearly the

whole of Queensland, where all the people are more or less connected with, and dependent upon, squatting, the people live agreeably together. But when population increases, and other interests spring up, the whole social body festers with sores —as if man were not brother to man.

The appropriating of select parts of country under the name of *agricultural reserves*, exclusively for the benefit of purchasers of land, was a most beneficial act on the part of the Queensland Legislature. The measure reflects the highest credit on the Government of that colony, standing out, as it does, in striking contrast to the 'go anywhere' system of New South Wales, and the 'house that Jack built' land legislation of Victoria. The land question is an interminable subject of discussion. The following extract from the *Queensland Guardian*, in reference to the most favoured part of that colony, the Darling Downs, which is called 'The Garden of Queensland,' will illustrate some of the causes of disaffection :

APPRAISEMENT OF RUNS ON THE DARLING DOWNS.

The following are the appraisements made by Mr. F. Gregory of the rent to be paid on the undermentioned runs, on the Darling Downs, during the five years' renewed leases, commencing January 1, 1866 :

Gowrie, Frederick Neville Isaac, 70,000 acres   £583 6s. 8d.
Goombunga, Frederick Neville Isaac, 50,000 acres   £123 6s. 8d.
Westbrook, J. D. M'Lean and W. Beit, 113,722 acres — £628 14s.
Rosalie Plains, W. Kent, jun., and E. Wienholt, 100,000 acres - £250.
Jingi Jingi, S. Murray, 128,000 acres   £208 6s. 8d.
Cooranga, T. J. P. and J. A. Bell, 125,000 acres — £412.

Jimbour, T. J. P. and J. A. Bell, 219,911 acres—£685 3s. 8a.

Fairy Land, S. Murray, 17,280 acres—£27.

Seven Oaks, ditto, 11,520 acres—£18.

Canago, ditto, 20,480 acres £32.

Pelican, ditto, 32,000 acres £50.

Irvingdale, R. Tooth, 88,154 acres £363 6s. 8d.

Tumaville, W. F. Gore and M. B. Baldock, 130,000 acres £478 14s. 8d.

Pilton, H. B. Fitz and W. Wilson, 34,788 acres—£153 8s.

Northbranch, W. F. Gore and M. B. Baldock, 80,720 acres £232.

Haldon, H. B. Fitz and W. Wilson, 43,295 acres—£118 6s. 8d.

Jondaryan, R. Tooth, 115,859 acres £523 6s. 8d.

Cecil Plains, J. Taylor, 172,801 acres—£405 6s. 8d.

Yandilla, W. F. Gore and M. B. Baldock, 229,360 acres—£708 2s. 8d.

Lagoon Creek Downs West, W. Kent, jun., and E. Wienholt, 21,760 acres—£70.

With reference to those assessments the *Queensland Times* says: 'The assessed rentals on certain stations on the Darling Downs, which appear in another column, show that, for the next five years, 1,800,000 acres of the best and most favourably situated land in the colony is to be held by its present occupants for about £6,000 per annum, or at a rate of a little over three farthings per acre. We had expected something better than this—especially as the idea of disposing of the fee simple of the poorest and the most remote runs in the north at half a crown an acre has been so scornfully scouted. And yet half a crown an acre purchase money would be equal (even at only five per cent.) to three halfpence an acre per annum, or just double what Mr. Gregory calls on the occupiers of the "garden of the colony" to pay for the next five years. There is something rotten in the state of Queensland. No doubt the present rental of these runs is a great advance on what was paid before, but this is nothing to the point. The rents of runs in South Australia, with fewer advantages than the Downs stations of Queensland enjoy, were some time since assessed at about sixpence an acre per annum, and this rental, in many instances, is now being paid. We regard these Queensland valuations as disgraceful. Sixpence an acre per annum would have been a moderate rent. The most miserable run in the colony, however distant from port, will have to pay a halfpenny per acre per annum ; and yet these stations, with railways being made to their gates, and enjoying every advan-

lage, are only to pay an average rental of three farthings. It has
been said that the lessees will probably not give up their leases,
but accept of the appraisement, and we rather incline to the same
opinion.'

The whole subject of squatting, in so far as
Queensland is concerned, is correctly stated in
the manifesto published by the Queensland Government, one hundred and thirty thousand copies
of which have been circulated in Great Britain
for the information of intending emigrants. The
squattages are let on fourteen years' leases, and
are to be revalued at that period. The rent
for the first four years is merely nominal, with a
view to the encouragement of enterprise in taking
up new country, and is increased according to
circumstances during the two succeeding periods,
each one of which will be five years. The quantity
of country held in one block is limited to two
hundred square miles, and must be stocked with
sheep or cattle to the extent of one-fourth of its
estimated capabilities during the first year. Grass
lands are estimated to carry and to fatten one hundred sheep or twenty head of cattle per square mile.
The rent for the first four years is ten shillings per
square mile ; during the first of the two succeeding
not less than 25l., nor more than 50l., per ‘ block '
of twenty-five square miles ; and, during the second
period of five years, not less than 30l., nor more
than 70l. per block.

Some new faculty would actually seem to be
necessary to enable one to understand many
antipodean matters rightly. It is somewhat strange,

and indeed altogether outré to European compre-
hension, that while purchasers of land in many of
the Australian colonies will be required to reside
on their property, and not be permitted to purchase
more than three hundred and twenty acres, the
squatter may hold possession of hundreds of
thousands of acres here, there, and everywhere,
whilst he may reside in Sydney, Paris, London,
or, indeed, anywhere he may choose.   In the
case of these absentees and large holders of
Crown land, there are evils connected with squatting which cannot be easily defended, as in the
case when one man holds as much land as
would provide for the comfortable settlement of
hundreds of families.   Thorough master of the
art of avoiding expense, the squatter very frequently takes no interest of any kind in
the individuals and the families in his employment.   A few tumble-down bark huts may be
all that represents the homestead of a property
valued at twenty or thirty thousand pounds.   One
of these large holders of Crown lands, a partner in
a company, boasted to me that he and his partners
could send into market every year twelve thousand
head of fat cattle, independently of spare stock,
such as 'boilers,' i.e., cattle only fit for boiling
down.   Australia was surely intended for other
purposes than the enriching of a few individuals.
The Crown lands are very frequently, in Government phrase, styled 'the waste lands of the Crown.'
They cannot, however, with propriety be called
waste lands, for they are applied to the only

purpose, speaking of them in general, to which they can ever be applied, grazing. Hundreds of miles of country may be travelled over, and not as much good land seen as would make a cabbage-garden or a ten-acre field for cultivation. If there is no favourable opinion to be entertained of absentees, credit is due to those squatters who do reside on their stations, giving employment to domestic servants, labourers and their families. Those men carry civilisation with them into the bush, and they will always be found alive and ready to lend a helping hand to every good work which may be going on around them ; and the fact is worthy of mention, that they are uniformly distinguished for unbounded kindness and hospitality to clergymen. Stations are of greater or less size, and, as I have remarked, they change hands very frequently. When they are sold, the usual practice is by public auction of the sheep, cattle, and horses upon the station at so much per head—the station, with all the improvements given in, stores, drays, and all that is used in the working of the estate, taken at valuation. The prices seem to be regulated by the prices of wool and tallow in the London market. Stations are sometimes sold, however, without stock, though somewhat rarely. An owner of several squattages, in whose house I was staying, incidentally mentioned in my hearing to a gentleman beside him, that he had purchased 'the B——k Run sheep at twenty-five shillings a-head.' This was enormous, as the selling price of sheep was not more than eight or ten shillings a-head. An explanation ensued—it proved to be an A 1 run, and would carry fifty thousand sheep : there were only twenty thousand sheep upon it.

The following advertisement, published in the *Sydney Morning Herald*, of a station for sale, belonging to a resident squatter, and situated in the Alpine regions, where the climate is favourable for English gardening and agriculture, contains much information of the minutiæ of squatting :

RICHARDSON and WRENCH have received instructions to Sell by Auction, at the Rooms, Pitt Street, Sydney, on TUESDAY, the 27th day of MARCH next,

At 11 o'clock.

FOR POSITIVE SALE,

TENTERFIELD.

_{*} Stores, Drays, Teams, Working Horses, Implements, Machinery, and all belongings necessary for carrying on such an important property, to be taken by valuation in the usual way by arbitration.

TERMS LIBERAL.

One-fourth Cash, residue by bills at 1, 2, and 3 years' date, bearing interest at the rate of 3 per cent. per annum, secured on the property by mortgage in the usual way.

Tenterfield is entitled to a lease for five years, from 1st January 1866, at £350 per annum.

Application has been made to the Government to set apart water reserves for the use of the back country, and to protect said reserves from free selection. The applications are in course of being granted.

TENTERFIELD.

This station is situated on the table-land of New England, on the head of the Severn River, or Tenterfield Creek, and 110 miles from the shipping port of Grafton, to which there is a very good road. Some part of the country consists of open plains, the principal portion being lightly timbered, well grassed, undulating ridges, and on all parts of the run are well-sheltered ridges.

It contains an area of about 180,000 acres, and is estimated as capable of depasturing 35,000 sheep and 2,500 cattle and their yearly increase in all seasons.

The IMPROVEMENTS at the head-station comprise a commodious and handsome cottage residence, containing nine rooms, and verandahs, arranged and finished in superior style; a well-stocked garden, orchard, and vineyard; also, a beautiful grove of English forest trees.

The outbuildings include kitchen and servants' rooms, laundry, stores, five-stall stable, groom's quarters, harness rooms, coach-house, &c.

Among the other improvements are the following: Woolshed, 100 feet long, shingled, with sawn and slabbed floor, battened catching-pens, powerful screw-press, sheep-room capable of holding 1,500 sheep, shingled, and the necessary yards attached. Wash-pool, with yards, large brick-built store, containing office and six other compartments, one of which is used for storing wool, and one for wheat, &c. Storekeeper's cottage of four rooms, with kitchen and meat-house. Blacksmiths' and carpenters' shops, men's huts, mostly built of brick, small stockyard, horse ditto, milking ditto, slaughtering ditto, &c., boiling-down establishment, with the necessary pots, yards, and other conveniences. Grass paddock, subdivided, of about 400 acres. Cultivation-paddock, of about 100 acres.

At the cattle-station, are

Large stock-yard, with spaying-pens, herding-paddock, grass ditto, of about 50 acres, subdivided. Dairy, stockmen's huts, &c., and

At the sheep-stations,

Fifteen huts, with the necessary yards to each, and hurdles for lambing, all now in full working order.

With the TENTERFIELD STATION will be included 320 ACRES OF PURCHASED LAND, on which the head-station improvements are erected. The following are the stock which will be sold with the station, viz. :

Sheep.—2,218 ewes, $1\frac{1}{2}$ years old.
    2,803 ditto, $2\frac{1}{2}$ do., with lambs at foot.
    2,608 ditto, $3\frac{1}{2}$ ditto.
    1,257 ditto, $4\frac{1}{2}$ ditto.
    3,558 ditto, $4\frac{1}{2}$ and $5\frac{1}{2}$ ditto.
      703 ditto, ditto, ditto, ditto, a stud flock.
    1,127 ditto, 6 and upwards.
    6,788 wethers, mixed sexes, in about equal proportions.
    1,158 mixed ages and sexes.
    2,121 wethers, $1\frac{1}{2}$ years old.
    1,311 ditto, $2\frac{1}{2}$ ditto.
    1,396 ditto, $3\frac{1}{2}$ ditto.
    1,510 ditto, $4\frac{1}{2}$ ditto.
    1,004 rams, $1\frac{1}{2}$ ditto, to aged.

Total : 29,562 more or less.

Cattle.—2,800, more or less, a mixed herd.

Implements, in which are included reaping machine, thrashing ditto, winnowing ditto, ploughs, harrows, &c., tools of various kinds, stores, about 1,000 bushels of wheat or flour therefrom, stack of oaten hay, about 8 tons, and about 70 bushels of maize.

The sheep are free from all contagious diseases. They are of very superior quality, and yield a heavy clip. Great expense has been incurred in introducing the choicest rams procurable ; of the present stock of rams, 5 are pure bred Rambouillet, 7 pure German, and all imported. About one-half the flock are young sheep, the progeny of the imported rams and stud ewes that have been carefully selected. Others are bred from the celebrated Glengallan, Rosenthal, and other first-class flocks. A large proportion of the Tenterfield clip averaged in London, in the last August sales, over 2s. per lb., the wool being only hand-washed. The sheep have been regularly classed, and the rejected and old ones sold off every year.

CHAPTER V

GOLD-DIGGING

DAME FORTUNE would seem, at some time or other, to have been careering in a chariot over the summits of the Australian Alps, sowing as she went handsful of gold dust, and pieces of gold ; but all that she scattered thus bears no proportion to the quantities which, as if she had been blindfolded, she permitted to escape from her chariot as it coursed along in a zigzag way, apparently without any determinate route or boundary, the gold running out from the chariot in streaks and patches, like meal, or wheat, on the road in the line of travelling of a dray filled with badly-tied sacks. The illustration is not precisely accurate, however, for the treasure is buried in the soil;

but it may serve to convey some idea of the distribution of gold. It is scarcely possible to wash a tin dishful of earth, sand, or gravel, in the gold-producing tracts of country, without discovering a minute particle of gold, a speck just large enough for the eye to discern in the bottom of the dish, after all the earth, gravel, or sand has been carefully washed out, the gold, in consequence of its greater weight, always sinking to the bottom. This is called 'prospecting,' and the number of specks in the bottom of the dish determines the richness or the poverty of the soil in gold. Prospecting is not confined to the surface of the ground, however, as a hole, several feet in length, is generally dug, or a shaft may sometimes be sunk in the same way as in sinking for a well, to test the ground underneath. Rewards are given to the discoverers of new gold-fields, and a bonus of several 'claims' granted of the gold-field which they have discovered. If a 'rich prospect' is fallen upon, and the ground is found to be payable, a new gold-field is said to have been discovered, and there is nothing wanting but 'diggers' to make matters 'go a-head.' If any of them are reported to be 'doing well,' and especially if any of them make 'large finds,' the news from the new gold-field is spread far and wide with the speed of lightning. Storekeepers, innkeepers, and others in the neighbourhood, on the main thoroughfares leading to the locality, and all others interested in the new field, give the most flattering accounts of how much this, and how much that party has made ; all being

stated with great accuracy, to save themselves
from the risk of some rather unpleasant consequences which have sometimes followed from
diggers who have come from long distances running
foul of, and awarding merciless punishment to,
those who gave false or exaggerated information.
The news from the new gold-field, which is heralded
by the press principally on the authority of local
correspondents, brings a 'rush' towards it. 'Distance lends enchantment to the view;' and it is
very frequently observed that those gold-diggers
who have been remote and unsuccessful are
the first to arrive at the new gold-field. Whilst
traversing a bush-track, where there were not
more than twelve grown-up persons residing
within sixty miles length of country, two men,
hangers-on at a wayside, or, as it is frequently
termed, an 'accommodation-house,' where I halted
for the night, took to the work of 'prospecting,'
discovered a rich prospect, found a cradle, commenced washing in the usual manner, and made
large earnings. The news soon spread abroad, and
within three weeks there were about fifteen hundred
persons collected within half a mile length of a
creek where the two men had been working. The
sudden change was very surprising, and it would be
difficult to imagine any other circumstance save the
discovery of gold which could have attracted so
large a population, within so brief a period, into
Nature's previously almost untenanted domain.
There was no road, merely bush tracks leading
from station to station very high and steep

mountains had to be crossed, ascended and descended ; some parts were very thickly timbered,
whilst creeks and gullies opposed, one would
have thought, almost insurmountable obstacles
to traffic. Gold ! what will the love of gold not
lead men to do? Hardships, dangers, difficulties, all the great bugbears which make people
shrink from doing what they are not inclined to
do, seemed all to disappear like an idle dream.
Provisions were sold at an enormously high price.
If eight bullocks could not ascend the mountain
with a loaded dray, twenty-four with a half-loaded
dray might, and must ; one team assisting the
other, the bullocks stimulated by endless shouting,
their drivers, worked to the highest pitch of
frenzied excitement, goading them, at the same
time, with the butt-end of their whip handles. One
by one the loaded drays, slowly, but perseveringly,
reach their destination ; up and down hill, through
deep ravines in the mountains, over gullies, creeks,
and swamps, assistance is always readily given by
the one to the other. An Australian bullock-
driver seems to flinch at nothing in travelling with
his dray. No matter how rough and mountainous
the country may be, if the bullocks can stand on
their feet, he will make them take the dray after
them. It is a marvellous sight when they are
coming down the face of a steep mountain,
with a heavy load ; but on a closer view one sees
that the apparently difficult operation is adroitly
managed by means of a heavy tree attached behind
the dray, trailing on the ground. Bullock-drivers

have more than a little of the arduous work in connection with gold-digging ; and it is to be hoped
that their usual heavy charges compensate for their
toil and adventure. They are the carriers on
the road ; there are numbers who are their own
carriers, and are provided with horses and carts
which contain all the necessary supplies of tools
and provisions. In the line of a 'rush,' and in the
great cavalcade of men on horseback, with their
blankets strapped before them on their saddles,
they are very conspicuous. The pedestrians are
by far the most numerous, however ; they have all
their *swags* on their backs ; some carry shovels and
picks, whilst others, grudging the labour of carrying
utensils, and relying on purchasing them from
the storekeepers, are without them. There are
vehicles, too, of every description, to be met with,
forming what seems to be an endless procession,
as if some entire settlement had broken up, or the
people were all hastening away from a plague ;
and not the least marked feature in the 'rush,' and
ceaseless stream of human life, are the neatly tilted
carts, in which are comfortably housed mothers
and their young families, with their goods and
chattels. The worst of it is to come. There is a
risk, a troublesome anticipation that John, the
father of the family, and his two partners, Peter
and James, who accompany the cart, might not
strike upon a 'good claim' There is some consolation, however, derived from the thought of
having no house, no fuel, and no water to pay for ;
besides, there is plenty of fresh air, beef and

mutton are usually cheap, and, if the wife is an industrious woman, she can provide for herself and live independently of her husband's earnings, by doing washing and cooking for diggers ; hence there is nothing to prevent the family from enjoying many domestic comforts. Where a family is residing, a plot of ground is very frequently observed near the dwelling, which is fenced, and cultivated as a garden. In addition, many of the diggers' families have cows and carry on dairy work. Houses of every conceivable construction are 'run up' in a very short time ; timber being usually abundant, whilst the bark of trees serves to cover the roof of ' shanty,' ' log-house,' ' hut,' ' house,' or by whatever name the erection is called. Stores and inns are of a more pretentious character, and some expense is incurred in the use of sawn timber in flooring and weather-boarding those establishments. Calico tents are the prevailing house accommodation, however, being easily erected, and as easily removed. Without perhaps a single exception, a ' claim,' which may be about the size of a cottage garden staked out by the Gold Commissioner and his officials, is taken up and worked by a ' party.' The party may consist of three, four, six, or eight persons, all well known to, and having confidence in, each other, and between whom disagreements very rarely take place.

A gold-field is a place of bustling industry. Every one seems to be intent on his own affairs, and indifferent to those of others, whilst there is an appearance of order, quietness, and regularity ob-

served, which would surprise many who have con-
jured up in their imaginations such scenes of
wildness and disorderliness as they may have read
of in public prints. Lines of streets may be sometimes passed, and the eye be greeted with all those
designations on sign-boards, such as tailor, shoemaker, watchmaker, bank, baker, surgeon, &c.,
which are to be met with in any large town, without a single omission.

There is 'rowdyism' to be witnessed sometimes
no doubt, especially on Saturday nights, when
groups of men gather round public-houses, some of
them 'knocking down their money' and 'giving
shouts,' but this remark is very far from applicable
to the general character of the digging population.
There are many most respectable persons and
families to be met with at a gold field ; many who
have received the highest education in schools and
universities, who have always moved in spheres of
good society, and who are in no way ashamed of
their employment ; a life, as I have heard some of
them say, of entire freedom and independence. As
a body, indeed, the diggers might compare favourably with any of the other labouring classes in the
community.

At some of the fields there are parties to be
seen finding gold in a manner which any one
sufficiently able to handle a pick and shovel would
seem competent for, there being mere digging and
washing of sand, clay, and gravel, in the beds of
water-courses, with 'surfacing.' In the process of
'surfacing,' the earth on the surface is dug one, two,

L

or three feet, thrown into a cart or wheelbarrow, and cast into a trough, into which water is conducted and kept constantly running. The earth, clay, and gravel, is continually stirred, by means of shovels and forks, by two men; and the gold, usually in very small quantities, about the size of threepenny pieces, falls to the bottom of the trough, and escapes along with small stones through a sheet of perforated iron at the further extremity. Large holes like gravel pits may also be frequently seen, in which the same operation is gone through with the gravel, earth, or· clay, which may have been dug out of them. This is called 'shallow sinking.' By far the most common, and it may therefore be supposed to be the most remunerative method of finding gold, however, is sinking shafts ('deep sinking' as it is termed), and the preliminary labour in this case is similar to that of sinking for a well, the object being to come upon the original deposits—Dame Fortune's streaks and patches. The work in this case is of a most laborious nature, and only such persons as Cornish miners, who, by the way, have proved themselves to be first-rate hands at gold-digging, and others who have made mining an occupation and a study, are properly competent for the task. A practical knowledge of geology is also necessary; and this every one learns quickly at the diggings from those two excellent teachers, observation and experience. The 'bed-rock' is a favourite word with the diggers, being the depth to which the shaft is sunk, and beyond which there is no labour required in sinking deeper; the shaft is said to be 'bottomed' when the bed-rock has been struck. The bed-rock reached, all that is necessary is to scrape with a trowel the sand and gravel which may be upon it, also the washing-stuff and whatever may be the thickness of the deposit; the material is then put into a bucket as it is collected; and, when the bucket is filled, it is attached to a rope hanging down the mouth of the shaft, and is drawn up by the man who is stationed at the windlass. This washing-stuff is destined to go through the same process as all other washing-stuffs; but in most cases it is put into 'cradles.' A great quantity of gold has sometimes been found in one of these bucketfuls after it has been washed; and when the 'claim' is rich, great care is taken of the washing-stuff after it reaches the surface, and is thrown into a heap beside the mouth of the shaft, in case night prowlers might make free with it. The process of tunnelling is carried on underneath, on the surface of the bed-rock, and to the same extent as the claim above. There is danger in this part of the operation, and lives have been lost from want of proper attention to the use of props for preventing the earth and stones from falling down overhead. Shafts are of various depths, according to the elevation or depression of the much-famed bed-rock, or the height and depth of the stratification of sand, gravel, or clay, in which the gold is found. Boulders of granite and solid rock have to be pierced through frequently, and blasting with gunpowder at great depths is not the least risk to the life of the gold shaft-sinker; water may also come in at times and stop operations altogether, whilst fresh air must be pumped down the shaft continually, to enable the digger to breathe freely in his narrow and confined cell. One man told me that he had been in a shaft six hundred feet deep. Next to the bed-rock, the 'lead of gold' is the great object of the shaft-sinker. If he has been fortunate in striking on the gold, there is a course or a direction in which it can be followed, and he is successful so long as he can follow the 'lead,' but if he loses the 'lead' all his labour is lost. A shaft may be sunk at very great expense—month after month being occupied in the work, and all of no avail. Even if the digger strikes the bed-rock, he may not strike the lead of gold, and in this case it is called a 'shicer,' a most ominous term with diggers.

There is a great amount of business done in shares of claims. A party of diggers may not have the pecuniary means to enable them to go to the bottom of the shaft, but storekeepers, and others who are possessed of money, are 'wide-awake,' and are always ready to have a chance of reaping a rich golden harvest easily, by advancing money to the party, and receiving in return a share in their claim. The washing-stuff is usually dug out before washing commences ; and those interested are present at the close of the day's labour for the purpose of seeing the drawer, or wooden box, into which the gold has fallen in the process of rocking the cradle. If a man lifted a piece of gold out of the cradle, or washing-stuff, unknown to the other men of the

party, it would be regarded as a serious misde-
meanour. Such occurrences are rarely, if ever,
heard of, however. There are many singular stories
told by the diggers of their 'claims.' After having
expended all their money in sinking a shaft, they
sometimes lose hope of ever coming to the bed-rock,
and occasionally sell their rights. The party who
purchase, however, after having sunk one or two
feet deeper, very often strike on a rich deposit of
gold. The gold differs very much in its size and
form, and one hears of 'fine,' or 'gold-dust,' 'scaly,'
and 'rough,' according to the character of the
country in which it is found. The fine, or gold-
dust, is found in granite country, where there are
no quartz rocks ; the 'scaly,' where quartz and slate
are intermixed ; and the 'rough,' where quartz
predominates. When the gold has the appearance
of being much water-worn, and thinly diffused, it
is called 'drift gold'; and it is understood that there
is some deposit, or bed of gold, from which it has
come. To alight upon these deposits is the great
object of research and attention on the part of
gold-diggers. A man, or a party, might do, as I
used to see one man do—old Bill Cowpers (whom
I knew as a bullock-driver, before the diggings were
heard of)—dig away at the side of a mountain and
'chance it.' Very few of the diggers, however,
would chance it as Bill did : he never seemed to
move from the place where he first commenced.
Perhaps it was very inconvenient for him to shift, as
he had an aboriginal woman living with him, which
might be a potent reason for his always remaining

at one place. Bill had evidently great faith in the
mountain. Six months might elapse, and with all
his labour he would not get any gold apparently;
he never seemed in any way desirous, however,
continued always dig, digging in the side of the
mountain, and washing, with the assistance of the
aboriginal woman, the gravel and clay which he
collected as carefully as if he had been getting gold
all the time. A lad who assisted him on one
occasion, when he came upon a rich spot, said, however, that he had got six hundred pounds' worth,
and that it would keep him and his 'gin' a long
time. Bill had been about twelve years beside his
hole in the mountain, when I saw him last, and he
is likely to die there.

Parts of country may be met with which are
entirely covered with quartz; ridges, hills, mountains,
and valleys, where the grass is short, or has been
recently burnt, glistening in the sun, as if covered
with snow. Where there is quartz, however, there
is not necessarily gold, and no universal rule of any
kind would seem to be applicable for enabling one
to find the eagerly-sought-for metal. Strong indications of its presence may be found, however, in
one place more than another, from the quartz having
the appearance of being much burnt; and also from
the presence of rounded pebbles, calcined stones,
black sand, or emery patches—garnets, sapphires,
&c., lying on the surface. There is a sign held out
in such cases to dig, but one might dig a long time
without finding more than a few specks in a tin
dishful of earth or gravel; he might be fortunate,

too, however, as I saw one man who had come upon
a nugget as large as a child's fist, about a foot
beneath the surface of the ground. News of this
kind spreads fast. There had been a few instances
of the same kind ; hundreds and thousands of people
were soon attracted to the spot ; a Gold Commissioner, with his staff of officials arrived, and
claims were taken up. It was no better, however,
than a lottery ; for one who was successful there
were twenty unsuccessful, whilst the majority of the
people went away poorer than they came. They
might have been more successful, and the new gold-
field ' gone ahead,' had water been more plentiful.
Without water, however, even a gold-field, however
rich, would seem to be almost valueless.

Quartz is said to be the matrix of gold, and
auriferous quartz is very often spoken of as the kind
of quartz in which the gold has been formed, and
still exists in its disintegrated state. This quartz
is sometimes discovered in the sides of mountains,
cropping out from beneath the surface, and the gold
is seen embedded in streaks and veins, in the most
minute particles, often just large enough to be seen
by the naked eye. ' Fosacking ' is the term given
to the employment of those who go about searching
for gold thus exposed on the surface of the ground,
and the tools of those persons consist merely of a
pocket-knife and a hammer. There is never much
hope entertained of the success of those who go a-
fosacking, however, and there are very few who
think of it.

When a discovery of this kind has been made—

gold in the solid rock—which is termed 'quartz reefs,' a company is immediately started for working it. Steam power and gear are necessary for crushing the quartz, and a great amount of capital is required for working the reefs to advantage. Skill is often as much needed as capital, however, and indeed, success depends altogether upon proper management. Experience often comes too late for correcting mistakes which have been made. Besides quicksilver and blankets, there are various appliances used to prevent the escape of the most minute particle of gold from the crushed quartz in the process of washing. Companies are not much heard of at the gold-fields, however, save in connection with quartz crushing. There are gold-fields in which there are no quartz rocks, and where very little quartz may be seen, though small pieces of gold are always found amongst the sand and gravel. The country on the surface is interspersed with large bluffs and boulders of granite; the gold, in such cases, is very fine, and is very properly called 'gold-dust,' being almost as fine as flour, whilst one rarely sees particles as large as the smallest pin-head. There is always the greatest abundance of garnets and emery in the bottom of the cradle or trough in which the gold is washed, and specimens may be found of all the precious stones, cairngorm, cornelian, agate, sapphire, emerald, ruby, topaz, and many others; and it would be unjust to the writer—himself the bearer of the first prospect of gold found in the northern diggings to Sydney—to omit mention of the diamond. A jeweller there, to whom I showed the prospect, pointed to a diamond among the small stones which were mixed with the gold. I mentioned the circumstance to several diggers; but they all seemed to think more of gold than of diamonds. There are also many interesting objects of natural science to be seen in the washing-stuff of the gold-digger, not the least of which, perhaps, are many varieties of petrified wood.

Steam power is used for other purposes besides quartz-crushing. A gentleman invited me on one occasion to look at his steam engine, which he had employed in pumping water out of a large hole in a creek beside a gold-field. He had thirty men engaged, at the rate of ten shillings per day, in shovelling the mud, sand, and gravel at the bottom of the hole, as the water was pumped out, into carts and wheelbarrows. A great amount of ingenuity was displayed in making use of the water pumped out, in washing the stuff that was taken from the bottom of the hole. The yellow grains of gold, when they were washed and sank to the bottom, seemed to stream at one small opening of the trough as plentifully and as regularly as flour from the spout of a mill. The person alluded to had netted twelve thousand pounds from the one water-hole. What one water-hole had done, what might not another do? so dictated reason; but there is neither reason nor common sense sometimes in connection with the finding of gold. He persevered, and persevered again, until he had lost all his former earnings.

This tale is so common that the words, 'gain to-day and lose to-morrow,' have almost passed into a proverb. Perseverance at gold-digging, of all known pursuits in the world, is the least likely to be attended with success.

During the *furore* in England, produced by the intelligence of gold-fields having been discovered in Australia, several gold-mining companies were started in London, with the usual announcements of 'Provisional Committee,' 'Interim Secretary,' &c. Shares were sold and resold, but what ultimately became of some of the companies it might be difficult to conjecture. There was one, however, which should not have blown up so readily as it did. No doubt, in this case, it was very dis-heartening, after a very large expenditure of money in the designing, purchase, and exportation of machinery, and the payment of the passage money of a large number of men, who were engaged as servants of the company, to hear that the machinery was of no use, after great expense in dragging it a long way into the interior ; and that the most of the hired servants had deserted as soon as they had reached the shores of Australia. A number of the men adhered to their engage-ments, however, whilst a more trustworthy manager of the company could not have been found any-where than the one who had been engaged. The position in which this gentleman found himself placed was not very enviable—at least he said so himself ; as he could get no tidings whatever of his employers. The company had broken up, and no

one would have anything to do with him. He
accommodated himself to the situation, however—
set to work with the men who had remained, to
find gold as others were finding it. Success
attended his efforts, and at last he found himself
in possession of a large quantity of gold. Not at
all relishing his somewhat questionable situation,
he decided on freeing himself from the concern—
paid the men their wages, and the debts he had
incurred for the company. He kept the remaining portion of gold and returned to England. It
may be interesting to the ' Provisional Committee '
and ' Interim Secretary,' to know that their
machinery is still in good order, and when I saw it
last, was still the cause of many curious inquiries
from passers-by, and the subject of endless con-
jectures as to its object.

It is not usual with the diggers, when they have
amassed a quantity of gold made what they
designate a ' pile '—to keep it in their possession
at the gold-fields ; though small quantities may be
freely parted with, and sold to bank-agents, storekeepers, and others. They have all a correct
knowledge of the value of the precious metal, and
have scales for weighing it in their tents. The
' Government gold escort,' a four-wheeled vehicle,
drawn by four horses, in which are seated armed
policemen, is entrusted with the conveyance of the
gold to the capital. The Gold Commissioner at
the gold-fields receives the packages (bags made
of chamois leather) from the diggers, bank-agents,
and others, for which he gives a duplicate or

acknowledgment : and the packages, after being
duly sealed and registered, are forwarded by the
Government escort, as addressed, to the mint, bank,
merchants, or friends of the sender.

It is understood that the mint gives the same
weight in sovereigns as the weight in gold, the
alloy in the sovereigns defraying the expense of
coinage, and supplying the difference in value of
the coined and uncoined gold. The Government
always endeavours to reimburse itself for expenses
connected with the gold-fields, and the subject of
revenue is considered in the shape of a small export
duty on the gold. A ' miner's right ' of ten shillings
a year, and an escort fee, however, are charges that
have not much place in the mind, especially of the
lucky digger.

Robberies may be heard of sometimes ; but,
everything considered, they are of remarkably
rare occurrence. There is an overawing power in
a large assemblage of people. There are so many
eyes turned from every direction upon one, like an
eye of omnipresence and omniscience, that it is
almost impossible for a daylight robber to escape
detection ; besides, the diggers are not men to be
quarrelled with ; not one of them would think of
crying ' police '—every one learns, in every part of
Australia, and it becomes engrafted upon one's
very nature by habit and experience, never to
permit one's self to be robbed, to take good care
of whatever one is in possession of, and to offer no
temptation to any person whatever. There is no
small number of persons, however, ' loafers ' and

'hangers-on,' who are no better than children, as they will take whatever they fancy, or whatever they can lay their hands on, when they find they can do so unobserved. 'Stolen waters are sweet,' and there can be no doubt of the great pleasure which they have in stealing.

When found in its native state, embedded in the earth, and mixed with the soil, gold in the hands of many of the diggers would seem to lose all its adhesive properties. Speaking generally, there is nothing with which people are usually found so loath to part with as gold. The truth of the saying, 'lightly comes, lightly goes,' will not at all apply, however, to the case of the digger, for the gold is not easily found, very great labour being required, and sometimes very great expense incurred in finding it ; at least, such is the case in most of the gold-diggings. ' Pains seek to be paid in pleasures,' would seem to approach much nearer the truth, and account for the amazing indifference manifested by many of the diggers in taking care of that of which they had so much difficulty in acquiring possession. The life of personal dis-comfort, the pangs of loss and disappointment, the great uncertainty with which the mind has been kept, as on a rack—all rebound with great force on the head of the lucky digger ; and success very quickly passes into, and terminates in excess. With nothing to live or hope for, with no views extending beyond the present, without any previous fixed habits of frugality, the majority of those who were the first at the diggings—wonderfully successful old convicts—threw away the money which they had obtained for their gold, as if the pleasure of throwing it away was the only motive which they had in seeking for and finding gold; and some of them might have been heard telling, as I have frequently heard them myself, in boastful language and in rivalry one with another, how fast they could throw it away, or 'knock it down,' as they termed it.   The mind sometimes cannot endure to be kept brooding over that of which it feels its incapacity to take any care and management; whilst there is a kind of relief experienced in getting rid of that which would be a source of care and anxiety to continue in possession of.   It was not till the last sixpence was gone, that some men whom I knew might be said to have returned to their normal condition, and were fit for work.   There is not an inn of any description to be met with anywhere, in which champagne does not figure prominently and invitingly, with its peculiar glasses and bottles, the name of the wine being marked in gilt, artistically-formed letters on an emblazoned label.   There is a studied attention in such cases to supply a demand of not unfrequent occurrence, that of men coming to 'knock down' their money—and it is always the most expensive liquor which such men call for, namely, champagne, for which they are charged fifteen or twenty shillings per bottle; but this will not satisfy, and nothing will satisfy them but a 'shout for all hands,' every one within hearing being asked to partake.   Some of them, in this state of mind, have been known to light their pipes

with bank-notes—an illustration of consuming
vanity and ostentation, and a manner of gratifying
the love of display of wealth, which might fairly
claim the merit of defying all competition.

Those who continue to lead a wandering and
unsettled life, notwithstanding the most solid quali-
ties of heart and mind, which would admirably
qualify them for taking an honourable place, and
attaining success in the many pursuits in the great
mart of the world's industry, are apt to become so
entirely changed in character as to be almost unfit
for any settled occupation. Everything seems to
have got out of joint with them they are restless
and dissatisfied—locomotion, like some poisonous
ingredient instilled into their veins, infects their
whole constitution of mind and body, and it is to
very little purpose that an antidote is administered,
in the shape of the advice, ' a rolling stone gathers
no moss.' There are chances waiting them yet ;
they must go, will go, and would continue going
until the end of the chapter of this earthly existence, were it not for the strong claims which the
great law of necessity imposes upon them, and
which compels them to go no longer when they
are not able to go. The greatest and saddest
drawback of the gold-digging life, besides the uncertainty which attends it, is the wandering and
unsettled mode of existence, which seems to be
almost inseparable from it. A claim may turn out
very well, but it is apt to get worked out ; another
claim is taken up, and it may turn out a 'shicer ';
then there are other gold-fields, where the diggers

are reported to be doing better, or a new gold-field is discovered, and there is always the hope of being more successful, so that the life of chance, like ' a Will-o'-the-wisp,' leads the unlucky digger from place to place ; and it is not trifling earnings of gold which he learns to be contented with. Seven or ten shillings a day would be thought very indifferently of, and would be said to be ' nothing.'

Every one practically acquainted with the gold-fields will advise young men to be cautious before engaging in the pursuit of gold-digging, or may urge them not to think of it. It is a most perilous situation for them—a life of the direst temptation. A man may be damaged in body, heart, and mind, much in the same way as a carriage may be damaged by bad usage in being taken from the beaten public highway, and made to jolt over ruts and rough, broken ground, the risk and the damage to the carriage being greater when it is built of green and unseasoned timber. It is almost impossible for young men to take that amount of care of themselves at the gold-fields which is necessary for their well-being. Personal discomfort and unpalatable diet are matters of no slight consideration, as depravity of living has an affinity of attraction for every other kind of depravity. Man is an expensive being, and it will not do to treat one's self cheaply. A life of excitement, irregularity, and uncertainty, without any of the advantages of improving social intercourse, are also matters of no slight consideration. New and strange faces start up, a new scene of life is entered on, and young men of pliable natures will ever be prone to yield, succumb, and accommodate themselves to circumstances, very bad circumstances, indeed, amid the great disturbing forces of gain, loss, and disappointment, added to the evil of working in slush, under the heat of the midday sun, with the constitution taxed above its natural strength. Hence there is always a ready recourse to ardent spirits for quelling the mental and bodily disturbance, and the practice is apt to become habitual, as the necessities of the hour and moment tend to supersede and to extinguish all other considerations.

The Yankees are remarkable for their adaptation to circumstances, for fertility of resources, and for singular talent in pushing and 'going ahead.' They are enterprising traders, and all the Southern Pacific Ocean, and various shipping ports, bear evidence of their commercial industry, in the interchange of signals and such inquiries between vessels on approaching each other on the wide ocean, as 'Cargo?' 'Where bound for?' Passengers on board British vessels are familiar with the names of Boston, New York, and other ports in America, and the phrase, '.American notions,' in the answer given as to the cargo. ' American notions ' consist of an immense variety of articles of merchandise which the United States seem to hold the prescriptive right of manufacture, such as cheap household, farming, and digging utensils, buggies, clocks, and many other things extensively used in the Australian colonies. Com-

M

municativeness and inquisitiveness are nearly related ; they seem to be excellent auxiliaries in
that industrious art, the ' pursuit of knowledge
under difficulties,' and no one would seem better
qualified to enlist them in his service than a
Yankee trader. When gold-digging commenced
in California, the writer was staying at an hotel in
Wellington, New Zealand, where a Yankee trader
was also staying. Seated at the dining-table, the
latter was discoursing of the business he was doing
very largely and most benignantly to some other
seafaring men, to whom he was occasionally putting
questions. Captains of vessels are known to do
a good deal of business on their own account,
in addition to taking charge of their ships and
cargoes, and it might be useful to hear what might
concern them. There was not much to arrest
attention until the Yankee trader, with a touch of
bravado, made the astounding announcement of
his intention to take *a cargo of coffins !* ' Coffins !
a cargo of coffins !' every one at table seemed to
say, at the same time looking most demurely at
the Yankee trader, as if he and his brig, the fast
sailing of which he was always boasting of, were
the veritable Charon and his boat! An explanation
ensued. ' Coffins,' he said, ' are selling high just
now in California ; I took,' he continued, ' a cargo
of potatoes from this to San Francisco when I was
here last ; they all went to smash before I got to
the Sacramento. I have returned for another
cargo, and I calculate, by putting them into coffins,
having all the carpenters I can get here making

them, I'll land the potatoes safely, and make an almighty dollar of the two!' To such an ingenious, money-making, and enterprising race of people the gold-fields of Australia could not fail to present attractions. At first, it must be confessed, they made themselves very obnoxious to the peaceably disposed portion of the people, in spouting republicanism, and exciting to rebellion against the British Government; and they all seemed to be dubbed majors, or captains, in virtue of the military rank which they held in the United States. Intermeddling with political affairs was rather a work of supererogation on their part, as there was the people's great champion and leader in Sydney espousing the cause of separation, and crying 'Cut the painter!' quoting on all occasions, as he continues to do still, American institutions as a textbook for instruction and guidance, and endeavouring to make every one believe, as he seems profoundly in the belief himself, that whatever is American is divine. The era of responsible government, and the advent of manhood suffrage, must have reconciled the Yankees to the country, however, as they were never afterwards heard of as meddling with politics. They were engaged more profitably to themselves and others, in introducing, if not inventing, various mechanical contrivances for facilitating the labour of digging for and washing gold. There was one gold-field with a population of nearly three thousand people, all in some way or other dependent on the diggings, where everything was at a deadlock from the want

of water to wash the earth in which the gold was
found ; nothing daunted, a number of American
citizens formed themselves into a company, and
entered into arrangements with the Gold Commissioners and the Government for the privilege
of selling water to the diggers. A water-course
was dug, communicating with a running stream
far out of reach, a ' race ' (as the water-course
is called) was formed, winding round and round
for fourteen miles, thus supplying the much-
needed water to the diggers in the different localities.
The labour was immense, and the engineering
skill which was displayed, especially in dams
and sluices, and the formation of aqueducts over
deep ravines in the mountains, was astonishing.
The company, however, reimbursed themselves
largely, and derived a great revenue from the sale
of water, which was charged for weekly. They
ultimately sold their interest in the water in shares,
and returned to the United States with, as the
diggers said, a ' pile.'

There are people to be met with at the gold-
fields from every country in Europe some from
the Cape of Good Hope, and some from the West
Indies. There are no foreigners, however, equal to
the Chinese in respect of numbers. They were
coming, shipload after shipload, so rapidly that
some fear was entertained of their outnumbering
the British population, were they permitted to come
as they had been doing. The result was the imposition of a poll-tax of ten pounds by the Legislature, which has nearly amounted to a prohibition.

Singly, they appear to be quiet, good-humoured, passive, and unresisting people. A very different opinion is formed of them, however, when they are found in large numbers together, being sulky, stubborn, overbearing, having the manner of persons possessed by a sense of their great importance. They are generally disliked by the other diggers. Not being so venturesome as others, a Chinaman prefers safe, though small, earnings to making a venture, as in sinking a shaft; and he is given to wash over again the stuff that has been washed by others, instead of finding out new stuff for himself. There are many of them at the diggings and townships engaged in business as storekeepers, bakers, butchers, and market gardeners. Marriages sometimes take place between them and English, Scottish, and Irish females. They are notorious gamblers and great cheats. A storekeeper related to me a clever artifice which some of them had resorted to for cheating him and many others. He had been putting sovereigns into his pocket, along with his silver change, but he could never see them to take them out again when he wanted them. This went on for some time, as he thought that the confusion of mind which he might have been in was the cause of the disappearance of the sovereigns. Having observed, however, that Chinamen were rather anxious to get change in silver, and were somewhat fastidious when they got it, his suspicions were aroused and he found, on looking at the silver in his pockets, that the half-crowns, shillings, and sixpences were coated with quick-

silver ! The mystery of the disappearance of the
sovereigns was at once solved. They had received
a coating of quicksilver from mixing with the
Chinamen's silver, and he had given away his
sovereigns to them in change as shillings ! When
first introduced, and before the gold-diggings
commenced, the Chinese had not perhaps the
opportunity of cheating, being engaged under
periods of indenture at very small wages, about
six pounds a year, as shepherds, cooks, and servants,
making themselves generally useful. They were
always known, however, to be engaged in cheating
one another. The superintendent of a station,
where I halted for the night, showed me a piece of
paper with some scrawls of ink upon it, which, he
said, he had just received from a Chinaman in
payment for five pounds' worth of store goods.
The Chinaman looked most woeful and confused
when told that it was not worth anything. Another
Chinaman, he said, had given it to him in payment for a horse, and said it was Englishman's
money for five pounds ; an imposition of the same
kind as that which an Englishman in China might
practise upon another in attempting to write the
Chinese language, and in giving him a document
purporting to be Chinese.

When the gold-diggings commenced, shepherds
were not receiving more than twelve pounds, and
stockmen seventeen pounds a year ; whilst labour
generally was very cheap, and all the labouring
classes, who could afford to pay the passage-money,
were going to California. It was at this time that

the Chinese were first introduced to supply the great demand for labour. Wages rose instantly on gold being found in Australia, and the labouring classes were largely benefited. When the gold was first discovered, people went with a determination to find it : hoping even against hope ; but they are not so much disposed now to 'chance it.' Rich and payable spots are not, therefore, so apt to be come upon, and this may account for the reported falling-off in the yield of the gold-fields. As to the gold-fields becoming worked out, exhaustion may occur in some places, that is, the gold may be found so thinly diffused as not to pay the labour of finding it, but there are so many large tracts of country of a similar character to that in which it is found, that new gold-fields will always be heard of, as in Western Australia, and gold-digging is likely to continue to take its place as a permanent and great industrial pursuit. Were the diggers to content themselves with small, though certain earnings, and not go about so much from place to place, it might be better for them, and complaints of the want of success would be more seldom heard of. The truth of the aphorism, 'Gold may be bought too dear,' has a singular confirmation at the very fountain-head. The statement is so current at the gold-fields, and has appeared so often in print indeed, I have seen it in some of the Melbourne newspapers that there must be some foundation for the truth of the assertion, that every ounce of gold obtained from the earth is produced at a cost of seven pounds. As much as

ten pounds per ounce has sometimes been reckoned
as the cost of its production. This is astounding.
The selling price of gold amounts only to about
three pounds seventeen shillings and sixpence per
ounce. Three pounds twelve shillings, and three
pounds fifteen shillings, are about the prices received by the diggers, according to quality. It is
not, therefore, the gold-diggers, but the traders,
storekeepers, innkeepers, merchants, and people in
England, with the farmers in California and Chili,
who have benefited most by the gold-fields in
Australia. Large benefits have also, no doubt,
been derived by stock-holders—sheep and cattle
having quadrupled in price. Sinking a shaft is an
expensive and laborious undertaking ; from the
bad state of the roads in a time of flood, and the
impossibility of travelling in a time of drought,
provisions are apt to become scarce, and flour,
sugar, tea, and all other commodities, rise to such
exorbitant prices that very large earnings indeed
are necessary to enable one to stand the contest ;
besides, a scarcity of water may occur, and this
adds immensely to the expense. The number of
persons of different grades of life with whom I
have met, who had been engaged in gold-digging,
had met with indifferent success, and had tired and
sickened of the occupation, is a good opinion on
the spot as to the unsatisfactory nature of a life of
gold-digging.

The newly discovered gold-fields of Western
Australia form at present the great theme and
object of attraction to gold-diggers.

CHAPTER VI

SHEPHERDING

The Shepherd's Mode of Life—Easy Way of Earning a Livelihood—Hutkeepers and Families—Resources for those Unaccustomed to Manual Labour—Wages—Rations—A Commercial Traveller and an Expatriated Irish Landlord—Shepherding a Stepping-stone to a Better Position—A Lucky Irishman—Newly-Arrived Emigrants—Scottish Highlanders in Trouble—Encamping Out.

A MAN walking slowly along a public highway, with a flock of sheep straggling before him, and nibbling at the grass on the roadside, is not unlike the shepherding of Australia. Indeed, any one capable of walking a few miles a day, with sufficient eyesight to observe the sheep before him, as he leisurely follows them, is deemed quite competent to perform the duties of a shepherd. It is not so in New Zealand, however, shepherding there more nearly resembling what it is in Great Britain; whilst a man who might suit for a shepherd in Australia might not suit in New Zealand. There are few things which seem so surprising as the facility with which a livelihood may be secured in Australia, without doing anything worthy of the name of labour—simply by shepherding. Many persons, who in the mother country would most unquestionably be the inmates of poor-houses, or the objects of public charity, can always manage to obtain here, by tending sheep, a comfortable subsistence for themselves and families, and even accumulate money if they are careful. It was an excellent method of getting rid of some noisome people who had been always crying out for relief, to send them to Australia; and it must have been very astonishing to many to think how it was possible for such helpless human beings, when they arrived there, to be able to provide for themselves. There were two persons, a man and his wife, both far advanced in years. The woman had lost the power of her limbs; but when stretched on a couch beside the fire, she was able to cook for herself and her husband. The man could not do much—but he could do a little; he could walk about a mile a day, and attend to some maimed sheep (foot-rot), resting himself the most of the time on a fallen tree; and this service entitled him to eight shillings a week, with rations for himself and wife.

Shepherding is a very indolent occupation, and it is pitiable in the extreme sometimes to see a man of fourteen or sixteen stones weight dragging himself along the ground, sitting on a fallen tree, lying down, basking in the sun, and doing work which might be done as well and which is very frequently done by a boy fourteen or sixteen years of age. Hutkeeping is a still lazier occupation. The man has nothing to do save to sit in the hut all day long, to cook his own victuals, to shift, when necessary, the hurdles in which the sheep are folded, and to inform the overseer of any of the sheep being missing when the flocks are put in at night. He sleeps in a covered box like a sedan-chair beside the sheep, to guard against any attack being made upon them by the native dogs, the noise and howlings of his own dog, the usual signal of their presence, awakening him. When a family is engaged for an out-station, there is an addition of wages in lieu of the hutkeeper; the wife taking care of the hut, the husband making himself responsible for performing all the other duties of the hutkeeper. There are usually two or three shepherds at an out-station, and the sleeping by the sheep-folds at night is always arranged in such a way that one of the unmarried shepherds may do it. When the married and unmarried all live comfortably together, the out-station the usual haggard, naked, woe-begone looking shepherd's hut is found very frequently, in such cases, to assume the appearance of a comfortable homestead. The wife, if a thrifty woman, employs her powers of persuasion with the men in assisting her to carry out her schemes of domestic management and economy; cows are kept, a garden is formed, and there are all the usual adjuncts of household comfort. The employing of families at stations is a great improvement upon the old system of hutkeepers; a home is provided for many a previously homeless wanderer, the humanising influences of society are brought within their reach, and they are saved from the great danger of becoming what is

called 'cranky,' a deficiency in their mental
powers, which has happened to some from being long
alone.   When there are in a family one or two boys
capable of taking charge of a flock of sheep, the
family is left in sole charge of the out-station ; and
the general arrangement is, when there are two boys
shepherding, that the father of the family stays at
home, employing his time to his own and his
family's benefit, in such work as cultivating the
garden, making shoes—if he is a shoemaker—and
attending, at the same time, to the boys in charge
of the sheep, and seeing that they do their duty
properly.

One of the singular attractions which Australia
presents, is the asylum which it provides for persons
who are incapable of doing manual labour, and the
ease with which a livelihood may be gained, and
the bread of industry won, independently of hard
labour.   Those who are unable to face the storm
and endure the stern realities of life in individual
effort and encounter with the world, may here,
in shepherding, always betake themselves to a
shelter, possessing and enjoying the peace and
comfort of a home, and be plentifully provided for.
Many persons in Australia, more especially those
who are the heads of families, who have never been
accustomed to manual labour, are subject to a
pressure that falls easily and lightly enough upon
those inured to toil, but is a most grievous burden
when borne by those who have never earned their
bread by the sweat of their brow.   A knowledge of
the land they live in, and its great pursuit, ' wool-

growing,' would, however, enable them to place themselves in a position in which they would be able to attain independence, and all the while receive the advantages of a settled home. A person whom I knew, who had been a commercial traveller in England, preferring a shepherd's life, had quietly and comfortably ensconced himself at an out-station with his wife and family, wholly free from expense. He appeared quite satisfied, and there was no word of grumbling, discontent, or disappointment to be heard from his lips; the cause being, I suppose, that he was well-informed, knew the kind of country which he had come to, and had been careful not to leave himself any ground for complaint or disappointment. His gay partner, with whom he had braved the 'perils of the deep,' to push his fortune in Australia, proved herself to be an industrious housewife; a well-cultivated garden, with cows, pigs, and poultry, testified to their industry and domestic comfort, whilst the flowers in front of their dwelling showed the lively interest which they had taken in their new situation. The commercial traveller, now a shepherd, was ambitious to 'get on,' was qualifying himself for an overseership, and hoped, he said, to be 'promoted from the ranks.' He was fond of reading, and he had certainly every facility, so far as regarded time, for indulging in his hobby. Whatever may have been the benefits generally of Sir Robert Peel's Encumbered Irish Estates Bill, it had brought about a great change in the fortunes of one person whom I knew, who said to me, that being at an out-station in the bush of Australia was somewhat different from living in state and being lord of the manor of one of the finest properties on the banks of the ——— However, he did not seem in any way disconcerted, he was, in fact, with his excellent wife and family, very happy and cheerful. Virtue seeks the shade, and there were many circumstances which concurred to render his situation agreeable. Their privacy was not liable to be intruded upon; they were all enabled to maintain their independence, and there was no hard work required of them ; the sons had received a superior education, and there was every prospect of their future advancement as overseers or superintendents. Their house was situated on the slope of a ridge which ran along the banks of a river, and out of reach of high-water mark. In the course of the channel of the river there were patches of alluvial soil. One of these patches, not far distant, had been taken possession of and cultivated by the previous occupant of the station. Maize was grown in sufficient quantities to feed pigs and poultry, whilst the ground was strewn with pumpkins and melons. There was also a handsome addition of garden produce, in the shape of a superabundance of peaches ; and if the man who had planted the peach stones had also planted grape and fig cuttings, there would have been a still more valuable addition. As it was, it was merely an accident that there were fruit-trees there at all, and the man at the time of planting them very likely thought little of the favour he was conferring on those who were to come after him.

They could have received the use of as many cows as they pleased – hundreds of them, in fact as stock-holders are too glad to get their cattle quartered to refuse any request for them.

There are a great many unpleasant associations connected with Australian shepherding, however; at first there were convicts, next exiles, then followed Chinese, with half-castes, and coolies from India; even savages from the Feejee Islands were introduced to help the sheep-farmers. Cheap labour was wanted, and the profits of grazing at the time could not afford, or were supposed not to afford, a sufficiently high rate of wages to attract emigrants from Great Britain. All this has passed away, however. The gold-diggings brought about a complete revolution in the rates of wages—those of shepherds rose from twelve to forty pounds a year, and even as high as sixty pounds, when a man undertook the watching of his flock at night, whilst rations were added. The rations for one man are the well-known weekly allowance of 10 lbs. of flour, 10 lbs. of meat, 2 lbs. of sugar, and a quarter of a pound of tea. The wages of shepherds, like those of every other description of labour, will be found, however, to vary at different periods, and in different parts of the country, in accordance with the law of supply and demand.

There is much interest attached to the occupation of shepherding, from the large number of people who are engaged in it, from the peculiar situation of individuals and families, and also from its having been hitherto the great starting point—the stepping-stone, or the spring-board—for enabling people to

make money for their future settlement in life. The
population of towns—storekeepers, innkeepers, and
others engaged in business—is recruited from the
shepherding class; farming is almost entirely in
their hands : whilst many, with esquires added to
their names, who may be seen driving in their
chariots, with horses in bright burnished silver-
mounted harness, commenced their Australian life
as shepherds. Those who take to the occupation
are saved all risk of loss, to begin with, having
nothing to lose ; taken from on board ship, it may
be, when landed, they are provided for, housed, fed,
and attended to like children in the arms of their
nurse; they acquire knowledge of the country,
of pursuits, manners and customs; thus the stability
of their fortune is not endangered in the same way
as that of one who first begins to settle on the land
devoid of experience, and who has to maintain himself and family all the while at his own cost.

Those who seem to profit most in shepherding
are families in which there are one, two, or three
boys, each capable of tending a flock of sheep. A
father of a family, thus favourably circumstanced,
incidentally mentioned to me in his house, that he
had saved by his sons' labour one thousand pounds,
and that he proposed to remove from the bush, and
settle in New Zealand. It is far from being desirable
that any one individual, or family, should continue
long shepherding, however ; from the solitary mode
of life, 'all, all alone,' Sunday and Saturday, from
one year's end to the other, constantly following
sheep, an instinctive aversion to the occupation is

soon felt, and there are many, in consequence, who leave to settle in a town or neighbourhood, leaving their places to be filled by others. An Irishman, named Michael O'Brady, whose hut I used to pass very frequently, and to whose wife, Bridget, I was indebted for many kindnesses, in receiving part of their rations, was the only one I have met who seemed quite determined to stick to shepherding as long as he could. Michael did not herd himself, however, and was always hanging about the house ; he had a large number of boys shepherding, and they were bringing him, he said, three hundred pounds a year. Michael seemed to have been made for Australia, or Australia made for him, and no two ever got on better together. ' I don't like work,' he once said to the writer, who had questioned him if he never thought of buying land and settling near a town. Michael arrived at the time when shepherds were leaving to go to the California gold-diggings, and was, therefore, a great prize. He was taken from the ship in which he landed, with Bridget and their crowd of young children, and conveyed in a dray, to a station far in the interior, by the sheep-farmer who hired him and his eldest . boy. This is not always the good fortune of many, however, and newly arrived emigrants are not unfrequently thrown into a state of great perplexity in not seeing employers waiting, as they anticipated, to engage them. The statements of some of these emigrants would appear pitiable in the extreme to those unacquainted with their real situation and the manners of the country. A paragraph, under the

N

heading ' Distressing Case,' appeared in a Queensland newspaper, but an old colonist, or one inured
to Australian life, would have failed to see anything
distressing in the case. Two families, the paragraph
stated, had arrived in an emigrant ship. The
fathers of those families, two stout, able-bodied men,
had travelled forty miles inland, looking for employment, and could not find any. They returned to
Brisbane and made their case known to the authorities, stating that they and their families were
destitute. An old colonist, however, would at once
have ' humped his swag,' and taken his family with
him ; he would not think a journey of forty miles
worth speaking about, as the further he travelled
inland, the more certain he would be of obtaining
employment, and a high rate of wages ; whilst he
would persevere in going from station to station,
until he had succeeded in finding a situation of some
kind or other.

The people are all very kind ; and the poorer
the families, the more certain one would seem to
be of being hospitably entertained ; whilst the
owners of stations are always remarkable for assisting persons who are looking for employment. I
know of only one case of travellers complaining of
want of hospitality. The complaint was made by
a number of Scottish Highlanders, who had not
been long from on board ship, and were wending
their way to a station in the interior. They stopped
me suddenly on the road, and one exclaimed, partly
in English and partly in Gaelic, with a movement
of his arm which the appetite of hunger seemed

only capable of causing, ' If we had met you '
(meaning, also, all the other people in the bush)
' as you have met us, in the Glen of ——, we would
have shown you how to treat men.' An explanation followed, when it appeared that they
had been a long time without food, and had been
refused assistance at a station which they had just
passed. They had failed to make their case clearly
known, and they were ignorant of the fact that the
district which they were traversing was overrun
with gold-diggers, whose repeated calls at the
houses of the settlers was too great a tax to be
borne patiently. The wants of the Highlanders
were supplied, however, by a most hospitable
gentleman, at the next station which they came
to.

Encamping out at night is a universal practice.
Indeed, an experienced Australian never dreams
in travelling of making to a house for lodgings,
unless it be to recruit his stock of provisions.
There are always drays going along the road,
and travellers on foot usually keep company with
the draymen in their favourite places of encampment, and it is always found to be more agreeable
to sleep out at night, under an awning, such as
that of a blanket, or a covering formed of a sheet
of calico.

CHAPTER VII

LOST IN THE BUSH

Bush Directions to Travellers —Bush of Australia and Bush of New
Zealand — Died of Starvation – Riding in a Circle—Lost Tra-
vellers—A Traveller gone Mad—Short Cuts and Hair-breadth
Escapes—Marked Tree Line-- Lost Children – Blacks Tracking
a Lost Child—A Mother and her Lost Child—Aboriginal
Guides.

THE directions which are usually given to a traveller who is endeavouring to find his way from
one station to another in the interior, where there
is no ' marked tree line,' or bush track, to guide
him, are much as follows : ' Keep down the side of
the river (or creek) for nearly three miles, until
you come to a cattle camp ; pass that and bear a
little to the right, and you will come to Rocky
Gully ; cross over it, and look for a ridge to the
left ; go over it, and keep right ahead, and you
will come to Oakey Creek ; follow it down, and
you will come to an out-station of Ballibullu.
There is a well-marked road from that to the head-
station. You cannot mistake it—it is only twenty
miles.' An experienced bushman would not be
likely to mistake such directions. He would know
how much a mile represented, he would know a

cattle camp when he saw it, and he could also distinguish Rocky Gully and Oakey Creek from all other creeks and gullies, as being prominent features in the country to be travelled over; places, such as creeks and gullies, being often named from some peculiarity that distinguishes them, such as the existence of water. It is very different, however, with one who is unaccustomed to bush travelling; if he sees one cattle camp he sees a hundred: and as to Rocky Gully and Oakey Creek, they cannot speak for themselves and say that they are the gullies and creeks which were to be come to. Over-anxiety is always certain to lead to a mistake, and the directions which have been given should be carefully attended to. A gentleman in travelling informed me that he had gone one hundred miles out of his way, in consequence of a mistake which he had committed in not following the direction indicated in words similar to those given above. He had turned off too soon—went right ahead as directed, continued his journey until he came to what he supposed was Oakey Creek, followed it down, and came to a part of the country far from where he had intended going to, when he discovered that, instead of following the fall of the water to the west, he had followed it to the east. The whole country has the appearance of being spread over with a network, in consequence of the chains of hills and mountains, which are thinly covered with trees. Hills bare of trees being rarely met with, it is impossible to see to any great distance in one direction, and thus mark out some object to steer one's course by ; and, as a consequence, travelling in a straight direction is seldom possible, from the intervening and frequently steep mountains, unless it may be far inland, where the country is much more level. The bush of Australia bears no resemblance to the bush of New Zealand, that of the latter country being dense, indeed, frequently impenetrable forest, not unlike the clumps of plantation which occur at intervals in the mountain districts of Scotland.

A gentleman, who had recently arrived from England, named St. George, with whom I sometimes met whilst travelling, had brought with him ten thousand pounds to invest in sheep-farming. Favoured with letters of introduction, he was profitably employing his time in going from station to station, endeavouring to acquire information and make himself acquainted with the modes of management of sheep, before completing a purchase. He trusted himself, on one occasion, to follow out a bush direction given to him, from one station to another (the distance was about twenty miles across the country) ; there was no marked tree line, or bush track, and he was requested to be very careful to look out, after he had crossed a chain of mountains, for a bridle-track which would lead him straight to the station which he wished to go to. The bridle-track was of vital importance to him, and he felt as if his very life depended upon it   He took the first track he came to, after he had crossed the mountains, and followed it all day, up and down hill, over fallen trees, branches, rocks, stones, and sometimes through close scrub ; still the path was very distinctly marked. The sun shone sometimes on his back, sometimes on his face, and he did not know what to think of it ; he always kept on the path, however, as directed, where he could see it, but the path, or supposed bridle-track, never seemed to bring him nearer the anxiously-looked-for station. Darkness finally set in, and, as he could not see his way any further, there was no alternative left but to remain in the bush all night. He was frightened to trust his horse by allowing it to graze freely, as experienced bushmen always do, by taking off the saddle and bridle, and making use of the stirrup leathers to tie the horse's fore feet to prevent it from straying any distance. He never let the reins out of his hands, greatly to his own as well as his horse's discomfort. The next day's journey was much the same as the preceding one—up and down hill, over rocks, dead timber, and through brushwood, still, after all his arduous labours and indefatigable perseverance, there was not the least appearance of being re-warded by a sight of a human dwelling. Faint from want of food, though fortunately there was plenty of water, and his mind not being in a very collected state, he gave himself up for lost, and with the object of removing all anxiety from the minds of his relatives in England, and showing that he had not come to his death by foul means, he wrote with a pencil on a slip of paper, ‘ Died of starvation,’ and pinned the paper to a shirt, which he hung on a branch of a tree. He then laid himself down on the ground, bidding farewell to the world. The shirt, however, was the cause of his being saved from the death which he had anticipated, and to which he had so complacently resigned himself, as it attracted next day the notice of a stockman who had most opportunely happened to come in that direction, and who conducted the traveller safely to the station which he had been endeavouring to reach. It transpired that Mr. St. George had been following cattle-tracks, and these are usually much more distinct and beaten than bridle-tracks. Cattle have often to travel long distances for water, and they follow one another in one path, in going to the summits of the hills and mountains for warmth at night, or in returning to the valleys to drink ; and, from going to and fro so frequently, their tracks become more beaten than the public highway.

The superintendent of a station narrated to me rather a curious misadventure of a traveller, who had just made his entrance into the bush, and who was as ignorant as Mr. St. George of the necessity of adhering to the famous direction for providing against the danger of being lost ; ' Follow the fall of water down ; sure to come to some place.' The inexperienced traveller had lost sight of the great public highway ; a fall of rain had made the grass to grow so quickly as to have made it rather difficult in some places to see the road ; he gallantly persevered on his journey, however, following, as he supposed, the right direction. The attention of

the superintendent was called to him in the early
part of the day, and as he was travelling where
there was no highway, the former naturally enough
concluded that he was well acquainted with the
country; and, from the fact of his always riding in
the same place, it was thought that he was looking
for lost horses or bullocks. Late in the evening,
the superintendent's attention was again called to
him, and, seeing that he always followed the same
route, was riding at great speed, and, as nearly as
he could guess, travelling in a circle, he began to
entertain misgivings as to the traveller's soundness
of mind. Riding up to him, the mystery was at
once solved. 'I was lost! I was lost!' exclaimed
the traveller, in an ecstasy of delight, 'but I knew
that I was coming to some place, the road always
getting more distinct.' The traveller had been
making the road himself; he had come upon his
own horse's tracks, had continued to follow them,
and had been riding round and round as in a circus.
To men placed under similar circumstances, the
mark of a hatchet upon a tree, or a footprint upon
the sand, will sometimes communicate far greater
happiness and purer feelings of delight than those
which could be communicated by entering into
possession of the richest earthly inheritance.

There is always a strong temptation to 'strike
across the country,' to use the common expression,
as a saving may thus be effected sometimes of
twenty or fifty miles in a journey of two or three
days. It is in attempting to make those 'short
cuts,' as they are called, that nearly all the cases of

being lost occur, and from which the numerous recitals of hair-breadth escapes derive their origin. Some of these hair-breadth escapes are certainly very remarkable. A stockman told me that, on cracking his whip in an unfrequented part of his run, he heard, as he thought, the sound of a human voice. On going to the place whence the sound proceeded, there was a man, in a most exhausted state, who had been lost for several days. Whilst making a near cut, which saved me fifteen miles in a day's journey, a shepherd, in charge of a flock of sheep, thus accosted me in passing : ' A man had a narrow escape here a few days ago ; it is easy enough getting in here, but it is another thing getting out.' It was a labyrinth of granite hills, surrounded by high mountains. ' I saw the mark of a man's foot,' continued the shepherd, ' and knew that there was some one about here who had lost himself — there were fresh marks the following day. I cried and *coocyed* without getting any answer. I brought my gun with me the next day, to make him hear. I heard his voice, and went to the place ; the man was nearly dead, and I had some difficulty in getting him to my hut.' It was very thoughtful on the part of the shepherd, and credit-able to him in the highest degree, as very few indeed would have taken the precaution which he took in anticipating the misfortunes of a fellow creature, and rescuing him from the jaws of death. This case contrasts most strongly with one which I heard of in New Zealand. A number of men who were travelling together — all new arrivals — had encamped for the night. During the night long, they heard and were disturbed with the sound of the well-known *cooye*. They gave no answer, however. The *cooye* was from another party, who had been lost for several days in the dense forest, and who, some time afterwards, were found dead from exposure and hunger at the place where they had cried out. Not to answer a *cooye* that is, *cooyeing* in return --is always accounted the greatest barbarity which one can be guilty of, but it was, no doubt, excusable in this instance, the new arrivals being ignorant of its grave and important meaning.

The boldness, or rather the foolhardiness, of some in attempting to do what they see others doing, without possessing the same knowledge of the country, and experience in travelling, frequently brings them into situations of great peril, and in one instance which came under my observation, was the cause of one man's death. I had traversed the same path -a bridle-track—frequently. It had been a 'marked tree line' of road, but the marks upon the trees were nearly all obliterated, and the route was only traversed by those who knew the country. The man, whom I had seen, attempted to follow this path, to 'short cut' it, and had lost himself. He was found, by the merest accident, by the owner of the station, after he had been wandering about for eight days in a maze of broken ridges, rather thickly timbered. He had lost the use of his reason, and, in a state of delirium, had stripped himself of all his clothing and was appeasing his hunger by devouring a black snake which he had succeeded in killing, and which he still held in his hand when he was found. The gentleman who found him conveyed him in a cart to his house. Medical assistance was procured, and every attention bestowed upon him, but he never rallied, and died a few days afterwards.

There is something peculiarly distressing and lamentable, however, when children, so helpless and entirely destitute of resources, are lost. Fortunately, instances are not numerous, but, when a case does occur of a child being lost, it is a source of bitter and poignant grief to the parents, who are almost more deserving of pity than the lost child, as an occurrence of the kind never takes place without the parents taking the blame of negligence on themselves for having permitted the child to go out of their sight. I officiated at the interment of one child which came to its death in this manner. The grief of the mother was too agonizing to admit of description, and it must have been greatly intensified from the fact of the remains having been found only a very short distance from the house.

Those in search of lost children are apt, very stupidly, to make so much noise in crying and shouting, that the child is frightened, and instinctively conceals itself. A very good illustration of this came under my notice at a station where I happened to be at a time when the child of a shepherd was lost. As soon as the intelligence reached the station, every man and boy about the place were instantly on horseback, with stock-whips in their hands, and a kennel of dogs at the horses'

heels, howling and barking. A stranger would
have been very apt to have mistaken all the ado
and excitement as an expedition in pursuit of a
bushranger, or a wild beast, rather than a search
for a lost child. Scattering themselves over the
ground surrounding the shepherd's hut, they commenced looking everywhere for the child. It was
rather open country, thinly dotted with trees, and
they could see long distances in every direction.
They were all filled with astonishment at their lack
of success, and could not help giving utterance to
their fears— to thoughts of the death and inscrutable
mystery of the child's disappearance. It was now
late in the evening ; and, as they could not see to
continue their search longer, they thought that they
might as well kill a native dog, which their own
dogs had been barking at, in a hollow log. Dismounting, and arming themselves with sticks to
strike the brute as it came out, one of the men,
looking into the hollow of the log, saw the child
which they had been searching for. The child had
been frightened by the wild screams, roars, and
cries, and had hid herself.

A family may live sometimes quite unconscious
of the dangers which they have been creating and
rearing around their dwellings. Houses are usually
at first erected where there is a clear, open sward
of grass, where large views may be obtained around,
and always where there is a permanent supply of
water. Where cows are kept, and dairying is
carried on, the soil is enriched ; and young trees
are apt to grow up vigorously and to form a scrub.

A girl, fourteen years of age, the daughter of most industrious parents, had gone to look for the cows in one of these scrubs, but she never returned. Ten days were fruitlessly spent in search of her by many persons; the air resounded far and near with cries to her; there was no answer, and those cries, especially by strange voices, had, in all probability, frightened her and caused her to go further away. The country was rather hilly and thinly covered with trees, as the country generally is. It was woeful to give over the search when the shades of evening had closed around them and to repair to their own houses, knowing that she whom they had been in search of was out in the cold, dewy nights, without shelter or covering, famishing for want of food ; and every morsel which they put to their lips served only to remind them, and the parents more particularly, that Jessie, the lost one, had not taken anything for so many nights and days. There did not happen to be any blacks about, but their services were now deemed indispensable. There were some at a neighbouring station, who came very readily when solicited to give assistance, but it was too late. They, however, did their part very well. On being told where the girl was last seen to enter the scrub, they went down instantly on their hands and knees, and, with their large, sooty eyes, scanned every blade of grass, fallen leaf, and twig, with as much care and delicacy as if they had been objects of infinite worth. Holding their eyes intently on the ground, and scanning it in this way as they

went along, they tracked the marks of her feet,
step after step, and over every inch which she had
traversed. It was tedious work for the blacks, but
they seemed proud of the great consideration in
which their services were held. The marks of her
feet led to a rocky eminence, nearly two miles distant from the house ; here the blacks directed the
attention of the anxious parents and others, who
were watching them with absorbing interest, to
some marks of blood on the rock, saying, in their
uncouth jargon : ' Feet bleeding on the head of
this fellow rock.' All the busy surmising as to
where she could possibly have gone were soon set
ta rest, and, as the blacks had conjectured, her
dead body was found on the summit of the rock.

There is always great satisfaction when the
remains of the lost are found. Uncertainty is the
most calamitous state which the mind can be
thrown into. The heart is choked, and there is an
unutterable anguish in the pent up and conflicting
emotions of hope and fear. In one case which I
knew of, a man, with his wife and family, had
committed the mistake of settling at a certain place
beside a dense scrub. The youngest child, the
only boy in the family, had been unguardedly permitted to enter it ; he was lost, and never found.
The bereaved mother drank deeply of the cup of
sorrow ; her mind was ever restless. She could
think of nothing, do nothing, but what concerned
the finding of her lost boy ; and no words of peace
and consolation could be heard until some trace of
him could be found. Thoughts of him were ever

recurring to her mind ; he might be found in one
place—he might be found in another—and her
requests to go in search were often attended to
when she was unable to go herself. All hope of
earthly care had fled from her dwelling ; a mantle
of death seemed to cover it ; the breeze which had
wafted the sweetest fragrance to her, seemed now
to bear the most poisonous exhalations ; death
and terror were couched in every fallen tree, and
their branches, waving in the wind, appeared to be
triumphing in the victory which they had obtained
over her and her boy. Sleep fled her pillow, and,
prostrated in body and mind, she sank into the
deep wat of suffering, of bereavement, and of
ceaseless wailing, and found an early grave.

The aborigines are of inestimable value to
inexperienced travellers. There are few stations
at which some of them may not be found loitering,
and young lads especially are always ready to
mount a horse and go a long distance for a trifling
reward.

CHAPTER VIII

DROUGHTS AND FLOODS

LIABILITY to severe droughts and to great flood are distinguishing characteristics of Australia, and it would be in vain for the most hopeful of the speculative admirers of the future of that Continent to attempt to gainsay or ignore those great facts, which tell severely on the cultivators of the soil, and render agriculture a most hazardous undertaking, save in some famed localities, as along the coast, and in the dividing ranges. One would be apt to suppose that floods would not be so disastrous to the farmer as droughts, but in many places, the whole of the land available for agriculture is situated on the margin of creeks and rivers, and a flood, when of unusual size, is as disastrous as a drought, in consequence of the losses sustained in the carrying away of fencing, crops, and sometimes even houses, whilst the land is frequently spoiled by the sand and *débris* which have been deposited. A drought, when of long continuance, is felt by all classes of the community, and is indeed a fearful visitation of Divine Providence. In a continuous journey of four hundred miles inland, during a time of severe drought, I did not observe a blade of green grass; bush fires prevailed everywhere; the dry and withered grass crumbled in the hand into powder, and the whole was set fire to with the object of preparing the ground for the new grass which was to grow after the expected fall of rain. The heaven was as brass, the earth as iron—the sun and moon had changed their appearance, were as if clad in sackcloth, or red as blood, when seen through a smoked glass. In consequence of the black vapours, with which the atmosphere was filled, from the bush fires far and near, the sun's rays, during the height of the day, poured down the most intense heat. The birds on the trees might be seen panting for breath;—water, cold, cold water! It is only under such circumstances that one can fully understand the apt illustration of Scripture story. The trees afford only miserable shelter, and there is no place so much coveted as the shadow of a rock for protection against the oppressive heat of the sun's rays. There is also great danger in travelling in the heat of the mid-day sun; and it is at such periods that 'the smiting of the sun by day'—cases of sunstroke—are reported as happening to those who incautiously expose themselves to the deadly heat without the aid of an umbrella or a proper covering for the head.

There was one well-authenticated case of a conflagration which had originated in a singular manner, related to me by the owner of the station where the fire had originated in the interior of Queensland. The day was broiling hot; there was no living object to be seen moving about anywhere, save a stray lizard, or a magpie in search of food, and the usual stock-yard attendants, carrion crows. The birds had sheltered themselves in the leafy branches of the trees, and the ants, which are usually so very busy in going to and fro in their thoroughfares on the ground, did not venture to come out of their nests. The cattle were all in their encampments, performing the offices of mutual kindness in constantly wiping away with their tails from one another the clouds of flies which were continually endeavouring to settle upon them. The sheep were gathered in clusters at the roots of trees, panting heavily from the oppressive heat, the shepherd in charge of them sitting drowsily on a fallen tree. Outdoor manual labour might be said to be impossible save to the blacks, and indoor labour might be said to consist chiefly in wiping the perspiration from the head and face, and in going to quench the thirst with the trickling drops which oozed from the canvas bags of water suspended in the verandah. It was on such a day of intense heat that my informant observed smoke arise near one of the outbuildings of the homestead. The smoke was increasing in volume, and the fire from which it proceeded became visible and was soon spreading fast in the direction of the dwelling-house, feeding itself on shreds of bark and chips of wood, which covered the ground thickly. The buildings would have been all in a flame in a short time had it not been for the timeous discovery. The origin of the fire was clearly traced to an axe which had been left outside, the powerful heat of the sun's rays having acted on the polished blade and ignited shreds of bark beside it.

The hot winds are supposed to be occasioned by the perpendicular rays of the summer sun falling on the sandstone ridges, and the large tracts of country covered with loose stones in the north-western interior. The winds passing over these parts of country are heated, and deprived of their moisture. They present an obstacle of a formidable character to the successful pursuit of cultivation over a great part of the interior. Though no dependence of any kind is placed on agriculture, there will be very frequently found at stations patches for growing maize, sorghum, and saccharatum, pumpkins, melons, and sometimes wheat. The work is regarded as having very much of the nature of a venture ; and a crop in one out of two, three, or five years will not be a disappointment. In districts where wheat can be grown, and where there is no convenience of carriage, or sufficient population to maintain a steam flour-mill, every homestead is provided with a portable iron hand flour-mill, to grind the wheat into flour, an operation in connection with which the aborigines sometimes make themselves very useful. One of the earliest clergymen in New South Wales narrated to the writer rather an interesting episode in his life in connection with a drought and the hand flour-mill. After a long journey to visit a family, he was greeted by the mother with the not very gratifying intelligence,' We have not a morsel of bread' 'there had been a drought during the preceding year, and flour was very scarce), 'but if you'll wait a little, the wheat is about ripe.' With sickle in hand she went to the ripe field, reaped a few handfuls, thrashed the ears, the cracking noise of the hand flour-mill instantly followed, and flour and bread were speedily produced from the recently upstanding ears of wheat.

Veils are in general use during hot weather in summer as a protection against the flies, which are very troublesome. In a time of severe drought, in travelling the main lines of road, veils are absolutely indispensable; and the fabric of which they are made requires to be of a much closer texture than that which is usually worn. It is impossible to travel even a short distance without being enveloped in clouds of dust; and the eyes, ears, and nostrils are all liable to be stuffed with fine sand. Veils would not seem, however, to form any protection against the 'sandy' and 'swelling blight' complaints of the eyes to which some persons, at this season of the year, are liable to be affected. The 'sandy blight' is so named from the painful sensation as of sand in the eyes; the 'swelling blight' is not painful, and is attributed to the sting of a small fly. They are both likely to be occasioned, however, by the dry, parched state of the atmosphere during the continuance of hot winds. They do not continue long, and are easily remediable by shading the eyes from the sun and washing them with weak goulard water.

However great the heat of the sun, whatever the state of the roads, and however arduous travelling may be, travelling must be done, at any cost or sacrifice; and bullock teams, with drays, are always to be met toiling slowly along, or, occasionally, horse teams, moving at a much brisker pace, the men in charge of them so besmeared with dust, their faces so black—the perspiration producing with the dust a coating of mud - that it is impossible to distinguish the white teamsters from those black ones, who are sometimes found in charge of bullock drays from far distant stations, and who have been taught the useful arts of life. The teamsters on the road bear no proportion to the number encamped at the water-holes and the crossing places of rivers, who have been unable to continue their journey in consequence of the weak state of their bullocks, and the loss of some of them by death. They are what is called 'stuck up'; cannot move out of their place, and must remain where they are until there is food on the road, or till they get fresh bullocks which are able to stand the journey. Carriage, as a necessary consequence, rises to a high price, and there is no alternative left to many, when crops have failed, but to betake themselves to an occupation of which they never thought before viz., carrying on the road showing how much manners and modes of

life may be influenced by a country, and how vain
it is to struggle against forces beyond all human
control. If a drought continues, and there is no
appearance of a change taking place, in the shape
of a fall of rain, the most doleful forebodings are
sometimes entertained by the stockholders in some
parts of the country, of the calamity which hangs
over them in the probable loss of their stock from
starvation and want of water ; whilst not a few
have their fears deeply embittered in reflecting on
the unfortunate error which they have committed
in burning so much of their runs. And it is in
cases of this nature that experience comes so much
to the aid of the Australian settler, in the making
of ' dams,' and guarding against the great danger
of ' overstocking.'

There were some stations where the extremely
distressing remedy was resorted to, of killing the
lambs and calves to save their mothers. A gentleman, whom I met on the road, said that he had
seen sixteen good horses dead in one water-hole.
They had gone there to drink, and had sunk in
the slimy bottom and perished. The superintendent of a cattle station said that he had lost
seven hundred cows ; another superintendent said
that he had lost about one-third of the stock, and
that this was about the loss sustained by many
other stations. The sheep-farmers, in some parts
of the country, also suffered great losses of sheep,
a fulfilment of predictions which I had heard from
very old colonists.

With respect to the very severe drought of 1865

and the beginning of 1866, which was felt over a great part of South Australia, Victoria, and New South Wales, I think I cannot do better than give the following notices, which occur in the *Sydney Morning Herald*, of January 20th, 1866, with reference to the last-named colony:

The first extract is remarkable as showing the uncertain nature of Australian weather. 'Just a week before Christmas (the middle of summer), the frightful heat of the weather was suddenly arrested, in the south and west, and for three days these districts were plunged into mid-winter. At Kiandra there was a heavy fall of snow, which covered the ground in some places to the depth of three feet; at Queenbean, hail, rain, and sleet prevailed—whilst on the heavy ranges south from that town, and on the opposite side of the Murrumbidgee, a wintry coating of snow lay until the Tuesday before Christmas. Since then there has been one unbroken series of fierce winds and burning heat. The thermometer at various places and times has ranged from 120 to 140 degrees in the sun, and from 80 to 101 degrees in the shade. Relief has been temporarily given by occasional thunder-storms, which, whilst they have deluged the particular localities over which they have burst, have been exceedingly partial in their distribution of the blessed and much-looked-for element—water. At Beza there has been no rain for the last ten months. At Ulladulla there has not been, for the last twelve months, a sufficient fall of rain to penetrate one inch into the ground. At the Wimmera, water is so scarce that the least

valuable of the horse stock is being shot, in order
to prolong the supply to the remainder ; and emus,
not usually seen in that quarter, come tamely up to
drink at the casks that have been filled for the
horses. A gentleman who recently travelled down
the Bland Creek, states that he saw no less than six
hundred head of dead cattle, in about twelve miles
from the creek. There are very few stations, in the
far west where a serviceable horse can be obtained.
Water is not to be had, except at distances ranging
from thirty-five to sixty-five miles apart, and, unless
these places are made, there is no chance of a
drink ; and, as is usual upon occasions like the
present, we hear occasionally of fearful deaths in
the bush, for the traveller who misses his road just
now is a doomed man. The long stretch of country lying between the Lachlan and the Murrumbidgee, and known as the Levels, from its flat and
unbroken character, has suffered perhaps as severely
as any part of the country ; and, as it has been
pretty thickly settled upon, this suffering is all the
more distressing. Many of the residents have now
to send long distances for water, and even that,
which is their whole dependence, will not, it is calculated, last more than six weeks longer, should no
rain fall in the interim. Those water-holes are also
almost unapproachable, from the large number of
dead and dying cattle that lie round them, the
former in all stages of decomposition. Owing to
the state of the country, it has become exceedingly
difficult to get carriage for loading any great distance
into the interior, unless at very high rates. Bullock

teams cannot possibly travel, and for horse teams, the carriers have to take with them all the food required for the consumption of their animals. A letter from Walget states that on one station, where one hundred and twenty thousand sheep had been guaranteed to the shearers, only sixty thousand could be brought into the shed; and that, on another station in the same district, only one hundred and thirteen thousand were shorn where there should have been one hundred and eighty thousand.' In each case the deficiency had been caused by deaths in the flocks, owing to the want of food and the scarcity of water. With reference to the large sheep farms in Walget, an estimate of the extent of land which goes to form one of them may be easily arrived at by calculating five, six, or seven, as the number of acres to a sheep which the land is estimated to carry. It is an observation which I have heard old Australians make, that when there were droughts in the south, there was rain in the north, and *vice versa*. This seems to have been the case in connection with this drought, as there was no want of rain in Queensland.

One hundred, or even ten yards, of a New Zealand stream or river, choked full of Captain Cook's watercress, would be a prize indeed in the interior of Australia at any time, but more especially during a time of long-continued droughts; it would be something agreeable and refreshing for the eyes, but it would be much more so to the palate in seasoning the unvarying round of beef, tea, and damper, or bread. The want of vegetables is often

severely felt. The wealthy stock-owners are usually
well provided in their stores with pickles and preserved potatoes, but these are too expensive articles
of consumption for the working people. Along the
coast, and on the dividing ranges, pumpkins, all
the varieties of melons, English vegetables and fruit,
such as peaches and apricots, are grown plentifully.
In the interior, however, and where hot scorching
winds prevail in summer, the fruit is roasted on the
trees, and no succulent vegetable of any kind is
able to stand the withering heat The human constitution, both bodily and mentally, is a delicate
one. It was manifestly the design of the Creator,
in providing such fruits as grapes, peaches, oranges,
melons, &c., as the peculiar productions of a warm
climate, that the constitution should be supported
and cherished, that men should not merely live, but
enjoy life ; and there would be less intemperance
heard of in Australia if those resources which nature
has provided were within reach of the people, during
the time of the occurrence of such droughts as those
which have been described. I have seen parts of
the country in the high dividing ranges, which,
visited by thunder-storms, were as green as an
emerald, with waving fields of grain, pumpkins,
melons, potatoes, turnips, cabbages, carrots, and all
the other varieties of English vegetables, growing
in the greatest profusion, and where they had never
been known to fail.

When rain falls—and if it has been general and
plentiful, a drought is very soon forgotten – the
whole surface of the earth soon begins to smile, a

carpet of the deepest green takes the place of all that was dry and withered—and it is not in human nature to resist the enchanting influence. 'A drought will not come back again,' is the expression whilst men dismiss from their minds all thoughts of the occurrence of another drought, more especially at the board of festive entertainment. The sudden change is remarkable, the grass grows rapidly, and there would seem to be no limit to the number of cattle, sheep, or horses, which the land is capable of carrying, or to the crops of grain which might be cultivated. The dryness of the air, and the heat of the sun, however, soon change the green appearance of the earth's surface into a brown colour. A drought is most severely felt during the spring and summer months, and may prevail throughout the whole of August, September, October, November, December, and January. Floods, of which there may be a succession, prevail during the autumn and winter months, February, March, April, May, June, July. If there is a continuation of two or three days' rain, which has been general, a flood will inevitably follow. Graziers look on, however, in such cases, with great indifference, unless they have teams on the road, and supplies for their stations unduly detained. It is very different, however, with the small settlers, and with gold-diggers, to whom travelling on the road with heavily laden drays is almost impossible. The rate of carriage rises to an exorbitant figure, and what with that rate and the consequent scarcity of provisions, living becomes very expensive.

There are storekeepers, however, who have anticipated all this, and who make a harvest both of
droughts and floods. I saw one river which had
risen forty feet within a few hours; there are
other rivers which overflow their banks, carrying
destruction in their course, sweeping away fencing,
crops, sometimes houses, and spoiling the cultivated
land. The newspapers relate the stereotyped tales
of floods, great losses, exploits of men with boats
on the river, near the coast, and persons saved and
drowned. There is such a scarcity of water in
many places, that the possibility of being deluged
with it is about one of the last things thought of,
and is regarded as something of the nature of
' being too good news to be true.' In rather a level
part of country in the interior where I had been,
and where it was difficult to get a drink of water, a
shepherd told me shortly afterwards that there was
an inland sea sixty miles in breadth—he meant
back waters. Whilst crossing a creek, a few days
after a flood, there was a hutkeeper standing with
a most rueful countenance ; he had lost, he said,
seventy pounds ; he was afraid to keep his money
in the hut, and for safety had concealed it in a
fallen tree ; but the flood had carried away the
fallen tree during the night, and with it his seventy
pounds. One of the earliest sheep-farmers in
Queensland told me that he once lost five thousand
sheep in consequence of a flood which he had not
anticipated—and which none of the other sheep-
farmers, who were also sufferers, had anticipated
the river had risen high and suddenly, and, as no

rain had fallen before, where they were situated, the flood had come upon them unawares.

Agriculture is largely engaged in by those who have other occupations and sources of income, independently of their farms, such as carriers, sawyers, storekeepers, innkeepers, &c. The greatest agriculturists are the graziers or squatters who are in districts where the climate is favourable ; and they have great advantages in folding their sheep on the cultivated land, thus cleaning it of weeds and enriching the soil. A failure in the crop of grain does not incommode them much, however, as their great mainstays are the crops of wool and the increase of stock. South Australia is the only one of the Australian colonies where wheat growing has taken its place as the leading industrial pursuit, and from which there are large exports of both wheat and flour every year to the other colonies. Chili and California are the two other principal places upon which the people in Victoria, New South Wales, and Queensland, have been hitherto largely dependent for supplies of flour.

CHAPTER IX

CONVICTISM

THERE is no word in the English language of which one requires to make a more studied use in Australia than the word 'convict.' It is entirely erased from the vocabulary of those who desire to 'live peaceably with all men,' and who have learned enough of the conventionalism of society to prevent them from offending against its rules and maxims. A celebrated writer, who did not form a very high estimate of human nature, said that 'man never forgives'; and it was with great truth that the King of Israel, amid a choice of evils, chose the least, and prayed, ' Let me not fall into the hand of man.'

The question, ' What will we do with our convicts?' is one that has taxed the ingenuity of those who have had more to do with them than any others — who have had them in their employment as 'assigned servants' from the Government. An old naval officer, who was eminently qualified to deal with them, had at one time a great number of them in his service engaged in felling trees, in fencing, &c.; but there was one who would not leave him after the expiration of his sentence. 'I have had him flogged times without number,' he said to the writer, who was staying one night at his house. 'Not a whit was the man ever the better— as incorrigible a scoundrel as ever was in this world; I have put a rope round his neck, and on horseback dragged him after me back and forward through that pond,' pointing towards a pond at some distance from the house, 'but it was all of no use'; and looking at me significantly he concluded, 'the man will not leave my service.' The incorrigible looked old and worn-out, and did not seem as if he were able to go very far. He must have been so habituated to punishment that it had become a kind of necessity to him, and likely he felt at times uneasy if he did not receive any; all that was human in his nature must have been well-nigh lashed out of him, leaving nothing but something of the nature of a spaniel dog. Though a stern and rigorous taskmaster, the officer alluded to probably acted justly and honestly towards his 'assigned servants'; and this was no doubt the ground of the incorrigible's attachment to him. But masters of this kind cannot be found always. One employer of convicts, who was of a most niggardly disposition, the owner of a large and valuable property, which had been made valuable by the labour of his

convict servants, paid the penalty of his life by a
blind selfishness in supplying them with bad quality
of rations, and keeping them long at work. The
residue of a large fire, which contained some charred
human bones, was all that remained to testify to
the mystery of his disappearance. The men who
had been in his employment, every one of whom
were convicts, declared themselves innocent, and
nothing could be brought home to them. One of
them, however, who acted as cook, and who was
always about the house, could not easily avoid
being suspected of knowing something regarding
his master's death. On regaining his liberty he
married, became a man well to do in the world,
with a fine young family of children growing up
around him. Compared to the taking away of life,
all other crimes would seem to be as shadows ; and
though he never confessed the murder there were
not wanting indications of a fearfully troubled mind,
especially in the fact that he frequently retired and
held communion with the dark places of the forest
at midnight hours.

'Truth is stranger than fiction.' A lad about
sixteen years of age was sentenced, at the Inverness
Circuit Court, to fourteen years' penal servitude for
sheep-stealing. The grazier who laid the accusation
against him deeply regretted afterwards that he
had done so, as his own sons had been the in-
stigators to the crime. The law must take its
course, however, and nothing that he could do
could avail to obtain the lad's release from the
hands of justice. Being much interested in him,

P

and acquainted with a settler in New South Wales, he gave him a letter to be delivered to the settler when he arrived there. For greater security he sewed the letter in the lining of the lad's jacket. The lad forgot all about the letter, until it dropped one day, when his jacket had gone to tatters. Singularly enough, the letter was directed to his employer, to whom he had been assigned by the Government. The document was of considerable service to him ; he was afterwards promoted to the situation of overseer, and a large number of men were placed under his charge. He gained the reputation of being an execrable tyrant, however, and he supplied all that he wanted in common sense and knowledge of mankind by the lash. The want of education, and knowledge of keeping accounts, were a sad hindrance to his advancement in the world. It was from the class of overseers who were at that time employed that many of the wealthiest settlers have sprung, and he almost stood alone in failing to avail himself of advantages and opportunities which had been so easily placed within his reach.

It has been said that guilt receives more protection than innocence : and it is remarkable what an amount of interest is taken in a great criminal—what sympathy is excited as to his fate—what a large place he occupies in public attention, and how strong is the desire for obtaining information regarding him. No item of intelligence concerning him comes amiss ; how he sleeps, what he says, and what he does are chronicled as subjects of the

greatest public concern ; whilst it is probable that
no sympathy or concern of any kind will be at the
same time extended to those who have been
grievously wronged and injured beyond all calcula-
tion by him. If a reprieve has been granted, and
the great criminal, instead of being sent to the
scaffold, is transported for life, the news is heralded
far and wide, and takes its place in the latest telegraphic intelligence, along it may be with announcements of the movements of the members of the Royal
family, and other matters of great national interest.
It may be interesting to those who take delight in
the horrible, to be informed that their sympathies
may be sometimes misplaced in behalf of a great
criminal, and that the satisfaction which they
receive on hearing that he is not to be executed is
sometimes unnecessary. I certainly knew of one
man who had been sentenced to be executed, and
who was reprieved (the sentence of death being
transmuted into transportation for life), who complained to me that he had not been executed. ' I
was ready to die then,' he said, ' but am not ready
now ; a worse man than ever I was.'

It serves to illustrate the large possession which
clergymen hold in the minds of those with whom
they have to do, that actions which they themselves
may think little of at the moment, sink down deep
into the hearts of others, and may serve, as in the
case of the person I am about to refer to, as subject
for some minds to ruminate on to the close of the
latest lifetime. The circumstances of the case of
this individual are somewhat extraordinary. He

was one of the 'Bonnymuir rebels' sentenced to
transportation for life; but had received a free
pardon, after a number of years' servitude, having
been all the time employed by Government—a great
advantage, he thought, preferable to having his lot
cast into the hands, it might be, of some ignorant
and tyrannical master. He was confined, he said
to me, forty days and nights in the 'den' of Stirling
Castle, with very little daylight and fresh air, and
scarcely enough of food to keep life in the body.
One of the town clergymen came to visit him and
the other prisoners ; he pleaded strongly with him
to bring him some food ; he came next day and
gave him a *bible*! The man never seemed to have
been able to forget this ; morning, evening, and
midday, it was the theme of his discourse, the
clergyman being the subject of deep, bitter, vehement
abuse and outcry. All the badness which this world
could produce was in that man, and a favourite
figure of speech of his was to make use of the
clergyman's name when he wished to express
horror or detestation of anything. 'I kept the
bible,' he said, and he showed it to me ; 'but —'
In all probability the clergyman was the last person
with whom he had any friendly intercourse at home,
and the pangs of hunger, disappointment, and insult
which he felt on being presented with the bible instead of food, had caused a deep wound in his heart
—a wound which always opened and bled at every
thought that occurred to him in his exile of the land
of his birth, his relations, and all that he had on
earth ; and it is always to the last link in the chain

that was broken during separation from home that
the thoughts of the exile are first cast, and the heart
looks first to be united to the last friendly or un-
friendly word that was spoken the last hillside that
was seen, the last parting farewell; and of how
much service would a little kindness have been to
this man, who believed that he was fighting for the
liberties of his country, if on leaving that land for
which he suffered, and was suffering so much, there
had been, as it were, some lovely spot in his fatherland upon which he might at times lay his weary
head and aching heart to rest? On regaining his
iberty he saved his earnings carefully, and purchased a piece of land. A knowledge of the
industrial pursuits of the colony, which he had
acquired during his servitude, enabled him to judge
correctly, and make a wise investment of his savings
and his own labour. The uncertainty of the seasons
dissuaded him from agriculture. Orange trees had
been introduced, and were found to suit the climate.
Accordingly, he prepared part of his land for the
purpose of an orangery; and within a very few
years the young trees which he had planted brought
him the means of an easy and comfortable livelihood. They had grown to a very large size, and
his small, unpretending dwelling-house was nearly
concealed in the midst of the thick green foliage,
all dotted over with oranges, like spheres of gold.

A laudable consideration was shown by the
Government to a class of convicts belonging to what
are usually styled ' the upper classes of society,' and
who were known by the name of ' specials.' A

settlement was set apart for them, and they were exempted from severe manual labour. One of them made himself very useful, like many others, by teaching in families ; he was wont to receive letters from his wife and daughters ; but it would have been kindness to him not to have written so fre-quently, as he became quite unmanned on hearing from any of them, and weeks would elapse before he could summon fortitude to open the letters and read their contents. There were many whose wives and families joined them in their exile ; in some instances this was an advantage, but unfortunately the habits of some of them were so entirely changed, that they might almost, with some propriety, be said not to be the same individuals ; and a union, however blest it might have been at home, did not always promise to be the same when entered on again under entirely different circumstances.

Many of them, who had received tickets-of-leave, and others who had served their time under Government for the full period of their sentence, bore the brunt of the battle with the aborigines in entering into the service of the pioneers, and were the first to take up country for grazing. The pastoral life, following flocks of sheep, and riding after cattle, was a much more agreeable and pre-ferable occupation to them than clearing land and working at farms under a scorching sun. They are now scattered over all the occupied interior, and are mostly debilitated old men, to whom the settlers gave the name of ' old crawlers.' There was one with whom I met who presented a frightful spectacle--very distressing to look upon. I had incidentally heard from the owner of a station that the blacks had been violent when he took possession of the country which he occupied, had killed some of his shepherds, and that one man, after being fearfully mangled, had recovered most unexpectedly. This was the very man. His head thrown back over his shoulders had remained fixed in the same position in which the blacks had left him, they having believed that he was dead. He was greatly shocked on learning that I had never heard of him in Scotland. 'I thought,' he said, 'every one had heard of *me* there.' On putting the question to him, his 'fame, it appeared, was founded on some burglaries which he had committed in the New Town of Edinburgh, and which had been blazed abroad as cases which had displayed great daring and dexterity!

There can be no doubt whatever of the material advantages of the boon, in fact which transportation was to a large number of criminals. They were placed in a much better position than they would have been in Great Britain and Ireland for acquiring wealth and independence. Many of them never served out the period of their sentence; good behaviour was rewarded by a ticket-of-leave, and they were entirely free to dispose of their labour to their own best advantage. They have been the most migratory class of the community, and will be found dispersed over all the Australian colonies. I heard an old clergyman in Tasmania, better known as Van Diemen's Land, stoutly main-

taining that there were fewer old convicts there in
proportion to free emigrants than in any of the
settlements in Australia ; and this notwithstanding
the immense number who had been transported
there. It is very common at the antipodes for
persons to change their names when they wish to
make a fresh start in life. It will not be always
found prudent to permit one's mind to be much
influenced against old convicts. I have known
some of them take pride in asserting that there
was more crime committed by free emigrants than
by old convicts. This may not be the case. There
is no denying, however, that the refuse of Great
Britain and Ireland has always been deemed
eligible as emigrants to the Australian colonies.

It is not easy escaping the conviction, and it
has never been, I presume, attempted to be denied,
that convictism has tended in no small degree to
give a distinct character and complexion to certain
phases of Australian life which it would not have
otherwise worn, and a knowledge of this constitutes
no small part of that much vaunted 'colonial
experience,' extolled as the foundation of success.
'What is the use of a friend,' I have heard one
man say, 'but to take the use of him ?' Very
comforting doctrine this, and the friendships of
some people are more to be dreaded than their
enmities. The following are not bad illustrations
of this kind of friendship. The Reverend Thomas
James was a young clergyman newly arrived from
England, entrusted with the establishment of a
mission in the interior of New South Wales, in

connection with the Church to which he belonged. The commencement is always the most trying and difficult part of the work. The giving of money to a ball, a horse-race, or a circus, people are always ready enough to understand the propriety of, but giving money towards the erection of a church, or the maintenance of a clergyman, is another thing altogether. A man will disburse a hundred pounds for a box at a theatre, or spend as much in one night's feasting, but a ' shilling !'—' no,' he ' could not afford it' towards a charitable object. He speaks the truth here quite correctly, ' he cannot afford it,' and it would be downright punishment for him to give anything ; the task would be as great as it would be for an infant to lift a millstone from the earth. It is all easily understood, a new class of sentiments are called into operation—the benevolent ones, naturally, perhaps not very strong, and weak from want of exercise, cannot bear the pressure of any weight being laid upon them. Many such persons are more to be pitied than condemned. If it comes to a parley, the amount of human ingenuity displayed in evading the question is astonishing. The man labours with all his soul to find out excuses, and pleads as strongly as if it was for his own life, that he might be spared ; and no general on the battle-field scans the ground more keenly, takes a wider range of vision in guarding the outposts, and providing against the danger of a sudden attack, that he may not be worsted in his conflict with the enemy. There is always more lost than gained by these contributors.

They are always certain to fall upon the stratagem
for escaping giving money by finding fault with
the object of it. The inventive faculty is set busily
to work, and when the object is a clergyman it
often appears as if all the faults are found with him
which can be found. The clergyman may not be
much to their favour or liking, but it is well for
these Crœsuses to be put in mind of the Divine
ordinance of the Christian ministry, that it is simply
for them to do their duty, leaving the clergyman
to do his ; and that if all were to act as they do,
Divine institutions would perish from the earth.
There was a mission fund, a building fund, and
other funds in favour of which the Reverend
Thomas James was endeavouring to enlist the
sympathies of the people amongst whom he was
labouring. He was a popular preacher, was well
received at the stations, embryo townships, and
gold-fields, which he periodically visited. In this
ardent monetary undertaking, it was almost impossible for him not to conceive a personal attachment towards a man who had always manifested
the greatest interest in his welfare, and who was a
liberal contributor to the funds. This person represented himself as coming into the district with
a view to commence a store on an extensive scale.
Mr. James had a heart above suspicion, and, as the
man had no house of his own at the time, he
kindly invited him to make his house his home.
The offer was thankfully accepted, and this was
really all that the person desired for his liberal
contribution to the funds, and the interest which

he had taken in Mr. James. He was known
everywhere afterwards as the clergyman's friend,
and was trusted by every one accordingly as a
highly respectable man. Accompanying Mr.
James in his journeys, he was admitted into the
privacy of domestic circles—knew all about the
mail and the money that was being sent down to
Sydney. The mail had been several times 'stuck
up' and robbed, but not a ray of suspicion ever
flashed across the mind of any one that it was the
clergyman's friend who had really been committing
all the depredations. As a crowning feat of
impudent rascality, and taking still greater advantages of the shelter which the clergyman un-
wittingly afforded him for carrying on his nefarious
business, he accompanied him to Sydney—paid all
the expenses of the journey, and procured an
introduction, through Mr. James, to the wealthy
merchants in connection with the church of the
latter. The merchants were delighted with the
new country connection, and the prospect of the
large profits with which these country connections
are usually attended. Mr. James's acquaintance
with their new customer was a sufficient guarantee
of the latter's trustworthiness, and they gave him
credit to the amount of three thousand pounds'
worth of merchandise. The packages of merchandise were forwarded to their destination up
the country, but never reached that destination.
The addresses were altered at a small shipping
port, where they were landed, put on board a vessel
for California, and nothing was afterwards seen or

heard of the clergyman's friend. White savages
are a thousand times worse than black. It is in-
sulting, in fact, to humanity to compare them to
human beings—they are like vultures, with out-
stretched wings, floating in the air, looking out for
prey or reptiles, creeping stealthily on the ground.
Perhaps, indeed, they may be compared with
nothing so favourably as the boa constrictor, which
first covers with its saliva the object it prepares to
devour. 'What a fool,' said a 'gentleman' once
to me in Sydney, 'your friend is; he has bought
that place from me; he might have had it a
thousand pounds cheaper; however, it is so much
in my pocket.' This 'Ninevite' happily united a
certain business with a lodging-house, which was
well known. My friend, with his wife and family,
had been staying at the lodging-house, paying for
their board. Strangers in the town, it was almost
impossible to be insensible to the attention bestowed
upon them, or indifferent to the advice tendered to
them in the name of the sincerest friendship.
They were honest, believing people, and considered
other people to be as honest as themselves. They
had been living in their sylvan solitude in the
interior for a very long period, by a life of per-
severing industry had saved a few thousand pounds,
and had come to pass the end of their days within
sound of the Sabbath bells in the beautiful town of
Sydney. In addition to the thousand pounds
which their ' friend ' confessed to have robbed them
of, he led them completely astray by false information, and might be said to have almost ruined

them, as they would have to begin the world anew. There are cool, calculating persons to be met with whose minds are whetted like a keen instrument in the pursuit of gain ; all mankind is their lawful prey, and when they succeed, they claim an intellectual superiority—esteem themselves 'clever'

whilst their villainies redound to their honour and credit. In colonial phraseology, ' pointers ' is the name by which such persons are usually distinguished and stigmatized ; that is, they follow the pursuit of gain as pointers do game, are always on the watch for ignorant and unsuspecting persons, whom they are never so likely to succeed in plundering as under the guise of friendship.

It is right to 'give the devil his due,' as the proverb says, and there should not be laid to the charge of convicts that which they have very little to do with, 'bushranging.' The bushrangers of the present day are young men who have grown up wild in the bush—mostly stockmen—who have become accustomed to galloping after horses and cattle, and to following a thieving mode of life, by taking horses and cattle to which they have no right. That it is not destitution which prompts many of them to lead a life of highway robbery is clear enough from the fact of some of them being very wealthy. One Jamieson, a mere lad, inherited, when in prison, twenty thousand pounds, which were forfeited to the Government. Hall, who was shot by a policeman, and whom the Hon. John Robertson called the ' king of the bushrangers,' was also a mere youth and the owner of a station.

Bushranging had not been heard of for about thirty years previously, and was not resumed until after the advent of manhood suffrage. It broke out when the people's passions were excited in the universal cry of ' Free selection before survey '— the right to go and settle anywhere they liked ; and, when the Legislature of New South Wales, pandering to the passions of the people, passed a law for them to go and settle anywhere they liked, with the addition of a bounty of fifteen shillings in the pound credit to all who would settle on the land.

The love of applause is common to young men in the bush, as it is common to young men elsewhere : and it must have been highly pleasing to these desperadoes to find their names, with accounts of the robberies which they had committed, prominently mentioned in the public press, with no less a personage than the Hon. John Robertson, who had been Premier, pronouncing one of them to be a ' king.'   In a different state of society, and in another country, these young men would have led a forlorn hope in entering the breach in a fortress, and would have filled the trenches with their dead bodies for their comrades to pass over. Under a good government they might have been valuable members of society.   Scores of mounted policemen, with Government contracts for their maintenance as if for an army, in pursuit of bushrangers, and a reward of five thousand pounds for the capture of five of them, dead or alive, is very expensive work.   It would be indicative of greater economy, one would suppose, if the Government of New South Wales, instead of making a law for people to scatter themselves, would form settlements, where they might all be brought within the healing influences of society, and receive the benefits of education and religion.

Whatever evils New South Wales may have inherited from convictism, demagogues have proved themselves the greatest criminals, and have done more injury than convicts.

CHAPTER X

THE Free Church of Scotland cut the ground
completely underneath my feet at the antipodes,
and left me with one solitary adherent, a Strathbogie man, and I know more of the Free Church of
Scotland than any one alive. I was present the
very day, an eye-witness, of the presentation to the
Rev. Robert Young, being laid on the table of
Auchterarder Presbytery the beginning of the ten
years' conflict and the Free Church of Scotland.
My solitary adherent, a Strathbogie man, Mr.
Gordon, M.L.A., New South Wales, suggested the
best thing I could do for myself was to leave,
'persecuted in one city flee to another.' There is a
parish here without a single Presbyterian Minister,
ten or twenty times larger than all the parishes of

Scotland. I will always find plenty to do. The Rev. Dr. Clark, of St. Andrew's, Edinburgh, well acquainted with me, offered me assistance from the Colonial Mission, of which he was the head. I declined to receive money from Scotland to fight against the Free Church ; a hundred pounds from the government and some of my own served me to get along. There was preaching at every place I halted for the night ; all called in to hear the parson, no matter what church they belonged to. At one place an old convict was much affected, could not cease from crying. Never knew or heard of such a thing as this before,. free forgiveness through Jesus Christ, my theme being ' wounded for our transgressions,' and he asked his employer to give me all the money that was coming to him. Sleeping out at night under the glorious starry firmament beside a creek or river, hobbling the horse and making a saddle a pillow, was of very frequent occurrence, and there was a terrestrial blessedness here which those who dwell in kings' palaces might justly envy only careful of the horse-rug in which I had wrapt myself, a snake did not get into the folds, and this was easily avoided by a fire blazing alongside. I never took kindly to the unvarying menu, salt junk and damper (bread made from dough put into a heap of hot ashes) ; a box of raisins and bag of ship biscuits I found far more serviceable. By stowing some of this in my valise, I felt proof against what was certain to occur, starvation in being lost in the bush, for there were really no roads, only blazes in the trees directing from one place to another, and some of these trees would disappear from bush fires. In passing, a shepherd said he had come on the remains of a man in some high ridges. It was evident here the lost one had been a stranger or he never would have gone to high ridges; when lost, he would have been familiar with the well known adage, ' Keep to the fall of the water, sure to come to some place.' It was an exciting time for me. There was a continual riding and tossing about on horseback, cattle stations and sheep stations six, ten, and twenty miles apart, often clambering over rocks and through brushwood to find out the abode of a shepherd who wanted his children baptized. In well regulated stations, Sunday will be found well observed, all doffing their Sunday attire at the head station, and attending religious service in the proprietor's house ; nothing possibly could be more commendable ; a line, however, requires to be drawn somewhere, and if drawn anywhere, drawn here, administering the sacrament ; one, well known to me, must have ' got mixed,' failed to understand where the lay element ceased and where the clerical element commenced. Certain it is he committed himself to baptize a child at his religious service on Sunday, and it is a most remarkable fact, that child was afterwards accidentally burnt to death, the only one instance I ever knew of a child being burnt to death. It is needless to say they would have nothing more to do with squatter baptisms. It was rather a large order from a customer or parishioner, Peter Mc Grathe, a journey of some hundreds of miles, to

baptize his children ; as well go the way of Peter
as anywhere else, must go somewhere. On arriving
at the out-station where Peter was employed, I
could not avow asking : ' What on all the earth
could have induced you to go so far inland ? ' The
answer was very intelligible : ' My wife would have
ruined me ; always shop, shopping ; I determined
to take her away, where she could not get near a
shop.' I had heard of needles being sold at a
shilling a-piece, and what the cost of a love of a
bonnet and all the paraphernalia of a lady in full
feather might be I really do not know, never having
had a wife, and knowing nothing at all of the
amenities that must exist between man and wife ;
had nothing to say in regard to this matter as to
Peter acting rightly or wrongly ; there is this much
I am certain of, Peter, according to his own account
of himself, was no fool. ' I have come to Australia
and mean to make the most of it. My boys are
all shepherding forty pounds a year each, thirty
pounds a year myself as hut-keeper, everything
provided except clothing. In a short time I will
have a few hundred pounds together and go and
settle in New Zealand.'

I must have owed my life sometimes to being
a good swimmer. There is one advantage in knowing to swim, confidence in crossing creeks and
rivers when in a flooded state, careful above all
things when it comes to swimming to keep clear of
the horse, fatalities occurring in the rider being
killed by a kick of the horse from being near it in
the water. If there are ' perils of waters ' there are

far greater perils in not being well-skilled in horse-
flesh, two young clergymen of the Church of
England situated as I was, in adjoining districts,
losing their lives, one by a fall from his horse, the
other by drowning. There are some horses trustworthy, others again, and the great bulk of them,
altogether untrustworthy. There are small sheets
of water ever presenting themselves, in travelling
over which a child might be supposed easily to
wade. An ill-bred lumbering beast of a horse at
the call of the rider would go slapdash into this
sheet of water, and drown itself and rider in a hole
twenty or thirty feet deep that has been scooped
out by a flood. A trustworthy horse would do
nothing of the sort, take good care of itself, and
therefore good care of the rider, unless it found
a stranger on its back, and there is no knowing
what might here take place ; and I know of no good
reason why a breeder of good horses should not be
canonised, his name emblazoned on the roll of
cardinals and other great people as a pillar of the
Church ; this much is certain, but for the fortunate
incident of meeting with a well-bred horse, I would
not be alive to-day to tell the tale. The sagacity
of this animal was amazing. Lost, as I was scores
of times, I had nothing more to do than to throw
the reins over the neck, and there it would lead me,
straight as an arrow, to the place I was going to,
if it had been there before. At any dangerous
crossing place, it would be certain to test the trustworthiness of the ground by beating with its fore-
feet.

The horse-racing and steeplechasing in Great Britain are poor tame exhibitions of a horse's prowess in comparison of what may be often witnessed in the Greater Britain, an old nag heading a mob of wild cattle or horses. Seeing what it has to do, it might be almost heard saying to the rider, ' Now, young man, look out, take good care of yourself!' Off it goes at a rattling pace, leaping over fallen timber, alighting on the ground again like a bird (learned this from youth upwards), down and up gullies, on, on, glorying in the chase, it may be from morning till night. The horses or cattle, never having had such a hard tussling as this, obliged to give in, can stand it no longer, the old nag with her greater powers of endurance proving one too many for them ; no help for it but to allow themselves to be driven into the stockyard as quietly as a flock of sheep. The old nag has done the whole business, the rider having had nothing to do but to take care of himself. The sorry part of the business is the little outcome of the old nag's heroic exploit, the owner of one of these mobs of wild horses telling me all he received for them was twenty-five shillings a-piece for export to India.

Of all the revolting sights under the canopy of heaven there surely never was anything to be compared to this, the murderous onslaught by stockmen with loaded rifles on those beautiful creatures, young calves, left to die on the ground as food for carrion crows. Inquiring as to their object in this, the answer was, ' We are exterminating the breed

of them.' Cattle, horses, and sheep it seems all tend
to deteriorate, and an infusion of new blood is
necessary to their growing to the perfection of their
nature, and know as little of the doctrine, survival
of the fittest, as bees, ants, and spiders. In these
days, when nature must be made to unlock and
deliver up all her secrets, it would be an admirable
subject of investigation for the savants, the fittest
of survival of the race of mankind. My old
class fellows, Lord Kelvin, Principals Caird and
Cunningham, might be safely entrusted as experts
to probe this matter to the very bottom. The
churches would be immensely interested in the
result of their research, seemingly in a maze and
haze about this raising such a dust, like the woman in
the gospel sweeping the house to find this precious
treasure, the survival of the fittest, in the lost piece
of silver. If they had only the good sense of the
woman to light their candle with the 'light that
lighteth every man that cometh into the world,'
they would see they were in search of the survival
of the fittest in those 'fit for the Kingdom.' 'Love
your enemies, bless them that curse you, do good
to them that hate you, and pray for them which
despitefully use you and persecute you.' Impossible, no one of the race of Adam can do this;
but there is nothing impossible to one of the race
of the second Adam, the Lord from heaven.

There is something in those Australian creeks
and rivers when in high flood, that will baffle the
skill of the best swimmer in the world. One whose
hospitality I enjoyed very often, on returning from

Sydney after arranging everything in regard to his station—and there will be frequently as many as twenty or thirty hands employed at a station—found the river in front of his homestead in high flood. He was an experienced man, and thought he knew all about floods ; all the *débris* was carried down, and apparently no danger in swimming across the river, and he must either do this or be out all night without food or shelter. There were the children on the other side standing and scream-ing with delight, ' Mother, mother, father has come ! ' Mother comes out with baby in her arms, and all the family are congregated on the margin of the swollen river seeing father swim across. He had not swam any distance, when a log underneath the surface came dashing against him, and carried him away in the foaming waters as a twig, no more seen for ever. It was a truly melancholy sight. I must have crossed that river dozens of times and not seen as much water in many parts of it that would suffice to drown a kitten, at other times a volume of water sufficient to float an ironclad. If the art of swimming is a desirable clerical acquisition in the lines of unpleasant places in Australia, the art of swimming would seem to be equally desirable in the clerical lines of unpleasant places in New Zealand. I give the story as told me by a Wesleyan Missionary in a sojourn there in the forties, regarding Bishop Selwyn. The dangerous coast of New Zealand was not at that time well surveyed, and he had the greatest difficulty in threading his way with his missionary craft in the

interminable labyrinths of bays and inlets and
sunken rocks far out to sea. He found one day
his missionary craft had sprung a leak. Nothing
daunted he threw himself over the side of his vessel,
dived underneath it, and stopped the leak with
pitch. The homily of the Bishop to his Maori crew
on the occasion is well worth recording. 'Noah's
ark was pitched within and without. The only
known preservative against all the woes and foes
of the world within and without is the pitch, the
atonement, the blood and righteousness of the Lord
Jesus Christ. Many are drowned in destruction
and perdition, sink and perish in the deep sea of
desperation and misery, all from want of the pitch.
You must here learn to be wise unto salvation,
and to work out your own salvation, and your
peace shall be as a river and righteousness as the
waves of the sea. Let all the sorrows and miseries
of the world come rolling and dashing against you
like the waves of the ocean, the pitch will come too.
Gaining experience in the daily use and handling
of the pitch in closing up every rent you will have
good hope of your frail vessel reaching safely the
haven of rest, where there shall be no more sea,
and a long story ever afterwards to tell of the
wonderful life-preserving pitch.'

Engaged in ministerial duty on the borders
of what is now Queensland, I was invited to a
merry gathering and to take a very prominent
part indeed   unite in wedlock a young lady to one
of two young gentlemen, not long arrived from
the mother land to take up country and engage

in that great business, squatting; the bait here
was and still remains in Northern Australia tremendous, as much land as all the kingdom of Fife
for five pounds a year. The young gentlemen
departed some time afterwards on their exploring
expedition, never anything more seen or heard of.
I never shared the opinion entertained by many—
killed by the blacks; there would have been
tidings of this in some of their belongings being
seen in their possession, roaming about the different stations. In a conversation with one of the
early pioneers of Queensland, he made some very
pertinent remarks in regard to the danger new
arrivals exposed themselves to in familiarity with
the aborigines. He mentioned particularly a
family of the name Fraser; he warned them
repeatedly of the peril they were exposing themselves to in allowing the blacks to come so near
their homestead, giving them sugar, flour, tobacco,
for some small services, or opossum skins.
The warning was unheeded. One day the stockman came galloping to his place in a great way;
the family were all killed by the blacks. On returning with him, the sight he saw was something
horrible, beyond description or conception; everyone of the family of ten speared, cut, and hacked
by boomerangs and wadys as ruthlessly as if they
had been a bed of nettles. I was at a station
where exactly the same thing took place; whole
family killed except two little girls, who were
fortunately from home at the time of the disaster,
and from the same cause, familiarity with the

aborigines. There are few stations in which there will not be found a solitary aboriginal, making himself most useful in going messages, mustering cattle and horses, and breaking-in buck-jumping horses, but these solitary aboriginals will always be found to belong to tribes in distant localities. It seems to be a law of existence of the aborigines, one tribe always at war with another tribe. It would have been vastly more to the advantage of the young gentlemen and all their sorrowing friends and relations, including the sadly disconsolate young widow, if they had ' stooped to conquer,' served two or three years' apprenticeship to an old squatter, tutored in here to all the innumerable and unmentionable little things so indispensable for *getting on* and succeeding in colonial life, always more to unlearn than to learn, and shuffling off all their old habits,.thoughts, and associations, getting hold of that rich mine of wealth in dearly purchased knowledge and experience. If the young gentlemen had ever succeeded in their perilous adventure, they would have found to their sad discomfiture they had been engaged in a wild goose chase. A new land regulation coming out putting a stop to all the traffic in land blocks and recognising no one's right to the land unless occupied by sheep or cattle. Here was an opportunity for my old acquaintance James Macgregor, whom I met shortly afterwards trudging along with sheep, cattle, dray with wife and the children whom I had baptized. James could shoe a horse, salt a bullock, erect a hut, anything in fact for one to get along. I had nearly forgotten all about James when he came in my way a long time afterwards; he had sold the station for fifty thousand pounds. If there is a tide in the affairs of men, which, when taken at the flood leads on to fortune, there would seem to be troubles connected with a fortune after it has been acquired, and here all James's troubles began, where others cease. He had no love for being a grand gentleman, driving about in his carriage; he would much rather be going on in his old 'jog trot' way. John Macfarlane, a man exactly of the same sort, told me all the money he brought with him from Scotland was half a crown; his station was sold for upwards of a hundred thousand pounds. Dying intestate, a dispute commenced about the successor to the property; the dispute has been going on for a number of years, and will continue to go on until those interesting gentlemen who take a lively interest in those dying intestate will discover some morning there is little or nothing remaining of the hundred thousand and upwards to dispute about. I never heard the word fortune coming from these two men's lips, if they ever thought of such a thing; simply carefully attending to the work of to-day, leaving to-morrow to take care of itself. If they had been looking and striving for this making a fortune, they would have been certain to have got into the meshes of the lien nets of the merchants, and have been striving all their lives long to make fortunes to others instead of fortunes to themselves.

Since the establishment of the Native Police and Black Trackers in Queensland, nothing would now appear to be ever heard of as the depredations by the blacks. The young gentlemen knew little of the land of droughts and floods to which they had come, and instead of being killed by the blacks, there was a far greater likelihood they had fallen into the very difficulty in which I fell shortly after leaving them, perished, as I nearly perished, from want of water. I went into the dry bed of a river in search of it day after day ; domicile after domicile, out-station after out-station deserted, the very silence of the grave reigned everywhere around ; no living thing to be seen anywhere ; the innumerable feathered songsters, that make the groves of Australia so truly delightful with their gambols and mirth and melody, had all departed ; they could not live where there was no water. One of the plagues of Egypt had set in, every green thing covered with lice. I need not say almost, I must have been completely delirious from raging thirst. In taking out all the best articles from my valise and laying them carefully down at the root of a tree, a ray of hope suddenly burst in, seeing crows flying in the direction I was travelling, a sure indication this, old hands will be heard to say, of water not being far off. At last, when I came to water, it was something terrible to drink it, and could scarcely avoid the feeling it would have been better never to have seen it. Sadly ruinous and destructive as those droughts are, and a gold field I visited during a drought, the cabbages were half a crown apiece. There is one great advantage of these droughts along with bush fires little known and appreciated, sweeping with the besom of destruction those vile pests, snakes, which would otherwise make of the land of Australia, so truly enjoyable, uninhabitable for man or beast. With the proverbial little things the most important things in life, it is worth observing how the neglect of very little things may be the occasion of indescribable suffering in a long journey during oppressive heat in the noonday sun. Faint, weary and worn, tired, jaded and torn, passing a clump of Marmosa trees beside a lagoon, I could not resist the temptation of dismounting, giving the horse a drink, and resting under the delicious shade the other trees, gum trees, afford little or no shade, the arrow-shaped leaves drooping to the earth like lady's earrings, the rays of the sun pass through them to the earth like water through a sieve I unguardedly fell asleep, and awoke with a pain in the ear truly horrible ; an insect had got in and was burrowing and scratching as if determined to make a tunnel through my head, as Sir Edward Watkin is of making a tunnel through the English Channel. Fortunately I was on my way homewards, and with the aid of a syringe and hot water succeeded in dislodging the vile thing. This neglect of the little thing was a handkerchief over my head. Leading a horse with a green hide halter (bullock's skin), on seeing a snake the horse I was leading suddenly pulled me off the horse I was

riding, and there I lay on the ground with the
bullock-hide halter firmly twisted round my wrist
tied to the horse's head, rearing and plunging in
front of me, the shoes of the hind feet just touch-
ing my head, dead, dead, another instant my brains
are dashed out.   The furious animal at length fully
exhausted in dragging me over stumps and stones,
the perspiration flowing from it as if it had just
come out of a boiling cauldron, stood.   But here
was a terrible difficulty ; my right arm was dis-
located and I could not raise it to undo the green-
hide halter firmly twisted round the wrist ; by a
great effort I succeeded in reaching the horse and
slipping the halter off the head.   The neglect of
the little thing here was simply to have had the
halter so loose in the hand as to be able to release
the hand at any time.   Singular, though smashed
almost to a jelly, not the slightest feeling of pain.
It must be the same in the battle-field, those
receiving great wounds feeling no pain.   The pain
next day, however, was something to think about,
crawling to a homestead, a few miles distant,
which I happily reached, and where, with medical
aid, soon got all to rights again.   Stockmen are
heard to say they cannot stand the jostling in the
saddle longer than ten or twelve years.   I had
been longer than twelve years in the saddle, and
gone through as much jostling in the saddle as
any of them.

CHAPTER XI

MATRIMONY

Young Gentleman—Hobson's Choice Chinamen - Hodge and his
Wife—Troubles of Shepherds Mary Jane, Fanny, and Elizabeth
—Troubles of a Parson Bridecake for the Funeral - Convict
Chaplain—Convict Damsels.

THAT rich luxuriant pasture, delighting so much
the hearts of pastors and their flocks in the Fatherland, marriage, has very little in common with the
scant herbage in the far interior of Australia.
There are so many minor influences at home
operating insensibly and all-powerfully, the eyes of
the world, friends, relations, that one is saved from
himself by these stout barriers, all everywhere
around him, that seldom is such a thing heard
of as a young gentleman taking that tremendous
leap, a foolish marriage. It is altogether different
in the interior of Australia, no hedges or barriers
of any kind, every one left to his own sweet will,
and in the matter of a wife nothing better than
Hobson's choice, this one or no one, there being
no others to choose from. I refused point blank
to marry a young gentleman to a young woman ;
the parties to the marriage, the parents of the
young woman especially, were most indignant,

threatened legal proceedings against me, there being no other clergyman nearer than a hundred miles to celebrate marriage. Some time afterwards the young gentleman thanked me for delivering him out of a fearful scrape. ' Blessed is he who considereth the poor,' not those who give to the poor, so much mischief being done in indiscriminate charity in depriving the poor of their self-respect and self-reliance ; and why should not this ' considereth' be as applicable in clergymen marrying couples, seeing that they were not unequally yoked together, some reason and judgment in the matter—no wild caprice—a paroxysm that has come suddenly on and will just as certainly suddenly go off ? I never would have anything to do in marrying Chinamen at the gold-fields, though this was done by others. There would have been some satisfaction here—no danger of shocking the marriage party—should I inadvertently make use of the words of a Highland clergyman in tying the matrimonial cord—' You two I declare one mutton John Chinaman would have understood mutton far readier than flesh. I felt I had a good case in Hodge, marrying him to one in the same position in life. Some time afterwards Hodge came and offered fifty pounds if I would unmarry him. ' What is the matter?' ' Slattern and wasp of a thing ; neither hands nor head, nothing but tongue. I am not going to be tied to a woman like that all my life.' ' Look here, Hodge ; you have been cursing Bridget with bad names. Why don't you cherish her as you promised to do, by calling·her all the good names you can think of, and have ever heard of? All these good names will be showers of blessings on Bridget's head, and you will find she will do everything to please you. You have fallen out ; here Bridget is as much to blame as you in breaking that solemn vow you both took, that when one was angry the other would not be angry.'

Riding along a shepherd came running, saying, ' Yer reverence, I want you to marry me to a woman in a dray,' pointing in the direction and naming the station. ' How long have you known her?' ' Since yesterday.' ' You are not going to marry a woman you know nothing of?' ' She says she came in an emigrant ship, and is looking for a situation.' ' Don't you believe a word of it ; some runaway.' ' I'll chance it.' ' All very well you chancing it, but how am I going to chance it ? I have no means of knowing anything about her, and might get into trouble in marrying another man's wife to you.' ' If I don't get her, some-one else will get her.' There was the force of argument in this appeal, and not wishing to do an unkind thing, I consented to marry him, taking good care to protect myself in the legal formula before witnesses. She was free and unmarried, and no lawful impediment to the marriage. It would have been wrong asking her many questions ; this would only have been tempting her to tell lies, and she was evidently nothing but a bundle of them, and so very like a hussey that came bawling after me, ' I have three husbands going about,

R

robbing one after another and making fools of the clergy.'

I had supreme satisfaction and delight in attending to the case of another shepherd who asked to be married ; not the slightest scruple, danger, or difficulty of any kind here in anyone coming down upon me in great wrath, and calling me to account. I asked the bride her age— seventy-two last February! What a mercy would it be to those maidens who marry in haste and repent at leisure, to take a leaf out of this bride's book and wait until they reached the respectable age of seventy-two, and be saved all repentance and in smooth waters to the end of their life. I asked the bridegroom what made him think of marrying this old woman tottering on the brink of the grave ? The answer was, ' She might live some years, and as long as she lived would be as good as thirty pounds a year to him as hut-keeper.'

The last persons whom a clergyman would wish to offend are those lordly gentlemen, the squatters, who bring the light and life of civilisation into the interior in their troupe of domestic servants, managers and others, who profess to be judges of a good article, come down here swooping most un- mercifully amongst the Mary Janes, Elizabeths, and Fannys, entailing no end of misery to families, and the poor parson in the outpouring of the wrath of his best friend in being instrumental in depriving him of his indispensable household servants. The writer knows more of this than he cares to acknowledge. ' There are as good fish in the sea as ever came out of it;' and why do not those intelligent men communicate at once with their relatives at home and tell them plainly they want a wife, and show they are well deserving of one in their highly honourable conduct, in refraining from inflicting misery on others to benefit themselves. There is surely something in that feeling in many quarters against marrying in the month of May. Here is the case of a marriage in the month of May, and that would seem to establish the correctness of the feeling, that Hymen holds high court and festival at the antipodes as in the Fatherland. In a long journey of forty miles to the residence of the bride, and timed to arrive at one o'clock in the afternoon, a gentleman, travelling along with me, suddenly dropped dead from his saddle as if he had been shot, and while in the very act of speaking to me. I was detained until one o'clock next morning to meet the marriage party, in going to a station to arrange about the removal of the dead body of my fellow-traveller. The veil of the newly-married wife, coming in contact with a lighted candle in signing the marriage certificate, was all in flames, and I pulled the veil off her head. That very night a messenger came after me to return and bury her husband, who had accidentally shot himself, and it was certainly something very remarkable to observe bridecake serving both for the marriage and for the funeral.

One who held the appointment of chaplain during the convict era, in a factory where the female

convicts were entombed, told me of the great
stroke of business he had done in marrying his
protégées to up-country Lotharios, always old
convicts. The convict damsels were all arranged
in a long line, as a string of beads or wild geese,
welcome to choose any one. There were never any
cases of denial—only too glad to get their liberty.
If they were all blanks and no prizes they all had
at least the high honour of being in her Majesty's
service. There is nothing that can come so near
to touch the hearts of the lovers of Australia as
those who bear its future destinies in the hollow of
their hands the mothers. There is no denying
the bad blood that has been introduced and the
blotches that have broken out on the fair face—
bushrangers. I have met some of these strong
young lusty fellows, and the impression made on
my mind was, they were altogether incapable of
smiling—if they ever so much as smiled all their
life long. It was no love of plunder that actuated
these desperadoes, for some of them were well-to-do
in the world. It was nothing but sheer downright
devilry ; their countenances were as wild and ferocious as leopards or tigers, and seemingly as incapable of being reclaimed as are those of being
domesticated ; they would have served as admirable models for a sculptor, of those we read of
possessed with devils and dwelling in the mountains, and the conditions here were exactly similar.
A mother's love ! No, they never knew a mother's
love ; they were cradled in curses, their souls
steeped and dyed with curses, and they were

taking revenge upon society for neglect in early youth ; evils fall by their own might, and like every other unclean thing in the world hastens to dissolution.   And of the many friends of man in the world not the least is the grave, where the wicked cease from troubling, and where the weary be at rest.

CHAPTER XII

DEMOCRACY AND ITS RESULTS ·

Antipodean Go-aheadism   The Clergy and Crooked Legislation—
A Gaol *versus* a Woollen Factory— Deprivation of a Town's
Rights and Privileges -- Losses of the People—Members of Par-
liament—Brains, but no Money—Mr. William Sykes and Bank
Failures--President of the Council and Chief Justice on the
Land Law   -Early Colonisation—Squattager Cities of Refuge--
Emporiums of Wealth for the Poor Radicalism -Scattering of
the People · Sufferings of the People.

THE Bishop of Armidale and Grafton said he had
been twenty-three years in the Episcopate, and
had spent thousands and thousands of pounds of
his private means in maintaining his position, and
if he retired to-morrow he would not have more
than 150*l.* a year to live upon.

The calamities of this clergyman of the Church
of England require explanation. The writer was
the first minister of the Church of Scotland in the
diocese, and this when Armidale might be heard
spoken of as the camp, and in the great lines of com-
munication, as innship is seen to arise, the origin
usually being an inn, serving also as a store and
post office. If there are any applications for land
a staff of Government surveyors will be making
their appearance, laying out a town, and suburban

lots, sites for churches, schools ; all these town and suburban lots are put up for sale at public auction. I was requested by the managers of the church to which I belonged to attend one of these sales and purchase some lots adjoining the site for their church. The following, who bid against me, may well serve as a *tableau vivant* of antipodean go-aheadism. *First*, the auctioneer, himself a Government official, with his Government salary and seven thousand pounds he was said to have earned in dabbling in lots put into his hands by the Government for sale ; in gold-digging parlance he had made his pile and was off. *Second*, a large speculator in land, who died insolvent. *Third*, a son of the Emerald Isle. I had known him as clerk, gold-digger, drover, commission agent, auctioneer. He could not get rich fast enough at these occupations ; there was one chance remaining, a seat in Parliament. With a glib tongue he had no difficulty in this, taking up the cry free selection before survey. He was not long in Parliament. By voting straight with the Government, he received a Government situation of five hundred pounds a year.

Fourth, a German Jew. The purpose of their bidding against me was very apparent in the German Jew, coming at the close of the sale, and offering the lot he had purchased, and for which I had also bid, if I would give him ten pounds for his bargain. I declined five pounds, no ; two pounds, no. Finding he could get nothing out of me he commenced gesticulating, muttering some words in German as if he had been bitten by a snake ; he

had indeed been bitten, but he had bitten himself
in losing instead of gaining, by the forfeit of the
deposit. What support could a clergyman expect to
secure from those confounded rascals, actually
robbing me of money carefully collected for church
purposes ? Society at the time was in such an
intricate state, there might be said to have been no
society at all, every one like Dugald Dalgety
fighting for his own hand. The members of the New
South Wales Parliament have withdrawn all the
money formerly given to the clergy, for their own
benefit. Voluntaryism ; there is certainly nothing
wrong in voluntaryism in the colonies. Putting
new wine into new bottles ; there is no disturbing
element as in the old country. Putting new wine into
old bottles, is the cry of disestablishment, breaking
the bottles in all the ties of Christian neighbourhood
and brotherhood. What the clergy in New South
Wales have to complain of is the badness of the
bottles ; all cracked, cracked legislators and crack-
brained members of Parliament. Here, about forty
miles beyond Armidale, Glen Innes, they have
erected a gaol at a cost of twelve thousand pounds,
and after standing there for about twelve years,
there has never been known to be a prisoner in it.
There surely never was such crack-brainedness ; if
they had erected a woollen factory instead, how
much more beneficial would this have been to the
people, and what an unspeakable mercy to the
young women in the neighbourhood, at their wits'
end in not knowing what to do with themselves.
Houses in the interior may be seen covered with

bullocks' hides instead of sheets of bark. What an immense industry might be carried on here in tanneries, there being nothing from which the people suffer so much as the boots and shoes, made by prisons in America, for which the highest prices are charged and will not stand a day's wear. It is doubtful if many or any of the legislators know of those wonderful places, cedar scrubs, about eighty miles from the high table land, containing the choicest timber for cabinet making, sassafras or satinwood predominating, as if an extraordinary providence had transported a part of Borneo to the very place where the timber was needed, all the other timber, that is, gum trees, being useless for cabinet making, and what an immense industry might be engaged here in cabinet making. The people could all live and thrive ; engaged in those industries, the droughts and floods not affecting them the slightest ; but there is no possibility of the people living and thriving on patches of land in the squatters' runs, here, there, and everywhere, and the people in the interior, the main producers of the wealth of the colony, had a far better preferential claim to Government support and patronage than rich gentlemen's sons in Sydney, and had the hundreds of thousands of pounds lavished upon a university in Sydney been laid out in encouraging woollen factories in the interior, this certainly would not have occurred. Multitudes of famishing people rushing from the interior and crowding the streets of Sydney, with untold miseries of deserted homes and families.

The tempter is always more to blame than the tempted, and the Government of New South Wales cannot release itself of its responsibilities to those people in their losses and miseries, having been led to their ruin by the common device, a cheap bargain in deferred payment.

There is no condition of agricultural success in the interior of Australia as in the interior of New Zealand. All this might have been anticipated, and was anticipated by the late President of the Council, Sir John Hay, when in opposition to the radical party; he had spent the best part of a long life in the interior, was acquainted with the land, people, and everything. It was also anticipated by the late Chief Justice, Sir James Martin, born and bred in the colony, with his legal mind, studying consequences and the remote bearings of everything. It is interesting to observe how correctly he anticipated what has taken place in addressing a crowd during a political ferment. Free selection before survey, ye howling idiots, ye will see thousands of starving people from the interior coming down upon you; the number from last accounts was fourteen thousand. The land in the interior suitable for the settlement of a population is small indeed; all this available land is to be found in the high dividing ranges, in alluvial flats occurring at intervals, the soil not washed away as at other places and carried by floods and lodged in large heaps in the interior, serving no purpose there for cultivation on account of floods, droughts, and hot

winds.   An alluvial flat of five thousand acres, close
to the town of Armidale, was surveyed and divided
into allotments for the benefit of the town.   To the
consternation of the residents all this their town
land was advertised to be sold in one day.   The
answer of the Government to their petition against
it was, we want the money.   The whole of the five
thousand acres was purchased by the squatter at
the upset price of 1*l*. an acre.

How easily could the five thousand pounds
have been obtained by laying hold of a cattle run
in the district, about ten miles in length, the same
in breadth, serving no purpose but the demorali-
sation of a family ; the stockman having turned
' free solicitor ' and earning a livelihood by stealing
his former master's cattle, putting the whole up for
sale in ten lots, the five thousand pounds got at
once without interfering with the town land.   But
no more of that nasty abominable huckstering in
deferred payment, nothing but a cheat, and all the
elements of moral and political degradation might
be found in the one thing, deferred payment, and
the tricks of trade in this are amply abundant and
sufficient in the world without the Government
resorting to them.

The next day the whole of the cows of the
people of Armidale town were driven from what had
formerly been their town land into the pound, and
no more heart-sickening sight was ever witnessed,
than that of a poor woman going about asking for
money to help her to get her cows out of the

pound, the sole means of support for herself and family. The member of Parliament for the district was standing by all the time this was going on ; he might not have known so much, but if he had any regard for his constituents, he must have known this much, that there was a Governor in the colony who could at once put a stop to this deprivation of the town rights and privileges, and one asks what is the use of members of Parliament? I have never seen any use of them except making a provision for themselves and friends in Government situations. I was introduced to a newly elected member of Parliament in the interior, with the request at the same time for money to help him in his parliamentary career. He might have been seen humping the swag, tramping it all the way to Sydney, and not long afterwards becoming a minister of the Crown ; unfortunately, he did not long survive to reap the fruits of the golden harvest that falls into the lap of those who have brains but no money. An old country like England can stand a great deal of radicalism and be none the worse, perhaps the better, there being so much inter-pellant power, but in a new colony radicalism with manhood suffrage at the end of the tether is a terrible infliction. Constitutions are said not to be made but to grow : but there is no such thing as growing in the radical creed, and there is no such thing as building up ; it must be always pulling down, and the holdings of vast numbers of people, the fruits of national labour and industry, lent out in the purchase of land at one or two pounds an

acre; must be brought down to the dead level of
five shillings an acre, Government everything, the
people nothing. Money got out of every one thing,
fairly or foully, to keep this great machine, Government, in motion for the special benefit, honour, and
delight of the Sydneyites, Paris being France and
Sydney New South Wales. In Mr. William Sykes
exploiting in the interior, the right man has been
taken by the hand for bringing in money to the
Government treasury, the purpose here being to
goad the squatters to purchase their runs. Mr.
Sykes has been credited with breaking into banks ;
it is quite a new experience making the banks
close their doors ; he has done this most effectually,
and it was impossible for the squatters to hold possession of their runs without heavy advances from
the banks in securing possession of favourite water
frontages, where Mr. Sykes would be certain to
enrich himself.

' A little wisdom required to govern ' is a very
old saying, and nothing could have been easier in
the Government of New South Wales than simply
to have followed the lines of Government laid down
from the very foundation of the colony, and which
had contributed to all its wealth and prosperity,
and if an archangel from heaven had laid down
those lines, nothing could have appeared so wise
and beneficent. Such a happy blending and uniting
of rich and poor, the squattages being factories for
taking in poor people and sending them out rich.
Great Britain might be seen here with her long out-
stretched arm of benevolence and money providing

for her miserable outcast children, and the squattages were 'cities of refuge' to many; if one
required to hide himself from the manslayer, he
could always hide himself here, no one knew anything about him and no one cared to know anything
about him, inquiry into character before employment being altogether unknown, shelter and provision for the most woebegone, and one who is held
capable of nothing else in the world is always held
capable of this, shepherding in Australia, and the
lazier the man always the better shepherd (this is
not the case in New Zealand), and that terrible
obstacle to finding employment, an encumbrance·
in a wife and family, is better recommendation for
finding employment. Mike and Jim might bolt,
getting disgusted with the lonely life, but there was
no risk of this taking place in Pat and Biddy and
the young Pats; Pat was a fixture, and Biddy if
she was a thrifty woman could go on changing and
live like a little queen, all the people knew what
they were doing, and what they had to effect. If one
wished to make a home for himself, there was this
only course open to him, settle near a town, where
the land was surveyed and ready for occupation,
the people all brought here at once within the pale
of moral and religious influences, and boys too long
shepherding losing the faculty of speech, recovering
from the affliction on being brought within the
healing influences of society, all these early lines
of colonisation have been done away with for no
reason whatever. Settle anywhere; nothing possibly
could be so disastrous and insane, and if a set of

savages or gypsies had been framing a land law, there is nothing more certain, their land law would have exactly corresponded with the land law of New South Wales. No use for towns, civilisation, Christianisation, or anything of that sort, squat down anywhere ; and there is not one hundredth part of the care and attention given to the people there is given to sheep and cattle. Exposed to all the perils of the scattering of the people, one of the just curses of the Almighty, an easy prey to every design-ing vagabond, and in the masterful art of extor-tion there will be none found so expert as Go-vernment employés. Here is a case of one, a licensed Government surveyor, pouncing upon a free selector in his lonely part, not finding all the money he re-quired, laying hold of a horse that was standing near, to the great grief of the daughter Mary, crying out the man has gone off with Nelly, a valuable brood mare ; the man was off indeed, rejoicing greatly in the facilities afforded him for the exercise of his predatory talents ; stolen waters are sweet, and there can be little doubt of many gloating and glorying over their ill-gotten gain plunder, and who have no more of the law of humanity in their souls than a carrion crow. Here was a scamp of a medical man, who to my certain knowledge arrived in the interior as poor as a ' church mouse,' telling me with great glee that he had got fifty pounds for one visit ; if he could not get money he was certain always to get horses, and I bought some from him myself ; he told me his income was as good as fifteen hundred pounds a year. If the scamp had been living with an equal population in the United Kingdom he would not have received fifteen hundred pence.

The following are a few extracts from lectures delivered in Sydney by the author as a protest on the part of the clergy against the action of the Government in the 'Scattering of the People,' one of the great curses of the Almighty :

Gathering and heaping up money is work that can be done any day by a coalheaver ; there are a great many things in the world far more valuable than money, and which money cannot purchase ; there is love, truth, justice, honour, humanity. Go anywhere sounds very well ; large, liberal. It is nothing but sound and fury, there is not a grain of reason or common sense in it. The Government has the means of knowing, and the people have not the means of knowing, where they may settle with the best likelihood of success, and I hold it is driving the people to ruin and destruction to permit them to settle where they choose. There are those who have great faith in mankind, and that a man when left to himself will always act best for his own interest. There never was a greater delusion ; habits are easily formed, bush habits like every other kind of habits. Society is a sacred contract, sealed and ratified in heaven, and established for the good of the individual. This sacred vessel the legislature of New South Wales has taken and broken and dashed in pieces to the ground. Society contains within itself all the elements of its own preservation, wickedness is kept down as a common enemy, virtue is cherished as a friend, and it is in such circumstances, *Vox populi vox Dei.* He was a very Solon in legislation, that honourable member who stood up in his high place in Parliament and called in the free solicitor to select near each other, and they would fight the squatters', 'love of our neighbour?' In the new departure of the Government, deferred payment in the purchase of the land, political life in the colony is well-nigh extinguished. Who would be so rude and wicked as to say anything against this liberal and benevolent Government that gives the people credit in the purchase of the land? The Government can well afford to be liberal with the land, but it has no right and business to be liberal with that which does not belong to it—the hearts and consciences of the people. The land is to be held sacred; in selling the land the Government was bound to give up full possession of the rights of the land, the man treated as a man and not a helot and slave, tied and bound to this Government, and have no heart and voice to cry out against the wrongs and oppression of Government. The British lion in Great Britain is a noble animal, stands by and sees that there is not a hair of your head touched; in Australia he is a ferocious brute, takes you into his mouth and swallows you.

FINIS

Spottiswoode & Co. Printers, New-street Square, London.

S

MESSRS. LONGMANS, GREEN, & CO.'S

CLASSIFIED CATALOGUE

OF

WORKS IN GENERAL LITERATURE.

History, Politics, Polity, and Political Memoirs.

Abbott.—A HISTORY OF GREECE. By EVELYN ABBOTT, M.A., LL.D. Part I.—From the Earliest Times to the Ionian Revolt. Crown 8vo., 10s. 6d. Part II.—500-445 B.C. Cr. 8vo., 10s. 6d.

Acland and Ransome.—A HAND-BOOK IN OUTLINE OF THE POLITICAL HISTORY OF ENGLAND TO 1890. Chronologically Arranged. By the Right Hon. A. H. DYKE ACLAND, M.P., and CYRIL RANSOME, M.A. Crown 8vo., 6s.

ANNUAL REGISTER (THE). A Review of Public Events at Home and Abroad, for the year 1892. 8vo., 18s.

Volumes of the ANNUAL REGISTER for the years 1863-1891 can still be had. 18s. each.

Armstrong.—ELIZABETH FARNESE; The Termagant of Spain. By EDWARD ARMSTRONG, M.A., Fellow of Queen's College, Oxford. 8vo., 16s.

Arnold.—Works by T. ARNOLD, D.D., formerly Head Master of Rugby School.

INTRODUCTORY LECTURES ON MODERN HISTORY. 8vo., 7s. 6d.

MISCELLANEOUS WORKS. 8vo., 7s. 6d.

Bagwell.—IRELAND UNDER THE TUDORS. By RICHARD BAGWELL, LL.D. 3 vols. Vols. I. and II. From the first Invasion of the Northmen to the year 1578. 8vo., 32s. Vol. III. 1578-1603. 8vo., 18s.

Ball.—HISTORICAL REVIEW OF THE LEGISLATIVE SYSTEMS OPERATIVE IN IRELAND, from the Invasion of Henry the Second to the Union (1172-1800). By the Rt. Hon. J. T. BALL. 8vo., 6s.

Besant.—THE HISTORY OF LONDON. By WALTER BESANT. With 74 Illustrations. Crown 8vo. School Reading-book Edition, 1s. 9d.; Prize-book Edition, 2s. 6d.

Buckle.—HISTORY OF CIVILISATION IN ENGLAND AND FRANCE, SPAIN AND SCOTLAND. By HENRY THOMAS BUCKLE. 3 vols. Crown 8vo., 24s.

Chesney.—INDIAN POLITY: A View of the System of Administration in India. By Lieut.-General Sir GEORGE CHESNEY. New Edition, Revised and Enlarged.
[In the Press.

Crump.—A SHORT INQUIRY INTO THE FORMATION OF POLITICAL OPINION, from the reign of the Great Families to the advent of Democracy. By ARTHUR CRUMP. 8vo., 7s. 6d.

De Tocqueville.—DEMOCRACY IN AMERICA. By ALEXIS DE TOCQUEVILLE. 2 vols. Crown 8vo., 16s.

Fitzpatrick.—SECRET SERVICE UNDER PITT. By W. J. FITZPATRICK, F.S.A., Author of 'Correspondence of Daniel O'Connell'. 8vo., 7s. 6d.

Freeman.—THE HISTORICAL GEOGRAPHY OF EUROPE. By EDWARD A. FREEMAN, D.C.L., LL.D. With 65 Maps. 2 vols. 8vo., 31s. 6d.

History, Politics, Polity, and Political Memoirs—*continued.*

Froude.—Works by JAMES A. FROUDE, Regius Professor of Modern History in the University of Oxford.

THE HISTORY OF ENGLAND, from the Fall of Wolsey to the Defeat of the Spanish Armada.
Popular Edition. 12 vols. Crown 8vo., 3*s.* 6*d.* each.
Silver Library Edition. 12 vols. Crown 8vo., 3*s.* 6*d.* each.

THE DIVORCE OF CATHERINE OF ARA-GON: the Story as told by the Imperial Ambassadors resident at the Court of Henry VIII. *In usum Laicorum.* Crown 8vo., 6*s.*

THE SPANISH STORY OF THE ARMADA, and other Essays, Historical and Descriptive. Crown 8vo., 6*s.*

THE ENGLISH IN IRELAND IN THE EIGHTEENTH CENTURY. 3 vols. Cr. 8vo., 18*s.*

SHORT STUDIES ON GREAT SUBJECTS. 4 vols. Cr. 8vo., 3*s.* 6*d.* each.

CÆSAR: a Sketch. Cr. 8vo., 3*s.* 6*d.*

Gardiner.—Works by SAMUEL RAW-SON GARDINER, M.A., Hon. LL.D., Edinburgh, Fellow of Merton College, Oxford.

HISTORY OF ENGLAND, from the Accession of James I. to the Outbreak of the Civil War, 1603-1642. 10 vols. Crown 8vo., 6*s.* each.

A HISTORY OF THE GREAT CIVIL WAR, 1642-1649. 4 vols. Cr. 8vo., 6*s.* each.

THE STUDENT'S HISTORY OF ENGLAND, With 378 Illustrations. Cr. 8vo., 12*s.*

Also in Three Volumes.

Vol. I. B.C. 55—A.D. 1509. With 173 Illustrations. Crown 8vo. 4*s.*

Vol. II. 1509-1689. With 96 Illustrations. Crown 8vo. 4*s.*

Vol. III. 1689-1885. With 109 Illustrations. Crown 8vo. 4*s.*

Greville.—A JOURNAL OF THE REIGNS OF KING GEORGE IV., KING WILLIAM IV., AND QUEEN VICTORIA. By CHARLES C. F. GREVILLE, formerly Clerk of the Council. 8 vols. Crown 8vo., 6*s.* each.

Hart.—PRACTICAL ESSAYS IN AMERICAN GOVERNMENT. By ALBERT BUSHNELL HART, Ph.D., &c. Cr. 8vo., 6*s.*

Hearn.—THE GOVERNMENT OF ENGLAND: its Structure and its Development. By W. EDWARD HEARN. 8vo., 16*s.*

Historic Towns.—Edited by E. A. FREEMAN, D.C.L., and Rev. WILLIAM HUNT, M.A. With Maps and Plans. Crown 8vo., 3*s.* 6d. each.

BRISTOL. By the Rev. W. HUNT.

CARLISLE. By MANDELL CREIGHTON, D.D., Bishop of Peterborough.

CINQUE PORTS. By MONTAGU BUR-ROWS.

COLCHESTER. By Rev. E. L. CUTTS.

EXETER. By E. A. FREEMAN.

LONDON. By Rev. W. J. LOFTIE.

OXFORD. By Rev. C. W. BOASE.

WINCHESTER. By Rev. G. W. KIT-CHIN, D.D.

YORK. By Rev. JAMES RAINE.

NEW YORK. By THEODORE ROOSEVELT.

BOSTON (U.S.) By HENRY CABOT LODGE.

Horley.—SEFTON: A DESCRIPTIVE AND HISTORICAL ACCOUNT. Comprising the Collected Notes and Researches of the late Rev. ENGELBERT HORLEY, M.A., Rector 1871-1883. By W. D. CARÖE, M.A. (Cantab.), Fellow of the Royal Institute of British Architects, and E. J. A. GORDON. With 17 Plates and 32 Illustrations in the Text. Royal 8vo., 31*s.* 6*d.*

Joyce.—A SHORT HISTORY OF IRELAND, from the Earliest Times to 1608. By P. W. JOYCE, LL.D. Crown 8vo., 10*s.* 6*d.*

Lang.—A HISTORY OF ST. ANDREWS. By ANDREW LANG. With Illustrations by T. HODGE.   [*In the Press.*

Lecky.—Works by WILLIAM EDWARD HARTPOLE LECKY.

HISTORY OF ENGLAND IN THE EIGHTEENTH CENTURY.

Library Edition. 8 vols. 8vo., £7 4*s.*
Cabinet Edition. ENGLAND. 7 vols. Cr. 8vo., 6*s.* each. IRELAND. 5 vols. Crown 8vo., 6*s.* each.

HISTORY OF EUROPEAN MORALS FROM AUGUSTUS TO CHARLEMAGNE. 2 vols. Crown 8vo., 16*s.*

HISTORY OF THE RISE AND INFLUENCE OF THE SPIRIT OF RATIONALISM IN EUROPE. 2 vols. Crown 8vo., 16*s.*

History, Politics, Polity, and Political Memoirs—*continued.*

Macaulay.—Works by LORD MAC-AULAY.

COMPLETE WORKS.

Cabinet Ed. 16 vols. Pt. 8vo., £4 16*s.*
Library Edition. 8 vols. 8vo., £5 5*s.*

HISTORY OF ENGLAND FROM THE AC-CESSION OF JAMES THE SECOND.

Popular Edition. 2 vols. Cr. 8vo., 5*s.*
Student's Edition. 2 vols. Cr. 8vo., 12*s.*
People's Edition. 4 vols. Cr. 8vo., 16*s.*
Cabinet Edition. 8 vols. Pt. 8vo., 48*s.*
Library Edition. 5 vols. 8vo., £4

CRITICAL AND HISTORICAL ESSAYS, WITH LAYS OF ANCIENT ROME, in 1 volume.

Popular Edition. Crown 8vo., 2*s.* 6*d.*

Authorised Edition. Crown 8vo., 2*s.* 6*d.*, or 3*s.* 6*d.*, gilt edges.

Silver Library Edition. Crown 8vo., 3*s.* 6*d.*

CRITICAL AND HISTORICAL ESSAYS.

Student's Edition. 1 vol. Cr. 8vo., 6*s.*
People's Edition. 2 vols. Cr. 8vo., 8*s.*
Trevelyan Edition. 2 vols. Cr. 8vo., 9*s.*
Cabinet Edition. 4 vols. Post 8vo., 24*s.*
Library Edition. 3 vols. 8vo., 36*s.*

ESSAYS which may be had separately price 6*d.* each sewed, 1*s.* each cloth.

Frederick the Great.	Lord Clive.
Lord Bacon.	The Earl of Chat-
Addison and Wal-	ham(Two Essays).
pole.	Ranke and Glad-
Croker's Boswell's	stone.
Johnson.	Milton and Machia-
Hallam's Constitu-	velli.
tional History.	Lord Byron,and The
Warren Hastings	Comic Dramatists
(3*d.* swd., 6*d.* cl.).	of the Restoration.

SPEECHES. Crown 8vo., 3*s.* 6*d.*

MISCELLANEOUS WRITINGS.

People's Ed. 1 vol. Cr. 8vo., 4*s.* 6*d.*
Library Edition. 2 vols. 8vo., 21*s.*

MISCELLANEOUS WRITINGS AND SPEECHES.

Popular Edition. Cr. 8vo., 2*s.* 6*d.*
Student's Edition. Crown 8vo., 6*s.*

Cabinet Edition. Including Indian Penal Code, Lays of Ancient Rome, and Miscellaneous Poems. 4 vols. Post 8vo., 24*s.*

Macaulay.—Works by LORD MAC-AULAY.—*continued.*

SELECTIONS FROM THE WRITINGS OF LORD MACAULAY. Edited, with Occasional Notes, by the Right Hon. Sir G. O. Trevelyan, Bart. Crown 8vo., 6*s.*

May.—THE CONSTITUTIONAL HISTORY OF ENGLAND since the Accession of George III. 1760-1870. By Sir THOMAS ERSKINE MAY, K.C.B. (Lord Farnborough). 3 vols. Crown 8vo., 18*s.*

Merivale.—Works by the Very Rev. CHARLES MERIVALE, Dean of Ely.

HISTORY OF THE ROMANS UNDER THE EMPIRE.
Cabinet Edition. 8 vols. Cr. 8vo., 48*s.*
Silver Library Edition. 8 vols. Cr. 8vo., 3*s.* 6*d.* each.

THE FALL OF THE ROMAN REPUBLIC: a Short History of the Last Century of the Commonwealth. 12mo., 7*s.* 6*d.*

Parkes.—FIFTY YEARS IN THE MAKING OF AUSTRALIAN HISTORY. By Sir HENRY PARKES, G.C.M.G. With 2 Portraits (1854 and 1892). 2 vols. 8vo., 32*s.*

Prendergast.—IRELAND FROM THE RESTORATION TO THE REVOLUTION, 1660-1690. By JOHN P. PRENDERGAST, Author of 'The Cromwellian Settlement in Ireland'. 8vo., 5*s.*

Round.—GEOFFREY DE MANDEVILLE: a Study of the Anarchy. By J. H. ROUND, M.A. 8vo., 16*s.*

Seebohm.—THE ENGLISH VILLAGE COMMUNITY Examined in its Relations to the Manorial and Tribal Systems, &c. By FREDERIC SEEBOHM. With 13 Maps and Plates. 8vo., 16*s.*

Smith.—CARTHAGE AND THE CARTHAGINIANS. By R. BOSWORTH SMITH, M.A., Assistant Master in Harrow School. With Maps, Plans, &c. Cr. 8vo., 6*s.*

Stephens.—PAROCHIAL SELF-GOVERNMENT IN RURAL DISTRICTS: Argument and Plan. By HENRY C. STEPHENS, M.P. 4to., 12*s.* 6*d.* Popular Edition. Cr. 8vo., 1*s.*

History, Politics, Polity, and Political Memoirs—*continued.*

Stephens.—A HISTORY OF THE FRENCH REVOLUTION. By H. MORSE STEPHENS, Balliol College, Oxford.   3 vols. 8vo. Vols. I. and II. 18s. each.

Stubbs.—HISTORY OF THE UNIVERSITY OF DUBLIN, from its Foundation to the End of the Eighteenth Century. By J. W. STUBBS. 8vo., 12s. 6d.

Thompson.—POLITICS IN A DEMOCRACY: an Essay. By DANIEL GREENLEAF THOMPSON, Author of ' A System of Psychology, &c. Cr. 8vo., 5s.

Todd.—PARLIAMENTARY GOVERNMENT IN THE COLONIES. By ALPHEUS TODD, LL.D. *[In the Press.*

Tupper. — OUR INDIAN PROTECTORATE: an Introduction to the Study of the Relations between the British Government and its Indian Feudatories. By CHARLES LEWIS TUPPER, Indian Civil Service. Royal 8vo., 16s.

Wakeman and Hassall.—ESSAYS INTRODUCTORY TO THE STUDY OF ENGLISH CONSTITUTIONAL HISTORY. By Resident Members of the University of Oxford. Edited by HENRY OFFLEY WAKEMAN, M.A., and ARTHUR HASSALL, M.A. Crown 8vo., 6s.

Walpole.—Works by SPENCER WALPOLE.
HISTORY OF ENGLAND FROM THE CONCLUSION OF THE GREAT WAR IN 1815 TO 1858. 6 vols. Crown 8vo., 6s. each.
THE LAND OF HOME RULE: being an Account of the History and Institutions of the Isle of Man. Cr. 8vo., 6s.

Wylie.—HISTORY OF ENGLAND UNDER HENRY IV. By JAMES HAMILTON WYLIE, M.A., one of H. M. Inspectors of Schools. 3 vols. Vol. I., 1399-1404. Crown 8vo., 10s. 6d. Vol. II. *[In the Press.* Vol. III.   *[In preparation.*

Biography, Personal Memoirs, &c.

Armstrong.—THE LIFE AND LETTERS OF EDMUND J. ARMSTRONG. Edited by G. F. ARMSTRONG. Fcp. 8vo., 7s. 6d.

Bacon.—LETTERS AND LIFE, INCLUDING ALL HIS OCCASIONAL WORKS. Edited by J. SPEDDING. 7 vols. 8vo., £4 4s.

Bagehot.—BIOGRAPHICAL STUDIES. By WALTER BAGEHOT. 8vo., 12s.

Boyd.—TWENTY-FIVE YEARS OF ST. ANDREWS, 1865-1890. By A. K. H. BOYD, D.D., Author of ' Recreations of a Country Parson,' &c. 2 vols. 8vo. Vol. I., 12s. Vol. II., 15s.

Carlyle.—THOMAS CARLYLE: a History of his Life. By. J. A. FROUDE.
1795-1835. 2 vols. Crown 8vo., 7s.
1834-1881. 2 vols. Crown 8vo., 7s.

Fabert.—ABRAHAM FABERT: Governor of Sedan and Marshal of France. His Life and Times, 1599-1662. By GEORGE HOOPER, Author of ' Waterloo,' ' Wellington,' &c. With a Portrait. 8vo., 10s. 6d.

Fox.—THE EARLY HISTORY OF CHARLES JAMES FOX. By the Right Hon. Sir G. O. TREVELYAN, Bart.
Library Edition. 8vo., 18s.
Cabinet Edition. Crown 8vo., 6s.

Hamilton.—LIFE OF SIR WILLIAM HAMILTON. By R. P. GRAVES. 3 vols. 15s. each.
ADDENDUM TO THE LIFE OF SIR WM. ROWAN HAMILTON, LL.D., D.C.L., 8vo., 6d. sewed.

Hassall.—THE NARRATIVE OF A BUSY LIFE: an Autobiography. By ARTHUR HILL HASSALL, M.D. 8vo., 5s.

Havelock.—MEMOIRS OF SIR HENRY HAVELOCK, K.C.B. By JOHN CLARK MARSHMAN. Crown 8vo., 3s. 6d.

Macaulay.—THE LIFE AND LETTERS OF LORD MACAULAY. By the Right Hon. Sir G. O. TREVELYAN, Bart.
Popular Edition. 1 vol. Cr. 8vo., 2s. 6d.
Student's Edition. 1 vol. Cr. 8vo., 6s.
Cabinet Edition. 2 vols. Post 8vo., 12s.
Library Edition. 2 vols. 8vo., 36s.

Marbot.—THE MEMOIRS OF THE BARON DE MARBOT. Translated from the French by ARTHUR JOHN BUTLER, M.A. Crown 8vo., 7s. 6d.

Montrose.—DEEDS OF MONTROSE: THE MEMOIRS OF JAMES, MARQUIS OF MONTROSE, 1639-1650. By the Rev. GEORGE WISHART, D.D. (Bishop of Edinburgh, 1662-1671). Translated, with Introduction, Notes, &c., and the original Latin, by the Rev. ALEXANDER MURDOCH, F.S.A. (Scot.), and H. F. MORELAND SIMPSON, M.A. (Cantab.). 4to., 36s. net.

Biography, Personal Memoirs, &c.—*continued.*

Seebohm.—THE OXFORD REFORMERS —JOHN COLET, ERASMUS AND THOMAS MORE : a History of their Fellow-Work. By FREDERIC SEEBOHM. 8vo., 14s.

Shakespeare.—OUTLINES OF THE LIFE OF SHAKESPEARE. By J. O. HALLIWELL-PHILLIPPS. With numerous Illustrations and Fac-similes. 2 vols. Royal 8vo., £1 1s.

Shakespeare's TRUE LIFE. By JAS. WALTER. With 500 Illustrations by GERALD E. MOIRA. Imp. 8vo., 21s.

Sherbrooke.—LIFE AND LETTERS OF THE RIGHT HON. ROBERT LOWE, VISCOUNT SHERBROOKE, G.C.B., together with a Memoir of his Kinsman, Sir JOHN COAPE SHERBROOKE, G.C.B. By A. PATCHETT MARTIN. With 5 Portraits. 2 vols. 8vo., 36s.

Stephen.—ESSAYS IN ECCLESIASTICAL BIOGRAPHY. By Sir JAMES STEPHEN. Crown 8vo., 7s. 6d.

Verney.—MEMOIRS OF THE VERNEY FAMILY DURING THE CIVIL WAR. Compiled from the Letters and Illustrated by the Portraits at Claydon House, Bucks. By FRANCES PARTHENOPE VERNEY. With a Preface by S. R. GARDINER, M.A., LL.D. With 38 Portraits, Woodcuts and Fac-simile. 2 vols. Royal 8vo., 42s.

Wagner.—WAGNER AS I KNEW HIM. By FERDINAND PRAEGER. Crown 8vo., 7s. 6d.

Walford.—TWELVE ENGLISH AUTHORESSES. By L. B. WALFORD, Author of ' Mischief of Monica,' &c. With Portrait of Hannah More. Crown 8vo., 4s. 6d.

Wellington.—LIFE OF THE DUKE OF WELLINGTON. By the Rev. G. R. GLEIG, M.A. Crown 8vo., 3s. 6d.

Wordsworth.—Works by CHARLES WORDSWORTH, D.C.L., late Bishop of St. Andrews.

ANNALS OF MY EARLY LIFE, 1806-1846. 8vo., 15s.

ANNALS OF MY LIFE, 1847-1856. 8vo., 10s. 6d.

Travel and Adventure.

Arnold.—SEAS AND LANDS. By Sir EDWIN ARNOLD, K.C.I.E., Author of 'The Light of the World,'&c. Reprinted Letters from the ' Daily Telegraph.' With 71 Illustrations. Cr. 8vo., 7s. 6d.

Baker.—Works by Sir SAMUEL WHITE BAKER.

EIGHT YEARS IN CEYLON. With 6 Illustrations. Crown 8vo., 3s. 6d.

THE RIFLE AND THE HOUND IN CEYLON. 6 Illustrations. Cr. 8vo., 3s. 6d.

Bent.—Works by J. THEODORE BENT, F.S.A., F.R.G.S.

THE RUINED CITIES OF MASHONALAND : being a Record of Excavation and Exploration in 1891. With Map, 13 Plates, and 104 Illustrations in the Text. Cr. 8vo., 7s. 6d.

THE SACRED CITY OF THE ETHIOPIANS: being a Record of Travel and Research in Abyssinia in 1893. With 8 Plates and 65 Illustrations in the Text. 8vo.

Brassey.—Works by LADY BRASSEY.

A VOYAGE IN THE 'SUNBEAM'; OUR HOME ON THE OCEAN FOR ELEVEN MONTHS.

Library Edition. With 8 Maps and Charts, and 118 Illustrations. 8vo., 21s.

Cabinet Edition. With Map and 66 Illustrations. Crown 8vo., 7s. 6d.

Silver Library Edition. With 66 Illustrations. Crown 8vo., 3s. 6d.

Popular Edition. With 60 Illustrations. 4to., 6d. sewed, 1s. cloth.

School Edition. With 37 Illustrations. Fcp., 2s. cloth, or 3s. white parchment.

THREE VOYAGES IN THE 'SUNBEAM'. Popular Edition. With 346 Illustrations. 4to., 2s. 6d.

Travel and Adventure—*continued.*

Brassey.—Works by LADY BRASSEY—*cont.*

SUNSHINE AND STORM IN THE EAST.
Library Edition. With 2 Maps and 141 Illustrations. 8vo., 21s.
Cabinet Edition. With 2 Maps and 114 Illustrations. Crown 8vo.,7s. 6d.
Popular Edition. With 103 Illustrations. 4to., 6d. sewed, 1s. cloth.

THE LAST VOYAGE TO INDIA AND AUSTRALIA IN THE 'SUNBEAM'. With Charts and Maps, and 40 Illustrations in Monotone (20 full-page), and nearly 200 Illustrations in the Text from Drawings by R. T. PRITCHETT. 8vo., 21s.

IN THE TRADES, THE TROPICS, AND THE 'ROARING FORTIES'.
Cabinet Edition. With Map and 220 Illustrations. Crown 8vo., 7s. 6d.
Popular Edition. With 183 Illustrations. 4to., 6d. sewed, 1s. cloth.

Curzon.—PERSIA AND THE PERSIAN QUESTION. With 9 Maps, 96 Illustrations, Appendices, and an Index. By the Hon. GEORGE N. CURZON, M.P., late Fellow of All Souls' College, Oxford. 2 vols. 8vo., 42s.

Froude.—Works by JAMES A. FROUDE.
OCEANA : or England and her Colonies. With 9 Illustrations. Crown 8vo., 2s. boards, 2s. 6d. cloth.
THE ENGLISH IN THE WEST INDIES: or the Bow of Ulysses. With 9 Illustrations. Cr. 8vo., 2s. bds., 2s. 6d. cl.

Howard.—LIFE WITH TRANS-SIBERIAN SAVAGES. By B. DOUGLAS HOWARD, M.A. Crown 8vo., 6s.

Howells. — VENETIAN LIFE. By WILLIAM DEAN HOWELLS. With 18 Illustrations in aqua-tint from original Water Colours. 2 vols. Crown 8vo., 21s.

Howitt.—VISITS TO REMARKABLE PLACES, Old Halls, Battle-Fields, Scenes illustrative of Striking Passages in English History and Poetry. By WILLIAM HOWITT. With 80 Illustrations. Crown 8vo., 3s. 6d.

Knight.—Works by E. F. KNIGHT, Author of the Cruise of the 'Falcon'.
THE CRUISE OF THE 'ALERTE': the Narrative of a Search for Treasure on the Desert Island of Trinidad. With 2 Maps and 23 Illustrations. Crown 8vo., 3s. 6d.   [*Continued.*

Knight.—Works by E.F.KNIGHT—*cont.*
WHERE THREE EMPIRES MEET: a Narrative of Recent Travel in Kashmir, Western Tibet, Baltistan, Ladak, Gilgit, and the adjoining Countries. With a Map and 54 Illustrations. Cr. 8vo., 7s. 6d.

Lees and Clutterbuck.—B. C. 1887: A RAMBLE IN BRITISH COLUMBIA. By J. A. LEES and W. J. CLUTTERBUCK, Authors of 'Three in Norway'. With Map and 75 Illustrations. Cr. 8vo., 3s. 6d.

Nansen.—Works by Dr. FRIDTJOF NANSEN.
THE FIRST CROSSING OF GREENLAND. With numerous Illustrations and a Map. Crown 8vo., 7s. 6d.
ESKIMO LIFE. Translated by WILLIAM ARCHER. With 16 Plates and 15 Illustrations in the Text. 8vo., 16s.

Pratt.—TO THE SNOWS OF TIBET THROUGH CHINA. By A. E. PRATT, F.R.G.S. With 33 Illustrations and a Map. 8vo., 18s.

Riley.—ATHOS : or the Mountain of the Monks. By ATHELSTAN RILEY, M.A. With Map and 29 Illustrations. 8vo., 21s.

Stephens.—MADOC: An Essay on the Discovery of America, by MADOC AP OWEN GWYNEDD, in the Twelfth Century. By THOMAS STEPHENS. Edited by LLYWARCH REYNOLDS, B.A. Oxon. 8vo., 7s. 6d.

Von Hohnel.—DISCOVERY OF LAKES RUDOLF AND STEFANIE: Account of Count SAMUEL TELEKI'S Exploring and Hunting Expedition in Eastern Equatorial Africa in 1887 and 1888. By his companion, Lieutenant LUDWIG VON HOHNEL. Translated by NANCY BELL (N. D'ANVERS). With 179 Illustrations, 2 Large and 4 Small Coloured Maps, giving Route of Expedition. 2 vols. 8vo., 42s.

THREE IN NORWAY. By Two of Them. With a Map and 59 Illustrations. Cr. 8vo., 2s. boards, 2s. 6d. cloth.

Whishaw.—OUT OF DOORS IN TSARLAND ; a Record of the Seeings and Doings of a Wanderer in Russia. By FRED. J. WHISHAW. Cr. 8vo., 7s. 6d.

Wolff.—Works by HENRY W. WOLFF.
RAMBLES IN THE BLACK FOREST. Crown 8vo., 7s. 6d.
THE WATERING PLACES OF THE VOSGES. Crown 8vo., 4s. 6d.
THE COUNTRY OF THE VOSGES. With a Map. 8vo., 12s.

Sport and Pastime.

THE BADMINTON LIBRARY.

Edited by the DUKE OF BEAUFORT, K.G., assisted by ALFRED E. T. WATSON.

ATHLETICS AND FOOTBALL. By MONTAGUE SHEARMAN. With 51 Illustrations. Crown 8vo., 10s. 6d.

BIG GAME SHOOTING. By C. PHIL-LIPPS WOLLEY, F. C. SELOUS, W. G. LITTLEDALE, Colonel PERCY, FRED. JACKSON, Major H. PERCY, W. C. OSWELL, Sir HENRY POTTINGER, Bart., and the EARL OF KILMOREY. With Contributions by other Writers. With Illustrations by CHARLES WHYMPER and others. 2 vols.   [In the Press.

BOATING. By W. B. WOODGATE. With an Introduction by the Rev. EDMOND WARRE, D.D., and a Chapter on 'Rowing at Eton,' by R. HARVEY MASON. With 49 Illustrations. Cr. 8vo., 10s. 6d.

COURSING AND FALCONRY. By HARDING COX and the Hon. GERALD LASCELLES. With 76 Illustrations. Crown 8vo., 10s. 6d.

CRICKET. By A. G. STEEL and the Hon. R. H. LYTTELTON. With Contributions by ANDREW LANG, R. A. H. MITCHELL, W. G. GRACE, and F. GALE. With 63 Illustrations. Cr. 8vo., 10s. 6d.

CYCLING. By VISCOUNT BURY (Earl of Albemarle), K.C.M.G., and G. LACY HILLIER. With 89 Illustrations. Crown 8vo., 10s. 6d.

DRIVING. By the DUKE OF BEAUFORT. With 65 Illustrations. Cr. 8vo., 10s. 6d.

FENCING, BOXING. AND WREST-LING. By WALTER H. POLLOCK, F. C. GROVE. C. PREVOST, E. B. MITCHELL, and WALTER ARMSTRONG. With 42 Illustrations. Crown 8vo., 10s. 6d.

FISHING. By H. CHOLMONDELEY-PEN-NELL. With Contributions by the MARQUIS OF EXETER, HENRY R. FRANCIS, Major JOHN P. TRAHERNE, FREDERIC M. HALFORD, G. CHRISTO-PHER DAVIES, R. B. MARSTON, &c.

Vol. I. Salmon, Trout, and Grayling. With 158 Illustrations. Crown 8vo., 10s. 6d.

Vol. II. Pike and other Coarse Fish. With 133 Illustrations. Crown 8vo., 10s. 6d.

GOLF. By HORACE G. HUTCHINSON, the Rt. Hon. A. J. BALFOUR, M.P., Sir W. G. SIMPSON, Bart., LORD WELLWOOD, H. S. C. EVERARD, ANDREW LANG, and other Writers. With 91 Illustrations. Cr. 8vo., 10s. 6d.

HUNTING. By the DUKE OF BEAUFORT, K.G., and MOWBRAY MORRIS. With Contributions by the EARL OF SUF-FOLK AND BERKSHIRE, Rev. E. W. L. DAVIES, DIGBY COLLINS and ALFRED E. T. WATSON. With 53 Illustrations. Crown 8vo., 10s. 6d.

MOUNTAINEERING. By C. T. DENT, Sir F. POLLOCK, Bart., W. M. CONWAY, DOUGLAS FRESHFIELD, C. E. MA-THEWS, C. PILKINGTON, and other Writers. With 108 Illustrations. Cr. 8vo., 10s. 6d.

RACING AND STEEPLE-CHASING. Racing: By the EARL OF SUFFOLK AND BERKSHIRE and W. G. CRAVEN. With a Contribution by the Hon. F. LAWLEY. Steeple-chasing: By ARTHUR COVENTRY and ALFRED E. T. WAT-SON. With 58 Illusts. Cr. 8vo., 10s. 6d.

RIDING AND POLO. By Captain ROBERT WEIR, J. MORAY BROWN, the DUKE OF BEAUFORT, K.G., the EARL of SUFFOLK AND BERKSHIRE, &c. With 59 Illustrations. Cr. 8vo., 10s. 6d.

SHOOTING. By Lord WALSINGHAM and Sir RALPH PAYNE-GALLWEY, Bart. With Contributions by LORD LOVAT, LORD CHARLES LENNOX KERR, the Hon. G. LASCELLES, and A. J. STUART-WORTLEY.
Vol. I. Field and Covert. With 105 Illustrations. Crown 8vo., 10s. 6d.
Vol. II. Moor and Marsh. With 65 Illustrations. Cr. 8vo., 10s. 6d.

SKATING, CURLING, TOBOGA-NING, AND OTHER ICE SPORTS. By JN. M. HEATHCOTE, C. G. TEBBUTT, T. MAXWELL WITHAM, the Rev. JOHN KERR, ORMOND HAKE, and Colonel BUCK. With 284 Illustrations. Cr. 8vo., 10s. 6d.

SWIMMING. By ARCHIBALD SINCLAIR and WILLIAM HENRY, Hon. Secs. of the Life Saving Society. With 119 Illustrations. Cr. 8vo., 10s. 6d.
[Continued.

Sport and Pastime—*continued.*

THE BADMINTON LIBRARY—*continued.*

TENNIS, LAWN TENNIS, RAC-
QUETS, AND FIVES. By J. M. and
C. G. HEATHCOTE, E. O. PLEYDELL-
BOUVERIE and A. C. AINGER. With
Contributions by the Hon. A. LYTTEL
TON, W. C. MARSHALL, Miss L. DOD,
H. W. W. WILBERFORCE, H. F.
LAWFORD, &c. With 79 Illustrations.
Crown 8vo., 10s. 6d.

YACHTING. By the EARL OF PEMBROKE,
the MARQUIS OF DUFFERIN AND AVA,
the EARL OF ONSLOW, LORD BRASSEY
Lieut.-Col. BUCKNILL, LEWIS HER-
RESHOFF, G. L. WATSON, E. F.
KNIGHT, Rev. G. L. BLAKE, R.N.,
and G. C. DAVIES. With Illustrations by R. T. PRITCHETT, and from
Photographs. 2 vols. [*In the Press.*

Campbell-Walker.—THE CORRECT
CARD: or, How to Play at Whist; a
Whist Catechism. By Major A. CAMP-
BELL-WALKER, F.R.G.S. Fcp. 8vo.,
2s. 6d.

DEAD SHOT (THE): or, Sportsman's
Complete Guide. Being a Treatise on
the Use of the Gun, with Rudimentary
and Finishing Lessons on the Art of
Shooting Game of all kinds, also Game
Driving, Wild-Fowl and Pigeon Shoot-
ing, Dog Breaking, etc. By MARKS-
MAN. Crown 8vo., 10s. 6d.

Falkener.—GAMES, ANCIENT AND ORI-
ENTAL, AND HOW TO PLAY THEM.
Being the Games of the Ancient Egyp-
tians, the Hiera Gramme of the Greeks,
the Ludus Latrunculorum of the Romans,
and the Oriental Games of Chess,
Draughts, Backgammon, and Magic
Squares. By EDWARD FALKENER.
With numerous Photographs, Diagrams,
&c. 8vo., 21s.

Ford.—THE THEORY AND PRACTICE OF
ARCHERY. By HORACE FORD. New
Edition, thoroughly Revised and Re-
written by W. BUTT, M.A. With a Preface by C. J. LONGMAN, M.A. 8vo., 14s.

Francis.—A BOOK ON ANGLING: or,
Treatise on the Art of Fishing in every
Branch; including full Illustrated List
of Salmon Flies. By FRANCIS FRANCIS.
With Coloured Plates. Cr. 8vo., 15s.

Hawker.—THE DIARY OF COLONEL
PETER HAWKER, author of "Instructions to Young Sportsmen". With an
Introduction by Sir RALPH PAYNE-
GALLWEY, Bart. With 2 Portraits of
the Author and 8 Illustrations. 2 vols.
8vo., 32s.

Hopkins.—FISHING REMINISCENCES.
By Major E. P. HOPKINS. With Illustrations. Crown 8vo., 6s. 6d.

Lang.— ANGLING SKETCHES. By
ANDREW LANG. With 20 Illustrations.
Crown 8vo., 7s. 6d.

Longman.—CHESS OPENINGS. By
FRED. W. LONGMAN. Fcp. 8vo., 2s. 6d.

Payne-Gallwey.— Works by Sir
RALPH PAYNE-GALLWEY, Bart.

LETTERS TO YOUNG SHOOTERS (First
Series). On the Choice and Use of a
Gun. With Illustrations. Crown
8vo., 7s. 6d.

LETTERS TO YOUNG SHOOTERS. (Second
Series). On the Production, Preserva-
tion, and Killing of Game. With Direc-
tions in Shooting Wood-Pigeons and
Breaking-in Retrievers. With 103
Illustrations. Crown 8vo., 12s. 6d.

Pole.—THE THEORY OF THE MODERN
SCIENTIFIC GAME OF WHIST. By W.
POLE, F.R.S. Fcp. 8vo., 2s. 6d.

Proctor.—Works by RICHARD A.
PROCTOR.

How TO PLAY WHIST: WITH THE
LAWS AND ETIQUETTE OF WHIST.
Crown 8vo., 3s. 6d.

HOME WHIST: an Easy Guide to Correct Play. 16mo., 1s.

Ronalds.—THE FLY-FISHER'S ENTO-
MOLOGY. By ALFRED RONALDS. With
20 Coloured Plates. 8vo., 14s.

Wilcocks. THE SEA FISHERMAN: Com-
prising the Chief Methods of Hook and
Line Fishing in the British and other
Seas, and Remarks on Nets, Boats, and
Boating. By J. C. WILCOCKS. Illustrated.
Crown 8vo., 6s.

Mental, Moral, and Political Philosophy.

LOGIC, RHETORIC, PSYCHOLOGY, ETC.

Abbott.—THE ELEMENTS OF LOGIC. By T. K. ABBOTT, B.D. 12mo., 3*s*.

Aristotle.—Works by.

THE POLITICS: G. Bekker's Greek Text of Books I., III., IV. (VII.), with an English Translation by W. E. BOL-LAND, M.A. ; and short Introductory Essays by A. LANG, M.A. Crown 8vo., 7*s*. 6*d*.

THE POLITICS: Introductory Essays. By ANDREW LANG (from Bolland and Lang's ' Politics '). Cr. 8vo., 2*s*. 6*d*.

THE ETHICS: Greek Text, Illustrated with Essay and Notes. By Sir ALEX-ANDER GRANT, Bart. 2 vols. 8vo., 32*s*.

THE NICOMACHEAN ETHICS: Newly Translated into English. By ROBERT WILLIAMS. Crown 8vo., 7*s*. 6*d*.

AN INTRODUCTION TO ARISTOTLE'S ETHICS. Books I.-IV. (Book X. c. vi.-ix. in an Appendix.) With a con-tinuous Analysis and Notes. Intended for the use of Beginners and Junior Students. By the Rev. EDWARD MOORE, D.D., Principal of St. Edmund Hall, and late Fellow and Tutor of Queen's College, Oxford. Crown 8vo., 10*s*. 6*d*.

Bacon.—Works by.

COMPLETE WORKS. Edited by R. L. ELLIS, J. SPEDDING, and D. D. HEATH. 7 vols. 8vo., £3 13*s*. 6*d*.

THE ESSAYS: with Annotations. By RICHARD WHATELY, D.D. 8vo. 10*s*. 6*d*.

Bain.—Works by ALEXANDER BAIN, LL.D.

MENTAL SCIENCE. Crown 8vo., 6*s*. 6*d*.

MORAL SCIENCE. Crown 8vo., 4*s*. 6*d*.

The two works as above can be had in one volume, price 10*s*. 6*d*.

SENSES AND THE INTELLECT. 8vo., 15*s*.

EMOTIONS AND THE WILL. 8vo., 15*s*.

LOGIC, DEDUCTIVE AND INDUCTIVE. Part I., 4*s*. Part II., 6*s*. 6*d*.

PRACTICAL ESSAYS. Crown 8vo., 2*s*.

Bray.—Works by CHARLES BRAY.

THE PHILOSOPHY OF NECESSITY: or Law in Mind as in Matter. Cr. 8vo., 5*s*.

THE EDUCATION OF THE FEELINGS: a Moral System for Schools. Crown 8vo., 2*s*. 6*d*.

Bray.—ELEMENTS OF MORALITY, in Easy Lessons for Home and School Teaching. By Mrs. CHARLES BRAY. Cr. 8vo., 1*s*. 6*d*.

Crozier.—CIVILISATION AND PRO-GRESS. By JOHN BEATTIE CROZIER, M.D. With New Preface, more fully explaining the nature of the New Orga-non used in the solution of its problems. 8vo., 14*s*.

Davidson.—THE LOGIC OF DEFINI-TION, Explained and Applied. By WILLIAM L. DAVIDSON, M.A. Crown 8vo., 6*s*.

Green.—THE WORKS OF THOMAS HILL GREEN. Edited by R. L. NETTLESHIP.

Vols. I. and II. Philosophical Works. 8vo., 16*s*. each.

Vol. III. Miscellanies. With Index to the three Volumes, and Memoir. 8vo., 21*s*.

Hearn.—THE ARYAN HOUSEHOLD: its Structure and its Development. An Introduction to Comparative Jurispru-dence. By W. EDWARD HEARN. 8vo., 16*s*.

Hodgson.—Works by SHADWORTH H. HODGSON.

TIME AND SPACE: a Metaphysical Essay. 8vo., 16*s*.

THE THEORY OF PRACTICE : an Ethical Inquiry. 2 vols. 8vo., 24*s*.

THE PHILOSOPHY OF REFLECTION. 2 vols. 8vo., 21*s*.

Hume.—THE PHILOSOPHICAL WORKS OF DAVID HUME. Edited by T. H. GREEN and T. H. GROSE. 4 vols. 8vo., 56*s*. Or separately, Essays. 2 vols. 28*s*. Treatise of Human Nature. 2 vols. 28*s*.

Mental, Moral and Political Philosophy—*continued.*

Johnstone.—A SHORT INTRODUCTION TO THE STUDY OF LOGIC. By LAURENCE JOHNSTONE. With Questions. Cr. 8vo., 2*s.* 6*d.*

Jones.—AN INTRODUCTION TO GENERAL LOGIC. By E. E. CONSTANCE JONES, Author of ' Elements of Logic as a Science of Propositions '. Cr. 8vo., 4*s.* 6*d.*

Justinian.—THE INSTITUTES OF JUSTINIAN : Latin Text, chiefly that of Huschke, with English Introduction, Translation, Notes, and Summary. By THOMAS C. SANDARS, M.A. 8vo. 18*s.*

Kant.—Works by IMMANUEL KANT.

> CRITIQUE OF PRACTICAL REASON, AND OTHER WORKS ON THE THEORY OF ETHICS. Translated by T. K. ABBOTT, B.D. With Memoir. 8vo., 12*s.* 6*d.*
>
> INTRODUCTION TO LOGIC, AND HIS ESSAY ON THE MISTAKEN SUBTILTY OF THE FOUR FIGURES. Translated by T. K. ABBOTT, and with Notes by S. T. COLERIDGE. 8vo., 6*s.*

Killick.—HANDBOOK TO MILL'S SYSTEM OF LOGIC. By Rev. A. H. KILLICK, M.A. Crown 8vo., 3*s.* 6*d.*

Ladd.—Works by GEORGE TURNBULL LADD.

> ELEMENTS OF PHYSIOLOGICAL PSYCHOLOGY. 8vo., 21*s.*
>
> OUTLINES OF PHYSIOLOGICAL PSYCHOLOGY. A Text-Book of Mental Science for Academies and Colleges. 8vo., 12*s.*

Lewes.—THE HISTORY OF PHILOSOPHY, from Thales to Comte. By GEORGE HENRY LEWES. 2 vols. 8vo., 32*s.*

Max Müller.—Works by F. MAX MÜLLER.

> THE SCIENCE OF THOUGHT. 8vo., 21*s.*
>
> THREE INTRODUCTORY LECTURES ON THE SCIENCE OF THOUGHT. 8vo., 2*s.* 6*d.*

Mill.—ANALYSIS OF THE PHENOMENA OF THE HUMAN MIND. By JAMES MILL. 2 vols. 8vo., 28*s.*

Mill.—Works by JOHN STUART MILL.

> A SYSTEM OF LOGIC. Cr. 8vo., 3*s.* 6*d.*
>
> ON LIBERTY. Cr. 8vo., 1*s.* 4*d.*
>
> ON REPRESENTATIVE GOVERNMENT. Crown 8vo., 2*s.*
>
> UTILITARIANISM. 8vo., 5*s.*
>
> EXAMINATION OF SIR WILLIAM HAMILTON'S PHILOSOPHY. 8vo., 16*s.*
>
> NATURE, THE UTILITY OF RELIGION, AND THEISM. Three Essays. 8vo., 5*s.*

Monck.—INTRODUCTION TO LOGIC. By H. S. MONCK. Crown 8vo., 5*s.*

Ribot.—THE PSYCHOLOGY OF ATTENTION. By TH. RIBOT. Cr. 8vo., 3*s.*

Sidgwick.—DISTINCTION : and the Criticism of Belief. By ALFRED SIDGWICK. Crown 8vo., 6*s.*

Stock.—DEDUCTIVE LOGIC. By ST. GEORGE STOCK. Fcp. 8vo., 3*s.* 6*d.*

Sully.—Works by JAMES SULLY, Grote Professor of Mind and Logic at University College, London.

> THE HUMAN MIND : a Text-book of Psychology. 2 vols. 8vo., 21*s.*
>
> OUTLINES OF PSYCHOLOGY. 8vo., 9*s.*
>
> THE TEACHER'S HANDBOOK OF PSYCHOLOGY. Crown 8vo., 5*s.*

Swinburne.—PICTURE LOGIC : an Attempt to Popularise the Science of Reasoning. By ALFRED JAMES SWINBURNE, M.A. With 23 Woodcuts. Post 8vo., 5*s.*

Thompson.—Works by DANIEL GREENLEAF THOMPSON.

> A SYSTEM OF PSYCHOLOGY. 2 vols. 8vo., 36*s.*
>
> THE RELIGIOUS SENTIMENTS OF THE HUMAN MIND. 8vo., 7*s.* 6*d.*
>
> THE PROBLEM OF EVIL : an Introduction to the Practical Sciences. 8vo., 10*s.* 6*d.*

Mental, Moral and Political Philosophy—*continued.*

Thompson. – Works by DANIEL GREENLEAF THOMPSON—*continued.*

SOCIAL PROGRESS. 8vo., 7s. 6d.

THE PHILOSOPHY OF FICTION IN LITERATURE. Crown 8vo., 6s.

Thomson. – OUTLINES OF THE NECESSARY LAWS OF THOUGHT: a Treatise on Pure and Applied Logic. By WILLIAM THOMSON, D.D., formerly Lord Archbishop of York. Post 8vo., 6s.

Webb.—THE VEIL OF ISIS: a Series of Essays on Idealism. By T. E. WEBB. 8vo., 10s. 6d.

Whately.—Works by R. WHATELY, formerly Archbishop of Dublin.

BACON'S ESSAYS. With Annotation. By R. WHATELY. 8vo., 10s. 6d.

ELEMENTS OF LOGIC. Cr. 8vo., 4s. 6d.

ELEMENTS OF RHETORIC. Cr. 8vo., 4s. 6d.

LESSONS ON REASONING. Fcp. 8vo., 1s. 6d.

Zeller.—Works by Dr. EDWARD ZELLER, Professor in the University of Berlin.

HISTORY OF ECLECTICISM IN GREEK PHILOSOPHY. Translated by SARAH F. ALLEYNE. Cr. 8vo., 10s. 6d.

THE STOICS, EPICUREANS, AND SCEPTICS. Translated by the Rev. O. J. REICHEL, M.A. Crown 8vo., 15s.

OUTLINES OF THE HISTORY OF GREEK PHILOSOPHY. Translated by SARAH F. ALLEYNE and EVELYN ABBOTT. Crown 8vo., 10s. 6d.

PLATO AND THE OLDER ACADEMY. Translated by SARAH F. ALLEYNE and ALFRED GOODWIN, B.A. Crown 8vo., 18s.

SOCRATES AND THE SOCRATIC SCHOOLS. Translated by the Rev. O. J. REICHEL, M.A. Crown 8vo., 10s. 6d.

THE PRE-SOCRATIC SCHOOLS: a History of Greek Philosophy from the Earliest Period to the time of Socrates. Translated by SARAH F. ALLEYNE. 2 vols. Crown 8vo., 30s.

MANUALS OF CATHOLIC PHILOSOPHY.
(Stonyhurst Series.)

A MANUAL OF POLITICAL ECONOMY. By C. S. DEVAS, M.A. Cr. 8vo., 6s. 6d.

FIRST PRINCIPLES OF KNOWLEDGE. By JOHN RICKABY, S J. Crown 8vo., 5s.

GENERAL METAPHYSICS. By JOHN RICKABY, S.J. Crown 8vo., 5s.

LOGIC. By RICHARD F. CLARKE, S.J. Crown 8vo., 5s.

MORAL PHILOSOPHY (ETHICS AND NATURAL LAW. By JOSEPH RICKABY, S.J. Crown 8vo., 5s.

NATURAL THEOLOGY. By BERNARD BOEDDER, S.J. Crown 8vo., 6s. 6d.

PSYCHOLOGY. By MICHAEL MAHER, S.J. Crown 8vo., 6s. 6d.

History and Science of Language, &c.

Davidson.—LEADING AND IMPORTANT ENGLISH WORDS: Explained and Exemplified. By WILLIAM L. DAVIDSON, M.A. Fcp. 8vo., 3s. 6d.

Farrar.—LANGUAGE AND LANGUAGES: By F. W. FARRAR, D.D., F.R.S., Cr. 8vo., 6s.

Graham.—ENGLISH SYNONYMS, Classified and Explained : with Practical Exercises. By G. F. GRAHAM. Fcp. 8vo., 6s.

Max Müller.—Works by F. MAX MÜLLER.

SELECTED ESSAYS ON LANGUAGE, MYTHOLOGY AND RELIGION. 2 vols. Crown 8vo., 16s. *[continued.*

History and Science of Language, &c.—*continued.*

Max Müller.—Works by F. MAX MÜLLER—*continued.*

THE SCIENCE OF LANGUAGE, Founded on Lectures delivered at the Royal Institution in 1861 and 1863. 2 vols. Crown 8vo., 21s.

BIOGRAPHIES OF WORDS, AND THE HOME OF THE ARYAS. Crown 8vo., 7s. 6d.

THREE LECTURES ON THE SCIENCE OF LANGUAGE, AND ITS PLACE IN GENERAL EDUCATION, delivered at Oxford, 1889. Crown 8vo., 3s.

Roget.— THESAURUS OF ENGLISH WORDS AND PHRASES. Classified and Arranged so as to Facilitate the Expression of Ideas and assist in Literary Composition. By PETER MARK ROGET. M.D., F.R.S. Recomposed throughout, enlarged and improved, partly from the Author's Notes, and with a full Index, by the Author's Son, JOHN LEWIS ROGET. Crown 8vo.. 10s. 6d.

Strong, Logeman, and Wheeler. INTRODUCTION TO THE STUDY OF THE HISTORY OF LANGUAGE. By HERBERT A. STRONG. M.A., LL.D., WILLEM S. LOGEMAN, and BENJAMIN IDE WHEELER. 8vo., 10s. 6d.

Whately.—ENGLISH SYNONYMS. By E. JANE WHATELY. Fcp. 8vo., 3s.

Political Economy and Economics.

Ashley.—ENGLISH ECONOMIC HISTORY AND THEORY. By W. J. ASHLEY, M.A. Crown 8vo., Part I., 5s. Part II., 10s. 6d.

Bagehot. — ECONOMIC STUDIES. By WALTER BAGEHOT. 8vo., 10s. 6d.

Crump.—AN INVESTIGATION INTO THE CAUSES OF THE GREAT FALL IN PRICES which took place coincidently with the Demonetisation of Silver by Germany. By ARTHUR CRUMP. 8vo., 6s.

Devas.—A MANUAL OF POLITICAL ECONOMY. By C. S. DEVAS, M.A. Crown 8vo., 6s. 6d. (*Manuals of Catholic Philosophy.*)

Dowell.—A HISTORY OF TAXATION AND TAXES IN ENGLAND, from the Earliest Times to the Year 1885. By STEPHEN DOWELL. (4 vols. 8vo.) Vols. I. and II. The History of Taxation, 21s. Vols. III. and IV. The History of Taxes, 21s.

Jordan.—THE STANDARD OF VALUE. By WILLIAM LEIGHTON JORDAN. 8vo., 6s.

Leslie.—ESSAYS IN POLITICAL ECONOMY. By T. E. CLIFFE LESLIE. 8vo., 6s. 6d.

Macleod.—Works by HENRY DUNNING MACLEOD, M.A.

THE ELEMENTS OF BANKING. Crown 8vo., 3s. 6d.

THE THEORY AND PRACTICE OF BANKING. Vol. I. 8vo., 12s. Vol. II. 14s.

THE THEORY OF CREDIT. 8vo. Vol. I. 10s. net. Vol. II., Part I., 4s. 6d. Vol. II. Part II., 10s. 6d.

Meath.—Works by The EARL OF MEATH.

SOCIAL ARROWS: Reprinted Articles on various Social Subjects. Crown 8vo., 5s.

PROSPERITY OR PAUPERISM? Physical, Industrial, and Technical Training. 8vo., 5s.

Mill.—POLITICAL ECONOMY. By JOHN STUART MILL.

Silver Library Edition. Crown 8vo., 3s. 6d.

Library Edition. 2 vols. 8vo., 30s.

Shirres.—AN ANALYSIS OF THE IDEAS OF ECONOMICS. By L. P. SHIRRES, B.A., sometime Finance Under Secretary of the Government of Bengal. Crown 8vo., 6s.

Political Economy and Economics—*continued*.

Symes.—POLITICAL ECONOMY : a Short Text-book of Political Economy. With Problems for Solution, and Hints for Supplementary Reading. By J. E. SYMES, M.A., of University College, Nottingham. Crown 8vo., 2s. 6d.

Toynbee.—LECTURES ON THE IN-DUSTRIAL REVOLUTION OF THE 18th CENTURY IN ENGLAND. By ARNOLD TOYNBEE. 8vo., 10s. 6d.

Wilson.—Works by A. J. WILSON. Chiefly reprinted from *The Investors' Review.*

PRACTICAL HINTS TO SMALL IN-VESTORS. Crown 8vo., 1s.

PLAIN ADVICE ABOUT LIFE INSURANCE. Crown 8vo., 1s.

Wolff.—PEOPLE'S BANKS : a Record of Social and Economic Success. By HENRY W. WOLFF. 8vo., 7s. 6d.

Evolution, Anthropology, &c.

Clodd.—THE STORY OF CREATION : a Plain Account of Evolution. By EDWARD CLODD. With 77 Illustrations. Crown 8vo., 3s. 6d.

Huth.—THE MARRIAGE OF NEAR KIN, considered with Respect to the Law of Nations, the Result of Experience, and the Teachings of Biology. By ALFRED HENRY HUTH. Royal 8vo., 21s.

Lang.—CUSTOM AND MYTH : Studies of Early Usage and Belief. By ANDREW LANG, M.A. With 15 Illustrations. Crown 8vo., 3s. 6d.

Lubbock.—THE ORIGIN OF CIVILISA-TION and the Primitive Condition of Man. By Sir J. LUBBOCK, Bart., M.P. With 5 Plates and 20 Illustrations in the Text. 8vo. 18s.

Romanes.—Works by GEORGE JOHN ROMANES, M.A., LL.D., F.R.S.

DARWIN, AND AFTER DARWIN : an Ex-position of the Darwinian Theory, and a Discussion on Post-Darwinian Questions. Part I. The Darwinian Theory. With Portrait of Darwin and 125 Illustrations. Crown 8vo., 10s. 6d.

AN EXAMINATION OF WEISMANNISM. Crown 8vo., 6s.

Classical Literature.

Abbott.—HELLENICA. A Collection of Essays on Greek Poetry, Philosophy, History, and Religion. Edited by EVELYN ABBOTT, M.A., LL.D. 8vo., 16s.

Æschylus.—EUMENIDES OF ÆSCHY-LUS. With Metrical English Translation. By J. F. DAVIES. 8vo., 7s.

Aristophanes.—The ACHARNIANS OF ARISTOPHANES, translated into English Verse. By R. Y. TYRRELL. Crown 8vo., 1s.

Becker.—Works by Professor BECKER.

GALLUS : or, Roman Scenes in the Time of Augustus. Illustrated. Post 8vo., 7s. 6d.

CHARICLES : or, Illustrations of the Private Life of the Ancient Greeks. Illustrated. Post 8vo., 7s. 6d.

Cicero.—CICERO'S CORRESPONDENCE. By R. Y. TYRRELL. Vols. I., II., III. 8vo., each 12s.

Clerke.—FAMILIAR STUDIES IN HOMER. By AGNES M. CLERKE. Cr. 8vo., 7s. 6d.

Farnell.—GREEK LYRIC POETRY : a Complete Collection of the Surviving Passages from the Greek Song-Writing. Arranged with Prefatory Articles, In-troductory Matter and Commentary. By GEORGE S. FARNELL, M.A. With 5 Plates. 8vo., 16s.

Harrison.—MYTHS OF THE ODYSSEY. IN ART AND LITERATURE. By JANE E. HARRISON. Illustrated with Out-line Drawings. 8vo., 18s.

Lang.—HOMER AND THE EPIC By ANDREW LANG. Crown 8vo., 9s. net.

Classical Literature—*continued.*

Mackail.—SELECT EPIGRAMS FROM THE GREEK ANTHOLOGY. By J. W. MACKAIL, Fellow of Balliol College, Oxford. Edited with a Revised Text, Introduction, Translation, and Notes. 8vo., 16*s.*

Plato.—PARMENIDES OF PLATO, Text, with Introduction, Analysis, &c. By T. MAGUIRE. 8vo., 7*s.* 6*d.*

Rich.—A DICTIONARY OF ROMAN AND GREEK ANTIQUITIES. By A. RICH, B.A. With 2000 Woodcuts. Crown 8vo., 7*s.* 6*d.*

Sophocles.—Translated into English Verse. By ROBERT WHITELAW, M.A., Assistant Master in Rugby School: late Fellow of Trinity College, Cambridge. Crown 8vo., 8*s.* 6*d.*

Tyrrell.—TRANSLATIONS INTO GREEK AND LATIN VERSE. Edited by R. Y. TYRRELL. 8vo., 6*s.*

Virgil.—THE ÆNEID OF VIRGIL. Translated into English Verse by JOHN CONINGTON. Crown 8vo., 6*s.*

THE POEMS OF VIRGIL. Translated into English Prose by JOHN CONINGTON. Crown 8vo., 6*s.*

THE ÆNEID OF VIRGIL, freely translated into English Blank Verse. By W. J. THORNHILL. Crown 8vo., 7*s.* 6*d.*

THE ÆNEID OF VIRGIL. Books I. to VI. Translated into English Verse by JAMES RHOADES. Crown 8vo., 5*s.*

Wilkins.—THE GROWTH OF THE HOMERIC POEMS. By G. WILKINS. 8vo. 6*s.*

Poetry and the Drama.

Allingham.—Works by WILLIAM ALLINGHAM.

IRISH SONGS AND POEMS. With Frontispiece of the Waterfall of Asaroe. Fcp. 8vo., 6*s.*

LAURENCE BLOOMFIELD. With Portrait of the Author. Fcp. 8vo., 3*s.* 6*d.*

FLOWER PIECES; DAY AND NIGHT SONGS; BALLADS. With 2 Designs by D. G. ROSETTI. Fcp. 8vo., 6*s.*; large paper edition, 12*s.*

LIFE AND PHANTASY: with Frontispiece by Sir J. E. MILLAIS, Bart., and Design by ARTHUR HUGHES. Fcp. 8vo., 6*s.*; large paper edition, 12*s.*

THOUGHT AND WORD, AND ASHBY MANOR: a Play. With Portrait of the Author (1865), and four Theatrical Scenes drawn by Mr. Allingham. Fcp. 8vo., 6*s.*; large paper edition, 12*s.*

BLACKBERRIES. Imperial 16mo., 6*s.*

Sets of the above 6 vols. may be had in uniform half-parchment binding, price 30*s.*

Armstrong.—Works by G. F. SAVAGE-ARMSTRONG.

POEMS: Lyrical and Dramatic. Fcp. 8vo., 6*s.*

KING SAUL. (The Tragedy of Israel, Part I.) Fcp. 8vo. 5*s.*

KING DAVID. (The Tragedy of Israel, Part II.) Fcp. 8vo., 6*s.*

KING SOLOMON. (The Tragedy of Israel, Part III.) Fcp. 8vo., 6*s.*

UGONE: a Tragedy. Fcp. 8vo., 6*s.*

A GARLAND FROM GREECE: Poems. Fcp. 8vo., 7*s.* 6*d.*

STORIES OF WICKLOW: Poems. Fcp. 8vo., 7*s.* 6*d.*

MEPHISTOPHELES IN BROADCLOTH: a Satire. Fcp. 8vo., 4*s.*

ONE IN THE INFINITE: a Poem. Cr. 8vo., 7*s.* 6*d.*

Armstrong.—THE POETICAL WORKS OF EDMUND J. ARMSTRONG. Fcp. 8vo., 5*s.*

Poetry and the Drama—*continued.*

Arnold.—Works by Sir EDWIN ARNOLD, K.C.I.E., Author of 'The Light of Asia,' &c.

THE LIGHT OF THE WORLD: or, the Great Consummation. A Poem. Crown 8vo., 7s. 6d. net.
Presentation Edition. With 14 Illustrations by W. HOLMAN HUNT, &c., 4to., 20s. net.

POTIPHAR'S WIFE, and other Poems. Crown 8vo., 5s. net.

ADZUMA: or, the Japanese Wife. A Play. Crown 8vo., 6s. 6d. net.

Barrow.—THE SEVEN CITIES OF THE DEAD, and other Poems. By Sir JOHN CROKER BARROW, Bart. Fcp. 8vo., 5s.

Bell.—Works by Mrs. HUGH BELL.

CHAMBER COMEDIES: a Collection of Plays and Monologues for the Drawing Room. Crown 8vo., 6s.

NURSERY COMEDIES: Twelve Tiny Plays for Children. Fcp. 8vo., 1s. 6d.

Björnsen.—PASTOR SANG: a Play. By BJÖRNSTJERNE BJÖRNSEN. Translated by WILLIAM WILSON. Cr. 8vo., 5s.

Dante.—LA COMMEDIA DI DANTE. A New Text, carefully revised with the aid of the most recent Editions and Collations. Small 8vo., 6s.

Goethe.

FAUST, Part I., the German Text, with Introduction and Notes. By ALBERT M. SELSS, Ph.D., M.A. Cr. 8vo., 5s.

FAUST. Translated, with Notes. By T. E. WEBB. 8vo., 12s. 6d.

FAUST. The First Part. A New Translation, chiefly in Blank Verse; with Introduction and Notes. By JAMES ADEY BIRDS. Cr. 8vo., 6s.

FAUST. The Second Part. A New Translation in Verse. By JAMES ADEY BIRDS. Crown 8vo., 6s.

Haggard. LIFE AND ITS AUTHOR: an Essay in Verse. By ELLA HAGGARD. With a Memoir by H. RIDER HAGGARD, and Portrait. Fcp. 8vo., 3s. 6d.

Ingelow.—Works by JEAN INGELOW.

POETICAL WORKS. 2 vols. Fcp. 8vo., 12s.

LYRICAL AND OTHER POEMS. Selected from the Writings of JEAN INGELOW. Fcp. 8vo., 2s. 6d. cloth plain, 3s. cloth gilt.

Lang.—Works by ANDREW LANG.

GRASS OF PARNASSUS. Fcp. 8vo., 2s. 6d. net.

BALLADS OF BOOKS. Edited by ANDREW LANG. Fcp. 8vo., 6s.

THE BLUE POETRY BOOK. Edited by ANDREW LANG. With 12 Plates and 88 Illustrations in the Text. Crown 8vo., 6s.

Special Edition, printed on Indian paper. With Notes, but without Illustrations. Crown 8vo., 7s. 6d.

Lecky.—POEMS. By W. E. H. LECKY. Fcp. 8vo., 5s.

Leyton.—Works by FRANK LEYTON.

THE SHADOWS OF THE LAKE, and other Poems. Crown 8vo., 7s. 6d.
Cheap Edition. Crown 8vo., 3s. 6d.

SKELETON LEAVES: Poems. Crown 8vo., 6s.

Longfellow.—THE HANGING OF THE CRANE, and other Poems of the Home. By HENRY W. LONGFELLOW. With Photogravure Illustrations. 16mo., 5s. 6d. net. [*Ready.*]

Lytton.—Works by THE EARL OF LYTTON (OWEN MEREDITH).

MARAH. Fcp. 8vo., 6s. 6d.

KING POPPY: a Fantasia. With 1 Plate and Design on Title-Page by ED. BURNE-JONES, A.R.A. Crown 8vo., 10s. 6d.

THE WANDERER. Cr. 8vo., 10s. 6d.

Macaulay.—LAYS OF ANCIENT ROME, &c. By Lord MACAULAY.

Illustrated by G. SCHARF. Fcp. 4to., 10s. 6d.

———————— Bijou Edition.
18mo., 2s. 6d., gilt top.

———————— Popular Edition.
Fcp. 4to., 6d. sewed, 1s. cloth.

Illustrated by J. R. WEGUELIN. Crown 8vo., 3s. 6d.

Annotated Edition. Fcp. 8vo., 1s. sewed, 1s. 6d. cloth.

Nesbit.—LAYS AND LEGENDS. by E. NESBIT (Mrs. HUBERT BLAND). First Series. Crown 8vo., 3s. 6d. Second Series, with Portrait. Crown 8vo., 5s.

Piatt.—AN ENCHANTED CASTLE, AND OTHER POEMS: Pictures, Portraits and People in Ireland. By SARAH PIATT. Crown 8vo., 3s. 6d.

Poetry and the Drama—*continued*.

Piatt.—Works by JOHN JAMES PIATT.

IDYLS AND LYRICS OF THE OHIO VALLEY. Crown 8vo., 5s.

LITTLE NEW WORLD IDYLS. Cr. 8vo., 5s.

Rhoades.—TERESA AND OTHER POEMS. By JAMES RHOADES. Crown 8vo., 3s. 6d.

Riley.—Works by JAMES WHITCOMB RILEY.

POEMS HERE AT HOME. Fcap. 8vo., 6s. net.

OLD FASHIONED ROSES : Poems. 12mo., 5s.

Roberts. — SONGS OF THE COMMON DAY, AND AVE : an Ode for the Shelley Centenary. By CHARLES G. D. ROBERTS. Crown 8vo., 3s. 6d.

Shakespeare.—BOWDLER'S FAMILY SHAKESPEARE. With 36 Woodcuts. 1 vol. 8vo., 14s. Or in 6 vols. Fcp. 8vo., 21s.

THE SHAKESPEARE BIRTHDAY BOOK. By MARY F. DUNBAR. 32mo., 1s. 6d. Drawing-Room Edition, with Photographs. Fcp. 8vo., 10s. 6d.

Stevenson.—A CHILD'S GARDEN OF VERSES. By ROBERT LOUIS STEVENSON. Small fcp. 8vo., 5s.

Whittier.—Works by JOHN GREENLEAF WHITTIER.

SNOW-BOUND : a Winter Idyl. With 10 Photogravure Illustrations by E. H. GARRETT. Crown 8vo., 6s. 6d.

AT SUNDOWN : A Poem. With Portrait and 8 Illustrations by E. H. GARRETT. Crown 8vo., 5s. 6d. net.

Works of Fiction, Humour, &c.

Anstey.—Works by F. ANSTEY, Author of ' Vice Versâ '.

THE BLACK POODLE, and other Stories. Crown 8vo., 2s. boards, 2s. 6d. cloth.

VOCES POPULI. Reprinted from ' Punch '. With Illustrations by J. BERNARD PARTRIDGE. First Series. Fcp. 4to., 5s. Second Series. Fcp. 4to., 6s.

THE TRAVELLING COMPANIONS. Reprinted from ' Punch '. With Illustrations by J. BERNARD PARTRIDGE. Post 4to., 5s.

THE MAN FROM BLANKLEY'S : a Story in Scenes, and other Sketches. With 24 Illustrations by J. BERNARD PARTRIDGE. Fcp. 4to., 6s.

ATELIER (THE) DU LYS : or, an Art Student in the Reign of Terror. Crown 8vo., 2s. 6d.

BY THE SAME AUTHOR.

MADEMOISELLE MORI : a Tale of Modern Rome. Crown 8vo., 2s. 6d.

BY THE SAME AUTHOR—*continued.*

THAT CHILD. Illustrated by GORDON BROWNE. Crown 8vo., 2s. 6d.

UNDER A CLOUD. Cr. 8vo., 2s. 6d.

THE FIDDLER OF LUGAU. With Illustrations by W. RALSTON. Crown 8vo., 2s. 6d.

A CHILD OF THE REVOLUTION. With Illustrations by C. J. STANILAND. Crown 8vo., 2s. 6d.

HESTER'S VENTURE : a Novel. Crown 8vo., 2s. 6d.

IN THE OLDEN TIME : a Tale of the Peasant War in Germany. Crown 8vo., 2s. 6d.

THE YOUNGER SISTER : a Tale. Cr. 8vo., 6s.

Baker.—BY THE WESTERN SEA. By JAMES BAKER, Author of ' John Westacott '. Crown 8vo., 3s. 6d.

Works of Fiction, Humour, &c.—*continued.*

Beaconsfield.—Works by the Earl of BEACONSFIELD.

NOVELS AND TALES. Cheap Edition. Complete in 11 vols. Cr. 8vo., 1s. 6d. each.

Vivian Grey.
The Young Duke, &c.
Alroy, Ixion, &c.
Henrietta Temple.
Contarini Fleming, &c.
Venetia. Tancred.
Coningsby. Sybil.
Lothair. Endymion.

NOVELS AND TALES. The Hughenden Edition. With 2 Portraits and 11 Vignettes. 11 vols. Cr. 8vo., 42s.

Comyn.—ATHERSTONE PRIORY: a Tale. By L. N. COMYN. Crown 8vo., 2s. 6d.

Deland.—Works by MARGARET DE-LAND, Author of 'John Ward'.

THE STORY OF A CHILD. Cr. 8vo., 5s.

MR. TOMMY DOVE, and other Stories. Crown 8vo., 6s.

Dougall.—Works by L. DOUGALL.

BEGGARS ALL. Crown 8vo., 3s. 6d.

WHAT NECESSITY KNOWS. 3 vols. Crown 8vo., £1 5s. 6d.

Doyle.—Works by A. CONAN DOYLE.

MICAH CLARKE: a Tale of Monmouth's Rebellion. With Frontispiece and Vignette. Cr. 8vo., 3s. 6d.

THE CAPTAIN OF THE POLESTAR, and other Tales. Cr. 8vo., 3s. 6d.

THE REFUGEES: a Tale of Two Continents. Cr. 8vo., 6s.

Farrar.—DARKNESS AND DAWN: or, Scenes in the Days of Nero. An Historic Tale. By Archdeacon FARRAR. Cr. 8vo., 7s. 6d.

Froude.—THE TWO CHIEFS OF DUN-BOY: an Irish Romance of the Last Century. By J. A. FROUDE. Cr. 8vo., 3s. 6d.

Haggard.—Works by H. RIDER HAG-GARD.

SHE. With 32 Illustrations by M. GREIFFENHAGEN and C. H. M. KERR. Cr. 8vo., 3s. 6d.

ALLAN QUATERMAIN. With 31 Illustrations by C. H. M. KERR. Cr. 8vo., 3s. 6d.

MAIWA'S REVENGE; or, The War of the Little Hand. Cr. 8vo., 1s. boards, 1s. 6d. cloth.

COLONEL QUARITCH, V.C. Cr. 8vo., 3s. 6d.

Haggard.—Works by H. RIDER HAG-GARD—*continued.*

CLEOPATRA. With 29 Full-page Illustrations by M. GREIFFENHAGEN and R. CATON WOODVILLE. Cr. 8vo., 3s. 6d.

BEATRICE. Cr. 8vo., 3s. 6d.

ERIC BRIGHTEYES. With 17 Plates and 34 Illustrations in the Text by LANCELOT SPEED. Cr. 8vo., 3s. 6d.

NADA THE LILY. With 23 Illustrations by C. H. M. KERR. Cr. 8vo., 6s.

MONTEZUMA'S DAUGHTER. With Illustrations by M. GREIFFENHAGEN. Cr. 8vo., 6s.

Haggard and Lang.—THE WORLD'S DESIRE. By H. RIDER HAGGARD and ANDREW LANG. Cr. 8vo., 6s.

Harte.—IN THE CARQUINEZ WOODS, and other Stories. By BRET HARTE. Cr. 8vo., 3s. 6d.

KEITH DERAMORE: a Novel. By the Author of 'Miss Molly'. Cr. 8vo., 6s.

Lyall.—THE AUTOBIOGRAPHY OF A SLANDER. By EDNA LYALL, Author of 'Donovan,' &c. Fcp. 8vo., 1s. sewed. Presentation Edition. With 20 Illustrations by LANCELOT SPEED. Cr. 8vo., 5s.

Melville.—Works by G. J. WHYTE MELVILLE.

The Gladiators.
The Interpreter.
Good for Nothing.
The Queen's Maries.
Holmby House.
Kate Coventry.
Digby Grand.
General Bounce.

Cr. 8vo., 1s. 6d. each.

Oliphant.—Works by Mrs. OLIPHANT.

MADAM. Cr. 8vo., 1s. 6d.

IN TRUST. Cr. 8vo., 1s. 6d.

Parr.—CAN THIS BE LOVE? By Mrs. PARR, Author of 'Dorothy Fox'. Cr. 8vo., 6s.

Payn.—Works by JAMES PAYN.

THE LUCK OF THE DARRELLS. Cr. 8vo., 1s. 6d.

THICKER THAN WATER. Cr. 8vo., 1s. 6d.

Phillipps-Wolley.—SNAP: a Legend of the Lone Mountain. By C. PHIL-LIPPS-WOLLEY. With 13 Illustrations by H. G. WILLINK. Cr. 8vo., 3s. 6d.

Robertson.—THE KIDNAPPED SQUATTER, and other Australian Tales. By A. ROBERTSON. Cr. 8vo., 6s.

Works of Fiction, Humour, &c.—*continued.*

Sewell.—Works by ELIZABETH M. SEWELL.

A Glimpse of the World. | Amy Herbert.
Laneton Parsonage. | Cleve Hall.
Margaret Percival. | Gertrude.
Katharine Ashton. | Home Life.
The Earl's Daughter. | After Life.
The Experience of Life. | Ursula. Ivors.

Cr. 8vo., 1*s.* 6*d.* each cloth plain. 2*s.* 6*d.* each cloth extra, gilt edges.

Stevenson.—Works by ROBERT LOUIS STEVENSON.

STRANGE CASE OF DR. JEKYLL AND MR. HYDE. Fcp. 8vo., 1*s.* sewed. 1*s.* 6*d.* cloth.

THE DYNAMITER. Fcp. 8vo., 1*s.* sewed, 1*s.* 6*d.* cloth.

Stevenson and Osbourne.—THE WRONG BOX. By ROBERT LOUIS STEVENSON and LLOYD OSBOURNE. Cr. 8vo., 3*s.* 6*d.*

Sturgis.—AFTER TWENTY YEARS, and other Stories. By JULIAN STURGIS. Cr. 8vo., 6*s.*

Suttner.—LAY DOWN YOUR ARMS *Die Waffen Nieder:* The Autobiography of Martha Tilling. By BERTHA VON STUTTNER. Translated by T. HOLMES. Cr. 8vo., 7*s.* 6*d.*

Thompson.—A MORAL DILEMMA: a Novel. By ANNIE THOMPSON. Cr. 8vo., 6*s.*

Tirebuck.—Works by WILLIAM TIREBUCK.

DORRIE. Crown 8vo., 6*s.*

SWEETHEART GWEN. Cr. 8vo., 6*s.*

Trollope.—Works by ANTHONY TROLLOPE.

THE WARDEN. Cr. 8vo., 1*s.* 6*d.*

BARCHESTER TOWERS. Cr. 8vo., 1*s.* 6*d.*

Walford.—Works by L. B. WALFORD, Author of ' Mr. Smith '.

THE MISCHIEF OF MONICA: a Novel. Cr. 8vo., 2*s.* 6*d.*

THE ONE GOOD GUEST: a Story. Cr. 8vo, 6*s.*

West.—HALF-HOURS WITH THE MILLIONAIRES: Showing how much harder it is to spend a million than to make it. Edited by B. B. WEST. Cr. 8vo., 6*s.*

Weyman.—Works by STANLEY J. WEYMAN.

THE HOUSE OF THE WOLF: a Romance. Cr. 8vo., 3*s.* 6*d.*

A GENTLEMAN OF FRANCE.. 3 vols. Cr. 8vo.

Popular Science (Natural History, &c.).

Butler.—OUR HOUSEHOLD INSECTS. By E. A. BUTLER. With 7 Plates and 113 Illustrations in the Text. Crown 8vo., 6*s.*

Furneaux.—THE OUTDOOR WORLD; or, The Young Collector's Handbook. By W. FURNEAUX, F.R.G.S. With 16 Coloured Plates, 2 Plain Plates, and 549 Illustrations in the Text. Crown 8vo., 7*s.* 6*d.*

Hartwig.—Works by Dr. GEORGE HARTWIG.

THE SEA AND ITS LIVING WONDERS. With 12 Plates and 303 Woodcuts. 8vo., 7*s.* net.

THE TROPICAL WORLD. With 8 Plates and 172 Woodcuts. 8vo., 7*s.* net.

THE POLAR WORLD. With 3 Maps, 8 Plates and 85 Woodcuts. 8vo., 7*s.* net.

Hartwig.—Works by Dr. GEORGE HARTWIG—*continued.*

THE SUBTERRANEAN WORLD. With 3 Maps and 80 Woodcuts. 8vo., 7*s.* net.

THE AERIAL WORLD. With Map, 8 Plates and 60 Woodcuts. 8vo., 7*s.* net.

HEROES OF THE POLAR WORLD. 19 Illustrations. Crown 8vo., 2*s.*

WONDERS OF THE TROPICAL FORESTS. 40 Illustrations. Crown 8vo., 2*s.*

WORKERS UNDER THE GROUND. 29 Illustrations. Crown 8vo., 2*s.*

MARVELS OVER OUR HEADS. 29 Illustrations. Crown 8vo., 2*s.*

SEA MONSTERS AND SEA BIRDS. 75 Illustrations. Crown 8vo., 2*s.* 6*d.*

Popular Science (Natural History, &c.).

Hartwig.—Works by Dr. GEORGE HARTWIG—*continued.*

DENIZENS OF THE DEEP. 117 Illustrations. Crown 8vo., 2s. 6d.

VOLCANOES AND EARTHQUAKES. 30 Illustrations. Crown 8vo., 2s. 6d.

WILD ANIMALS OF THE TROPICS. 66 Illustrations. Crown 8vo., 3s. 6d.

Helmholtz.—POPULAR LECTURES ON SCIENTIFIC SUBJECTS. By Professor HELMHOLTZ. With 68 Woodcuts. 2 vols. Crown 8vo., 3s. 6d. each.

Lydekker.—PHASES OF ANIMAL LIFE, PAST AND PRESENT. By R. LYDEKKER, B.A. With 82 Illustrations. Crown 8vo., 6s.

Proctor.—Works by RICHARD A. PROCTOR.

And see Messrs. Longmans & Co.'s Catalogue of Scientific Works.

LIGHT SCIENCE FOR LEISURE HOURS. Familiar Essays on Scientific Subjects. 3 vols. Crown 8vo., 5s. each.

CHANCE AND LUCK: a Discussion of the Laws of Luck, Coincidence, Wagers, Lotteries and the Fallacies of Gambling, &c. Cr. 8vo., 2s. boards, 2s. 6d. cloth.

ROUGH WAYS MADE SMOOTH. Familiar Essays on Scientific Subjects. Crown 8vo., 5s. Silver Library Edition. Crown 8vo., 3s. 6d.

PLEASANT WAYS IN SCIENCE. Cr. 8vo., 5s. Silver Library Edition. Crown 8vo., 3s. 6d.

THE GREAT PYRAMID, OBSERVATORY, TOMB AND TEMPLE. With Illustrations. Crown 8vo., 5s.

NATURE STUDIES. By R. A. PROCTOR, GRANT ALLEN, A. WILSON, T. FOSTER and E. CLODD. Crown 8vo., 5s. Silver Library Edition. Crown 8vo., 3s. 6d.

LEISURE READINGS. By R. A. PROCTOR, E. CLODD, A. WILSON, T. FOSTER, and A. C. RANYARD. Cr. 8vo., 5s.

Stanley.—A FAMILIAR HISTORY OF BIRDS. By E. STANLEY, D.D., formerly Bishop of Norwich. With Illustrations. Cr. 8vo., 3s. 6d.

Wood.—Works by the Rev. J. G. WOOD.

HOMES WITHOUT HANDS: a Description of the Habitation of Animals, classed according to the Principle of Construction. With 140 Illustrations. 8vo., 7s. net.

INSECTS AT HOME: a Popular Account of British Insects, their Structure, Habits and Transformations. With 700 Illustrations. 8vo., 7s. net.

INSECTS ABROAD: a Popular Account of Foreign Insects, their Structure, Habits and Transformations. With 600 Illustrations. 8vo., 7s. net.

BIBLE ANIMALS: a Description of every Living Creature mentioned in the Scriptures. With 112 Illustrations. 8vo., 7s. net.

PETLAND REVISITED. With 33 Illustrations. Cr. 8vo., 3s. 6d.

OUT OF DOORS; a Selection of Original Articles on Practical Natural History. With 11 Illustrations. Cr. 8vo., 3s. 6d.

STRANGE DWELLINGS: a Description of the Habitations of Animals, abridged from 'Homes without Hands'. With 60 Illustrations. Cr. 8vo., 3s. 6d.

BIRD LIFE OF THE BIBLE. 32 Illustrations. Cr. 8vo., 3s. 6d.

WONDERFUL NESTS. 30 Illustrations. Cr. 8vo., 3s. 6d.

HOMES UNDER THE GROUND. 28 Illustrations. Cr. 8vo., 3s. 6d.

WILD ANIMALS OF THE BIBLE. 29 Illustrations. Cr. 8vo., 3s. 6d.

DOMESTIC ANIMALS OF THE BIBLE. 23 Illustrations. Cr. 8vo., 3s. 6d.

THE BRANCH BUILDERS. 28 Illustrations. Cr. 8vo., 2s. 6d.

SOCIAL HABITATIONS AND PARASITIC NESTS. 18 Illustrations. Cr. 8vo., 2s.

Works of Reference.

Maunder's (Samuel) Treasuries.

BIOGRAPHICAL TREASURY. With Supplement brought down to 1889. By Rev. JAMES WOOD. Fcp. 8vo., 6s.

TREASURY OF NATURAL HISTORY: or, Popular Dictionary of Zoology. With 900 Woodcuts. Fcp. 8vo., 6s.

TREASURY OF GEOGRAPHY, Physical, Historical, Descriptive, and Political. With 7 Maps and 16 Plates. Fcp. 8vo., 6s.

THE TREASURY OF BIBLE KNOWLEDGE. By the Rev. J. AYRE, M.A. With 5 Maps, 15 plates, and 300 Woodcuts. Fcp. 8vo., 6s.

HISTORICAL TREASURY: Outlines of Universal History, Separate Histories of all Nations. Fcp. 8vo., 6s.

TREASURY OF KNOWLEDGE AND LIBRARY OF REFERENCE. Comprising an English Dictionary and Grammar, Universal Gazeteer, Classical Dictionary, Chronology, Law Dictionary, &c. Fcp. 8vo., 6s.

Maunder's (Samuel) Treasuries *—continued.*

SCIENTIFIC AND LITERARY TREASURY. Fcp. 8vo., 6s.

THE TREASURY OF BOTANY. Edited by J. LINDLEY, F.R.S., and T. MOORE, F.L.S. With 274 Woodcuts and 20 Steel Plates. 2 vols. Fcp. 8vo., 12s.

Roget.--THESAURUS OF ENGLISH WORDS AND PHRASES. Classified and Arranged so as to Facilitate the Expression of Ideas and assist in Literary Composition. By PETER MARK ROGET, M.D., F.R.S. Recomposed throughout, enlarged and improved, partly from the Author's Notes, and with a full Index, by the Author's Son, JOHN LEWIS ROGET. Crown 8vo., 10s. 6d.

Willich.—POPULAR TABLES for giving information for ascertaining the value of Lifehold, Leasehold, and Church Property, the Public Funds, &c. By CHARLES M. WILLICH. Edited by H. BENCE JONES. Crown 8vo., 10s. 6d.

Children's Books.

Crake.—Works by Rev. A. D. CRAKE.

EDWY THE FAIR; or, the First Chronicle of Æscendune. Crown 8vo., 2s. 6d.

ALFGAR THE DANE: or, the Second Chronicle of Æscendune. Cr. 8vo., 2s. 6d.

THE RIVAL HEIRS: being the Third and Last Chronicle of Æscendune. Cr. 8vo., 2s. 6d.

THE HOUSE OF WALDERNE. A Tale of the Cloister and the Forest in the Days of the Barons' Wars. Crown 8vo., 2s. 6d.

BRIAN FITZ-COUNT. A Story of Wallingford Castle and Dorchester Abbey. Cr. 8vo., 2s. 6d.

Lang.—Works edited by ANDREW LANG.

THE BLUE FAIRY BOOK. With 8 Plates and 130 Illustrations in the Text by H. J. FORD and G. P. JACOMB HOOD. Crown 8vo., 6s.

Lang.—Works edited by ANDREW LANG *—continued.*

THE RED FAIRY BOOK. With 4 Plates and 96 Illustrations in the Text by H. J. FORD and LANCELOT SPEED. Crown 8vo., 6s.

THE GREEN FAIRY BOOK. With 11 Plates and 88 Illustrations in the Text by H. J. FORD and L. BOGLE. Cr. 8vo., 6s.

THE BLUE POETRY BOOK. With 12 Plates and 88 Illustration in the Text by H. J. FORD and LANCELOT SPEED. Crown 8vo., 6s.

THE BLUE POETRY BOOK. School Edition, without Illustrations. Fcp. 8vo., 2s. 6d.

THE TRUE STORY BOOK. With 8 Plates and 58 Illustrations in the Text, by C. H. KERR, H. J. FORD, LANCELOT SPEED, and L. BOGLE. Crown 8vo., 6s.

Children's Books—*continued.*

Meade.—Works by L. T. MEADE.
DEB AND THE DUCHESS. Illustrated. Crown 8vo., 3*s.* 6*d.*
THE BERESFORD PRIZE. Illustrated. Cr. 8vo., 5*s.*
DADDY'S BOY. Illustrated. Crown 8vo., 3*s.* 6*d.*

Molesworth.—Works by Mrs. MOLESWORTH.
SILVERTHORNS. Illustrated. Cr. 8vo., 5*s.*
THE PALACE IN THE GARDEN. Illustrated. Crown 8vo., 5*s.*
THE THIRD MISS ST. QUENTIN. Cr. 8vo., 6*s.*
NEIGHBOURS. Illustrated. Cr. 8vo., 6*s.*
THE STORY OF A SPRING MORNING, &c. Illustrated. Crown 8vo., 5*s.*

Reader.— VOICES FROM FLOWERLAND : a Birthday Book and Language of Flowers. By EMILY E. READER. Illustrated by ADA BROOKE. Royal 16mo., cloth, 2*s.* 6*d.* ; vegetable vellum, 3*s.* 6*d.*

Stevenson.—Works by ROBERT LOUIS STEVENSON.
A CHILD'S GARDEN OF VERSES. Small fcp. 8vo., 5*s.*
A CHILD'S GARLAND OF SONGS, Gathered from ' A Child's Garden of Verses '. Set to Music by C. VILLIERS STANFORD, Mus. Doc. 4to., 2*s.* sewed ; 3*s.* 6*d.*, cloth gilt.

The Silver Library.

CROWN 8vo. 3*s.* 6*d.* EACH VOLUME.

Baker's (Sir S. W.) Eight Years in Ceylon. With 6 Illustrations. 3*s.* 6*d.*

Baker's (Sir S. W.) Rifle and Hound in Ceylon. With 6 Illustrations. 3*s.* 6*d.*

Baring-Gould's (Rev. S.) Curious Myths of the Middle Ages. 3*s.* 6*d.*

Baring-Gould's (Rev. S.) Origin and Development of Religious Belief. 2 vols. 3*s.* 6*d.* each.

Brassey's (Lady) A Voyage in the 'Sunbeam '. With 66 Illustrations. 3*s.* 6*d.*

Clodd's (E.) Story of Creation : a Plain Account of Evolution. With 77 Illustrations. 3*s.* 6*d.*

Conybeare (Rev. W. J.) and Howson's (Very Rev. J. S.) Life and Epistles of St. Paul. 46 Illustrations. 3*s.* 6*d.*

Dougall's (L.) Beggars All; a Novel. 3*s.* 6*d.*

Doyle's (A. Conan) Micah Clarke : a Tale of Monmouth's Rebellion. 3*s.* 6*d.*

Doyle's (A. Conan) The Captain of the Polestar, and other Tales. 3*s.* 6*d.*

Froude's (J. A.) Short Studies on Great Subjects. 4 vols. 3*s.* 6*d.* each.

Froude's (J. A.) Cæsar : a Sketch. 3*s.* 6*d.*

Froude's (J. A.) Thomas Carlyle: a History of his Life.
1795-1835. 2 vols. 7*s.*
1834-1881. 2 vols. 7*s.*

Froude's (J. A.) The Two Chiefs of Dunboy. 3*s.* 6*d.*

Froude's (J. A.) The History of England, from the Fall of Wolsey to the Defeat of the Spanish Armada. 12 vols. 3*s.* 6*d.* each.

Gleig's (Rev. G. R.) Life of the Duke of Wellington. With Portrait. 3*s.* 6*d.*

Haggard's (H. R.) She : A History of Adventure. 32 Illustrations. 3*s.* 6*d.*

Haggard's (H. R.) Allan Quatermain. With 20 Illustrations. 3*s.* 6*d.*

Haggard's (H. R.) Colonel Quaritch, V.C. : a Tale of Country Life. 3*s.* 6*d.*

Haggard's (H. R.) Cleopatra. With 29 Full-page Illustrations. 3*s.* 6*d.*

Haggard's (H. R.) Eric Brighteyes. With 51 Illustrations. 3*s.* 6*d.*

Haggard's (H. R.) Beatrice. 3*s.* 6*d.*

Harte's (Bret) In the Carquinez Woods, and other Stories. 3*s.* 6*d.*

Helmholtz's (Professor) Popular Lectures on Scientific Subjects. With 68 Woodcuts. 2 vols. 3*s.* 6*d.* each.

Howitt's (W.) Visits to Remarkable Places. 80 Illustrations. 3*s.* 6*d.*

Jefferies' (R.) The Story of My Heart: My Autobiography. With Portrait. 3*s.* 6*d.*

Jefferies' (R.) Field and Hedgerow. With Portrait. 3*s.* 6*d.*

Jefferies' (R.) Red Deer. With 17 Illustrations. 3*s.* 6*d.*

Jefferies' (R.) Wood Magic : a Fable. 3*s.* 6*d.*

Knight's (E. F.) The Cruise of the ' Alerte ': the Narrative of a Search for Treasure on the Desert Island of Trinidad. With 2 Maps and 23 Illustrations. 3*s.* 6*d.*

The Silver Library—*continued.*

Lang's (A.) Custom and Myth: Studies of Early Usage and Belief. 3s. 6d.

Lees (J. A.) and Clutterbuck's (W. J.) B.C. 1887, A Ramble in British Columbia. With Maps and 75 Illustrations. 3s. 6d.

Macaulay's (Lord) Essays and Lays of Ancient Rome. With Portrait and Illustrations. 3s. 6d.

Macleod (H. D.) The Elements of Banking. 3s. 6d.

Marshman's (J. C.) Memoirs of Sir Henry Havelock. 3s. 6d.

Max Müller's (F.) India, what can it teach us ? 3s. 6d.

Max Müller's (F.) Introduction to the Science of Religion. 3s. 6d.

Merivale's (Dean) History of the Romans under the Empire. 8 vols. 3s. 6d. ea.

Mill's (J. S.) Political Economy. 3s. 6d.

Mill's (J. S.) System of Logic. 3s. 6d.

Milner's (Geo.) Country Pleasures : the Chronicle of a Year chiefly in a Garden. 3s. 6d.

Newman's (Cardinal) Apologia Pro Vita Sua. 3s. 6d.

Newman's (Cardinal) Historical Sketches. 3 vols. 3s. 6d. each.

Newman's (Cardinal) Callista : a Tale of the Third Century. 3s. 6d.

Newman's (Cardinal) Loss and Gain : a Tale. 3s. 6d.

Newman's (Cardinal) Essays, Critical and Historical. 2 vols. 7s.

Newman's (Cardinal) An Essay on the Development of Christian Doctrine. 3s. 6d.

Newman's (Cardinal) The Arians of the Fourth Century. 3s. 6d.

Newman's (Cardinal) Verses on Various Occasions. 3s. 6d.

Newman's (Cardinal) The Present Position of Catholics in England. 3s. 6d.

Newman's (Cardinal) Parochial and Plain Sermons. 8 vols. 3s. 6d. each.

Newman's (Cardinal) Selection, adapted to the Seasons of the Ecclesiastical Year, from the ' Parochial and Plain Sermons'. 3s. 6d.

Newman's (Cardinal) Sermons bearing upon Subjects of the Day. 3s. 6d.

Newman's (Cardinal) Difficulties felt by Anglicans in Catholic Teaching Considered. 2 vols. 3s. 6d. each,

Newman's (Cardinal) The Idea of a University. 3s. 6d.

Newman's (Cardinal) Biblical and Ecclesiastical Miracles. 3s. 6d.

Newman's (Cardinal) Discussions and Arguments. 3s. 6d.

Newman's (Cardinal) Grammar of Assent. 3s. 6d.

Newman's (Cardinal) Fifteen Sermons Preached before the University of Oxford. 3s. 6d.

Newman's (Cardinal) Lectures on the Doctrine of Justification. 3s. 6d.

Newman's (Cardinal) Sermons on Various Occasions. 3s. 6d.

Newman's (Cardinal) The Via Media of the Anglican Church, illustrated in Lectures, &c. 2 vols. 3s. 6d. each.

Newman's (Cardinal) Discourses to Mixed Congregations. 3s. 6d.

Phillipps-Wolley's (C.) Snap: a Legend of the Lone Mountain. With 13 Illustrations. 3s. 6d.

Proctor's (R. A.) Other Worlds than Ours. 3s. 6d.

Proctor's (R. A.) Rough Ways made Smooth. 3s. 6d.

Proctor's (R. A.) Pleasant Ways in Science. 3s. 6d.

Proctor's (R. A.) Myths and Marvels of Astronomy. 3s. 6d.

Proctor's (R. A.) Nature Studies. 3s. 6d.

Stanley's (Bishop) Familiar History of Birds. 160 Illustrations. 3s. 6d.

Stevenson (Robert Louis) and Osbourne's (Lloyd) The Wrong Box. 3s. 6d.

Weyman's (Stanley J.) The House of the Wolf : a Romance. 3s. 6d.

Wood's (Rev. J. G.) Petland Revisited. With 33 Illustrations. 3s. 6d.

Wood's (Rev. J. G.) Strange Dwellings. With 60 Illustrations. 3s. 6d.

Wood's (Rev. J. G.) Out of Doors. 11 Illustrations. 3s. 6d.

Cookery, Domestic Management, &c.

Acton.— MODERN COOKERY. By ELIZA ACTON. With 150 Woodcuts. Fcp. 8vo., 4s. 6d.

Bull.—Works by THOMAS BULL, M.D.

HINTS TO MOTHERS ON THE MANAGE- MENT OF THEIR HEALTH DURING THE PERIOD OF PREGNANCY. Fcp. 8vo., 1s. 6d.

THE MATERNAL MANAGEMENT OF CHILDREN IN HEALTH AND DISEASE. Fcp. 8vo., 1s. 6d.

Cookery, Domestic Management, &c.—*continued.*

De Salis.—Works by Mrs. DE SALIS.

CAKES AND CONFECTIONS À LA MODE. Fcp. 8vo., 1s. 6d.

DOGS: a Manual for Amateurs. Fcp. 8vo., 1s. 6d.

DRESSED GAME AND POULTRY À LA MODE. Fcp. 8vo., 1s. 6d.

DRESSED VEGETABLES À LA MODE. Fcp. 8vo., 1s. 6d.

DRINKS À LA MODE. Fcp. 8vo., 1s. 6d.

ENTRÉES À LA MODE. Fcp. 8vo., 1s. 6d.

OYSTERS À LA MODE. Fcp. 8vo., 1s. 6d.

PUDDINGS AND PASTRY À LA MODE. Fcp. 8vo., 1s. 6d.

SAVOURIES À LA MODE. Fcp. 8vo., 1s. 6d.

SOUPS AND DRESSED FISH À LA MODE. Fcp. 8vo., 1s. 6d.

SWEETS AND SUPPER DISHES À LA MODE. Fcp. 8vo., 1s. 6d.

TEMPTING DISHES FOR SMALL INCOMES. Fcp. 8vo., 1s. 6d.

De Salis.—Works by Mrs. DE SALIS—*continued.*

FLORAL DECORATIONS. Suggestions and Descriptions. Fcp 8vo., 1s. 6d.

NEW-LAID EGGS: Hints for Amateur Poultry Rearers. Fcp. 8vo., 1s. 6d.

WRINKLES AND NOTIONS FOR EVERY HOUSEHOLD. Cr. 8vo., 1s. 6d.

Harrison.—COOKERY FOR BUSY LIVES AND SMALL INCOMES. By MARY HARRISON. Cr. 8vo., 1s.

Lear.—MAIGRE COOKERY. By H. L. SIDNEY LEAR. 16mo., 2s.

Poole.—COOKERY FOR THE DIABETIC. By W. H. and Mrs. POOLE. With Preface by Dr. PAVY. Fcp. 8vo., 2s. 6d.

Walker.—A HANDBOOK FOR MOTHERS: being Simple Hints to Women on the Management of their Health during Pregnancy and Confinement, together with Plain Directions as to the Care of Infants. By JANE H. WALKER, L.R.C.P. and L.M. L.R.C.S. and M.D. (Brux.). With 13 Illustrations. Cr. 8vo., 2s. 6d.

Miscellaneous and Critical Works.

Armstrong.—ESSAYS AND SKETCHES. By EDMUND J. ARMSTRONG. Fcp. 8vo., 5s.

Bagehot.—LITERARY STUDIES. By WALTER BAGEHOT. 2 vols. 8vo., 28s.

Baring-Gould.—CURIOUS MYTHS OF THE MIDDLE AGES. By Rev. S. BARING-GOULD. Crown 8vo., 3s. 6d.

Boyd ('A. K. H. B.').—Works by A. K. H. BOYD, D.D.

AUTUMN HOLIDAYS OF A COUNTRY PARSON. Crown 8vo., 3s. 6d.

COMMONPLACE PHILOSOPHER. Crown 8vo., 3s 6d.

CRITICAL ESSAYS OF A COUNTRY PARSON. Crown 8vo., 3s. 6d.

EAST COAST DAYS AND MEMORIES. Crown 8vo., 3s. 6d.

LANDSCAPES, CHURCHES AND MORALITIES. Crown 8vo., 3s. 6d.

LEISURE HOURS IN TOWN. Crown 8vo., 3s. 6d.

LESSONS OF MIDDLE AGE. Crown 8vo., 3s. 6d.

OUR LITTLE LIFE. Two Series. Cr. 8vo,. 3s. 6d. each.

OUR HOMELY COMEDY: AND TRAGEDY. Crown 8vo., 3s. 6d.

RECREATIONS OF A COUNTRY PARSON. Three Series. Cr. 8vo., 3s. 6d. each. First Series. Popular Ed. 8vo.,6d. swd.

Butler.—Works by SAMUEL BUTLER.

Op. 1. EREWHON. Cr. 8vo., 5s.

Op. 2. THE FAIR HAVEN. A Work in Defence of the Miraculous Element in our Lord's Ministry. Cr. 8vo., 7s. 6d.

Op. 3. LIFE AND HABIT. An Essay after a Completer View of Evolution. Cr. 8vo., 7s. 6d

Op. 4. EVOLUTION, OLD AND NEW. Cr. 8vo., 10s. 6d.

Op. 5. UNCONSCIOUS MEMORY. Cr. 8vo., 7s. 6d.

Op. 6. ALPS AND SANCTUARIES OF PIEDMONT AND CANTON TICINO. Illustrated. Post 4to., 10s. 6d.

Op. 7. SELECTIONS FROM OPS. 1-6. With Remarks on Mr. ROMANES' 'Mental Evolution in Animals'. Cr. 8vo., 7s. 6d.

Op. 8. LUCK, OR CUNNING, AS THE MAIN MEANS OF ORGANIC MODIFICATION? Cr. 8vo., 7s. 6d.

Op. 9. EX VOTO. An Account of the Sacro Monte or New Jerusalem at Varallo-Sesioa. 10s. 6d.

HOLBEIN'S 'LA DANSE'. A Note on a Drawing called 'La Danse'. 3s.

Miscellaneous and Critical Works —*continued.*

Halliwell-Phillipps.—A CALENDAR OF THE HALLIWELL - PHILLIPPS COLLECTION OF SHAKESPEAREAN RARITIES. Enlarged by ERNEST E. BAKER, F.S.A. 8vo., 10s. 6d.

Hodgson. — OUTCAST ESSAYS AND VERSE TRANSLATIONS. By W. SHADWORTH HODGSON. Crown 8vo., 8s. 6d.

Hullah.—Works by JOHN HULLAH, LL.D.
COURSE OF LECTURES ON THE HISTORY OF MODERN MUSIC. 8vo., 8s. 6d.
COURSE OF LECTURES ON THE TRANSITION PERIOD OF MUSICAL HISTORY. 8vo., 10s. 6d.

Jefferies.—Works by RICHARD JEFFERIES.
FIELD AND HEDGEROW : last Essays. With Portrait. Crown 8vo., 3s. 6d.
THE STORY OF MY HEART : my Autobiography. With Portrait and New Preface by C. J. LONGMAN. Crown 8vo., 3s. 6d.
RED DEER. With 17 Illustrations by J. CHARLTON and H. TUNALY. Crown 8vo., 3s. 6d.
THE TOILERS OF THE FIELD. With Portrait from the Bust in Salisbury Cathedral. Crown 8vo., 6s.
WOOD MAGIC : a Fable. With Vignette by E. V. B. Crown 8vo., 3s. 6d.

Jewsbury.—SELECTIONS FROM THE LETTERS OF GERALDINE ENDSOR JEWSBURY TO JANE WELSH CARLYLE. Edited by Mrs. ALEXANDER IRELAND. 8vo., 16s.

Johnson.—THE PATENTEE'S MANUAL: a Treatise on the Law and Practice of Letters Patent. By J. & J. H. JOHNSON, Patent Agents, &c. 8vo., 10s. 6d.

Lang.—Works by ANDREW LANG.
LETTERS TO DEAD AUTHORS. Fcp. 8vo., 2s. 6d. net.
BOOKS AND BOOKMEN. With 2 Coloured Plates and 17 Illustrations. Fcp. 8vo., 2s. 6d. net.
OLD FRIENDS. Fcp. 8vo., 2s. 6d. net.
LETTERS ON LITERATURE. Fcp. 8vo., 2s. 6d. net.

Macfarren.—LECTURES ON HARMONY. By Sir GEO. A. MACFARREN. 8vo., 12s.

Matthews.—PEN AND INK : Papers on Subjects of more or less importance. By BRANDER MATTHEWS. Crown 8vo., 5s.

Max Müller.—Works by F. MAX MÜLLER.
HIBBERT LECTURES ON THE ORIGIN AND GROWTH OF RELIGION, as illustrated by the Religions of India. Crown 8vo., 7s. 6d.   [*continued.*

Max Müller.—Works by F. MAX MÜLLER.—*continued.*
INTRODUCTION TO THE SCIENCE OF RELIGION : Four Lectures delivered at the Royal Institution. Cr. 8vo., 3s. 6d.
NATURAL RELIGION. The Gifford Lectures, 1888. Cr. 8vo., 10s. 6d.
PHYSICAL RELIGION. The Gifford Lectures, 1890. Cr. 8vo., 10s. 6d.
ANTHROPOLOGICAL RELIGION. The Gifford Lectures, 1891. Cr. 8vo., 10s. 6d.
THEOSOPHY OR PSYCHOLOGICAL RELIGION. The Gifford Lectures, 1892. Cr. 8vo., 10s. 6d.
INDIA : WHAT CAN IT TEACH US ? Cr. 8vo., 3s. 6d.

Mendelssohn.—THE LETTERS OF FELIX MENDELSSOHN. Translated by Lady WALLACE. 2 vols. Cr. 8vo., 10s.

Milner.—COUNTRY PLEASURES : the Chronicle of a Year chiefly in a Garden. By GEORGE MILNER. Cr. 8vo., 3s. 6d.

Perring.—HARD KNOTS IN SHAKESPEARE. By Sir PHILIP PERRING, Bart. 8vo., 7s. 6d.

Proctor.—Works by RICHARD A. PROCTOR.
STRENGTH AND HAPPINESS. With 9 Illustrations. Crown 8vo., 5s.
STRENGTH : How to get Strong and keep Strong, with Chapters on Rowing and Swimming, Fat, Age, and the Waist. With 9 Illus. Cr. 8vo, 2s.

Richardson.—NATIONAL HEALTH. A Review of the Works of Sir Edwin Chadwick, K.C.B. By Sir B. W. RICHARDSON, M.D. Cr., 4s. 6d.

Roget. — A HISTORY OF THE 'OLD WATER-COLOUR SOCIETY' (now the Royal Society of Painters in Water-Colours). By JOHN LEWIS ROGET. 2 vols. Royal 8vo., 42s.

Rossetti.—A SHADOW OF DANTE : being an Essay towards studying Himself, his World, and his Pilgrimage. By MARIA FRANCESCA ROSSETTI. With Illustrations and design on cover by DANTE GABRIEL ROSSETTI. Cr. 8vo., 10s. 6d.

Southey. — CORRESPONDENCE WITH CAROLINE BOWLES. By ROBERT SOUTHEY. Edited by E. DOWDEN. 8vo., 14s.

Wallaschek.—PRIMITIVE MUSIC : an Inquiry into the Origin and Development of Music, Songs, Instruments, Dances, and Pantomimes of Savage Races. By RICHARD WALLASCHEK. With Musical Examples. 8vo., 12s. 6d.

www.ingramcontent.com/pod-product-compliance
Lightning Source LLC
Chambersburg PA
CBHW020853020726
47497CB00005B/1388